ALWAYS MINE

The Foretold Series - Book Two

Michele James

PRAISE FOR THE FORETOLD SERIES

Warrior Mine

"If you enjoy adventure and romance you'll love this book. You'll fall in love with Lara and Talon and their exploits. Just when it seems everything is settled the author surprises you. I enjoyed the descriptive style and the historical facts James has included in the book. I highly recommend Warrior Mine. I couldn't put it down because what happens next is anyone's guess. I look forward to the next book Michele James will write in this series." ~Alessandra H

"Absolutely intriguing story. Didn't want to put it down. Sorry when it was over. Wanted more! This is perfect for a sequel. Michele James is a great historical romance writer. It shows she puts a lot of research into the era she has her characters in. Read her other 4 books. This one tops them all. Loved it!!" ~AAB

PRAISE FOR THE DESTINED SERIES

The Lion & The Swan

"What an amazing book! Well developed characters, complex and entertaining plot, beautifully described details and settings. Very difficult to put down. It cries for a sequel! Book two, hurry!" ~ conniecutie

"The purity of love between Assad and Oona is undeniable and beautiful. I adore Oona's strength and dedication to her sister. Assad was the perfect alpha, sensitive, strong, and passionate. Great, and moving tale." ~Andrea

The Stallion & The Tigress

"Love these books! Fun, witty, sensual and adventurous!!! Should be made into movies!!" ~Laura L. Sockey

"The strong woman (and the way her chief rival woos her) is wonderful. Especially because the leading lady is every bit as strong as her suitors! She chooses! I love the horses and the races and the way historical places and people are shown. This book stands alone, but it's also so cool that when you read Book 1 The Lion and the Swan, you get some of the backstory of this romance. Can't wait for Book 3 in this Destined Series. ~Kathleen Canney Lopez

"In this myth, the heroine, as her nickname suggests, is as powerful if not more so than any man. The men melt at the sight of her, but only one man will do, no matter the obstacles and there are many. The races by themselves are beautifully rendered. Kudos to the author for this romantic masterpiece. The book although number 2 of 3 is complete and stands alone." ~Plume Sobriquet

The Eagle & The Lynx

"Compelling read featuring a strong, righteous female lead. Intriguing romance and well-developed plot complete with subversion, betrayal and redemption. Looking forward to the next generation in the saga of The Destined!" ~jwrvt

"Book three of the Destined series brings the romance, adventure, and steamy love scenes of the first two books." ~MCB

The Stag & The Owl

"This final book in the series doesn't disappoint. Alina feels her true love has betrayed her but things change and Roark falls for his prisoner. Their many adventures and misadventures as they try to get Alina to safety are so well written and described. Almost hate to see this series end but what a wonderful way to end!" ~secret1

"Following the history of how all the women are linked by blood and love. To find love only to lose it due to someone's lies and deceit.

4

Time and patience wins the heart of the man she loves. Great reading!!" ~dkinghorn

www.BOROUGHSPUBLISHINGGROUP.com

ALWAYS MINE
Copyright © 2023 Michele James

ISBN: 978-1-957295-53-4

For Lauri, Randy, Hank the Tank, and Louie

ACKNOWLEDGMENTS

I'd written *Warrior Mine* as a stand-alone novel, but after publication, readers asked for a sequel. Luckily, I had set myself up for one with Lara's and Talon's daughter, Isabeau, and their godson, Wil. *Always Mine* is their second chance romance and book two of the Foretold series.

Thank you to my readers for suggesting this, and to Michelle for catching a major plot hole, and for talking me off the writer's ledge.

P.S. Book three in the series is brewing!

ALWAYS MINE

PROLOGUE
A Dream

Crossroads Keep, July 25, 795

Issy

"*Happy birthday, Issy.*"

Wil's eyes shone as dark as the lacquered mahogany box he held out to Issy. She ran a fingertip over the shiny black stone inlay in the shape of a horse at full gallop embedded in the lid.

"*It's beautiful, Wil.*"

Wil handed the box to her, his smile shy and hesitant. Two things he seldom was.

She opened the box and stared down at the ruby heart that pulsed with a light from within. "It's yours, Issy. Always."

"*Wil, I...*" *She held his gaze, and her own heart dropped to her feet as the jeweled heart in her hands fell to the floor and shattered into a thousand blood-red shards. When she looked up again, Wil was gone, vanished into a vast, hazy nothingness.*

CHAPTER ONE

The Return

June 802

Wil

Wil sat astride Charger, the Frisian stallion Talon had given him as a gift when he'd left Oloron nearly seven years ago. He shaded his eyes from the noon sun and looked down from the eastern pass into the valley he hadn't returned to since the day he left right after his seventeenth birthday.

He'd ridden Charger headed for Tours with a letter written by Talon, Count of Oloron, recommending him to King Charles. The king had read the letter and told Wil he remembered well the auspicious night Wil was born.

After Wil's three years of service in the army spent fighting in Saxony, Corsica, and Sardinia, Charles had put him under the tutelage of Gaston, the captain of his personal guard, and two months later Wil became a member of that elite troop.

He'd spent the next three years traveling to every corner of the Carolingian kingdom with Charles, serving not only as his personal guard, but often times as a courier and a confidant, thanks in large part to the education he'd received at Crossroads Keep.

Wil had been in Rome with Charles on Christmas Day in the year 800. The day Charles had been crowned Holy Emperor of Rome. The Pope had chosen Charles over Irene of Athens, Empress Queen of Byzantium, and the DeVittorio family of Lombardy had backed

Charles in this decision. The family had more sons than land in Lombardy, and so Dante DeVittorio, the third son, was to inherit the land given to them by Charles as a reward for their loyalty, and his older sister, Carina, twenty-six and unmarried, would live with him there and run his household.

Charles had chosen Wil to be in charge of escorting the brother and sister to Oloron, to introduce them to Count Talon and Countess Lara, who were to house them until their manor was built, and to help them learn how to raise crops and livestock on their land, which bordered Crossroads Keep's lands to the north.

Charles had also chosen Burrell, a stout and steady palace guard who was exceptionally deadly with his war axe, and, like Wil, knew the Lombard tongue, to accompany them along with the three men-at-arms, one lady's maid, and three wagons full of household goods and grapevines traveling with the DeVittorios.

They'd left Lombardy a month ago, taking the southern road along the Mediterranean Sea to avoid crossing over the southern Alps, yet even with the month of travel to prepare himself, Wil wasn't sure if he was looking forward to seeing Isabeau or dreading it.

Or even if he would see her again.

Though she was heir to the Oloron estate, she could've married and be living somewhere else. She could be dead. Though he didn't think that was possible.

Their connection couldn't be severed that completely without him sensing it.

Not that he hadn't tried.

Wil hadn't spoken to her since the night of her sixteenth birthday, when she'd refused his proposal, his love.

He'd ridden three hundred leagues north and east to get away from Isabeau, and he'd spent the years traveling the world. He'd met counts and countesses, kings and queens, even an empress, and the pope. He'd discovered a man could find plenty of highborn company amongst the ladies of their courts, and had tried his damnedest to forget Isabeau in the beds of other women.

He thought he'd succeeded, until he sat here on the eastern edge of Oloron Valley.

"How much farther?" Dante asked, pulling his horse up alongside Charger.

"As you see." Wil pointed down into the valley that sprawled out before them.

Woodlands edged the mountains surrounding the valley, and rivers and streams snaked through green pasturelands dotted with livestock, and fields planted with summer crops.

The rooftops of the town and the toths lining the roads had grown in number since the last time he'd looked down at the valley, and the road running north and south connecting to the main road running east and west looked to have been widened.

He smiled. Count Talon had been busy continuing to improve the lands and the lives of the people under his care. Wil looked to the far west end of the valley and spied Crossroads Keep. "We'll make the count's keep before sunset."

Charles had sent Talon a missive telling him when to expect the DeVittorios and how he expected Talon to host them. The missive had said nothing about Wil escorting them, as that hadn't been decided yet.

Wil had attempted to decline the job, but Charles had insisted, telling him it was well past time he returned home. His return would be a surprise, and as eager as he was to see his family and childhood friends again, it was Isabeau's reception that worried him.

"Where is my land?" Dante asked for the hundredth time since they'd left Lombardy.

This time, at least, Wil could show him. "Your family's land is there. North of the river that runs beyond those last two manor houses." He pointed to where Phillipe and Dardinel had lived. "There's good crop and pastureland there."

Dante nodded and took his own survey of the valley. "That is Oloron Manor?" He indicated the manor house closest to the eastern border.

"It is."

"What is the border line between Oloron and Crossroads lands?"

"I don't know." Wil assumed there was one, but it had never been a topic of discussion when he'd been growing up. Besides, it could have changed between then and now.

"But the manor and lands of Oloron are the Guiscard daughter's inheritance?"

Dante had been asking about the Guiscard family and their lands and horses the entire journey, and though Wil knew they were questions anybody would be asking, Dante asking them rubbed him the wrong way. Dante rubbed Wil the wrong way altogether.

"Last I knew," he told him.

Wil may not have liked the man much, but he had to admit Dante was good at reading people. He had a sneaking suspicion that Dante was good at playing them as well. He glanced over his shoulder at Carina, who favored her brother with the same light brown hair and blue eyes. She was still a pretty woman, yet it had been obvious her family had lost hope of her ever finding a husband.

They doted on her fourteen-year-old sister, and had blatantly pinned their hopes on her catching a titled husband back in Lombardy, sending Carina with Dante, younger than her by two years, to run his household until he found a suitable bride among the Franks. Which Wil had no doubt he would do. He was young and handsome, and a landowner. Wil hoped whoever he took to wife would be kind to Carina and let her continue to live with them.

If not, he worried what would become of her. She was the third child in the family, with two older brothers, two younger, and then her sister, the princess. Yet for growing up in the middle of so many siblings, she was incredibly meek and way too subservient to her brother for Wil's liking.

He chuckled, thinking of how Issy would have reacted to one of her brothers trying to lord over her, and then sobered. His first sight of Oloron in almost seven years and he was thinking of her as Issy.

"Lady Carina," Burrell, who had made himself her protector during the journey, asked, "would you like to rest a bit before we descend into Oloron?"

She looked to her brother, waiting for him to answer.

"No." Dante took up the slack in his horse's reins. "Now that we are finally here, let us continue on. I am *ansioso,* anxious to meet this Count Guiscard and his family."

As they descended into the valley, Wil took note of the finished palisade surrounding Oloron manse that had only begun to be built when he'd left. There was another building, which looked to be a stable almost as large as the house, and several other smaller buildings he didn't remember being there before.

The count and countess had named Isabeau, their firstborn, heiress to the manor and its lands when she was an infant. They'd installed Berta, Wil's grandmother, and Anglbert, her husband and one of Talon's oldest comrades and friends, to run the manor house until Isabeau was old enough to take it over. They'd been in their sixties when Wil had left seven years ago, but they were a hardy old pair, and he hoped they were still alive.

He wondered if Isabeau lived there now with a husband and children. After all, she would be twenty-three years old next month. And she was not only titled and well off, but a true beauty.

In Wil's mind, any husband of hers was a faceless shadow, while she was as clear to him as if she were standing before him. Slight of build, at sixteen she'd only come up to his chin, and he'd easily grown half a foot since then.

Her legs had been long and slim and her figure neat and trim. Her hair a mass of auburn curls down to the middle of her back, and her eyes a silvery gray that could be as soft as a dove's breast or as cutting as a falcon's wing.

He remembered her how she was, when she was his Issy.

Now, she was likely someone else's.

Wil sat up straighter in his saddle and squared his shoulders. Whoever's Issy she was now wasn't his concern. His concern was to introduce the DeVittorios to the Guiscards and to help them settle into their new home. Then he would leave Oloron and return to his duties as a king's guard.

They took the road west toward Crossroads Keep, drawing crowds as they passed. Apparently, the people knew they were coming.

Nobody seemed to recognize Wil, which wasn't surprising. He'd grown in height and heft in the years he'd been gone, had grown a beard, and wore armor and a helmet with the king's colors.

A few of the young women smiled and giggled as they rode past, and Dante smiled and waved at them as Carina looked about her with an expression on her face as placid as the roan mare she rode.

Wil had spoken with her daily for the month they'd been traveling, and he still couldn't have said what she truly thought about uprooting her life and moving here with her brother. Whether she was sad or happy to have left her family and home. Eager or resigned to start a new life in a new place.

When Wil had left Oloron to start his new life, a life without Isabeau, he'd felt all those things and more. Sadness, confusion, and then anger.

Anger at himself for never considering Isabeau didn't love him as he loved her. Anger at her for making him love her and not loving him back. Anger at the world for making him live in it without her.

He'd left Oloron because he couldn't stay and watch her love another man. Any other man. If it hadn't been for the grueling life of training, marching, and fighting against the Saxons his first year as a soldier, when he would fall asleep on any dry piece of earth he could find, Wil wasn't sure where he'd be now. Probably drowned in a barrel of wine somewhere unsavory.

The resignation had set in sometime during his second year away, and had stayed with him since, even as he'd made a new life for himself. A good life full of action, travel, and worldly experiences where he'd seen and learned more than he ever would if he'd stayed in Oloron. A life in which he'd met men and women of every court of every king from Gaul to Byzantium, and had slept with too many of the women to keep count. Beautiful, educated, charming, seductive women, whose only faults were that they weren't Isabeau Juditha Guiscard.

They rode southwest, past the main village, where Wil had spent many a market day helping his father and brother sell their leatherworks. Willem LeCuir's saddles were renowned throughout Gaul thanks to Count Talon and King Charles, who'd paid Wil's father a princely sum for the design of those saddles. A design the royal leather workers had been using for over twenty years.

As they rode farther west, they came upon Wil's family home, which had grown from a single-story wood and thatch house to two separate two-story houses of stone and wood, with a leatherwork building twice the size of his father's original shop. To have a saddle made by Willem LeCuir was a sign of wealth and rank. A sign men paid for well.

Wil glanced over at Burrell, who knew of Wil's family and a little of his growing up here in Oloron, and shook his head. As much as he'd have liked to stop and say hello to his parents and brothers first, that wasn't what he was here for. Besides, they'd have plenty of time to visit and catch up. Wil was to stay here with the DeVittorios until they were settled into their new home and lives. Which meant he'd be here through the summer and into the fall.

Another half league west, they rode past fields green with summer wheat. This was Aunt Marta and Uncle Denys's property, which had once belonged to Countess Lara when she was the valley's healer, along with the witch who'd raised her, Sophie the Sixth. The house that stood there now had been built over the ruins of Lara's and Sophie's house, burnt to the ground when Nithard Midered, Lara's uncle and the illegitimate Count of Oloron, had tried to burn her and her unborn child, true heirs to Oloron, alive in it.

Isabeau had been that unborn child.

The property looked much the same from the road as Wil remembered it, though the house itself had been added on to. The north wing, which had been built when Wil was young and Denys and Marta's twins had been born, had been added onto again, making it three times the size of the original house.

Wil smiled to himself. The valley and its people had continued to thrive under Talon's and Lara's rule, which was one of many reasons the couple were favorites of Charles.

Lara's adventure as Hamm, a cook's boy during the march to Spain, and how she'd captured the heart of Charles's stalwart Captain Guiscard, was another.

How Charles loved to tell that story, along with the story of the night of Wil's birth, which Wil had heard countless times growing up. He supposed it'd been auspicious, the king being in Oloron the night of his birth, him becoming liege to Charles seventeen years later and serving him directly for the past four years.

But what it meant now that Wil was returning to Oloron, he hadn't a clue.

He sat up straighter and rolled his shoulders back.

In another quarter league, he'd be finding out.

The watchtower called out their arrival, and by the time they rode through the open gates, they were met by a crowd at the center of which stood Count Talon and Countess Lara.

As tall and broad shouldered as ever, with streaks of gray in his black hair and beard, the count quickly took them in, his steel-eyed gaze giving nothing away. Beside him, Countess Lara stood as keen-eyed and handsome a woman as Wil had ever seen. Her gaze followed her husband's, lingering on Dante a moment and then meeting Wil's.

Her lips lifted at the corners as a sylph of a young woman with auburn curls escaping the long braid down her back and eyes the color of rain stepped up beside her.

Wil doffed his helmet and dipped his head to her, watching as recognition filled her eyes.

"Hello, Isabeau."

***

Issy

"Wil?" Issy grasped the pendant she was never without beneath her tunic. The pendant Wil had given her on her sixteenth birthday, of which she'd dreamed every night for the past seven nights, waking up gasping and shaking and clutching it in her fist. Aware that all eyes were on them, she let go of the pendant, catching the quick flick of Wil's gaze. "Your parents must be so glad you're back."

After almost seven years of imagining this moment, of thinking and planning what she would say to him when and if she ever saw him again, speaking of his parents was all she'd managed.

"They don't know I'm here yet," he told her, his voice even deeper than she remembered. He turned his attention back to her father, dismissing her presence as if it didn't matter in the least. "My duty was to bring my charges directly to the count."

Issy took in Wil's well-worn but sturdily made boots, leather breeches, and plain linen tunic beneath his vest of lacquered leather with the king's blue on his breast plate, the lacquered wrist cuffs and the helmet he set on his saddle's pommel.

A long sword was sheathed at his saddle, and he wore a short sword and knife at his waist. His earthen brown, wavy hair brushed his ears, and his beard, of which he'd had only the first few, wispy whiskers when he'd left, was cut short and neat, framing his full mouth and the strong line of his jaw. His tall, lanky body had filled out in all the right places, and he sat his Frisian stallion with an air of pride and strength.

He dismounted and was followed by a young, handsome man dressed in a tunic and breeches of fine linen and a leather vest.

Another man, sturdily built and dressed more like Wil with a soldier's vest, lacquered wrist cuffs, and a war axe sheathed at his side, dismounted his warhorse and gave a hand to a woman who looked much like the handsome young man, helping her dismount a sedate mare. The others in their party stayed seated on the wagons and their horses.

"Count Talon, Countess Lara," Wil said, "may I introduce Lord Dante De Vittorio and his sister, Lady Carina."

Issy's mother and father stepped forward, as did Dante De Vittorio. His sister, Carina, stayed a step behind her brother, chin down and hands folded at her waist as Dante clasped the count's arm. Issy hid her smile as her mother stepped around the men.

"Come, Lady Carina." The countess gently pulled the docile woman by the hand. "You must be tired from your long journey. Let us go inside where you may rest up before supper. Shall your maidservant come with us?"

Carina glanced back at the wagons, where a bedraggled woman of about thirty years sat waiting. "Oh, yes. Of course," she said with a heavy accent. "Thank you."

Though she'd much rather have stayed outside with her father, Wil, and Dante De Vittorio with his charming smile and shining blue eyes, Issy followed her mother and Lady Carina into the keep's manor house. She and her mother showed Carina and her maid up to the bedchamber they'd be sharing, telling them to take their time freshening up and to later join them in the dining hall, where Enid and the kitchen staff had set out a repast of breads, cheeses, cut up summer apples, and pitchers of ale and wine.

"I think Lady Carina looked a bit put out to be sharing a room with her maid," Issy commented as she and her mother descended the stairs.

"I think you're right," her mother agreed. She glanced back up at the closed door to Issy's childhood bedchamber and gave a slight shrug. "With any luck, it will only be for a few months. Harald isn't exactly thrilled to be sharing his room with Orlando for the duration."

Issy gave an unladylike snort. At seventeen years of age, Harald would definitely chafe at his thirteen-year-old brother invading his private rooms, while Lando was likely looking forward to it. He idolized his older brother, especially since Geoff had moved into Oloron Manor, awaiting his wedding with Desiree. The wedding was to be held on August first, a little over six weeks from now, and Desiree would be moving into Oloron Manor with Geoff once they were married.

"Are Dante and his men to stay in Geoff's old room then?" Issy asked.

"They are. Enid offered to stay with Marta and her family while the Lombards are here, so they could have use of her room, but your father wouldn't hear of it."

Widowed last year, Enid had moved into the manor house not long after. She was as much a lifelong friend of the countess as she was head cook at the keep. She was also sister to Patience LeCuir, Lara's closest friend and Wil's mother.

"Let's hope this Dante isn't as displeased about sharing a room with his menservants as his sister seemed to be about sharing hers," her mother said as they entered the dining hall. "Though they could stay in the guard barracks." She pulled out her chair and sat. "I suppose it will depend on what their young master decides."

Issy took her seat beside her mother as the sound of men's voices filled the entryway. "It appears we'll be finding out soon enough."

Women's voices answered the men's in the Lombard tongue, and then the group entered the dining hall and took their proffered seats across the table from the count and countess. Issy sat to her mother's left, and her brothers to their father's right, with her father's guards, Tree and Oswald, flanking them. Wil and Burrell sat to either side of Dante and Carina, putting Wil directly across from Issy.

She met Wil's gaze, so familiar and yet so different. Growing up, he must've sat across this table from her a thousand times. Then, all they'd had to do was look at each other to know what the other was thinking.

Now, he was a stranger to her. A handsome stranger with big, dark, expressive eyes beneath thick black-brown brows, and a short-cropped beard shadowing the hard line of his jaw, full mouth, and carved cheekbones. The lanky, gangly boy she'd known had grown into a tall, broad-shouldered, exceptionally handsome man.

A man she didn't know.

Whose eyes and face she could no longer read.

She had no idea what he was thinking as he stared back at her. Was he happy to be home? To see her? Or was he still as angry at her now as he'd been the day he left?

She was saved from any more musings as Geoff burst into the hall, his gaze going straight to Wil, who stood.

"Wil." Geoff wrapped him in a bear hug, then stepped back and clasped his arm. "Welcome home."

"Geoff." Wil held on to Geoff's arm with one hand and clapped him on the shoulder with his other. They stood nose to nose, grinning from ear to ear. The first smile Issy'd seen Wil crack since he'd ridden through the keep's gates. "It's good to see you."

She may not be good at reading Wil any longer, but recognizing the surprise on Dante's and his men's faces at the warm welcome between her brother and Wil didn't take any special knowledge or skill.

Burrell, Wil's fellow king's man, didn't give the two men a second glance as he tucked into the bread and cheese, though he did glance at Carina and her maidservant, who couldn't seem to take their eyes off Geoff as he took a seat next to Wil's.

Their father's twin in looks and build, Geoff was a man to catch any woman's eye, but he belonged to Desiree, and Desiree was one of Issy's closest friends.

"Geoff and Desiree are getting married," she blurted out. "On August first."

All eyes turned to Issy, who smiled innocently at her brother as Carina and the maidservant, whose name she really needed to learn, deflated in their seats.

"Congratulations, Geoff," Wil said. "You always did have your eye on Desiree."

Geoff puffed his chest out. "As it turns out, she had her eye on me as well."

Wil grinned and nodded, though he said nothing and wouldn't meet Issy's gaze.

"You'll come to the wedding?" Geoff asked. "If you're still here, that is."

"Of course."

"How long do you plan on staying?"

"I'm to stay until the DeVittorios are settled in their new home and have no more need of me."

Geoff glanced around the table. "All of you are staying here at the keep?"

"That was the plan."

"You should stay with us at Oloron Manor," he told Wil. "We have rooms there sitting empty."

"We?" Wil said.

"I live there with Issy," Geoff explained. "Along with Berta and Anglbert, though they have their own cottage on the grounds now. Desiree will be joining us after the wedding."

"What of Lady Isabeau's *marito*, her husband?" Dante asked.

Issy's cheeks flushed hot as she met Wil's curious gaze, and then turned to address Dante, head high and spine straight. "I have no husband."

Dante gave her a dazzling smile. "Then I say we should accept Geoff's kind offer." He turned to her parents. "Unless, of course, you prefer we stay here in your house, Count Talon."

Her father and mother held one of those quick, unspoken conversations between themselves. They had a long, happy marriage, the kind of marriage Issy wanted. The kind she knew in her bones Geoff and Desiree would have.

"If Isabeau agrees to this, it's fine by us," her father answered.

Issy's first instinct was to say no, she didn't agree to having a house full of strangers, and she absolutely didn't want Wil living with her for the next three to four months.

But Geoff was right. They had rooms enough to house the De Vittorios and their servants without them having to share four or five to a chamber, and it was obvious Geoff was eager to have his old friend, Wil, there.

She glanced at Wil, who looked no more thrilled about the idea than she was, and then at Harald, who mouthed "please" to her, eager, no doubt, to not have to share his room with Orlando.

"It would be our honor to have you stay with us," she told Dante, who bestowed another dazzling smile on her.

She chanced a quick glance at Wil, his jaw clamped tight, apparently as equally displeased to be staying in her house as she was to have him there.

"It's settled then," her father said. "Tonight, you'll rest up here, as planned, and tomorrow, we'll help you move into Oloron Manor."

CHAPTER TWO

Animales

Wil

"This'll be just like old times," Geoff said as he and Wil directed the menservants to put Wil's and Burrell's cots along the wall by the window in line with Geoff's four-poster bed. "You sleeping over in my room and being all moon-eyed over my sister."

"No." Wil ignored the quick look from Burrell. "It won't." He waited for the servants to leave the room. "For one thing, you're a betrothed lord in waiting and I'm a soldier. For another, I am not and will not be mooning over Isabeau."

"Uh-huh."

"Our friendship ended seven years ago."

"She dreamed it, you know."

A chill ran down Wil's spine. He knew the countess had foretelling dreams. But Isabeau? She'd never said anything to him about them. "What do you mean?"

"She dreamed you'd leave her. The day after her birthday party I heard her sobbing in our mother's arms, telling her you were leaving here, leaving her, and that she'd dreamed of it the night before."

"I didn't know."

"You do know you broke her heart when you left."

"After she broke mine," Wil ground out.

He turned on his heels and strode past Burrell, who wasn't even trying to pretend he wasn't listening anymore.

Wil slammed the door shut and headed down the stairs, silently cursing country life and having everyone thinking they have a say in a man's personal affairs. He hadn't known any different growing up here, but once he was in the army, he'd realized nobody knew a thing about him he didn't reveal himself. And he hadn't revealed much.

Not that he'd had much to hide, other than his broken heart, but he'd liked being able to start anew. The letter from Count Talon was Wil's introduction to Charles, but he'd advanced from horse soldier to king's guard on his own merits.

A position he intended to return to as soon as his duty to the De Vittorios was done here.

He'd left the keep after supper last night to go visit with his family, which now included Wyatt's pregnant wife, Priscilla, and their one-year-old son, Perrin, who lived in the new house on the property. They had welcomed him home with hugs and tears, and heartfelt joy that still warmed him from the inside out. He truly was glad to be close to them again, but his proximity to Isabeau chafed him raw.

He rounded the bottom of the stairs and was making his way to the kitchens when a loud, feminine shriek had him running back up, taking the stairs three at a time with Oswald on his heels. Geoff and Burrell ran out of Geoff's door, following them to the room where Carina's panicked voice was coming from.

"*Volpe. Volpe. Selvaggia volpe.*"

Burrell rushed the doorway, but Wil held him back.

Isabeau stood inside the chamber Carina was to share with Paola, her maidservant, waving her hands and shaking her head, a red fox sitting obediently at her feet. "No. No *selvaggia.*" She told the women. "Foxy's a pet. She's like a dog, a, ah…"

"*Cagna,*" Wil said, stepping into the room.

"No, no *cagna.*" Carina stayed pressed against the edge of the bed. "*Volpe.*"

"*Si, si. Ma lei non e savaggia,*" Wil explained. "She's not wild. *Lei e animale domestica*. She's tame."

"Yes, a tame pet." Isabeau bent down and picked up the vixen, who licked her chin. She ruffled the fox's fur, kissed her nose, and set her back down. "See?"

Wil walked over, knelt down, and held his hand out for the fox to sniff. "Is this the same orphaned kit you were raising before I left?"

"She is."

Wil scratched the vixen's chin. "I thought you meant to return her to the wilds."

"I tried." Isabeau bent down alongside him, and Wil caught a whiff of lavender. Storm-gray eyes met and held his for a moment before she scooped up the fox. "She kept finding her way back to me."

Isabeau stood, holding Foxy close. Her auburn braid, several shades darker than the vixen's coat, fell across the fox's chest. Wil stood too, closing his arms around Carina with an "oompf" as she flew into his chest.

Burrell took a step toward them, his hand on the hilt of his waist knife. Wil held a hand out, palm up. "She's in no danger," he told Burrell.

"*Grazie*, Wil. *Voi salvato me.*"

Wil caught Isabeau's eye roll and narrowed his own at her.

"*Sei benvanuta,*" he told Carina, who shook in his arms like a sparrow that'd barely escaped being eaten by the vixen. "It was nothing."

"Perhaps we should arrange a tour of the property for our guests," Isabeau suggested. "So we can introduce them to the animals and people who live here to avoid another misunderstanding."

"*Animales*?" Carina looked from Isabeau to Wil, who had to smile.

Knowing Isabeau, Foxy wasn't the only wild animal she'd rescued who'd decided life was better as her pet than out in the wilds.

"I'll arrange it with Dante," Wil said.

"No need." Dante strolled into the room, a pleased smile on his face as Wil peeled Carina's arms from around his waist and stepped away from her. "I heard most of what transpired."

Dante reached down and tried to pet the vixen on the head. Wil hid his grin as Foxy dodged his hand to hide behind Isabeau's skirt and Dante gave one of his nonchalant shrugs.

"Will now do?" Isabeau asked, glancing around the room.

"*Si, si, mio signora bellissima.*" Dante gave Isabeau a courtly dip of his head as Wil chuffed. "I will gather my men."

The apples of her cheeks a rosy shade of pink, Isabeau dipped her head in return. "I'll put Foxy away in my chambers and then meet you down in the common room."

Wil and the others had only stepped into the common room when Isabeau joined them and led the way through the dining hall into the kitchens.

"This is Lucinda," Isabeau introduced a middle-aged woman with brown hair streaked with gray tied into one long plait down her back, a welcoming smile, and a friendly demeanor. "Lucinda, this is Dante DeVittorio, his sister, Lady Carina, and their men and maidservant. And this is Wil LeCuir and Burrell, the king's men."

"LeCuir," Lucinda said, eyeing Wil. "You're Willem and Patience's middle son?"

"I am," Wil said, not at all surprised she knew who he was, though he didn't remember her. "It's a pleasure to meet you, Lucinda."

"Lucinda is the head cook and housekeeper for the manor." Isabeau indicated the large, clean, indoor kitchen where three separate worktables were set up. One for meats and cheeses, one for produce, and one for grains and baking. "If you have any special needs or requests, please go to her."

"Not to you?" Carina asked Isabeau.

Isabeau gave a short laugh. "I may be lady of the manor, but Lucinda runs it. I tend to deal more with the farming and the livestock." If she saw Carina's wrinkled nose, she ignored it.

"We serve breakfast and supper in the dining hall," Lucinda informed them. "But yer welcome to anything in the larders any time of day."

"What about at night?" Dante asked.

"The kitchen closes after supper," she told him in a firm yet kindly manner that put Wil in mind of his grandmother, who'd run the kitchens at Crossroads Keep for years, until she and Anglbert had been made stewards of Oloron Manor. "So that Marie and Yvette," she indicated two young women standing beside one of the tables, "may clean up and go home to their own families."

"But what if a man found himself *affamato*, famished, in the middle of the night?"

Lucinda tsked. "Of course, you may make yerself something to eat after the kitchens have closed." She narrowed her eyes on Dante. "But you had better clean up after yerself."

"Yes, ma'am." Dante gave her a quick grin and a quicker salute, and Lucinda grinned back at him, apparently won over by his charm.

He bestowed a smile on the two kitchen maids, who blushed prettily as they dipped their knees to him, and then he turned to Isabeau, who seemed more amused than impressed by his display. He held his crooked arm out toward her, and she hesitated a moment, met Wil's hard glare, then took Dante's arm.

Wil clenched his jaw and followed them out the kitchen door to the outside ovens and worktables, where the scent of baking bread filled the air, and a stout, gray-haired couple strolled toward them.

"Wilric, lad. Welcome home."

Wil unlocked his jaw and broke into a huge grin. "Anglbert." He stepped into the graybeard's open arms and returned the man's hug. Then he stepped back and kissed the woman's soft, fleshy cheek, wet with tears. "Grandmother."

"Oh Wil, my dear boy." His grandmother smiled through her tears and enveloped him in her welcoming arms. "It's so good to have you home again."

Wil sniffed and squeezed his grandmother tight. "I'm happy to see you again too."

"Leave off, lad." Anglbert tapped him on the shoulder. "Your poor grandmama is turning purple for lack of air."

Wil let go so quickly, his grandmother stumbled back a step, but she was laughing, and her cheeks were only a little pink.

"I'm fine, dearie," she assured her husband. "But look at you. You've grown into such a fine, strapping man. I think you're finally taller than your brother, Wyatt."

Wil grinned and stood up straighter. He'd been telling his older brother he was going to grow taller than him since he was four years old. "I am." He held his thumb and forefinger half a finger apart. "We measured ourselves last night."

"Ahem."

Wil turned to where Dante stood, clearly annoyed at being ignored. Isabeau stood between him and Carina, her hand no longer on Dante's arm. As if she'd ever needed his arm to walk out of her own door.

"Auntie Berta, Uncle Anglbert." Isabeau held her hands out to each side of her. "May I introduce our new guests, Dante DeVittorio, his sister, Lady Carina, and their men and maidservant." She indicated Burrell, who stood off to the side. "This is Burrell, Wil's friend and fellow king's man."

Anglbert nodded to Burrell, who could've passed as a younger version of her "uncle," who stepped forward and offered his hand to Dante. "Welcome," he said as Dante shook his hand. He dipped his head to Carina. "Lady."

"We're off on a tour of the property and the animals," Isabeau explained. "Foxy gave Lady Carina a scare earlier."

"Oh dear." Berta tsked. "You'll get used to the critters soon enough. Have you met Heinz yet?"

Carina shook her head. "Heinz?"

"Our guard pig," Isabeau said.

"You have a guard pig?" Wil was more amused than surprised. Isabeau had always had a menagerie of animals she cared for. Her father had even built a small stable at the keep to house the wilder ones while she healed their various illnesses and injuries.

"He's actually Randolph's, the head stable master and Lucinda's husband," Isabeau explained. A loud snort drew their attention to a middle-aged man with cropped blond hair and a short beard walking out of the stable, a huge, white boar with gray patches trotting alongside him. "Here they are now."

"Don't let either of them scare you, dearie," Berta told Carina. "They may both be a bit crusty on the outside, but they're soft as mush on the inside."

Carina nodded but didn't look like she really believed Berta. Isabeau waved Randolph over and grabbed cut up apple pieces from one of the worktables, motioning for Wil and the others to follow her out into the courtyard.

"Stay, Heinz." Randolph stopped several paces from them and held his hand down low. The pig stood at his knee, snout high, snuffling and sniffing the air around them.

"Randolph." Isabeau stepped forward and stood between them and the stable master and his boar. "These are our new guests, Dante DeVittorio, his sister, Lady Carina, their men and maidservant. Also, meet Wilric LeCuir and Burrell, the king's men."

Randolph dipped his head to Dante and Carina and then met Wil's gaze. "Wilric LeCuir. I've heard a fair bit about you since me wife and I moved here a few years ago. Your parents must be pleased you're back."

"They are. As am I."

Neither of them said another word as they stood there, sizing each other up. Since Randolph and Lucinda hadn't lived in the valley when Wil was growing up here, the only things he'd know about Wil was what he'd heard from others. And Wil didn't know anything about them, other than Isabeau trusted them enough to have them working on her manse.

That Randolph was openly leery of strangers and protective of the place didn't bother Wil in the least. In truth, it made him inclined to like the man. He held out his hand, and Randolph grasped and shook it.

"Good to meet you, Randolph."

"Wilric."

"Call me Wil."

Randolph gave his hand one last shake. "Wil."

"I want to introduce them to Heinz," Isabeau told Randolph.

Randolph nodded, then squatted down next to Heinz and laid an arm across the boar's shoulders. "You know Mistress Isabeau," he told the boar. "She's brought some new friends for you to meet."

The boar snorted as if it were listening and answering. Isabeau held out an apple slice and the pig took the slice with a happy snuffle. She handed a slice each to Wil and the DeVittorios.

"Offer Heinz an apple slice and introduce yourself," she said. "Once he's taken food from you, he's your friend forever. Though it doesn't hurt to keep feeding him treats every few days."

Neither Dante nor Carina made to move, so Wil stepped up. "Hello, Heinz. I'm Wil," he said as the pig gently took the apple slice from his hand.

Heinz easily outweighed Wil by several stone, and he'd seen the damage a wild boar could do to a man with those small tusks of his.

"We're friends now, right?"

Heinz snorted while shaking his head up and down. Wil laughed. He turned to Carina and motioned for her to come forward. Several small, hesitant steps later, she stood beside him, cowering into his side as Burrell stood to her other side, her hand fisted around the apple slice Heinz had already sniffed out. "Hold out your hand, palm flat, like you would for a horse," Wil told her.

Her big, blue eyes were fixed on Heinz. "I…I cannot."

Wil took her hand in his and unfurled her fingers. "Trust me," he said, and she nodded.

He held her hand out in his, steadying it as Heinz took the proffered slice of apple. As soon as the boar had taken the apple and Wil let go of her hand, she snatched it back and folded it into her skirts.

"There now, that wasn't so bad, was it?" he asked kindly, ignoring Isabeau's arched brows.

"No." Carina wiped her hand on her skirt and hugged Wil's side.

"My turn." Dante thrust his apple slice at Heinz, and the boar jerked its head back with a snort.

"Easy, Heinz." Randolph soothed the boar, petting him gently on the rump. "Master DeVittorio didn't mean to startle you." He looked up at Dante. "Jes move a little slower, not so aggressive like."

Dante looked like he was about to throw the apple at Heinz, but then he glanced at Isabeau's knit brows and pursed lip. He bent down and held out the apple in the palm of his hand, a smug smile tugging at the corners of his mouth as Heinz took the fruit. He straightened and wiped his hand on his breeches.

"Now that is done, shall we continue on?" he said to Isabeau, his more usual charming smile plastered on his face. "I am interested to see these stables and horses I hear so much about."

***

Issy

Issy led the way to the stable, her pride and joy. She pointed out the individual outside pens, attached to each stall by a door in the outer wall.

"They allow the horses in the stable to be outside in the open air if they choose when they aren't able to be pastured. My father did the same with his stable."

Wil took in the pens and nodded his approval. Dante gave them barely a glance as he strode ahead of Issy into the stable. He'd mentioned wanting to see her horses and learn about her breeding program last night at supper, so she'd told Randolph not to put them out in their pastures this morning, as was their usual routine. Which was why both of her stallions were pawing at the floors of their stalls.

"This is Kolossus." Wil's eyebrows rose as she introduced her Frisian stallion, large even for his breed. "My father and Phillipe brought him back for me five years ago when they went to Frisia to trade some of their broodmares for new stock. He's a gift I received when I inherited Oloron Manor. Ebony, one of my pregnant mares, is out of him and Onyx, as is Jolie, a two-year-old mare I'll breed next year."

Wil's eyebrows rose a tick at mention of Onyx, the mare she'd been gifted by her parents as a newborn filly for her sixteenth birthday, but he said nothing.

"Sabine, another of my mares, had a colt out of him. I traded the colt to my father for my broodmare, Lyts, who I'll show you shortly. My father, Phillipe, and I keep a book of all the bloodlines. That way we don't interbreed, keeping our lines strong and diverse."

Dante nodded his approval. "I have heard this about Oloron's famous Frisians, how you are so particular about bloodlines."

"It's true," Issy said proudly. "Which is why we have requests for our horses from Spain to Byzantium to Frisia."

"Who are you trading with in Spain?" Dante asked.

"A Basque named Inigo."

Wil's brows rose to his hairline. "Our Inigo?"

"One and the same."

"How did that come about?"

"Inigo became leader of his village six years ago and sent a messenger to my parents, asking if the peace they'd maintained for the past twenty years could expand into some trade. After much discussion among all parties involved, it was agreed upon and the valley's been trading with the Basques since."

"Does Charles know?"

"He does. He and my father have standing orders for all the whale oil Inigo can move."

"Trade is always better than raiding and war," Wil commented.

Issy considered asking him what he remembered when Inigo had kidnapped them, but now wasn't the time or place. She continued the tour, eager to see his reaction to what she was about to show him next.

"Over here," she pointed several stalls down, "is the most gorgeous, elegant horse I've ever seen."

"If you don't mind, *fratello*," Carina held the backs of her fingers to her nose, "my ladies and I will wait outside for you."

Dante waved them off and then waved at Issy to continue. Issy opened her mouth to tell Dante… what… that he was her guest, not her lord and master, but then she glanced at the amused expression on Wil's face, snapped her mouth shut, and strode over to Sultan's stall.

She stood, suppressing her grin as first Wil, then Dante, then Burrell, and Dante's three menservants sucked in their breaths while admiring the long-legged, slender-bodied, white stallion with the lightest of gray dappling, dark gray stockings, and an even darker mane and tail.

"*Mio Dio*." Dante clapped his hands together, startling Sultan, who snorted and stepped back from the stall gate. "He is *magnifico*."

Issy stepped up to the gate and held her hand out. "His name is Sultan," she said as the stallion sniffed and blew into her palm. "He's a—"

"Turkmene," Wil said. "A Turkoman horse from the northern steppes of Persia."

Issy grinned. Like her father, Wil must've traveled much of the known world as a soldier and king's man. It wasn't surprising he knew Sultan's breed. "He is."

"How did you come by such a horse?" Wil asked. "The Turkmen value their horses more than they do most people, and guard their breeding lines as closely as royalty."

"My father told me about the Turkmene horses he'd seen on his travels many years ago. I wrote to Charles, telling him of my dream to crossbreed Frisians and Turkmenes, to mix a Frisian's girth and strength with a Turkmene's speed and endurance. He wrote to Irene of Byzantium, and she sent me Sultan as an unbroken yearling four years ago, with the agreement that I return a crossbreed colt of his to her."

"What happens if you do not complete this bargain with the Empress Irene?" Dante asked.

Issy knew the DeVittorios had been rewarded the lands Dante was here to claim now for backing Charles over Irene as Holy Roman Emperor. She also knew about the rift that had grown between Charles and Irene since he'd been crowned emperor two years ago, and that the odds of Irene coming after her promised colt were slim to none.

But Issy was a Guiscard, and Guiscards upheld their oaths.

"I have no intention of finding out," she told Dante.

Dante hesitated a moment before nodding. "*Buona. Buona.* That is good. Have you any foals out of Sultan yet?"

Either Dante was unaware of the insult he'd given Issy, insinuating that she'd even consider not holding up her end of the bargain, or he didn't think it was worth apologizing for. She glanced at Wil and Burrell, who were both glaring at Dante, and decided to let the insult go and put it to a difference in cultures.

"Sultan has sired a yearling colt out of Sabine."

"May we see it?"

It? Issy furrowed her brows and put it to a language barrier. "He's out in the pasture for the day. We can add him to our tour."

"*Buona.* That will please me greatly."

Issy inclined her head in response, the insult she'd intended to let go of still ruffling her feathers.

Wil stepped up and held out his hand for Sultan to sniff and then ran his hand down the proud arch of the stallion's neck. "What's he like to ride?"

Issy grinned. "Like the wind."

"You ride this stallion?" Dante sounded surprised.

Wil chuckled.

"He's fast and smooth. He's sure-footed, and doesn't tire," she told Wil, ignoring the other gaping men. "Wait until you see him jump."

"Do you have jumps set up here?" Wil asked.

"What do you think?" He and Issy had loved taking their horses over the jumps set up at Crossroads Keep, and each of them had won local jumping contests as teenagers. Whichever one of them hadn't won had always taken second place to the other.

"I would like to see more of your breeding stock," Dante said before Wil could answer.

"Of course." Issy led the way over to the stalls of her two pregnant broodmares. "This is Lyts." The smallish Frisian mare came to the gate for a nose rub. "She's due the end of summer with Sultan's foal." She stepped over to the next stall, where a larger Frisian broodmare stood contentedly munching oats from her bucket. "This is Ebony. She's due next month as well. Sabine, my other Frisian broodmare, is out in the pasture with her colt, Silver, Sultan's colt I mentioned earlier, along with Jolie, Sabine's dam, and Onyx, my personal mare."

Wil's dark gaze met Issy's. "I haven't seen Onyx since the night she was born."

The night he'd proposed marriage to her and she'd refused him. The night he'd kissed her. A kiss whose memory had never left her, and still stood out among all others.

Not that she'd been kissed by many other men. Only three. And only one of them could be called a man; the other two had still been boys. But then Wil had also been a boy. A nearly seventeen-year-old boy the memory of whose kiss still warmed Issy's blood.

"I remember," she said, swiping at her flushed cheeks.

Wil said nothing, though his gaze sought the silver chain to the pendant he'd given her that night, and then dropped lower to where the pendant nestled between her breasts. Issy reached for the pendant, and then dropped her hand, torn between wanting to hold it up and show Wil that yes, she still wore it in memory of her best friend who'd abandoned her, and throwing it in the face of the handsome stranger who'd returned.

"That's enough of the stable," she said instead and headed for the door. "Let's continue our tour. Remi," she called the stable boy over. A simple lad who had a way with animals, he'd been orphaned when his mother died two years ago, and Issy had taken him in as a stable hand. "Please tell Randolph the horses can be let out to pasture now."

"Yes, Mistress." He stopped and stared at Wil. "Hey, I know you."

"Hello, Remi." Will shook the lad's hand. "I'm Wil, Willem LeCuir's son. We've both grown a bit since I was last here."

Remi's face split into a huge grin. "I 'member you. You, Master Geoff, and Mistress Isabeau stopped the mean boys when they was hurting me."

Issy remembered that day. A gang of boys from the next province over had caught Remi, who couldn't have been more than eight years old, alone in the woods. The gang had been pelting him with rocks and calling him horrible slurs when she, Wil, and Geoff had come upon them. They'd lit into the ruffians and sent them on their way with the warning to never cross their border again along with a fine collection of bruises, bloodied noses, and black eyes to show they meant it.

Wil met Issy's gaze and grinned, and for a moment, the Wil she'd known was back. He clapped Remi on the shoulder. "It's good to see you again."

"Are you the new guests staying here? The guests I'm to be my best for?"

Wil laughed. "I've accompanied your new guests here." He indicated Dante and his men. "This is Dante DeVittorio. He and his sister, Lady Carina, will be staying here for a while."

Remi gave a quick bow. "Sir De Vittorio."

Dante stared down his nose at Remi and said nothing.

"And this is Burrell, my fellow king's man, and Sergio, Dante's man, along with Marco and Carlo." Wil introduced the men. "You'll be seeing a lot of them while we're here."

Burrell and Sergio both stepped up and shook Remi's hand as Marco, a large, hulking man, and Carlo, younger and with a quicker smile, looked on. Issy swore Remi's chest swelled up and out.

"I'll be gettin' Randolph now, Mistress," Remi said, and hurried out, still grinning from ear to ear.

Carina and her maidservant, Paola, rejoined them outside as Issy led the way to the Stray's Stables, named after the small barn her father had built for her at Crossroads Keep, and which she used for the same purpose, to house and tend to injured and sick animals.

Currently, it housed two orphaned squirrels, a fawn with a broken leg, and a one-eyed owl who'd more or less taken up permanent residence.

"This is Aristotle," she introduced the brown and gray feathered eagle owl sitting on a perch made out of branches that spanned a corner of the stable next to a small, open window, and a nesting box on the other end of the stable. "He lost an eye a few years ago, and decided he liked living here even after it healed." She pointed to where the branch poked out the window. "He comes and goes as he pleases, and thinks he rules the roost."

"Is he friendly with people?" Wil asked, while Carina huddled against the open door and Dante walked past the squirrel's cage and over to the fawn's stall.

"Once he gets to know you," Issy answered. "Which can take some time and a lot of mice offerings."

"There is a *fulvo*, a fawn here with a splinted leg," Dante said, incredulous. "Why bother, when it will surely eat your crops as a *cervo*, a stag?" He indicated the squirrels, which were climbing the forearm Wil had lowered into their cage. "The squirrels too. They will steal your nuts and seeds. Why not save yourself the trouble of hunting or trapping them later on and eat them now?"

Wil chuckled and shook his head as Issy took a deep breath in and let it out slowly. She knew Dante's questions would be what most men would ask. Men who didn't know her.

"I prefer to give them a fighting chance to live as nature intends," she explained.

"Who takes care of them?" Carina sniffed daintily. "Who feeds them and cleans up after them?"

"I do," Issy told her. "Remi helps. He's quite good with creatures in need." She looked to Wil. "Wallace likes to come help. He's been working with my mother and Denys, learning to become a healer, along with Blanche, one of Denys and Marta's twins."

"My little brother told me this last night." Wil tried to shuck the squirrels clinging to his sleeve. "Though I got the impression him coming here was as much for Blanche's company as for the animals."

Issy didn't argue with Wil's assessment. In truth, she thought he had the right of it. "Come on, Acorn, Chestnut, playtime with Uncle Wil is over." She pulled the squirrels from Wil's cuffs, not missing how much larger his forearm had grown, and pulled the slatted roof to their cage closed. "I'm setting up a stall for them in a few days, so they'll be able to climb to their hearts' content."

Wil walked over to the fawn's stall. "How long before the splint comes off?"

"If Spot's leg continues to heal well, we'll take his splint off in a month or maybe a little less."

A gaze as dark as the fawn's met Issy's, a gaze she recognized for the second time today. A small smile tugged at the corners of Wil's mouth. "It's good to see some things haven't changed around here."

Issy gave him a quick smile, and over his shoulder caught the grim line of Dante's mouth. "I'll, ah, take you to the yearling's pasture now."

She pointed out the beehives on the edge of the orchard at the property's northern border as they made their way to the horse pastures. "The bees eat the nectar from the orchard and the wildflowers we grow next to their hives, which gives the honey a distinct taste, and pollinates the orchard. We sell Oloron honey in markets four provinces away, and we'll be adding six more hives next spring."

"Is your mother still selling Sophie the Sixth's love potions?"

Wil's question caught Issy by surprise. "She is. She says as long as the women keep asking for it, the men keep drinking it, and marriages keep following, she'll keep making it."

"Has she shared the recipe with you yet?"

Issy grinned.

"She did, didn't she?"

Issy shrugged.

"Love potion?" Carina's blue eyes grew wide. "And the woman, she offers it to the man she wishes to marry?"

Issy nodded. "Typically, that's how it works. Though a few men have offered it to the women they wanted to marry."

"And this works too?"

"It's responsible for at least one hundred marriages that I know of," Issy told her.

"Perhaps we can make that one hundred and one." All eyes turned to Dante, who was smiling at Issy. "I am meant to be looking for a wife here after all."

"Ah, yes, well," Issy stammered, not sure if she was reading too much into his words and his smile, though by the glare in Wil's eyes, she wasn't. "I'm sure once your presence here and the fact you're looking for a wife become known, we'll be selling love potions galore."

"Has a woman ever offered you a love potion?" Carina asked Wil, who coughed and cleared his throat as Burrell glowered.

"No," Wil answered.

"Whyever not?" Carina pressed.

"There was no need," Wil said, his dark gaze sweeping Issy's. "The entire valley knew who I was in love with, all except for her."

"What happened?"

"She refused me."

"Who would refuse you?" Carina exclaimed, then clapped her lily-white hand over her mouth.

"Right, well." Issy turned on her heels and called out over her shoulder. "Let's continue on to the foal's pasture, shall we?"

CHAPTER THREE

Borders

Wil

Wil had eaten supper at Oloron Manor many times in his youth. His grandmother, Berta, and her second husband, Anglbert, had run the manse as stewards for the count and countess until Isabeau was of age to claim her inheritance on her eighteenth birthday.

This was the first time he'd be supping here as Isabeau's guest. The first of many suppers to come. Tomorrow, he'd ride over with the DeVittorios to survey their land and buildings and determine what work would be needed to make the manse not only livable, but profitable.

Dante had visions of setting up his manse much like Count Talon had set up Crossroads Keep with farming, livestock, and breeding horses, as well as a vineyard. Which was a huge part of why Charles had wanted Talon to take Dante under his tutelage, and why Talon would be riding over with them tomorrow, along with Phillipe, who was partners with Talon in the horse breeding business, and Dardinel, who ran the farming side of the estates.

Wil walked into the dining hall where the high table, apparently used only for formal suppers, was left vacant and the household was seated at the two long tables. Isabeau sat at the center of one, with Berta and Anglbert to her left and Geoff to her right. A pretty blonde sat to Geoff's right, and Dante sat directly across from Isabeau with Carina and Sergio, while his and the manse's men-at-arms spread out along the rest of the table and the servants sat at the other.

"Wil." The pretty blonde beside Geoff jumped up, her curls bouncing, and Wil went to her and gave her a hug.

"Hello, Desiree." He stepped back, holding her hands in his and grinning into her big doe-brown eyes. "You've grown up since last I saw you."

A faint pink crept across her cheeks. "So have you," she said with a light laugh.

"All right, all right." Geoff stood and pulled Desiree into his shoulder. "Leave off, LeCuir. She's spoken for."

Wil chuckled. The Guiscards were well known for their ardor and protectiveness. Once they fell in love, that was it. No one but their chosen would do. He glanced at Isabeau, who had once been his chosen, though he hadn't been hers. It assuaged his pride a bit that she hadn't chosen anyone else yet either. But only a bit.

Burrell sat beside Sergio, so Wil took a seat beside Carina, across from his grandmother and Anglbert. It felt odd to not be sitting beside Geoff or Isabeau, as he would have before he'd left Oloron, but he was attached to the DeVittorios while here.

"This looks and smells delicious, Lucinda," Isabeau complimented as the head cook supervised as the platters of cheeses with grapes, roasted mutton, summer squashes, field greens, and freshly baked loaves of rye were served. She nodded to the other two kitchen maids. "Thank you, Marie, Yvette."

"I had the best of teachers." Lucinda dipped a knee to Berta, who beamed her approval.

She and the maidservants took their seats at the second table, and everyone tucked in to the meal. Wil, who'd been eating either camp or palace food for the last seven years, depending on where he was and what his duties were, hadn't realized how much he'd missed good country cooking.

Randolph and Remi came into the dining hall while Wil was stuffing his belly with his second helping of meat and bread, and Randolph spoke quietly into Isabeau's ear as Remi waved to Wil and took a seat at the second table. Isabeau nodded at whatever it was Randolph told her, and then he took his seat beside Lucinda.

"Is it the custom here," Dante asked Isabeau, "for the servants to eat with the family?"

Isabeau glanced about the hall as knives stilled and forkfuls of food hung midair. "It is," she answered. "Unless it's a formal meal. Is it not where you are from?"

"At the lower country estates, perhaps," he said, a touch of disdain in his voice. Or perhaps Wil was only imagining it. "Not in the *classe superiore*. No."

"Well." By the tone of Isabeau's one word, Wil hadn't been the only one to imagine Dante's disdain. "We don't pretend to be anything but country folk here, Signore DeVittorio."

Dante held a hand up as several muffled coughs filled the uneasy silence. "I meant no insult or disrespect," he apologized, and then flashed one of his charming smiles. "It is just one of many differences in our cultures. I am sure we will discover many more."

Isabeau dipped her head and glanced questioningly at Wil, who had been around enough landed Lombardy families to know that the DeVittorios were an especially proud and pretentious family. Still, he kept his face expressionless. His job was to help the DeVittorios assimilate, not cause friction between them and their hosts.

Though, if Isabeau outright asked him at some point, he wouldn't lie to her.

The meal continued in silence, until Lucinda and the maidservants went into the kitchens and came back carrying four pies.

"Strawberry, raspberry, or a mix of both?" Lucinda asked Carina first.

"*Niente*. None for me, thank you," Carina declined.

"Which do you suggest?" Dante asked Isabeau.

"Take your pick. They're all delicious."

"Which is your *preferita*, your favorite?"

Isabeau glanced over at Wil, who pressed his lips tight to keep from laughing out loud. If Dante thought fawning over her like this was a way to impress the Issy whom Wil had known, he was sorely mistaken.

"I, ah, I'm partial to strawberry," she said.

Lucinda cut and served slices of strawberry to Isabeau and Dante. She served Geoff and Desiree slices of raspberry without asking, and then looked to Wil.

"The mix of berries, please." He groaned in anticipation as Lucinda handed him his plate. "Now this, I've missed."

"They don't feed you pie in the palace?" his grandmother, who hated to think of anybody going without a proper meal, asked.

"They do," Wil answered. He took a bite and it didn't disappoint. "But not like this. I don't know what the difference is, where the berries are grown maybe, but the palace cooks have nothing on your cooking, Grandmother. Or yours, Lucinda."

"Nobody does," Anglbert agreed. "It was your grandmother's cooking that first caught my attention."

"Did she then offer you this Sophie the Sixth's love potion?"

All eyes turned to Carina.

"There was no need for her to." Anglbert gave Berta a quick sideways hug and a kiss on her beaming cheek. "I was pretty much sweet on her from the first day I met her. Not as badly as your father had it for your mother." Anglbert wagged his bushy eyebrows at Isabeau and Geoff. "The poor man kept falling off his horse and bleeding all over the place."

"The way our mother tells it, she hated our father at first sight," Geoff said. He laid his hand over Desiree's and gave it a gentle squeeze. "Unlike Desiree here, who's been in love with me since practically the day she was born."

"It's true," Desiree admitted. "My parents say the first time I smiled was when Geoff grinned down at me in my cradle."

Geoff lifted her hand and placed a kiss on her fingers. "And we haven't stopped smiling at each other since."

Isabeau rolled her eyes with an exaggerated groan that had half the table laughing. But not Wil.

"It must be nice to have such a steady, unwavering love," he said.

Isabeau's gaze met his, all laughter gone from them.

"So," Carina spoke to Desiree. "You did not offer any love potion to him?"

"I did offer him a vial," Desiree admitted. "When I was fifteen."

"Which was her way of telling me I could court her properly," Geoff finished. "And which I drank willingly."

Carina shook her head. "I do not understand."

"That's the thing about Sophie the Sixth's Love Potion, and the secret to its success," Isabeau explained. "A woman, or man, offers a vial to their intended, and if their intended accepts and drinks it, it means they're interested. If not…" She shrugged.

"Have you ever offered a man a love potion, Lady Isabeau?" Dante asked.

Wil swallowed what felt more like a rock than wine, waiting for Isabeau's answer.

Isabeau shook her head. "No, I haven't."

"To repeat my sister's question to Wil earlier today, whyever not?"

Isabeau glanced around the table, held Wil's gaze for a heartbeat, then looked back at Dante, lengthening her spine. "I've never felt the need or desire for a husband."

"For any, ah, particular husband?" Dante pushed. "Or for men in general?"

It took Isabeau a moment to realize what Dante was asking her, then her mouth opened and her eyes grew wide. "Oh," she said, and then laughed lightly. "Yes, I like men in general, and no, there's been no man in particular whom I'd wish to wed."

"Perhaps you simply have not met the right man yet," Dante said with a suggestive grin that Wil wanted to wipe from his face.

Pink spread across the apples of Isabeau's cheeks. "Perhaps."

***

Wil sat astride Charger, surveying the land Charles gave the DeVittorios. The southern part of the DeVittorios' land bordered the northern edges of Phillipe's and Dardinel's, and the eastern part bordered the northern edge of Isabeau's. A river that came down from the western mountains and ran east across the valley separated the DeVittorios' land from the others, with a stone bridge crossing over the river, and the mountains to the west and north created their own natural borders.

An old wood and stone house and stable lay in ruins in the northeastern corner of the land bordering the river, and only a few rotting posts remained of the pasture fencing. The land had lain fallow for the past thirty years, but it was loamy and fertile, and Dante was excited about tilling the fields and planting the grapevines he'd brought with him from Lombardy. Vines his family were renowned for and would eventually bring new trade to the valley.

"The vines will do well up against the mountains," Dante said. "There, they will be *protetta*, protected from the wind. The horses can be pastured in the southeast along the river, with the farm animals next to them and the crops to the southwest."

"I recommend planting crops more east than west," Dardinel told him. "They'll get more daylight that way. The western mountains tend to throw a long shadow."

To a man, they looked west toward the Pyrenees.

"You are Dardinel, the farmer, yes?" Dante asked, though they'd been introduced when Dardinel and Phillipe met them on the road.

"I am," Dardinel answered. A farmer who carried a long sword sheathed at his saddle, and knew how to wield it.

Wil had explained to Dante during their journey from Lombardy how Talon and his men had come to Oloron Valley as a troop of king's horse soldiers, and how several of them had decided to stay and start new lives here along with their captain, Talon, the newly landed Count of Oloron.

Wil eyed the forty and some years old soldiers and grinned. He'd bet his hard-earned coin that any one of them could still beat Dante in any kind of physical contest. The Lombard's hands were almost as soft as his sister's, without a blemish or callus on them. His servants had done almost everything for him on their journey here. Wil had never even seen Dante feed or saddle his own horse, much less pay any attention to it. Even when riding the chestnut gelding, whose name Wil had never heard spoken, Dante didn't talk to the horse or give it a friendly pat on the neck. Why he intended to breed horses on his land, Wil couldn't figure, other than he'd heard Dante's father mention starting their own line of horses to rival the Guiscards'.

Still, it wasn't Wil's problem what the DeVittorios did with their land, or why, only to settle them on it and introduce them to people who could help them manage it. At least Dante seemed to listen to Dardinel's suggestions for growing crops other than grapes. And agreed with Count Talon and Phillipe that the manor house and stable should be built where the previous ones had been, close to the road and the river.

They rode west to the open, fallow fields, where Talon and Phillipe helped lay out a plan to pasture the livestock along the western border, with the horses in a paddock closer to the stable and the crops in a field between the two.

"Did you bring any breeding stock with you?" Phillipe asked Dante.

"No." Dante shook his head. "I planned on buying livestock from breeders here." He held two fingers up. "*Due* milk cows, *tre* or *quattro* beef cows and a bull, a small herd of sheep, chickens."

"What about horses?" Talon asked. "Charles wrote that you were interested in breeding horses."

"I am," Dante answered. "Once I get the stable built and pastureland fenced, I will be prepared to buy some broodmares from you, as well as have my father send some of our broodmares and a stallion."

Talon glanced at Phillipe. "I'm sure we have a few good broodmares we'd be willing to sell, once we've seen the stallion you intend to breed them with."

"My father will send the stallion once I have the broodmares."

Talon held Phillipe's gaze longer this time.

"That's not how we do it," Talon told Dante. "We approve the stallion before we sell the mares to breed with him. The same with any broodmares we breed our stallions with."

Dante looked from Talon to Phillipe to Wil.

"Wil has seen our stallion," he told them. "Remember, Wil? The bay stallion in our stable? He will, how you say, *garantire*, for our stallion."

"I did see him," Wil said. "Once. In a stall. Not long enough or well enough to say if he'd be a good breeder or not."

"You saw him for as long as you saw Isabeau's Frisian and Turkmene yesterday. You were very *gratuito* of them as breeders," Dante argued. "Why would you not say the same about our stallion?"

"Because I know and trust the Guiscards' sense of horses," Wil told him. "I don't know yours well enough to trust or vouch for it."

Dante pressed his lips tight and narrowed his eyes at Wil, who stared right back at him. Wil might be here to help Dante, but he wasn't his man. His duty was to Charles, and his loyalty was Talon's, his godfather's. If Dante thought Wil was going to roll belly up and piss himself because Dante was angry with him, he had another think coming.

"This is something we can deal with further down the line," Talon said diplomatically. "First, you need to draw up a plan for your manor and stable and hire a crew to cut lumber and stone and build it. We'll put the word out for anyone interested to show up at the town marketplace next Saturday."

Dante gave a curt nod, jerked his horse's head around, and kicked the gelding into a canter back toward the road, Sergio and Marco following. Talon held back and rode alongside Wil.

"You don't care much for the young master DeVittorio, do you?"

Wil looked his godfather in the eyes. "No. I don't."

"Why not?"

"Let's just say Dante DeVittorio admires himself enough for the both of us."

Talon ran a hand back through his hair. "Anything more specific I should know about?"

Wil shook his head. "No. Not that I'm aware of."

"You'll let me know if there is?"

"You'll be the first, Captain."

***

Issy

Issy pulled Onyx up next to the horse pasture on their daily ride around the property, a habit she had learned from her father. Oswald and Gil, her men-at-arms, rode daily patrols as well, but Issy liked seeing things for herself.

Sabine and her colt grazed alongside Jolie and the other mares, Lyts's and Ebony's pregnant bellies glistening black under the late morning sun, Sultan standing guard close by. Kolossus, in the next pasture over along with Tug, the manses draft gelding, Maman, Issy's first saddle horse, now retired to a life of leisure, and half a dozen sheep and goats each, whinnied his displeasure at being kept away from the mares, while the mares lazily whisked their tails and ignored him.

Issy wished she could be as calm and indifferent to the two men currently occupying her house and thoughts as those mares were to the stallions. As happy as she was to see Wil again, he wasn't the same Wil she'd known. He was harder, mentally and physically, which wasn't surprising since he'd spent the past seven years as a soldier and a king's guard. He'd grown into a man in those years. A very handsome man. The roundness of his boyish face had been carved into chiseled cheekbones and a strong jaw, making his dark brown eyes look even bigger and deeper beneath his thick brows and high forehead, with a wary watchfulness about them that hadn't been there before.

He wore his earth brown hair, the curly tips bleached a lighter brown by the sun, cut above his ears rather than to his shoulders now, emphasizing his corded neck and broad shoulders. His chest was just as broad, tapering to a trim waist, and his arms flexed with muscles defined by years of riding and wielding weapons. The leather breeches he wore hugged well-muscled thighs, and though she would still describe him as long and lanky, there was a controlled but lethal power to his movements. That, along with his new wariness, put her in mind of a lone wolf she'd come across in the mountains a few times last summer.

Dante reminded her more of a wolf pup. Shrewd, cocky, proud, yet still trying to figure its position in a new pack. Which made sense, him being the third son of a wealthy family that had sent him to another country to build a life separate from, yet always attached to theirs. Their name. Their reputation.

A life she was now somehow supposed to help him build.

His sister, Carina, was more of a lapdog, bred to be pretty and witless and trained to obey her brother's every whim and marry for the good of the family. Though Issy was fairly certain Wil had caught her eye, she didn't see Dante approving of his sister marrying a lowly man-at-arms, even if he was the king's man, any more than she saw Carina going against her brother, no matter how many tame foxes and greedy boars the gallant Wilric LeCuir saved her from.

Issy set Onyx to a leisurely pace back to the stable with Foxy trotting alongside them, stopping to sniff at and mark her favorite fence posts and bushes. The stalls for the men's horses were empty, which meant they were still at Dante's property, where they were to meet up with her father, Phillipe, and Dardinel.

She gave Onyx a good brushing and a bucket of oats and was walking out of the stable when Dante, Sergio, and Marco rode up.

She glanced up the road and saw her father and Wil looking to be deep in conversation as they approached at a slow walk.

Dante dismounted and tossed his reins to Sergio. He caught Issy's curious gaze and took the reins back, giving the chestnut gelding a pat on its neck.

"What's his name?" she asked.

"Mattone," Dante said. "It means brick."

"Because of his color?"

"I believe so. He came to me with the name."

Issy let the gelding sniff her hand and then rubbed the white blaze that ran from his forehead to his nose. "He seems to be a good-natured soul."

"Soul?" Dante cocked his head at Issy. "Ah, *si, si*, he is."

He stood holding Mattone's reins as her father and Wil rode up and dismounted.

"Daughter." Her father held his arms out and enveloped her in his embrace.

Issy buried her face into his chest and breathed in the scent of love and safety. "Father."

He kissed the top of her head and let go his hold of her. "I better get going. I left Orlando at Willem's on my way over and should probably rescue him from your brother's unending questions."

"Tell Mother I'll be over tomorrow with Berta and Lucinda to help plan the Summer Solstice and welcome supper for the DeVittorios." She kissed her father's cheek and then glanced at Wil, who had followed her father into the army and king's service, while her younger brother Orlando wanted nothing more than to become a famous leatherworker like Wil's father.

Issy had followed her father and Uncle Phillipe into the horse breeding business, while Wil's youngest brother Wallace, and Blanche, one of Denys and Marta's daughters, had taken to the healing arts under Denys and Countess Lara's tutelage. Issy had learned her share of the healing arts as well, but much preferred tending animals to people.

Her father mounted Bolt and nodded to the others. "Wil, Dante, we'll see you tomorrow as well."

"Sergio," Dante called, and his man came trotting out of the stable. "Will you unsaddle Mattone and let him out in his pen?"

Sergio looked confused for a moment, then took the gelding's reins. "*Si, maestro.*"

"Mattone?" Wil said.

Dante scoffed. "That is my horse's name."

"Is it?"

Issy thought it odd Wil hadn't known the horse's name after traveling with the DeVittorios for a month. The Wil she'd known would've remembered all the horses' names before the people's. The look on his face as he glared between Dante and herself was even odder.

Turning his back to Wil, Dante reached his hand out toward Foxy, who nipped at the air between them and skittered behind Issy's skirts.

"She's probably still nervous after yesterday," Issy offered Dante, who wore an offended expression.

"Or she just doesn't like you," Wil said, then turned on his heel and led Charger into the stable.

CHAPTER FOUR

Con Permisso

Issy

The night air was warm and the tables set out in the courtyard of Crossroads Keep were laden with the bounties of summer. There were bowls of bitter greens and succulent squash, cut up peaches and plums, freshly baked rye breads, wheels of herbed cheeses, a goat roasting on one spit, and a buck that Issy's father, Geoff, and Wil had shot yesterday roasting on another. A casket each of ale and wine had been tapped, ten tubs of honey from Oloron Manor set out, and a dozen fruit pies sat cooling.

Torches lit the yard filled with the valley's people there to welcome the summer along with the DeVittorios. In the seven days he'd been here, Dante had already made his presence known among the ladies, who'd taken to calling him the Charming Lombard.

His sister, on the other hand, had kept close to the manor, but now had four men surrounding her chair offering to fetch her a cup of wine or a brawny arm to lead her around and introduce her to the crowd of curious villagers, a dour-faced Burrell never more than two steps away from her.

Issy was about to go over and rescue her when Wil walked up and held his hand out to Carina, who placed her soft, lily-white hand into his and stood with a grateful smile. Issy glanced down at her own tanned, roughened hands and stuffed them into her skirt pockets as Wil said something to Burrell and then led Carina away. Lengthening her spine and lifting her chin, she made the rounds of the yard as Wil and Carina did the same, greeting people and making small talk until it was time to eat.

She sat at the table of honor between Carina, who sat quiet as a mouse to the countess's right, and Desiree, who chatted her ear off while Issy pushed the sumptuous food around her plate, watching girls and women she'd grown up with casting flirtatious looks at Wil and Dante. Dante flirted back, causing them to burst out in twitters every time he smiled at one of them, while Wil ignored them for the most part, much as he'd been ignoring Issy ever since he'd arrived.

If they saw each other at the manor, it was only in passing, and he picked the seat farthest from her at the supper table every night. She told herself if Wil was still holding a grudge against her, that was his problem, not hers, the stubborn ass. Refusing his proposal of marriage was a decision she still stood by. If they'd have married, it would've ruined their friendship, which at the time had been the most important in her life. He'd been the most important person in her life next to her parents and brothers, and she'd always thought she was his.

Until he'd left her.

If anything, she should be angry at him for ending their friendship in such a manner. And she was. Yet beneath the anger lay a hurt so deep, she'd woken from dreams of watching him disappear into nothingness for years afterward. In fact, they'd only stopped three months ago, and then a week before he'd arrived back in her life, she'd started dreaming of losing the pendant he'd given her.

She didn't realize she'd pulled the pendant out and was rolling it between her fingers until Carina's voice broke through her musings.

"… a beautiful pendant. Was it a gift?"

Issy dropped the pendant back beneath her bodice. "Yes it was. My best friend at the time gave it to me for my sixteenth birthday."

"At the time?" Carina said. "You are no longer best friends?"

Issy looked over at Wil and met his dark, intent stare. "No," she told Carina, knowing full well Wil was listening to every word. "We're not."

"I am sorry for you then," Carina said, her voice tinged with sadness. "It is hard to lose a best friend."

Issy searched Carina's blue eyes and saw a deep sorrow there. "You had to leave your best friend back in Lombardy when you came here."

It was more statement than question, and Carina simply nodded and gave a wistful little smile.

Issy laid her hand over Carina's on the table. "I am truly sorry for you as well."

Tears welled in Carina's eyes. "Thank you, Lady Isabeau."

Issy gave her hand a quick squeeze. "Call me Isabeau or Issy, please. There is no need for Lady this and Lady that between us, is there?"

Carina smiled, pulled her hand from under Issy's, and swiped at her damp eyes. "No, there is not."

"Good," Issy said, and she meant it. "I think we can become quite good friends, Carina."

"As do I."

Issy beamed. She would much rather be friends with Carina than not, and was genuinely glad for this turn in their relationship. Especially since they'd be living in the same house for the next few months. It was awkward enough stepping on eggshells around Wil. And Dante made her uncomfortable in a way she couldn't explain. Now, at least, she wouldn't have to worry about Carina too. Not that they were much alike, but you didn't have to be akin to a person to like them.

Pleased that they'd seemingly overcome their differences, Issy chose a piece of strawberry pie from the plates laid out on the table and tucked into it. She noticed Carina didn't take any pie; she hadn't eaten any of the desserts offered to her at Oloron Manor either, which meant either she didn't care for sweets or was watching her trim figure. Issy considered asking her which it was but figured that was a conversation for after they were better acquainted.

With the meal finished, the tables were cleared and stacked by the outdoor kitchens. Musicians set up and started warming their instruments as men and women formed couples for the first dance, which Issy's parents would lead.

Issy and Wil had partnered for many a dance in the past, and she found herself holding her breath as he approached where she stood alongside Carina and a few other single women. Once again, Wil offered his hand to Carina, who blushed prettily as she laid her hand in his and followed him onto the dance floor. Issy let her breath out in a huff.

"Lady Isabeau, you look *molto carina*, very pretty tonight in your lovely dress." Dante stood in front of her with a charming smile and held his hand out. "Would you care to dance?"

She glanced at the other women watching her, and then smoothed the skirts of her lavender gown. "Yes, of course. Thank you, Sir DeVittorio."

"Dante. Please."

"Dante." Issy placed her hand in his, thinking it odd that she'd gone to first names with brother and sister the same night after seven days of cool politeness.

He led her next to Wil and Carina, and as it was a circle dance, Wil took Issy's other hand as Geoff, dancing with Desiree, took Carina's.

The drummer started the beat and the lute and tambourine players joined in. The dance started out slowly, gradually and continually picking up in pace. Dante was quick on his feet and quicker to laugh, his smooth hand holding tight to Issy's.

Wil's calloused hand was both strange and familiar, larger and stronger than she remembered, yet moving in time with hers as if they'd never stopped dancing together.

By the end of the dance, they were all panting and laughing, and Wil's fingers trailed across Issy's as he let go his hold, while Dante held tight.

"Shall we dance the next together as well?" he asked.

Issy glanced over Dante's shoulder at Wil's scowling visage, and then at the line of wistful ladies watching them. "Thank you for asking, Dante, but I don't think you should disappoint the other ladies eager to dance with you."

Dante gave an exaggerated sigh. "I shall conform to your wisdom in this, Lady, for I know you would not lead me astray."

"I, ah, no, I would not."

"So." He lifted her hand and held it aloft, his blue eyes smiling into hers. "Who should I ask to dance next?"

"There is Christine, Desiree's younger sister."

He glanced over at the pretty young blonde smiling shyly at him, bent low over Issy's hand, and kissed the back of her fingers. "I shall do my duty, my Lady."

He walked over to Christine and spoke, eliciting a huge grin as he led her to the dance floor. While his charm seemed to thrill other women, it made Issy uneasy when he focused it on her. She knew no ill of him, and he'd never crossed any lines. Maybe she wasn't used to a man plying her with so many sweet words and fine manners.

She looked around the courtyard, at the men she'd known her whole life. Good, honest, hardworking, hard fighting men. Men who were honorable if a little rough around their edges. Whose manners might not be so fine, but who could be counted on to do the right thing. Men like her father. Like Wil. Who stood off to the side of Carina while she conversed with Phillipe's and Dardinel's wives, his dark gaze on Issy.

***

Wil

Wil watched Isabeau disappear beyond the crowd into the night while he only half listened to the conversation between Carina, Doralice, and Annette, two women who'd been honorary aunties to him growing up, and who were gentle yet persistent in drawing

Carina out of her shy shell. When Carina laughed out loud at something Doralice said, Wil relaxed.

"Ladies," he excused himself and headed for the casket of ale.

He poured himself a cup and watched as another circle of couples prepared to dance, and was approached by a bevy of young women, some of whom he recognized and others he didn't.

"Welcome home, Wil," a pretty, round-cheeked brunette said as the others formed a half circle around him.

"Thank you, Bonnie," Wil answered, figuring he'd guessed correctly that she was one of Denys and Marta's twins when she smiled up at him. And whom he likely wouldn't have guessed if his younger brother, Wallace, hadn't already introduced Wil to her twin, Blanche. They'd been in side braids when he'd left.

"How long's it been?" she asked.

"Close to seven years."

"You've changed."

"I'd say we all have."

"Do you remember me?" a brown-eyed girl on the verge of young womanhood asked.

Will shook his head. "I'm afraid I don't."

"I'm Adele, Dardinel and Annette's daughter. I was only eight when you left."

"Adele. I do remember you. Your brother was…"

"Dustin. I'll be sure to introduce you again once he's done dancing."

Wil nodded.

"Is it true you know King Charles?" asked one of the nameless young women he didn't recognize.

"I do."

"And you were with him in Rome when he was crowned emperor?" another spoke up.

"I was."

"What was Rome like?" two others asked in unison.

"Was it as grand as they say?" another chimed in before he could answer.

Wil glanced over their heads, lifted his chin, and smiled as if answering someone else's beckoning. "Ladies," he said. "If you'll excuse me."

He walked away from a chorus of disappointed sighs and turned from the courtyard and the open curiosity he elicited, and headed toward the stable. Of course, it'd been much the same when he'd first joined Charles's personal guard and he'd faced a barrage of questions about his life.

Living in a palace wasn't all that different from living in a country village where everyone thought they had a right to know a person's business. Growing up here, Wil hadn't known any different, and by the time he was traveling from palace to palace or kingdom to kingdom with Charles and his household, he'd figured out how to be circumspect in his answers without seeming rude. But it didn't mean he liked being questioned by people who were little more than strangers to him.

Friends, he didn't mind so much.

Geoff had asked him a few questions about his time away, as had Talon, and Wil's parents and brothers. Isabeau, on the other hand, hadn't asked him a single question about the past seven years.

In truth, she'd barely spoken more than three words to him since he'd voiced his opinion on Dante and Foxy four days ago. Not that she'd spoken much to him before that. She'd been as adept at avoiding him as he'd been at avoiding her. Neither one of them eager to ask or answer questions better left unspoken between them.

He wandered his way to the stable and went inside, not at all surprised to find Isabeau in there, rubbing the nose of one of the horses and speaking in its ear. The horse's ears twitched and pricked in his direction, and Isabeau's hand stilled mid-stroke.

"Isabeau."

"Wilric."

Wilric? So, she was angry with him. Or responding to him calling her Isabeau, which he'd never done before he'd left. Before, she'd always been Issy. His Issy.

She dropped her hand to her side and faced him, her gray eyes sharp as a falcon's wing. "Why are you still so angry with me?"

Wil chuffed. In many ways she was the same Issy she'd always been. Honest and direct, almost to a fault. That, she'd gotten from her father. Her beauty, she'd gotten from her mother. A beauty that had grown and blossomed from girlish to womanly in the years he'd been away.

Why she wasn't married yet, he couldn't figure, and took some solace in. He couldn't've been the only man she'd refused in the past seven years.

"I'm not," he said. He'd gotten past being angry with her years ago. Hadn't he?

"So… you simply don't like me anymore?"

"I don't know you anymore," he told her.

Her eyes went from soft and forlorn as a dove's coo to sharp and fierce as a falcon's cry.

"Who do you know now? The lady Carina?"

"I've come to know her, yes. She's a sweet and gentle lady."

"Unlike me."

"You said it, not me."

Isabeau set her jaw and narrowed her eyes. A look he remembered well.

"She's a dormouse."

Wil leveled his gaze on hers. "A dormouse you, my falcon, are not to swoop down on and shred to pieces."

Her eyes lit up at him calling her his falcon, and then narrowed again. "You needn't worry about me, Wilric LeCuir. I'll leave the ravaging up to you. The big, bad wolf."

"Me? A big, bad wolf?"

"If the pelt fits."

Wil laughed. He'd missed this Issy, more than he'd known. "I have no interest in ravaging Carina, or any other woman in Oloron for that matter. As soon as I've fulfilled my duty and seen the DeVittorios settled in their new home, I'll return to serve Charles."

"Well, if that's the case, you should probably let all the other unmarried women in Oloron know too, so they can stop fawning over you."

"Fawning?" Wil snorted. "Like Dante does over you?"

"He doesn't fawn over me any more than he does over any other woman," she insisted.

"If you say so, Little Mule," he said, using his old pet name for her.

Isabeau opened her mouth, then snapped it shut. "I do say so, you stubborn ass," she hissed, her eyes widening at the quick twitch of Wil's lips before he pressed them tight.

She strode past him, her skirts swinging, and he gave his grin full rein.

"There's my Issy."

She glared over her shoulder at him, and he laughed, short and quick. Though he hadn't exactly enjoyed the subject matter, he had enjoyed their banter. He'd missed arguing with her and ruffling her feathers. He'd even missed being called a stubborn ass.

He'd missed her.

He trailed her out of the stable and back toward the party, grinning at her squared shoulders and determined stride. She knew he was behind her, and he knew how hard it was for her not to scowl over her shoulder. She slowed her stride and Wil followed her line of sight to where Dante stood away from the crowd, watching her and Wil approach, a frown on his face.

"Where have you two been?" he demanded as he stepped in front of Isabeau, blocking her way.

"Excuse me?" she said, her surprise evident in her voice.

Dante held both hands up, palms out. "Pardon me, Lady Isabeau, I did not mean to insinuate anything untoward occurred between you and Wil—"

"What, exactly, is it you're not insinuating?" Wil growled, stepping up beside Isabeau.

Dante held his hands higher. "*Niente. Niente.* I am insinuating nothing." He turned an apologetic smile on Isabeau. "I was only concerned for your, how you say… reputation."

Isabeau didn't say a word, though her arched brows and tight lips said plenty.

"It is only, in my country," Dante explained, "a lady does not go into a place alone with a man who is not her husband."

Isabeau looked to Wil, who wanted nothing more than to pummel Dante, but couldn't. "It's true," he said, her instant smile of forgiveness toward Dante irritating Wil as much as Dante's accusation. "It's also true," he told Dante, "that here it is not so, especially if the man and the woman are old friends reminiscing about their childhoods."

"Ah, *buono, buono.* I am glad to be told this." Dante beamed at Isabeau. "Since I wish to formally ask your father for his *permisso* to court you, Lady Isabeau."

Isabeau's jaw dropped. "You want to ask my father's permission to court me?"

"*Si. Si.* In my country, this is how it is done. With your *permisso*, of course."

Wil raised his brows at Isabeau and gave her his best "I told you so" smirk. That the Lombard had been interested in Isabeau from the moment he'd laid eyes on her had been obvious to anyone watching. And Wil had been watching. Closely.

She lifted her chin at Wil's smirk and then turned a dazzling smile on Dante.

"I'll think about it."

***

Issy

Issy woke in her comfortable, familiar bed, with a jumble of strange and disconcerting feelings. Dante had gone directly from asking Issy's permission to court her to asking her father for his. Her father had responded exactly as she'd expected. He'd told Dante it was up to Isabeau who she accepted as a courter. Since she told him she'd think about it, she was more than annoyed he went to her father thinking he'd get what he wanted.

She rolled onto her back and stretched out her arms and legs, then wrapped her arms around Foxy and buried her face in the fox's ruff.

By telling Dante she'd think about him courting her, she worried she'd set something in motion she wasn't sure she wanted. She was twenty-two, almost twenty-three years old, an old maid by many standards, and Dante was handsome, charming, and was looking to go into horse breeding along with farming and a vineyard, all goals compatible with hers for her land. Land that bordered his. He intended to build a life here, unlike Wil, who would be leaving in a few months' time.

She gave Foxy a smacking kiss on her nose and got out of bed, walked over to the washbasin, and splashed water on her face. She donned her leather riding skirt, linen tunic, and boots, combed and wrangled her hair into a braid, and headed downstairs to breakfast where Wil, Dante, Burrell, Sergio, and Geoff sat eating porridge in uncommon silence.

Dante beamed at her, Geoff cocked his head, and Wil stood, picked up his bowl, and started for the kitchen door.

"I was going to work Sultan today," Issy announced. Wil stopped at the door and turned around. "If anyone wants to come watch."

Wil dipped his head and then pushed through the door, disappearing into the kitchen. High, feminine giggles floated into the dining hall before the door swung closed, followed by Dante's burst of "*Finalmente.* I have been waiting to see this horse in action."

Issy gave him a strained smile and went into the kitchen in time to see Wil's backside walking out to the outside kitchens. Lucinda filled a bowl with porridge, then watched askance as Issy sat at the worktable to eat it rather than join the men at the dining table.

She ate without tasting, thanked a perplexed Lucinda, left through the door to the outside kitchens, tossed Heinz an apple, went to the stable, and saddled Sultan herself.

"When Geoff and Dante get here," she told Remi, "let them know we're out in the exercise paddock."

"Yes, Mistress."

Issy swung up onto Sultan's saddle. "Have you seen Wil this morning?"

Remi stopped chewing his bottom lip and nodded. "He saddled his horse himself too and rode out." He chewed on his lip some more. "Did I do something wrong, Mistress?"

"What makes you ask that?"

"'Cos neither you nor Wil let me saddle your horses."

"No, Remi. It's nothing you did. It's Wil and I, we're quarrelling."

"Over him not liking you an' Dante maybe courting?"

Issy gave a wry smile. Gossip traveled fast, and there wasn't much Remi missed. "Something like that," she told him.

She walked Sultan over to the exercise paddock, where Wil was putting Charger through his paces. She pulled the Turkmene up to the fence and watched. Wil had always been a good rider, but seeing him on Charger, trotting and cantering, then taking the stallion in an easy gallop around the jumps, she was beyond impressed. Wil and Charger moved as one as the warhorse cut first right then left, then came skidding to a halt before pivoting on his hind legs and wheeling around in one direction and then another.

She grinned as Wil pressed his thighs tight and the stallion charged the jumps, feinting away at the last moment to the slightest pull of his reins. Wil's commands were so subtle they'd be invisible to the casual observer. Something Issy had never been when it came to Wil.

Once, she'd known him as well as she knew herself. At least she'd thought she had. Up until he'd proposed marriage. At the time, she'd only ever seen him as her best friend, like a brother, but now… Now he was no longer her best friend, or a friend at all. Now he was a stranger. A strapping, handsome stranger who showed bits and pieces of her old friend, and seemed to dislike her more than not.

So why had their arguing in the stable last night felt so right? Different, but right.

Sultan stamped his hooves and snorted, eager to get out into the paddock. Issy had never known a horse that loved to run and jump as much as he did. He was as smooth gaited and sure-footed at a full gallop as he was fast, and when he soared over a jump, Issy felt like she was flying.

She loved all her horses, especially Onyx, who was as smart, strong, steady, and faithful as a horse ever was, but there was something almost otherworldly about Sultan. Issy never felt like she owned him, but like he allowed her to tend to him and take care of his needs, and in return he deigned to let her ride him.

Charger snorted at Sultan, and Wil dipped his head to Issy and took the stallion on a cooldown lap as Dante, Sergio, Geoff, and Burrell came walking toward the paddock. Wil dismounted and led Charger out of the gate, keeping a safe distance between the two stallions and circling back around, claiming a spot at the fence as the others arrived.

Geoff went to stand by Wil, along with Burrell, and Sergio followed five feet behind Dante, who headed toward Issy and Sultan. Issy could feel Sultan tense as Dante neared, and she tensed as Dante came straight at them. Sultan danced sideways, putting some distance between them and bringing a frown to Dante's face.

"Your stallion is a bit, how you say, *alta tensione*."

Issy looked to Wil.

"High-strung," Wil said.

"He doesn't care for strangers." Issy defended Sultan, though what Dante said wasn't untrue. She tried to explain. "Where most horses would be like dogs, Sultan is like a cat. He doesn't give you his trust without you earning it."

"How long did it take you?" Wil asked when Dante said nothing.

"He was here seven days before he let me touch him. Two and half months before he'd take a saddle. And another seven days before he'd let me ride him."

Wil whistled low. They'd both helped her father saddle-break horses through the years, a process that normally took three days, not three months.

"Well," Dante said. "Now we are here to see if he was worth so much of your time."

Issy turned Sultan's head for the paddock. "Oh, he is," she said over her shoulder. "And you will."

She walked Sultan around the paddock the first loop, then sent him into a trot the second, a canter the third, and then an easy gallop, catching the impressed expressions on Dante's and Wil's faces as they watched the long-legged, high-stepping stallion go through his paces.

"Shall we jump now, Sultan?"

The horse pricked his ears forward and turned for the first jump, stepping more than jumping over the two-foot-high log. The next jump was a three-footer, which Sultan didn't even break stride to go over.

"Okay, boy," Issy said as they headed for the four-footer. "Here we go."

She gave him his reins and hugged her legs tight as he approached the jump, slowing enough to bunch his legs under him and sail over the jump. He hit the ground running and they circled the paddock, gaining even more speed, and took the same jump again, clearing it by a good foot. She took Sultan on a cool-down circle and trotted over to the grinning men.

"*Magnifico.*" Dante clapped, and Sultan snorted and backed up. "He is *magnifico.*"

Issy patted Sultan on the neck and looked to Wil, who knew his horses.

"He truly is a magnificent horse," he said. "You've done well with and by him."

Issy beamed.

"He will make an excellent stud for our stable," Dante said.

Issy's, Wil's, and Geoff's heads snapped around, while Burrell and Sergio slowly shook theirs.

"Our stable?" Issy asked.

"*Si.* When we are married and join our lands and stables, Sultan and I will both be busy making *bambini.*"

He smiled suggestively at Issy, who sat staring at him with her mouth agape.

"You do want children?" Dante asked. "Do you not?"

Muffled laughter came from where Wil and Geoff stood, and Issy snapped her mouth shut.

"You are getting ahead of yourself, Master DeVittorio," she told the still smiling Dante. "I told you I'd think about it. We are a long way from being married and making babies. Now, if you will excuse me."

She turned Sultan and galloped for the far fence, jumping it and riding west through the pastures and fields. She rode for the river and then followed it to the oak marking where the southern border of her land met with the northern border of her parents'. The same oak she and Wil had climbed a hundred times, hidden from the rest of the world on the platform their fathers had built among the sturdy branches as they shared their thoughts and secrets.

She tied Sultan to another, smaller oak with a patch of summer grass beneath it and left him to graze as she climbed the tree house oak and perched on a gnarled branch as thick as a man's torso that ran along the shoreline.

Her cheeks flushed hot at how Dante had proclaimed he and Sultan would be busy making babies and at Geoff's and Wil's amused laughter at her reaction. But mostly, her blood ran cold at how Dante assumed they'd be joining their lands and stables. Not if, but when, they married.

Issy loved running her own estate, with the help of others of course, but in the end, she had the final say in things. Things she didn't like the idea of sharing decisions about. Especially her horses.

Maybe if, over time, Dante proved himself knowledgeable about horses and their breeding, she'd consider sharing the running of her stable. Maybe. He'd have a lot to prove before then. Issy refused to be rushed into any of it, despite what Dante seemed to think. She'd have to be sure and explain her position to him. The sooner the better.

If it caused him to change his intentions, the thought of which didn't upset her at all, well then, so be it.

"Arrgh."

She shook her head as if she could shake some sense into her decision making, and saw Sultan lift his head and twitch his ears. She peeked around the oak's massive trunk and then climbed onto a higher branch and hid as best she could among the leaves and smaller branches as Wil rode up, dismounted, and tied Charger off to a tree on the opposite side of the oak to Sultan.

"I know you're up there, Little Falcon," he said, using her nickname in a voice both familiar yet strange, its deep masculinity resonating in her belly. "Shall I come up, or do you want to fly down?"

Issy almost told him to come up, but the thought of being alone with him in the intimacy of their old haunt had her scrambling down. She dropped onto the ground, landing on her feet and standing no more than two paces from him.

"Why are you here?" she demanded.

Wil laughed, short and harsh. "You always were direct."

Issy lowered her chin and raised her brows.

"So, I will be the same for you." He held her gaze for a moment, his own serious. "Don't fall for Dante's smiles and flattery. End this foolishness now, before it's too late."

"Why would I do that?" she asked, though she'd been considering it moments before.

"You don't know him, or him, you."

"If I decided to allow him to court me, isn't that the point? To learn about each other, and learn to care for each other?"

"Dante doesn't care about anyone but himself. He's only interested in your lands and horses."

Wil's words knocked her breath out of her chest. Like herself, he could be honest to a fault, but she'd never known him to be cruel. But she didn't know him anymore, and the man standing before her seemed intent on being callous and unfeeling,

"Nobody could ever want me for me?" she said through grit teeth. "Is that what you're saying?"

Wil held her narrowed gaze with his own, dark and unfathomable. "You know that's not what I'm saying," he rumbled. "If you recall, I wanted you for yourself. Once."

Issy lifted her chin. "But not anymore."

Wil opened his mouth, then clamped it shut. He cocked his head and stared at her for what felt like an eternity. "Take what I've said seriously," he ground out, and then he turned on his heels, strode over to Charger, and rode off, leaving Issy more confused than ever.

CHAPTER FIVE

Intentions

Wil

Wil, along with Dante, Talon, and Sergio, spoke to several men at the marketplace and chose Mason, a local builder who guaranteed a workforce of twenty men, to build the Lombard's new house and stable, and fence in his pastures. They hired six others to plant the vines, guaranteeing them three months' work and pay, and a chance to stay on in various positions if they and Dante agreed to terms.

Sergio would remain Dante's manservant and right hand when it came to running the estate, and Marco would be his livestock and stable master, with Carlo in charge of the farm and vineyard. Señor DeVittorio had chosen the men to travel and settle with Dante, and he'd chosen them for their specific talents, and because they were all unwed and supposedly looking for wives. Though Wil was pretty sure Sergio and Paola were sweet on each other.

Carina had stayed at the manor, too shy to venture out into such a public place yet.

Wil's father, Willem, and his brothers, Wyatt and Wallace, showed up shortly after the hiring had been finished, and Wil helped them set up their stall of leather goods, as he'd done every other Saturday of his youth.

"It's good to have you back, Wil," his father said at least five times, grinning and clapping Wil on the shoulder each time, and earning him an eyeroll from one or both of his brothers.

Wil didn't have the heart to remind his father that he wasn't back for good. He simply smiled and nodded, enjoying his time with his family while he could, and exchanging greetings and well wishes with the valley's people during market day.

He also kept an eye on Isabeau at her stall selling her manor's honeys, cheeses, herbs, and two dozen bottles of Sophie's Love Potion that she'd concocted with her mother over the past several days. Lucinda manned the stall as well, with the stalwart Oswald keeping watch over them, and Dante going back and forth between charming the women customers, making the rounds of the other sellers, and trying to be attached to Isabeau's hip. Once, he was standing so close to her that she turned around with an armful of cheeses and bumped into him, causing her to drop two of the cheeses and shoo Dante away. Dante doubled down and hovered even closer, too dense to notice her stiff movements and too full of himself to care.

"Some things haven't changed," Wyatt said, offering Wil a skin of water as he sat on the bench beside him.

Wil waved off the offer. "What are you talking about?"

"You watching Isabeau, scowling at any other man who dares pay her attention."

"He's not just any other man," Wil grumbled. "He's landed and titled and trying to court her."

"So I heard." Wyatt sat back, playing with the wedding ring on his finger. "Everybody heard at the welcome feast." He glanced over at Dante making a show of offering Isabeau a vial of love potion. "He's certainly not shy about his intentions."

Isabeau took the vial, shook her head, and set it down with the few remaining vials.

Wil chuffed. "He's a preening peacock."

Wyatt's booming laugh caught Isabeau's attention.

"Tell me what you really think," Wyatt said as Isabeau stared at them, then rearranged her tubs of honey.

"I think Isabeau's a grown woman who knows what she wants and can take care of herself. She's not mine anymore to worry about."

"Are you still hers?"

The question caught Wil off guard. As his older brother, Wyatt had known Wil better than almost anyone. He'd been there the day Wil had met Isabeau for the first time, when at one and a half years old Wil had taken one look at five-month-old Isabeau, whose parents had just brought her down from the mountain where Lara had been hiding with her, kissed her on her cheek, and claimed her. "My See." My Issy.

She'd been his Issy and he'd been her Wil from that moment until the day he'd left sixteen years later. She was no longer his, but was he still hers?

For years, he'd sworn to himself he was over her. Then he'd seen her again. Her auburn mane framing her perfect face. Skin the color of cream with high-cut cheekbones, a pert nose, and full lips widening into a smile that could dazzle the sun itself. Her slight but womanly figure was more alluring than he remembered, and her eyes remained intriguing: turning from a gray as soft as a dove's breast to sharp as a falcon's wing. He'd watched, beguiled, when her slender fingers grasped the pendant he'd given her for her sixteenth birthday.

He looked at his brother and shrugged. "Hell if I know."

Wyatt shook his head, then fixed his gaze over Wil's shoulder. "Here comes your new best friend."

Wil turned around expecting to see Isabeau, but it was Dante walking over to them. "Not funny," he said to Wyatt, who chuckled.

They stood as Dante approached and Wil reintroduced him to his father and brothers, who he'd met at the welcoming feast.

"Ah, I have been wishing to meet the famous LeCuir leather artisans," Dante said. He glanced around the stall filled with belts, satchels, knife sheaths, harnesses, bridles, riding tack, and saddles. "*Bene, bene.* Your pieces are as exquisite as they say."

"Thank you," Wil's father said. "We pride ourselves on doing good work for fair prices."

"I am certain you do. I look forward to doing business with you."

Willem waved a hand around. "Feel free to look around, let me know if you have any questions."

"I do, actually." Dante met Wil's curious gaze with a smug smile. "I would like to order a saddle as a betrothal present."

"For whom?" Wil's father asked.

"For the lady Isabeau."

"Jumping ahead of yourself, aren't you?" Wil scoffed.

Dante smirked. "I do not think so. I prefer to be a, how you say, *optomista*." He jutted his chin at Wil. "Not a *pessimista*."

Wil picked up the water skin on the bench, uncorked it, and took a swig. "I prefer to be a *realista*," he told Dante, saluting him with the skin. "You might want to make the saddle a birthday present instead." He corked the skin, set it down, and stood. "Father, brothers, I'll be back after I stretch my legs a bit."

He strolled over to Isabeau's stall, where he counted four bottles of love potion left on the table.

"'I'd only sold two dozen vials total over the past couple of years," Isabeau told him. "You and the Lombards being here have increased the demand by quite a bit."

Wil glanced around the marketplace, rife with villagers who'd known each other most, if not all, of their lives. "The lure of strange, single men looking for wives is hard to beat."

"Or once familiar, still single men returned," Isabeau said with a pointed grin. "You and Dante were responsible for selling half a dozen vials each, with the other eight spread out amongst Dante's men and Burrell."

"Really?" Wil puffed out his chest and got a chuff from Isabeau. He chuckled, glad to see a bit of his old friend coming out. She was shaking her head, and then caught sight of something over his shoulder. He followed her gaze to find Dante watching them, his usual smile gone. "What did you tell the six women who bought vials for your betrothed?"

"Betrothed?" Her eyebrows shot halfway up her forehead.

"According to Dante, it's only a matter of time."

"I told him I'd think about it, and that's a long way away from deciding on whether I want him to court me," she said hotly.

"Apparently, you need to explain it to him again."

"Why did you tell me this?" Isabeau pierced him with her falcon's gaze. "Why do you care if he courts me?"

"I don't," he lied.

"Yet you've warned me off him twice now. Why?"

"I don't like him," Wil told her. "I don't like him, I don't trust him, and I don't want to see you or your family taken in by him."

"Then why did you escort him here? Why are you staying to help him settle here?"

"Charles asked me to, as a personal favor."

"A soldier's duty to his liege lord."

"Exactly."

"And when you're done settling this snake in the grass in our valley of simple, naive country folk?"

Wil let out a bark of laughter. "The last thing I would call your father, or your mother, is simple or naïve."

"What would you call me?"

Beautiful. Fiery. Elusive. Maddening. A woman he used to know almost as well as he knew himself. "A mystery."

His answer must have surprised her, because she didn't say a word.

"To answer your previous question, I'll be leaving Oloron and returning to the king's service after the DeVittorios are settled in their new home."

Isabeau blinked, her lips pressed tight.

"In the meantime, please keep your eyes and ears as open to the Lombard as your mind." He reached out and laid his hand on her shoulder, giving it a gentle yet firm squeeze. "Despite what you may think, my lady Isabeau, I don't wish to see you hurt."

She shrugged off his hand. "What about your lady Carina?" she snapped. "Should I not trust her? Or is her doe-eyed, vapid meekness an act too?"

Your lady Carina? Wil cocked his head at Isabeau, who wasn't normally so peevish. At least the Issy he'd known hadn't been.

"Lady Carina," he assured her, "is a sweet, timid innocent. Unlike her brother...or others."

Her eyes went from falcon fierce to cold steel. "You can be such an insufferable ass, Wilric LeCuir."

Wil burst out laughing. "There's my little mule."

***

Issy

Oswald pulled the wagon up alongside the outdoor kitchens and Issy jumped down from her seat almost as soon as it stopped rolling. Foxy came running out from the stable ahead of Randolph, Remi, and Heinz and leapt into Issy's arms.

Issy hugged her close. "At least somebody loves me," she grumbled into Foxy's ruff. She set the fox down and met Randolph as he approached the wagon. "Everything good?"

"Aye, Mistress. The broodmares have been given their evening oats. Remi and me'll bring the others in from pasture soon as we've helped unload the wagon."

Issy nodded her approval. "I'll be at the Stray's Stables for a while."

Randolph tipped his cap. "I'll send Remi for ye when supper's on."

Wil, Dante, Sergio, and Burrell rode into the yard, and she strode right past them, not breaking her stride as Dante called out after her,

"Lady Isabeau, where ever are you going?" A pause, and then, "Where is she going?" directed at Wil.

"I don't know," Wil answered. "But when her feathers are ruffled like that, it's best to leave her alone."

Whatever Dante said in response was lost in a crowd of voices and the clank of the wagon's gate dropping open. Issy glared back over her shoulder and chuffed. Everyone there was helping unload the wagon but Dante, who was heading for the kitchens.

"Come on, Foxy," she told the vixen, slowing her pace now that she was away from the others. "Let's go check on Spot and see how Acorn and Chestnut are doing in their new enclosure."

The fawn's splint was clean and intact, the straw in his stall freshly strewn, and his food and water bowls were both full. She stepped over to the newly set-up stall for the squirrels, who were chattering and racing up and down the oak branches spanning the height and width of the enclosure. She peered through the slats covering the space between the gate and the ceiling, and saw that their food and water bowls were full as well.

"Remind me to thank Remi later," she told Foxy, who was busy sniffing out bits and pieces of nuts and fruit dropped outside the slats.

Aristotle opened one eye, glaring at her for disturbing his sleep, then fluffed his feathers and turned his back to her. Issy paced back and forth across the small confines of the barn, trying to collect her thoughts and make sense of the last ten days.

Wil's and the DeVittorios' arrival had disturbed her life in almost every way imaginable. She knew Geoff was only being hospitable, and practical, when he'd invited them to stay at Oloron Manor, but having them here had complicated things to no end.

She felt bad for what she had said to Wil about Carina. Not that Carina wasn't doe-eyed or meek, but the vapid had been mean-spirited. Luckily, Wil wasn't the type to tell Carina what Issy had called her, so the names would go no further, and he was much kinder and closer to the truth, she was sure, when he'd called Carina sweet, timid, and innocent. So, why did his defending Carina stick in Issy's craw? Especially when she'd declared to Carina that they could become good friends, and meant it.

Dante was a whole other situation. Granted, it'd only been three days since she'd told him she'd think about a courtship, something she'd never said to any other man, but it'd been a disappointing three days. Dante hadn't spent time with her sitting and talking, or taking walks or rides together and finding out more about each other. The only things Dante had done were to give her flirty smiles and declare he was ready to start making babies.

To be honest, Issy hadn't exactly changed her daily routine to make herself available, but he'd been bold enough to ask to court her. If she really meant she'd think about it, maybe she should be the one to invite him for a walk or a ride, just the two of them.

Then there was Wil, whose return had brought back every unresolved feeling she'd ever had about him, along with a few new ones. She'd been missing and mourning the boy she'd known, her best friend, since the day he'd left. She missed him still.

The man who'd returned was someone and something else altogether. Not necessarily in a bad way. He'd always been good-looking, but now he was jaw-dropping, belly-stirring handsome. There was an intriguing worldliness to him that made her want to sit with him next to a hearth fire, sipping wine and asking him question after question about his life since he'd left Oloron, listening to the deep timbre of his voice as he told her tales of his adventures until night gave way to dawn. To hear his descriptions of all the interesting places he'd been and people he'd met. To crawl into his lap and find out if his kiss was truly as wondrous as she remembered.

"Don't be a fool," she said, startling Foxy and Aristotle. "Do not." She shook her head. Adamant. "He's leaving again in a few months," she told Aristotle. "He's shown no interest in me that way," she told Foxy. "I'm not sure he even likes me as a friend anymore." She paced over to Spot's stall. "I'm contemplating

Dante's courtship," she said, and remembered his confusion as to why she would bother healing the fawn. "Aren't I?" She looked to the squirrels, who watched her from the oak branch. "Should I be?" She clapped her hands over her face and shook her head. "I'm so confused."

She dropped her hands and looked from animal to animal, but they had no answers. She knew who would though.

She clapped her hands and Foxy jumped up into her arms. "We'll go see my mother tomorrow and ask her." She ruffled the vixen's fur. "For now, let's go eat supper. I'm starving."

***

"What do you think I should do?"

Issy sat across from her mother at the small table in her parents' bedchamber, Foxy at her feet. She'd explained her predicament and thoughts about Wil and Dante, except for those about kissing Wil, and waited for her mother's sage advice.

"Have you dreamed about either of them?" her mother asked.

"Uh…" She hadn't expected her mother to ask that, though it really shouldn't have surprised her. Her mother had always been open with their family about her own foretelling dreams, and her father swore by them. Plus, Issy had confided in her mother about the dream she'd had the night before Wil proposed. "Not about them, exactly. But I did have a recurring dream for several nights before Wil and the DeVittorios arrived."

"Tell me."

Issy took a deep breath in and let it out slowly. "I'd wake in my bed in the morning, not wearing my pendant, with no memory of where I last put it. I search for it everywhere, my bedchamber, my old room here, Wil's childhood bedroom, my stable, the stable here." She clutched the pendant under her tunic, relieved to find it there. "Thinking it lost to me forever, I wander aimlessly, a hole in my soul as vast as the night sky." Her voice caught, the emptiness from her dreams overwhelming her for a moment. "Eventually, I wind up at our, Wil's and my, oak tree by the river. I start to climb it, but for every step up I take, the tree grows another ten, until I'm looking a hundred feet up into its branches." She closed her eyes. "Then I see it." She opened her eyes. "My pendant, hanging from the highest branch, twisting and turning in the breeze, until a sudden gust of wind blows. It breaks loose and drops, hurtling down toward me. I reach out for it, feel it hit my palm and fist my hand around it…and I fall." Her heart was in her throat, pounding in her ears as it did in her dreams. "Then I wake up."

Her mother sat speechless, her hazel eyes studying Issy closely. "It's always the same?" she finally asked.

"Sometimes the places I search differ, but the rest is always the same."

"And they stopped the day Wil and the DeVittorios showed up here in Oloron?"

"Yes."

Lara nodded, then tilted her head. "My dreams are always shorter, more specific." She tilted her head to the other side. "What do you think it means?"

Issy clapped her hands over cheeks and shook her head. "I don't know. I mean, obviously, it's about Wil and me losing him. Me searching for the pendant could be me searching for him." She dropped her hands. "For years after he left, I looked for him everywhere, all the time, hoping against hope that I'd see him coming around a corner, giving me that quick, half grin of his. Calling me Issy." She swallowed the lump that had formed in her throat. "The tree house oak was our favorite hiding spot, our secret place, it's where I daydreamed constantly about running into him the first few years he was gone." She shrugged. "Then I grew up and gave up on those dreams."

Her mother laid a hand over Issy's and gave it a gentle squeeze. "I'm so sorry, Issy. Your father and I knew you were heartbroken when he left, but we had no idea how deeply it affected you, or how long."

Issy turned her hand in her mother's and held it. "When I saw how much it upset you and Father, as well as Willem and Patience, who'd lost their son, I learned to hide it. As time went on, the hurt lessened."

"But not the hope that he'd return someday."

Issy said nothing. She didn't need to.

"Why do you think you fall in your dream while clutching your pendant?"

Issy shook her head. "I have no idea." She met her mother's gaze. "Do you?"

"I do, but I don't think you're going to like it."

Issy let go of her mother's hand and placed both of hers in her lap. "I'd like to hear it, all the same."

A small smile played at her mother's lips and eyes. "It's called falling in love for a reason," she said. "When you start to fall, the where and when and how you land is unknowable." She held Issy's gaze, her own serious. "What you need to figure out, my smart, beautiful, headstrong daughter, is who you're in love with, the boy you knew or the man he is now."

"A man who's leaving in a few months to resume the life he's made for himself and seems quite content with."

Her mother looked over at the cot in the corner of the room, the same one she'd slept on as an indentured servant to the captain Talon Guiscard twenty-odd years ago.

"Twenty-five years ago, I asked Sophie the Sixth if after losing her first husband three years into their marriage, and then losing Orlando after only five years together, was it worth it to love a man you were almost certain to lose. A man you would be grieving longer than loving."

Her mother had told Issy many stories about Sophie the Sixth, the healer witch who had raised her mother since infancy. About how wise, learned, and prophetic she was. How not only Lara, but the entire valley heeded her words. "What did she say?"

Her mother smiled, sad and bittersweet. "She said that she hadn't been grieving either of them longer than she loved them, for she loved them still, and always would."

"Yes, but I've already grieved Wil as a friend for seven years. I don't want to love him as a man only to grieve him for the rest of my life."

"Is that why you told Dante you'd think about letting him court you?"

Her mother's question was like a bucket of cold water in Issy's face.

"I... don't... know," she admitted. She recalled Wil's smirk when Dante had asked her, and how it had goaded her response. "Maybe."

"Wilric LeCuir aside," her mother said, "do you truly wish to be in a courtship with Dante?"

"I don't know that either. I mean, he's interested in me, he's intelligent, charming, handsome, and he intends to make his life here in Oloron. It would be practical to join our lands and families. Other than Wil not liking him, I don't know anything bad about him."

Which wasn't exactly true. Neither Foxy, Heinz, or Sultan liked him either.

"Well, the good thing is, you've only said you'd think about it, which leaves the decision in your hands. You've already got family and land of your own, so you don't need to marry him, or anyone else, until and unless you choose to," her mother said. She patted Issy's hand. "So, I recommend you do exactly that. You continue *thinking about it*, and take your time getting to know Dante, to see if there is more to him and you than practicality before making the decision to marry him. You are my and your father's daughter, Isabeau Juditha Guiscard, and I would strongly advise you against marrying where there is no passion and no desire."

CHAPTER SIX

Courtship

Issy

Issy rode Onyx alongside Dante on Mattone as they took the road to his new estate, Foxy trotting along with them, dashing in and out of the tall grasses bordering the road. Issy had offered to ride over with him, and Dante had instantly agreed, yet it bothered her that she'd had to be the one to suggest it in order to spend time alone together. She hoped it would help them get to know each other better, and if it went well, perhaps Dante would begin to put some effort into getting to know her. Because so far, he'd been acting as if his announcing his intentions was all it would take to win her affections.

As they rode, her mother's words stuck in her head. *I would advise you not to marry where there is no passion and no desire.* Words Issy knew in her heart were good advice and true. Hadn't she told Wil almost the same thing when she'd refused his proposal, because her love for him had been that of a sister for a brother? Something she no longer felt for him. In truth, her feelings whenever she saw him or thought of him now were anything but sisterly.

"Lady Isabeau?"

She pulled her attention back to Dante. "I'm sorry, I didn't hear what you said."

"You were, how you say, gathering wool?" He gave her a smile that felt more than a bit condescending. "Do not worry. I take no offense."

"You're too kind."

"*Si, si.*" He waved off her comment, completely missing her barb, which was probably a good thing. "As I was saying, this road connecting our properties is well maintained, making it an easy distance between our houses." He met her gaze and held it. "Of course, soon enough, we will not need to make the journey between houses, only to maintain our lands."

"We'll see."

"Why do you say we will see?"

Issy took a deep breath in and let it out slow and steady. Now was as good a time as any to set him straight.

"We don't yet know each other, Dante," she said, his name sounding strange on her tongue. "We need to get to know each other, to learn if we're compatible."

"Ah, I see. You are a woman who wishes for *amore*, for love and romance in her marriage."

"I am."

"Then I am your man." He smiled and waved his arm with a flourish. "I will provide to you all the love and romance your heart desires."

"We'll see," she repeated.

Dante grinned, his blue eyes bright with the challenge. "Yes, we shall."

***

Wil

Wil tied Charger to the rail outside the stable and set to brushing the stallion after his ride to the oak tree and back. He stripped off his jerkin and tunic, enjoying the warmth of the noon sun on his skin, letting its heat ease the muscles of his neck and shoulders, tense from gritting his jaw as he rode, thinking about how Isabeau had suggested she and Dante ride over to his lands together this morning at the breakfast table and Dante's instant agreement.

He set down the brush and began to work his way through Charger's mane with a comb

when he heard voices. Recognizing Isabeau's full-throated laughter, he looked up to see her and Dante riding toward the stable talking and smiling, looking happy and at ease with each other.

Wil growled low, causing Charger to cast a chary glance his way.

"Sorry, boy." Will patted Charger on the shoulder and went back to combing the stallion's mane while keeping one eye on the approaching couple.

They stopped outside the stable's door, where Dante acknowledged Wil with a dip of his head and Isabeau's eyes widened at the sight of his bare chest. Wil let a smile tug at the corners of his mouth, and may have flexed a muscle or two, then broke into a grin as Isabeau lifted her chin and dismounted from Onyx. Dante called out for Marco, his newly named stable master, who came trotting out along with Remi to take his and Isabeau's horses.

Dante offered Isabeau his arm and she accepted it. They started for the manor house, when Dante placed his hand over Isabeau's and turned to face Wil, catching him staring daggers at the Lombard's back. "Do not forget," Dante told him. "The builder will be here this afternoon to draw up the plans for my new house and stable."

"I'll be there."

"Dressed more like a gentleman than a field hand, I should hope." Dante stood with a smug, self-satisfied smile on his face that faltered a bit as Isabeau pulled her hand from his arm and pressed her lips tight, her gaze holding Wil's.

Wil smiled, placating and insincere, and bowed low with a flourish of his arm. "As you wish, Master DeVittorio." *You preening peacock.*

Dante dipped his head as if acknowledging a lesser man's due, while Isabeau pressed her lips even tighter, her eyes twitching up at the corners before Dante took her by the elbow and led her back to her house as if it were already his.

As if she were already his.

Wil concentrated on combing out Charger's tail, letting the rhythmic motions calm his ire. He returned the stallion to his stall, made sure his hay trough and water bucket were full, then went to the wash bucket and splashed cold water on his face and chest. He grabbed a towel and rubbed his chest and arms, then donned his tunic and jerkin, ran his fingers through his hair and headed for the manor house, where three strange horses were tied off at the railing by the front entrance.

On Talon's recommendation, the builder they'd hired for the DeVittorios' estate was a man in his early thirties named Mason, who was sitting at the table in the dining hall between Dante and Sergio. Two other men, who Wil assumed to be Mason's workers, sat directly across from him and Dante, and Carina sat to Dante's left, along with Isabeau and Paola, who was to be in charge of running the household alongside her mistress.

"Ah, here he is," Dante said as Wil took a seat next to Mason's men.

"Here I am," Wil said, though why Dante wanted him here, he wasn't sure. It wasn't like Wil had any experience building houses.

"And here is Count Guiscard." Dante stood along with the others as Talon entered the room.

The count waved at them to take their seats. "Call me Talon," he told them. "Count is for official occasions." He slapped Wil on the shoulder and took the empty seat next to him. "Wil."

"Captain."

Wil caught the quick twitch of Isabeau's lips, and the grim line of Dante's.

"Well then," Dante said. "Shall we begin?"

Talon had been right about Mason. He listened to all of Dante's requirements for the manor house and stable, including attaching outdoor pens to the stalls like Isabeau and her father had done, as well as a smithy, a bathhouse, a smokehouse and a barn for storing wine barrels. He then asked Carina about her preferences for the kitchens and any structures for the kitchen garden, and to Wil's surprise, she answered him without hesitation, or even glancing at her brother for his input. Though she did ask for, and was given, Paola's tacit approval.

As Mason drew out basic floor plans for all the buildings, he would glance occasionally at Carina, who would smile shyly and blush prettily. Wil wasn't the only one to notice. As their looks and smiles grew bolder, Dante's scowls grew more ominous. What Dante had against his sister becoming attached to Mason, Wil could only guess. And all his guesses had to do with Dante's looking down on Mason as an untitled commoner, a commoner who owned his own parcel of land, or a selfish wish on Dante's part to keep Carina running his household rather than her own, no matter her wishes.

Not that it was any of Wil's business, but he liked Carina, and his dislike for her brother had only grown since Dante made his intentions known regarding Isabeau. Wil decided then and there that he'd help Carina and Mason get to know each other better any way he could.

He caught Isabeau staring at him, her head tilted and her brows furrowed. He glanced meaningfully from Mason to Carina, and Isabeau's gaze followed and her brows raised. Wil gave her a quick nod, and noticed her watching Mason and Carina more closely, a small smile playing at the corners of her mouth.

Wil coughed, catching Isabeau's attention, and he dipped his head at the scowling Dante. She opened her mouth in a silent "Ah," and then whispered something in Carina's ear that caused Carina to blush profusely and nod quickly.

"What are you and my daughter playing at, Wil?" Talon asked under his breath.

"Just trying to help out a friend," Wil answered.

"Isabeau and Carina are friends now?"

"They are becoming so, yes."

"And you and Dante?"

"Despise each other."

"Yet you will stay and help him settle here while he tries to court my daughter?"

"I will fulfill my duty to my king."

"Fulfilling your duty to your king is a good and honorable thing," Talon said. "Until it is time to move on to other duties."

"Such as?"

"Fulfilling your duty to yourself and those you love."

Wil met and held Talon's piercing gaze, so like his daughter's. "She doesn't want me that way, Captain. She's made it perfectly clear."

"I love my daughter, Wil. But she doesn't know what she wants right now."

"I'm leaving as soon as the Lombards are settled."

"I left my love once too," he said, his voice catching. "I almost lost her forever because of it. The smartest thing I ever did was come back to her. For her."

Wil had no answer. Not for Talon. Not for himself. Certainly not for Isabeau, who watched him and her father with a quizzical brow.

"What do you think, Wil?"

Wil looked at Dante. "About...?"

"About where to set up a training paddock for the horses."

Wil concentrated on the plans laid out on the table and what he remembered of the property. "I'd say this area here, between the stable and the horse pasture." He looked to Talon and then Isabeau, the two people Dante should've been asking. They both nodded their assents.

"*Bene, bene.*" Dante clapped his hands. "We can meet at the property tomorrow?" he said to Mason. "Work out any adjustments the land dictates."

"Tomorrow it is." Mason rolled up the plans. "Then we can figure the materials and costs, and if everything is agreed upon, we can start the work as soon as you're ready."

"May Carina and I ride over to the property with you tomorrow?" Isabeau asked Dante, her smile and voice dripping honey so sweet and so unlike Wil's little mule, he figured she was up to something, and he felt certain he knew what she intended.

"Of course, you may, *mio amore bellisima*." Dante spoke to Isabeau, and then turned to Wil. "After all, it will be your home one day too."

***

"Break time," Mason called out as Isabeau pulled the wagon up. "Food's here."

Wil and Burrell tossed the log they were carrying onto the pile to be cut into lumber and joined the rest of the crew at the wash buckets. Burrell had been here almost daily for the past week, as had Wil, but for the two days he'd spent visiting his family. Used to the physical life of a soldier, it gave them something to do and kept them in good physical shape, plus, the sooner the work was completed and the DeVittorios moved in, the sooner they could return to their lives as king's men. A life Wil seemed keener to return to than Burrell.

In his mid-thirties and normally taciturn, lately Burrell spoke more and more of leaving the king's service and settling into a quiet life in a country village with a sweet wife. Wil asked him once if he had a lady or a place in mind, and he'd only smiled and said nothing, though Wil wasn't blind. He'd noticed Burrell was sweet on Carina since almost the first time they'd met. Unfortunately for Burrell, Carina seemed to be as infatuated with Mason as the builder was with her. Neither of whom Wil could see Dante agreeing to marrying his sister. Not because they weren't both good, hardworking men who adored Carina, but because they were untitled and poor.

Certainly, they were both harder working than Dante, not that he was hard to beat. The Lombard only showed up in the late mornings to check on the progress being made, leaving the day-to-day details to Mason, under Sergio's supervision. Luckily, the two of them worked well together, free from Dante's interference.

Splashing water over his face and hands, Wil dried them with a towel before heading over to the table set up with planks of wood and sawhorses for the noon repasts Isabeau and Carina had been bringing the crew every day since they'd dug the first marker post.

Mason was the first to the wagon, where he helped Carina down from the bench seat while Isabeau jumped down on her own. Oswald, who rode guard for them, tied his horse to the wagon and let the gate down. He handed a tray laden with cold meats and cheeses to Isabeau, which she carried over to the table, followed by Carina with a tray of breads, and Mason with a bowl of peaches and plums.

Oswald tapped the barrel of ale in the wagon and the men lined up with their cups in hand. Once they had their ale, they took their seats, with Mason sitting to one side of Carina and Burrell on the other. The men and Carina dug into their food while Isabeau, as was her usual, wandered around the property.

Wil figured it was her way of letting Carina and Mason have some time without her as a chaperone, as well as her way of keeping some distance from him, something they'd both become adept at. It was easy during the day when they were both busy. At supper, they simply talked with everyone but each other, though their glares and glances across the table spoke plenty. After supper, she and the other ladies would go up to their chambers, leaving the common room and the ale to the men.

The first time Dante had offered to walk her up the stairs to her room, Wil and Geoff had almost choked on their ale, and had actually choked and sputtered when she'd accepted. Now, seven nights later, it had become Dante's habit to escort her up the stairs, and Wil's to act like it didn't matter in the least to him when she smiled and took Dante's arm.

Wil would have thought it odd Isabeau came here every noon with Carina rather than in the morning with Dante, who never missed a chance to describe it as "their" manor, if it hadn't been obvious she was doing what she could to help Carina and Mason carry on their budding romance.

He tore off a piece of bread, slapped a chunk of cheese on it and took a bite, strolling over to where Isabeau was peering at the layout for the stable. "You're looking very proud of yourself."

Isabeau glanced from Wil to the table and back to Wil, her wide eyes all innocence. "Whatever would I be feeling proud about?"

"Your not-so-subtle encouragement of a certain couple's flirtation."

Isabeau shrugged. "I haven't a clue who you're talking about."

Wil chuckled. "Uh-huh."

Carina's laughter trilled out over the coarser laughter of the men, and it occurred to Wil he'd never heard her laugh before.

"Well, I, for one, approve," he said, feeling a bit disloyal to Burrell. Though Carina had never shown any romantic inclinations toward him. "I'm glad you and Carina have become friends. What does your suitor think of all this?"

"Dante? He thinks it's good of us to bring the workers food."

Wil chuffed. "That's not what I meant."

"He doesn't know," Isabeau admitted. "Carina told me she'd like to keep it that way."

"Her brother will never approve of her courting, much less marrying, Mason."

"She knows this," Isabeau said. "Which is why she wants to keep their budding feelings for each other a secret, at least until the estate is built and running and she's found someone to run the household for her brother alongside Paola should she and Mason go further with their relationship."

"Someone like you?"

All the amusement left her eyes. "Dante and I are nowhere near that decision."

"Does he know that?"

Isabeau opened her mouth and then snapped it shut. She knew Wil had heard Dante mention their marrying more than once. She'd look Wil's way every time, her exasperation evident if you knew what to look for.

And Wil knew exactly what to look for with her.

"You should go eat," she said, "before all the food is gone."

Wil took a bite of his bread and cheese and turned toward the table, then turned right back around.

"Tell me you're not seriously considering courting that preening peacock, Issy."

Her eyes widened at him calling her Issy, then narrowed. "What do you care?" she hissed. "You left. You're leaving again. So, go."

"You are so stubborn, Little Mule."

"And you're still an insufferable ass."

***

Issy

"Get up, Tug." Issy gave the draft horse's reins a gentle slap, bracing her feet against the floorboard as the wagon lurched forward.

"What were you and Wil arguing about?" Carina asked as soon as they turned onto the road.

"You and Mason."

"He's not going to tell Dante, is he?"

"No." Issy shook her head. "Wil would never give a secret away that wasn't his. Besides, he likes you and Mason."

"But not my brother."

Issy snorted. "No, he doesn't like your brother. Has it been that way from the start?"

"Yes. My brother thinks Wil is, how you say, all *muscolo*, no *intelligenza*. And Wil thinks Dante is a…"

"Preening peacock."

They both broke into laughter.

"Wil is not wrong," Carina said. "I love my brother, but he is a bit of a *gallo della passeggiate.*"

"Cock of the walk?" Issy translated.

"*Si.* Yes. You do not mind this about him?"

Issy shrugged. "It's not my favorite side of him."

"What is?"

Issy met Carina's waiting gaze. It was a fair question. One she'd been asking herself quite a bit lately.

"His charm. His good looks. His joy for life." Yet even as she went down the list of Dante's good points, Wil's brooding eyes came to her. Wil, who was leaving her again, whom she'd told to go. "His plan to build a life here in Oloron."

"Do you love him?"

"Dante?" Issy shook her head. "No. But I do like him."

"You are willing to marry for like?"

Wil's proposal, her refusal to marry him without passionate love came rushing back to her. "There was a time I would have said no," she answered. Her mother's warning not to marry without desire and passion rang in her ears. A warning Issy would have agreed with before the DeVittorios had come into her life. But now, she wasn't so sure. There was her age to consider, along with the fact that no other men had shown any interest in her for years now. Likely because she'd scared them away with her talk of never needing to marry, which she'd meant at the time. "Now, I'm not so certain." She forced a smile. "You, however, will be marrying for love sooner than later, I predict."

Carina gave a slow shake of her head. "Only if Dante allows it. Which I am afraid he will not, because he considers Mason below me in rank. Which is why I must continue to hide how we feel for each other from my brother for as long as I can." She laid a hand over Isabeau's. "Thank you for helping me with this. You and Wil and Sergio. I owe all of you for this."

"It's good of Sergio to help keep your secret. But why does he do it? Why does he keep it from Dante?"

Carina's smile was as close to devious as Issy had ever seen her.

"Sergio is sweet on Paola, as she is on him. I help keep their trysts from my brother, and I have promised I will vouch for them to be married once we are settled in our new home."

Issy tried to think of an instance where she had seen them act anything but friendly to each other, and couldn't. She'd have to pay closer attention.

"I don't want to come between you and your brother," she told Carina. "But he is your brother, not your father, or your master. He cannot actually stop you from courting or marrying Mason. In the end, the choice is yours."

"If I married against his wishes, against my family's wishes, they would disown me." She faced Issy. "Your family would not do this to you if you did not marry as they wished?"

Issy laughed, short and quick. "My family knows better than to try to force me to marry someone I didn't wish to."

Carina grinned. "Yes. I can see that about you."

"What I see about you," Issy said, "is that your family is three hundred leagues away. And if Dante disowned you, Mason would still marry you. He has his own land, a home, a thriving trade, it's not like you'd be living in poverty."

"All things to consider," Carina said, her usual mask of indifference back in place. "If it ever comes to that."

Issy liked this new Carina peeking out of her cocoon of complacency. She wanted to let her new friend see that it was possible to get the life you wanted, if you fought for it. And she knew the women who could prove it.

"You know what we need?" she asked, and then answered her own question. "We need an afternoon under the old oak with Sophie the Sixth."

"The dead witch?" Carina looked at Issy as if she'd sprouted horns.

"Exactly."

CHAPTER SEVEN

Under the Old Oak

Issy

Two days later, on a sunny Sunday afternoon, Issy drove the wagon to Marta's with Carina and Berta sitting next to her, Foxy snug in her box in the wagon's bed, which was laden with three of Berta's pies, three loaves of rye, and two jars of honey.

On the way there, Issy explained much of Lara's and Sophie's history to Carina, with Berta adding bits and pieces, and then launching into a retelling of the day the Basques kidnapped the women they were on their way to meet, along with Issy and Wil as babies, and how their men had gone after them and saved them.

"Do you remember anything about that?" Carina asked Issy.

"I was only a year old," Issy told her. "Wil was two. We really only know what we've been told by our mothers and aunties, though they do like to tell us how much fun it wasn't trying to keep two toddlers on a horse's back for days at a time."

"Then when they got older," Berta added, "it was impossible to get them off their horses." She chuckled. "We always said, as long as the two of them were together, they'd be fine."

"What happened to change that?" Carina asked. "You two barely acknowledge each other at supper."

"Here we are." Issy ignored Carina's question, turned Tug off the road and onto the path to Marta's house, and then pulled up the draft horse. "Whoa, Tug."

She glanced over toward the river where a table sat beneath the old oak, and where her mother, Patience, Enid, and Doralice were busy setting the table with trays, bowls, pitchers, and cups. She jumped down from the bench seat and then helped Berta and Carina. When Issy opened the wagon's gate, Foxy leapt out, then she handed Berta one of the pies.

"Mother." Marta came out of the house carrying a pitcher full of knives and forks, and hurried over to Berta. She gave her mother a quick kiss on the cheek. "I'm so glad you made it."

Berta tsked. "As if I'd miss an afternoon meeting under the oak with Sophie and the Survivors."

Issy caught Carina's perplexed brow and handed her a pie. "Just follow them," she said, pointing Carina toward the oak.

Issy carried the last pie over, and then went back for the breads and honey while Carina was being reintroduced to the other women. Foxy finished sniffing all her favorite places and trotted at Issy's heels to the table.

"Shall we?" Issy's mother said.

The women nodded, except for Carina, who looked more perplexed than ever as Marta handed out cutting knives.

"Come on." Issy waved at Carina to follow her over to the flower and herb garden, where they cut red, white, and yellow roses from bushes Sophie had planted fifty years ago, as well as purple iris, pink peony, and fragrant sprigs of lavender and rosemary. Then they walked over to the oak and stood in a semicircle around Sophie's grave, marked with a stone of granite.

One by one, Berta, Enid, Patience, and Marta knelt at the gravesite and whispered words only they and Sophie could hear before laying their bouquets on her grave.

"What were they saying?" Carina asked Issy.

"Traditionally, we thank her for everything she did for us, for the entire valley," Issy explained as Doralice, who, like Issy, had never met Sophie in person, but still owed much to, knelt and spoke low to her grave. "And whatever personal message we wish to pass on to her."

Doralice stood, and it was Issy's turn.

"I wish I'd known you in life," she told Sophie. "Mother says we would've been great friends, and Father says you were a force to be reckoned with." She gave a small smile, imagining the snow-capped healer who had caused grown men to quake with fear at what she saw in them. "Without you, my mother would've never lived, my parents would've never met, and I'd have never been born, so thank you for that. And for tending to the people of this valley so well for so long." Issy laid her flowers on the grave. "You will never be forgotten, Sophie the Sixth."

As she stood, her mother stepped up, her green eyes welling with tears. Issy went to stand beside Carina as her mother knelt and laid flowers on Sophie's grave, then placed her palm on the warm earth and silently communed with the woman who had loved her, raised her, and taught her the healing arts, as well as how to deal with her foretelling dreams and fiery temper. She smiled as tears ran down her cheeks, then kissed her fingertips and touched Sophie's gravestone before turning on her knees and laying her hand on Wolf's grave.

Issy had vague memories of Wolf, who had passed when she was six years old, and though the family had kept dogs in the years since, they had all been family dogs. None of them had belonged to her mother the way Wolf had, or she to them. Her father had asked her mother once why, and she'd said that she was busy raising her own pack of wolves, an endearment they used to this day when referring to their children.

"Who are the other two graves?" Carina whispered as Issy's mother stood and smoothed her skirts.

"Goats," Issy replied.

"Goats?"

"Marta's husband, Denys, buried two of my mother's goats to make Nithard think Wolf and my mother, who was pregnant with me, were dead after he tried to have her killed again by burning us alive in the house my mother lived in." Carina's jaw dropped open. "It worked, letting my mother and me and Wolf hide out until my father came back for us and my mother to claim her right as heir to the Oloron estate." Issy lifted her chin toward the house that stood there now. "As a reward, they built this house for Denys and Marta and gifted them the land."

"How many attempts on her life has your mother survived?"

"The first," Issy counted off, "which was more an attempt to kill her reputation, was when Nithard declared her an indentured servant to my father, who was captain of a troop of horse soldiers garrisoned at the keep. Which she earned her freedom from after serving as a cook's lad on the army's march into Spain.

"The second was when Ranulf, Nithard's son, sent his four henchmen after her and they chased her up the mountain until my father caught up with them. He, my mother, and Wolf fought them off and killed all but one, Lothair, though my father was gravely injured and my mother hid with him in the mountains and healed him.

"The third was when Nithard tried to burn her alive and she hid in the mountains again, gave birth to me, and waited for my father to return.

"And the fourth was when Nithard hired the Basques to kidnap us with the intent to kill my mother and me, and sell the others as slaves. That's why we call ourselves the Survivors. All the women here today, plus Wil, were the ones kidnapped. Marta only escaped being hauled up the mountain with the rest of us because she was six months' pregnant and my mother convinced the leader of the Basques she wouldn't survive the journey."

Carina stared open-mouthed at the women as Issy's mother went to stand at one end of the table with Marta standing at the other. Issy touched Carina's arm and they walked over and stood next to each other in the middle of the table across from Enid, Patience, and Doralice.

"Welcome, ladies." Lara held both arms out to them and motioned for them to sit as she took her seat. "It's always a pleasure to spend an afternoon with you, my fellow survivors, under the old oak with Sophie the Sixth, to whom we all owe, well, everything." The women smiled and nodded. "And a special welcome to Carina DeVittorio, our new friend come to live amongst us, and who, my daughter tells me, is in need of our hard-earned, womanly advice when it comes to a certain builder she's sweet on."

"You did not," Carina hissed at Issy, her cheeks a furious red.

"Oh yes, I did." Issy wasn't the least bit remorseful. "Trust me. You'll be thanking me soon enough."

"So, dearie, what's the problem with you and your young man?" Berta asked as the food was being passed around.

"I do not, I, um, he, ah…"

"Carina's besotted with Mason," Issy answered for her. "And Mason's besotted with Carina."

"So, where's the problem?" Patience asked, dribbling a spoonful of honey onto her piece of bread.

Issy glanced at Carina, who pressed her lips tight and shook her head.

"Carina's afraid her brother, Dante, won't approve."

"Of what?" Enid jumped in. "Mason is a healthy, honest man with a thriving trade who's well respected in this valley."

She speared a peach slice and popped it into her mouth, waiting as Issy nudged Carina with her elbow.

"I am afraid my brother will not approve because Mason is neither titled nor landed."

"I thought he owned the land his house and shop are on," Patience said.

"He does," several of the women said simultaneously.

"But not enough to be landed in Dante's mind, if I am correct?" Lara said, and Carina nodded.

Patience pointed her knife at Carina. "Do you require your brother's permission to court him?"

Issy met her mother's gaze and grinned, both of them appreciating Patience's directness.

"Do you?" Patience repeated as Carina hesitated.

"No," Carina answered. "I do not require it, but I...I do wish for it."

"Dante's trying to court you now, right?" Marta asked Issy, who half shrugged half nodded. "Can't you talk to him about his sister and Mason, sweeten his ear a bit?"

"I can talk to him," Issy said. "But I'm not sure how much influence my opinion will have on him."

"Tell him you're worried about sharing the running of a household with his sister," Patience suggested.

Carina held up a slim, soft hand. "While I appreciate all of your concern and advice, he, that is Mason, and I have not even spoken of courting yet, much less marriage."

Issy snorted. "I've been watching the way you two look and speak to each other every day for the past nine days. You're already courting."

Carina blushed from her neck to her hairline. "How can I know for certain?"

Issy pulled a vial of Sophie's love potion out of her skirt pocket and set it on the table in front of Carina.

"That's how," she told her. "Next time we take food to them at the work site, you ask Mason to walk with you and you offer him this. If he accepts it and drinks it, he's yours."

"If he does not?" she asked so plaintively that the women all smiled kindly.

"He will," Doralice spoke up for the first time. "Desiree told me that Geoff told her that Mason had been questioning him on how to go about asking Dante's permission to officially court you."

"He has?"

"He has," Doralice assured her. She reached across and patted Carina's hand. "I was in your place at this very table once."

"And was blushing about as much as Carina here is now," Enid said to kind laughter.

"My point is, listen to these women," Doralice told Carina. "There are several lifetimes' worth of knowledge and experience speaking here. And while they can be a bit crude sometimes," she gave Enid a glance only friends of twenty-plus years could give and receive without taking offense, "they wish only to help you and your young man build a happy life together here."

Carina nodded and wrapped her hand around the vial of love potion. "Thank you," she said to the table of grinning women while pocketing the vial. "Truly."

"Now that we've sorted Carina and Mason," Patience said, looking directly at Issy, "what are we to do about Issy and Dante?"

"What do you mean, what are you," Issy waved her arm around the table, "to do? There's nothing you need to do."

"From what my mother tells us," Enid said, "there's about as much spark between you as a campfire in a downpour."

Issy glared at Berta.

Berta stared right back. "Am I wrong?"

Issy opened her mouth, snapped it shut, blew a frustrated breath out. "No."

"Do you love him?" Patience asked.

"No," she admitted. "But I like him."

Patience pursed her lips and shook her head. "I've known your mother since we were toddlers and I've known you since you were in your mother's womb, Isabeau Juditha Guiscard. The worst thing you could do is marry a man you don't love with every fiber of your being. You're terrible at hiding your feelings. If you marry for like, you and your husband will both be miserable."

"Don't you think I know that?" Issy cried, the truth of her auntie's words like a punch to her gut. "That's why I refused Wil all those years ago."

"Wil asked you to marry him?"

All eyes turned to Carina.

"He did," Issy said. "On my sixteenth birthday."

"And?" Carina demanded.

Issy was beginning to miss Carina the quiet dormouse.

"I told him I loved him as a brother, and that I couldn't marry my brother." Issy met and held Patience's understanding gaze. "He left here two months later."

"That is the bad blood between you?"

Issy nodded. "That's why he hates me."

She caught the quick, meaningful glances between the women.

"Have you ever heard the saying that 'love and hate are two sides of the same coin'?" Berta asked her.

Issy chuffed. "Of course, I have. But that's not what's going on between Wil and me."

"If you say so, dearie."

Issy scrunched her nose at her auntie, ignoring the other women's light laughter. "I do say so," she said. "Now pass the peaches please, I'm starving."

***

Wil

Wil took a seat at the supper table on the opposite side and as far down from Isabeau and Dante as he could without being obviously rude and still affording him a discreet distance from which to watch them.

As far as he could see, Dante was more interested in what Isabeau was—landed, wealthy, and outwardly beautiful—than in who she was: diligent, intelligent, and caring. As beautiful on the inside as on the outside. Dante only seemed to care about how Isabeau affected him, not about her.

How could he? He didn't understand the most basic thing about her, which was how fiercely loyal she was, not only to her family and friends, human and animal, but to her home, to Oloron. Isabeau was a woman who would go to the ends of the earth for the man she loved, the man Wil once hoped to be. Yet any man who truly loved her would never ask her to leave her home, a home that was hers by blood, and that she'd made her own by hard work and love.

If Dante really thought she'd happily leave Oloron Manor for his new place, he had another think coming. Even if they were only a league's distance from each other.

"Lady Carina." Anglbert caught her attention as Lucinda and Yvette were serving the platters of cold ham and roast chicken. "How did you like your day under the old oak with Sophie the Sixth and her coven of lovely witches?"

"Oh, you." Berta tsked and pushed at Anglbert's shoulder. "Don't listen to him, dearie," she told Carina. "We're no more witches than other women."

Wil raised his brows but said nothing. He'd grown up with stories about Sophie the Sixth and her premonitions and curses, and Isabeau had let it slip once when they were younger that her mother had foretelling dreams. Dreams that always came true one way or another. According to Geoff, Isabeau had inherited her mother's foretelling dreams, and she'd dreamt of him leaving her the night before she'd left him, in a manner of speaking.

"*Si*, I had a wonderful time," Carina answered Anglbert. "It was very ah, *illuminante*. I now know why Isabeau is so…"

Spirited, bold, stubborn, Wil filled in his own description.

"… strong and sure and able to manage her own estate so *in modo efficiente*." Carina smiled at Isabeau and Berta and then across the table at Desiree sitting beside Geoff. "Why it seems as if all daughters here are this way, because they were raised to be so by strong mothers."

"Not only daughters," Geoff said, feigning insult and ignoring his betrothed's eye roll.

"Ah, *si*," Carina said. "Sons also. I learned of the kidnapping by the Basques these women went through, along with Wil, and how they survived it." She met Wil's gaze. "Do you remember any of this ordeal?"

"Not really," Wil told her. "Just vague memories of riding horses and chasing Issy around campfires."

Isabeau's head shot up and her gray eyes bored into his as Wil realized he'd called her Issy. At least he hadn't called her "my Issy."

"Did you know, brother," Carina continued blithely on, "Wil and Isabeau were inseparable friends as children?"

"What changed?" Dante asked, glancing from Isabeau to Wil with an innocent look on his face that Wil didn't believe for a moment.

"I left Oloron," Wil answered.

"Why?"

It was an honest enough question, and while Wil normally didn't like letting people in on things in his life he didn't consider their business, he figured Dante had a right to know the answer to why he'd left since it involved the woman Dante wanted to court. He met Isabeau's watching gaze and posed the silent question to her. She gave him a one-shouldered shrug.

"I asked Isabeau to marry me and she said no. I wasn't going to stick around and watch her marry someone else."

For the first time since he'd known Dante, the Lombard was silent, along with everyone else at the table except for a few coughs and clearing of throats.

"This is why you do not like me," Dante told Wil. "Because she said no to you and yes to me."

Wil hadn't liked Dante from almost the first moment he'd met him, but he wasn't going to go there now. "It doesn't help," he admitted.

Isabeau's eyes widened at Wil, then narrowed on Dante. "I've only said yes to considering a courtship, not to marrying you."

"Speaking of courting," Wil said to Dante before he could reply to Isabeau. "If a man wished to court Carina, I assume you would want him to ask your permission first."

He kept his face expressionless as he waited for Dante to answer, ignoring the quick gasps and dropped jaws all around the table.

Dante's jaw, on the other hand, was clamped tight. He tugged the wrists of his sleeves one by one, rolled his shoulders back, and lifted the corners of his pressed lips. "Of course I would. Any man who wished to court my sister must have the honor to ask me first."

"That's what I thought," he told Dante, who glanced back and forth between Carina and Wil.

"Well, lad," Anglbert burst out. "Aren't you going to ask permission to court the girl?"

Wil caught Carina's eye and winked as Berta elbowed her husband.

"It was more a general knowledge question than a personal one," he said.

"You are not asking me permission to court my sister?" Dante sputtered.

"No, I'm not."

"Good," Dante said. "Because I would not have given it."

"Why not?" Wil asked. Not that he couldn't have guessed, but he wanted Dante to say it, out loud.

Which he did, without hesitation.

"Because you are beneath her in breeding and wealth."

The sharp intake of breaths could be heard all around the table, along with Anglbert's fork hitting his plate. Dante yanked at his cuffs again, glaring across the table at Wil.

"You obviously don't know this yet," Wil told Dante. "But breeding and wealth are not the true measure of a man or woman."

Next to him, Burrell grunted, and across from him, Isabeau was glaring holes into the side of Dante's blond head.

"Well said, lad," Anglbert harumphed.

"Well said, indeed," Geoff added as he wrapped an arm around Desiree's shoulder and hugged her to him.

"I meant no insult to anybody," Dante said, palms up with an apologetic smile. "But it is the way of the world."

"Not here in Oloron, it's not," Isabeau told him sharply. "Here, it is as Wil said. Here, we measure a person by what they say and do, what they have gained through their own hard work rather than by what they've been given from birth."

Wil grinned. *There's his fierce little falcon.*

Dante waved a hand around the hall. "Were you not given this estate because of your birth?"

"I was," Isabeau said. "But I haven't sat on my laurels and reaped the rewards of others like my great-uncle did before me. I've worked hard to improve this estate, and I share the rewards with those not born to wealth and titles who have worked alongside me."

"As I intend to do with the land given to me," Dante told her. "With my sister working beside me until a suitable," he raised his brows at Wil, "husband is found for her."

As if by unspoken agreement, everyone at the table returned to eating, though Wil noticed that Isabeau pushed more food around her plate than she ate, a sure sign of her agitation. That and the furrow between her brows. The main course cleared and the fruit and cheese brought out, she ate a few strawberries and then pushed back from the table.

"If you'll excuse me," she said to no one in particular. "I have some things that need tending to."

Wil exchanged looks with Geoff as Dante barely acknowledged Isabeau's leaving before he took a cup of wine into the common hall, signaling for Sergio to follow him. Wil stood and headed out the kitchen doors. If he knew Isabeau, the things that needed tending were her hurt feelings and temper, and she'd be dealing with them in either the horse's or Stray's Stables.

Halfway to the horse stable, he heard snuffling behind him and turned around to find Heinz following.

"I don't have any treats with me." He showed the boar his empty hands. Heinz snorted and Wil chuckled. "Come on then, guard pig, let's go see if we can find a carrot for you in the stable, and maybe your mistress as well."

Heinz led Wil to the bucket by the door, snuffling happily as Wil fed him four pieces of broken-up carrot, and then trotted off. Wil grabbed another couple of carrots with their tops still on and went over to Sultan's stall.

"You really are quite something," Wil told the stallion, who he'd been slowly making friends with over the past three weeks. "I can see why your mistress has you stabled at night, lest some scoundrel with a sense of horseflesh made off with you in the dark." He ran his hand up and down the stallion's broad nose. "You'd easily be worth a thousand gold solidi or more in a thief's market."

"More like two thousand." Isabeau peeked her head out over Lyts's stall as Foxy wriggled under the gate and scooted over to Wil and rolled belly up, chirping as he rubbed her belly with the sole of his boot. "I see you've at least been making friends with the animals."

"Meaning compared to not making friends with certain humans?"

"If the boot fits." She glanced down at Foxy, now chewing playfully at the toe of Wil's boot, then met Wil's gaze, her own serious. "Why don't you like Dante?"

"He's a rich, spoiled pretty boy who looks down his nose at everything and person he doesn't consider worth his notice without ever having actually accomplished anything his entire life other than being born to a wealthy family."

Wil scuffed the toe of his boot on the floor and rubbed the back of his neck, considering whether to continue. He didn't want to anger her to the point where she became ruffled and refused to hear what he had to say, but then again, she'd asked. "He doesn't love you, Issy." Her eyes flashed wide. "He doesn't even know you and he doesn't make any effort to. All he knows or cares about is your family name and wealth, that you are a suitable wife for his purposes."

Isabeau opened the stall gate and stepped out, shutting it behind her and closing the chasm between her and Wil in three strides.

"Kiss me," she said.

Wil stepped back. "Shouldn't you be asking Dante this?"

"I'm asking you."

Wil cocked his head. "Like, a brotherly peck on the cheek?"

Isabeau's fierce gaze pierced his self-erected armor. "You choose."

Wil had chosen Issy the first time he'd laid eyes on her almost twenty-three years ago, and despite everything he'd said and done to prove to himself otherwise, he still chose her. He stepped closer and hooked his finger beneath the silver chain hanging round her neck. He ran his finger under the chain, over her collarbone, and along the hem of her tunic over the swell of her breasts. The warmth of her flushing skin sent heat coursing through his veins.

He stared down into gray eyes swirling with a storm of emotions, and all the hurt, anger, and pent-up passions he'd held in all these years surged through him. He wrapped one hand around her neck and the other around her waist, pulling her close. She sucked her breath in as he pressed her even closer, the small of her back a perfect fit for his splayed hand, his cock nestled in the softness of her belly. She smelled of lavender and strawberries, and when she leaned into him rather than pull away, he ran his hand up her back and held her face in both his hands.

"My little mule," he rumbled.

She smiled and laid a palm on his cheek. "My stubborn ass."

He lowered his mouth to hers, smiling against her lips and trailing featherlight kisses across her bottom lip. She dropped her hand from his cheek to his chest, and Wil touched his lips to hers, kissing her slowly, gently, then growing in need and fervor as he ran his hand through her hair and splayed his palm around the back of her head, holding her close and deepening his kisses. Isabeau mewled, the sound reverberating from his mouth to his cock, and Wil groaned.

"Mistress Isabeau?"

Isabeau went still, and Wil dropped his hands to his sides with a low growl.

"Remi?" Isabeau swiped at her flushed cheeks and took two steps back from Wil. "What is it?"

Remi stood gape jawed, glancing back and forth between Isabeau and Wil.

"Did you need me for something, Remi?" Isabeau asked, her voice kind but shaky.

"Um, uh, Master Dante sent me to find you. He wants to speak with you back in the house."

"The peacock can't even be bothered to come looking for you himself," Wil grumbled.

"We should both be glad he didn't," Isabeau hissed back.

"Why is that?" Wil asked. "Afraid we would've come to blows?" The possibility of which made him grin.

Isabeau glared at Wil. "Dante is much too civilized to get into a brawl over..." she threw both hands up in the air, "...whatever that was."

"Whatever that was?" Wil grabbed her by the upper arm and whispered low into her ear. "That was the kiss you asked for. A kiss from the man who chose you, always. Until now."

He let go his hold of her arm with a snort of disgust, turned, and strode out of the stable.

CHAPTER EIGHT

Kiss and Tell

Issy

Issy stood at the door to the stable and looked down the long line of men standing along a road leading to the framework of a manor house being built. The nameless, faceless man at the head of the line stepped up and kissed her, his lips as dry and tasteless as old leather. His perfunctory kiss over, he stepped away to disappear in the ether as the next man stepped up, his kiss as dull and emotionless as the first man's, and the next, and the next.

She stood there being kissed by one anonymous man after the other, neither feeling nor caring, until one man's lips warmed hers with their soft touch, growing in heat and need and force as his mouth plundered hers. He tasted of desire and passion, and his large, tactile hands pressed her close as she leaned into the hard breadth of his chest. Isabeau moaned into the wet heat of his mouth and he growled low, the sound resonating in her bones. He broke their kiss, and she stood staring into dark brown eyes beneath thick brows, the corners of his full mouth twitching up.

"Wil."

Issy bolted straight up in bed, her heart beating in time with the throbbing between her legs. She threw her tangled bedcovers off and swung her legs over the side of the bed, sitting on its edge and calming her breath. She'd been having the same dream every night for the past seven nights, ever since she'd asked Wil to kiss her in the stable, the only difference being that some dreams she ended up kissing Dante instead of Wil. In those dreams, Dante's kisses were only slightly more stirring than the dry, tasteless kisses of the numberless, faceless men before him. Those dreams, she woke up from with a dull emptiness in her chest, unlike the stirring deep in her belly Wil's dream kisses left her with.

As well as his two real-life kisses, seven years apart.

In those seven years, she'd been kissed by three other men, all of them vying to be her suitors. Not one of them had come close to eliciting the excitement and emotions that Wil's first kiss had roused in her, and she'd secretly hoped she'd romanticized his kiss all these years. Then she'd gone and asked him to kiss her, however he chose to, and he'd obliged. And now she knew she hadn't romanticized that first kiss at all. If anything, it had only shown her the possibilities of what a kiss could be. Possibilities his second kiss had shown her even more of. Possibilities she found herself wanting, craving, more of.

Of course, it was always possible Dante's kiss in real life could stir her as much as Wil's. The only way she'd ever know for sure was to ask him to kiss her, since he was too much of a gentleman to do so without asking her *permisso* first. So why hadn't she asked him yet?

Unable, or unwilling, to answer her own question, Isabeau stood and went to the washbasin, where she splashed water on her face and dressed in a plain work tunic and skirt, then went downstairs to break her fast.

She looked for Wil among the men at the table, even though she knew he'd spent the night at his parents' house, as he'd done every night since their kiss in the stable, and smiled as she met Dante's gaze. He stood and pulled the chair out next to his.

"*Amore mio.*"

"Thank you." Issy sat and ladled herself a bowl of porridge and then spooned some sliced peaches over it. "I'm planning to release the squirrels today after my morning ride," she told Dante. "Would you like to come with me?"

"On your morning ride, *si*. To release your squirrels, no."

Issy considered sweetening her offer by pointing out that they'd be alone while releasing the squirrels, it could be the perfect time to ask him to kiss her, then decided not to, more than a bit angry at the fact that she'd had to be the one to think of ways to be alone with him.

Wil's kiss and her response to it, to him was…heated, and she admitted to herself she was afraid Dante's kiss wouldn't measure up. That her dream would come true.

She finished her porridge in silence and then pushed back from the table. "I'll meet you in the stable," she told Dante, who'd been chattering away in Italian with Sergio.

"We will go together, *bella signora*."

Dante stood and left his empty bowl as Issy carried hers into the kitchen. She set it in the sink and grabbed a bruised peach. He followed her through the door to the outdoor kitchens, where Heinz was waiting for his morning scraps.

"Here you are, Heinzie." Issy gave him the peach and chuckled at the boar's snort of thanks.

"Get away." Dante shooed Heinz as the pig nosed the leg of his breeches. "I have nothing for you, *suino*."

Issy bit her tongue and continued on to the stable, where Foxy ran through the open door ahead of her to greet Remi, running circles around the grinning lad's feet.

"Hey, Foxy girl." Remi bent down to pet the vixen, who nipped at Dante's boot as he strode a hand's breadth past her.

"Bad dog," Dante snapped down at her.

"She's not a bad dog," Remi said, standing and defending her. "She's a good fox."

"*Idiota*," Dante swore under his breath, then yelled out, "Marco, saddle my horse."

Thankfully, Remi hadn't heard what Dante had called him, or if he had, he didn't react. But Issy had.

"Would you saddle Onyx for me, Remi?" she asked the lad. "Then let Sultan out to pasture."

"Yes, Mistress."

"Thank you, Remi. I appreciate all your help. Which reminds me, when I'm back from my ride, I'm going to pack up Acorn and Chestnut and release them, would you like to come with me?"

Remi bobbed his head up and down. "Can I give 'em extra food afore we go?"

"I'm sure they'd like that. If you could pack some extra food to leave with them too, that'd be a big help."

As he went to saddle Onyx, Remi's grin smoothed her ruffled feathers, which immediately flared out again as Dante grabbed for Sultan's bridle when the stallion poked his head over his stall gate, and quickly drew his hand back as Sultan nipped at it and tossed his head with a snort.

"*Diavolo*," Dante cursed.

"Did you call my horse a devil?"

"He tried to bite me."

"Because you grabbed for his bridle." *Idioto.*

"He needs to learn who is his master."

"You are not his master."

Dante's blue eyes flashed icy cold, then resumed their usual charming demeanor. "My apologies, *amore mio.*"

Issy took a deep breath in and blew it out. "Perhaps it would be better if you kept away from Sultan for a while, then we can slowly work on reintroducing you two."

"You are the horse mistress."

"Yes, I am."

Dante dipped his head, yet Issy had the distinct feeling he wasn't as contrite as he acted.

"Your horses," Marco said as he and Remi led Mattone and Onyx up to them, saddled and ready to ride.

"Thank you, Remi." Issy swung up onto Onyx's saddle and took the reins. "If you could saddle up Maman while I'm gone and pack up supplies for Acorn and Chestnut, we'll take them to their new home as soon as I get back."

Waiting outside, astride Mattone, Dante smiled at Issy as if she should be thrilled he'd deigned to accompany her. He was so clueless he didn't recognize the depth of her anger about how he'd treated her animals, and how he treated Remi and everyone and everything he deemed below him.

As much as she hated to admit it, Wil was right about Dante. He was a preening peacock with little to no thought for others. She led the way, giving him her back and musing on how and when she would tell him what she'd decided about giving him *permisso* to court her.

They rode past the Stray's Stables and the bees' boxes, where Randolph was collecting honey from the hives while the bees flitted from the lavender blooms to the wildflowers bordering their field, their legs heavy with yellow and orange pollen balls. From there, they rode the fences to the horse pastures, where Sabine and Silver grazed contentedly alongside Jolie, Lyts, and Ebony, their pregnant bellies round and firm.

Kolossus was in the next pasture over with Tug, Maman, and the estate's two milk cows, six goats, and half a dozen sheep. Issy had four beef cattle she pastured at Phillipe's along with his and the keep's and several other owners' cattle, forming a herd of sixty cattle that had turned out to be quite profitable for the valley.

"Are you planning on keeping any beef cattle?" she asked Dante, intending their conversation stay to practical matters.

"I have not decided yet. I am thinking to concentrate on the vineyard and horses first."

"Your manor house and stable seem to be on schedule. You could stable your broodmares before winter, get them used to their new home before breeding season in the spring and summer. When were you expecting your broodmares to arrive?"

"My father planned on sending them here this September, and now that I have seen your family's horses, I plan on buying at least two of your Frisian mares."

"That makes sense," she said, dismounting from Onyx and walking her along the fence line. "Which of our studs are you looking at using?"

"Your father's stallions," Dante answered as he dismounted and led his horse alongside Issy's. "Bolt and Dane."

Issy nodded her approval.

"And Sultan, of course."

Issy raised her brows slightly. "I'm not saying no, but I'm not saying yes to studding Sultan out to other breeders yet. Much will depend on Lyts's and Ebony's foals this year, and who I breed him with next spring. I want to establish his line with my mares first," she explained. "Of course you understand."

The corners of his pressed lips lifted. "Oh yes, *si, si*, I understand. I understand, you want to make your line the best." He gave her a full smile. "There is always the possibility we will be married by then anyway, and your line will be our line."

Issy said nothing.

As if summoned by their conversation, Remi walked up to the mares' pasture and led Sultan into it. As soon as he unclipped the lead rope, Sultan sprinted off, shaking his head and kicking up his heels, snorting and whinnying. The mares whinnied in answer and Silver ran over to his sire and started a game of chase.

"Silver is a fine-looking colt," Dante observed. "Do you plan on keeping him or selling him?"

"I haven't decided yet," Issy said. She had more than a soft spot for Sultan's first-born colt. Silver was something special, a culmination of years of dreaming and planning and working toward a horse bred for strength, speed, stamina, and intelligence, all things Silver showed great promise of. She laughed as Silver first ran from Sultan, then chased him. "No," she decided then and there. "I'm not selling him. I'm keeping him."

"What of your deal with Queen Irene of Byzantium?"

"She can have the next colt out of Sultan, which, hopefully, Lyts or Ebony will produce soon."

Dante pursed his lips. "You are very *decisivia*."

"Thank you." Issy decided to take his comment as a compliment. She made another decision too. She tied Onyx off to the fence and waited as Dante did the same with Mattone.

"Dante, I—"

He stepped up and pressed his lips to Issy's, taking her by surprise. Stunned, she stood stiffly as he placed a hand on her waist and began to move his lips, slowly, gingerly, placing soft kisses from one corner of her mouth to the other. His lips were cool and tasteless, his kisses measured, practiced. His hand never moved or applied any but the slightest pressure, his touch neither asking for or stirring her to any kind of response. He stopped kissing her and stepped back, holding both her upper arms and grinning as if he expected her to swoon at his feet.

Issy stood there mute and gave him a weak smile. Had he even noticed she hadn't kissed him back? He let go his hold of her, watching her, waiting, she was sure, for her to say something about how wonderful his kisses were. How moved she was by them.

Only she wasn't.

Not in the least.

His kisses had affected her in life as they had in her dreams, which was not at all.

"We, ah, we should continue our ride," she said, skirting around him and what she needed to do. But not yet. Not until she'd calmed down and figured out the best way to tell him they wouldn't be courting. "Remi will be waiting for me."

***

Wil

A short whistle caught everyone's attention at the building site.

"DeVittorio's coming."

Carina and Paola jumped up from the table and hurried over to the wagon Carina had driven over, in itself a testament to Isabeau's influence on her. Wil scooted closer to Mason, closing the gap where Carina had been sitting between them, as Sergio did the same with the empty space Paola had been occupying next to him.

Typically, Dante only checked on his estate's progress in the mornings, leaving the day-to-day supervision to Sergio, so why was he here now with that smug smile on his face? Wil speared a strawberry, popped it into his mouth, and waited, knowing Dante couldn't keep anything that made him smile like that secret for long.

"Brother," Carina greeted him from the wagon, where she and Paola were stacking the empty baskets they'd brought the food in. "Did you wish to join the men's repast?"

"No, no." He waved the men, who'd made no effort to stand at his arrival, back down. "I was riding the Oloron property with my betrothed and thought I would continue here, see what can be combined so we do not duplicate unnecessarily."

"Your betrothed?" Carina cast a quick glance at Wil. "You proposed? Isabeau accepted?"

Dante gave a nonchalant shrug. "No, not yet, but soon." He met Wil's scowl and grinned. "After what passed between us this morning, I am certain she will say yes when I do ask."

He was still grinning at Wil, waiting, Wil was sure, for him to ask what had happened between him and Isabeau that morning. Wil clamped his jaw tight. He'd be damned if he was going to play into the peacock's game. He turned his attention back to his plate and ate the last strawberry as the other men exchanged curious glances.

"Well." Dante tugged at the sleeves of his tunic. "Since I am certain you all wish to know, I will tell you." He held Wil's gaze as he spoke. "Our relationship has become, ah, how you say, *fisico e fisica*. Physical. It was…" He touched the tips of his fingers to his mouth and then splayed them open with a flourish. "*Magnifico*."

Dante's dramatics earned him a few "Congratulations," and even more eye rolls around the table. Wil said nothing. Did nothing.

He'd been supping with his family and sleeping over at his parents' house since his and Isabeau's kiss in the stable five days ago, purposely avoiding her and only catching glimpses of her from a distance in the hope it'd make all of this, her, Dante, their sort of courting, Wil's eventual leaving, easier.

It hadn't worked.

He'd been crazy to think it would. If he hadn't forgotten about her after seven years apart, what made him think staying away for a few days would? All it had done was make him stew over that damned kiss and how she'd responded to it, melting into his arms and kissing him back with the passion she'd always had simmering beneath her surface.

Had Dante's kiss stoked that same passion? A low growl rumbled up his chest and out his throat at the thought.

"I'm off," he announced as he stood and cleared his plate from the table, handing it to Carina.

"Where to?" Burrell asked.

"I've got a bit of business to tend to elsewhere." Remi had told Wil that morning that he and Isabeau were going to release the squirrels this afternoon, and Wil had a good idea where she was doing it. She'd always released any wildlife she'd raised at the oak on the property line, next to the river. Their tree house oak. A nice, private place to have a talk with her and find out if what Dante said had any truth to it.

He swung up onto Charger's saddle and rode away, turning west and following the fence line to the river, telling himself if she truly was about to become betrothed to Dante, then he'd back off and wish them both every happiness. If she wasn't… He honestly didn't know what he'd do.

That he still had feelings for his Issy was obvious. He hadn't fooled anyone except himself, and maybe her. That her feelings for him were no longer sisterly had been obvious as well in her response to his kiss.

She had kissed him back.

Passionately.

But would passion be enough? And enough for what?

He still intended on returning to Charles's service when he was done babysitting the DeVittorios, a fact he'd announced often.

He'd offered Issy nothing but his kiss, his passion, whereas Dante had offered for her hand, along with a life of wealth and comfort in the valley that was her home. A valley she had no intention of leaving.

Why would she leave? She may have been born the daughter of a count and countess, but she'd become who and what she was by her own merit and hard work. She owned and ran a profitable estate in a verdant valley surrounded by family and friends who loved and respected her. The love came from who she was and always had been at her core, a spirited, curious-minded, kindhearted girl. The respect came from who she'd grown into, a woman with a spine of well-honed steel, an open, educated mind, and a heart as fierce as it was compassionate. A woman who knew what she wanted and made it happen. A woman who normally did not suffer fools, so why did she not only suffer, but encourage, Dante DeVittorio in his pursuit?

Determined to ask her exactly that, Wil slowed Charger to a walk as they neared the oak, where Onyx and Maman grazed under its shade. Isabeau sat with her back against the oak's trunk, facing the river.

"Hey, Wil." Remi's head popped up from the tall grass along the river's edge. He waved. "We let Acorn and Chestnut go and they ran up the tree."

Wil dismounted from Charger and left the stallion to graze alongside the mares.

"See?" Remi pointed up into the oak, where the two young squirrels chattered down at them from a branch above the tree house platform.

"I do see," Wil said with a grin at Remi and a nod at Isabeau. "They seem quite happy."

"That's 'cos we left 'em a supply of nuts and seeds and fruits in the tree house," Remi explained. "Mistress Isabeau says they'll be needing it at first, and that we'll bring 'em more 'til they figure out how to live on their own 'n all."

"Mistress Isabeau is right," Wil said. About animals. About people, she still had some to learn.

She wasn't naïve, but she'd been cradled in the bosom of her family and Oloron Valley her entire life, whereas Wil had been out in the wider world. Where Isabeau's natural inclination was to see the best in all creatures, Wil had become more realistic about what people were capable of doing.

One of the things he'd always loved about her was the way she gave of herself so freely without expecting anything in return. As far as Wil could see, the only things Dante gave freely were his smiles and charm, and he only gave them out for what he would receive in turn. Wil hoped he could make Isabeau see this too.

"May I?" He indicated the ground beside her.

"Of course."

Wil lowered himself onto the ground and had a lap full of fox almost as soon as his backside hit dirt.

"Well, hello there, Miss Foxy." He ruffled the vixen's fur and rubbed her belly as she rolled around in his lap, chittering and gently mouthing his hand, her tail wagging nonstop. Then she stilled, perked her ears up, jumped off his lap, and ran into the reeds along the shoreline. Wil chuckled. "What's the longest she's ever sat still?"

Isabeau laughed lightly and shook her head. "Maybe to the count of three. Even then, her nose and ears are still twitching. She's as good as any cat in keeping the stables and grain bins rodent free though." She glanced up into the oak, where the squirrels had stopped chirping out their predator warnings. "Luckily, she's learned to leave the ones I tend to in the Stray's Stables alone. At least while they're there. Foxy and Aristotle both. Though they are wild animals, so…" She shrugged. "All I can do is give them a fighting chance."

"I suppose that's all any living creature can ask for."

"I suppose." She tilted her head and eyed him closely, and for a moment, the years fell away and he was sitting beside his best friend in all the world. The girl who had come to mean the world to him, until she'd rejected him. Well, not him, but his proposal of marriage.

She'd tried to explain her feelings to him in the two months between his proposal and his birthday, the day after which he'd left Oloron. But his pride had been hurt and he'd refused to listen. He'd refused her offer of continuing friendship and left his family, his friends, everyone and everything he'd ever known, and gone out into the world on his own.

He didn't regret his decision, or the life he'd lived since. He'd traveled across a great deal of Europe and parts of Byzantium, experiencing places and people most knew nothing of, and gaining an invaluable education of the world, its lands, peoples, and politics. Yet for all the world he'd seen, sitting here beside Issy under their oak was the only place he truly felt at home.

A home he'd be leaving again before winter whether or not she married Dante. He tried to convince himself it shouldn't matter to him if she did, that she could make her own decisions and live with them, but he knew in his bones that Dante wasn't the right man for Isabeau, and he would be no kind of friend if he didn't tell her how he felt. If he didn't protect her from making a huge mistake.

"I hear congratulations are in order," he said.

"For what?"

"Dante showed up at his property and announced your whatever you're doing has progressed to becoming, physical, and that you two were as good as betrothed."

Her eyebrows rose to her hairline. "He said what?"

"That you're sort of courting—"

"I know what you said he said," she snapped. "What I want to know is why he said it."

"So, it's not true?"

"No." She shook her head, then shrugged. "Well, partly."

"What part?"

"We kissed," she said, and Wil's gut twisted. "Actually, he kissed me." Wil saw red. "But we didn't become betrothed." She scrunched up her nose and shook her head. "It was worse than kissing one of my brothers."

Wil felt the weight that'd settled on his heart lift.

They both burst out laughing, causing the squirrels to scold them from the branches and Foxy and Remi to come running over, which made them laugh even harder. Every time their laughter started to quiet down, they looked at each other and burst out laughing again. They laughed until they were rolling on the ground with tears in their eyes, tears that seemed to wash away the years and hurt between them.

"I'm sorry, Issy," Wil said, wiping the tears from his cheeks as their laughter died down.

Her gray eyes full of fight and light held his. "For being an insufferable, unforgiving, stubborn ass?"

"Yes, Little Mule, for being all of that and more."

The fight in her eyes dimmed. "I'm sorry too," she said with a rueful smile. "I never meant to hurt you. You were my best friend. I missed you. I still do."

Wil reached over and gave her braid a gentle tug. "I miss my friend too. Think we can be friends again?" he asked. "I'd like to try."

Issy nodded. "So would I."

"Me too," Remi said, sitting cross-legged in the grass and twirling a leaf that Foxy kept biting at. "I wanna be friends."

"You are our friend," Issy told the lad. "Isn't he, Wil?"

"Of course, you are," Wil seconded. "Best friends."

"Does this mean you'll be supping with us again?" Remi asked Wil. "Now you aren't angry with Mistress Isabeau no more?"

Wil chuckled. "Yes, Remi. I'll be supping with you again."

"Yipee," Remi shouted, sending Foxy scurrying into Issy's arms.

"Your mother will be disappointed," Issy told Wil. "She told my mother how much she enjoyed having you home again, even if only for a while."

"While I've enjoyed being with my family, it felt strange being mothered after all these years," Wil admitted. "I mean, the house isn't the same house I grew up in. It's not really home anymore."

Issy laid her hand on his forearm. "It may have changed some, but Oloron was, is, and always will be your home, Wil. We'll always be your family."

Wil leaned back against the oak's trunk and closed his eyes with a sigh.

Issy was right. No matter where he went in this world, Oloron would always be his home.

It felt good to be home, good to have his friend back. He sat soaking up the summer sunlight, enjoying the peace and contentment for however long it lasted. Which might not be long at all, because he still hadn't done what he came here to do, and he had no idea how Issy would react.

He opened one eye and peered sideways at her, only to find her eyeing him.

"While I hate to disrupt our newly resurrected friendship," he said, opening both eyes and sitting up straight. "There's something specific I came to ask of you."

"I'm listening."

Wil met and held her curious gaze, his own dead serious. "Don't let Dante court you, Issy. He's not half the man he pretends to be, and he only sees the half of you he wants to. He's not the man for you."

Issy pressed her lips tight and tilted her head. "So, who is?"

Me, was what Wil almost said. What his heart wanted him to say. But his head was telling him that no matter how right it felt to hold her in his arms, no matter how passionate their kisses, he'd be leaving soon.

Leaving her. Again.

His own shattered heart he could survive, he'd survived it before. He didn't want to break hers again too. Especially as a lover, which was all he could offer her.

"I don't know," he said instead. "All I know is it's not him."

She stood and smoothed the dirt from her skirts, her eyes as cutting as a falcon's wing.

"Remi, Foxy," she said. "Time to head home."

***

Issy

Issy sat at the supper table, happy as she hadn't been since the day Wil returned to Oloron, escorting the DeVittorios and acting like a complete stranger to her. It was good to have her friend back, even if his kisses confused her to no end. Unlike Dante's, which had told her what she already knew and had been slow to admit.

Dante was not the man for her. Not even close.

She'd decided on the ride back from the oak that she'd invite him to ride with her on morning rounds tomorrow, find someplace private they could talk, and break their short-lived, mismatched pre-courtship.

For now, she was intent on enjoying supper with her family and friends. Lucinda had roasted a lamb along with carrots, turnips, and beets, and baked three strawberry pies when told Wil would be supping with them. Desiree was supping with them as well, and had brought a basketful of fragrant cut roses from her mother's garden, which sat in a pitcher in the middle of the table.

"How's your mother doing with the wedding planning?" Issy asked.

"Better than my father, who cries and bemoans his little girl leaving him at least three times a day," Desiree said with an indulgent smile. "He was the same with Priscilla before she married Wyatt."

Geoff patted her hand. "Phillipe'll forgive us as soon as we give him a grandchild."

Desiree blushed as prettily as her mother, Doralice, and concentrated on spooning carrots and beets onto her plate. Chuckling, Geoff planted a kiss on her cheek and served himself a helping of roast lamb.

"Where will the wedding be?" Carina asked.

"At Crossroads Keep," Geoff answered. "On the first of August, two weeks from today."

"You and your household are all invited of course," Desiree told Carina and Dante. "We're telling everyone to bring a bedroll and plan on spending the night at the keep." She grinned at Lucinda as the cook carried four loaves of freshly baked ryes in on a tray and set them on the table. "Lucinda, Berta, Enid, and Marta are cooking a morning-after breakfast for everyone."

"Guaranteed to cure any lingering effects from the night before," Lucinda said, waggling her brows.

"Thank you," Carina told Desiree. "We would be honored to attend."

Dante cleared his throat and Carina shrank back in her seat and lowered her eyes to her lap.

"My sister is correct," he told Geoff, though it was Desiree who'd offered their invite. "We would be pleased to celebrate your wedding with you." He caught Issy watching him and grinned. "Perhaps it will help with the planning of our wedding, *mi amore*."

"Mmmm." Isabeau gave a noncommittal hum. She glanced around the table, her own cheeks flushing warm at all the curious gazes fixed on her, and then put all her attention into cutting her meat and vegetables into bite-size pieces.

"How'd the squirrel release go?"

Issy looked up from the food she was pushing around her plate at Anglbert's question. "It went well. Last Remi and I saw them, they were scampering around the oak's branches, stashing nuts into the hollows."

"And Wil," Remi piped up. "Wil was there too."

"What?" Dante exclaimed. "Why?"

"Because that's where Issy always releases wildlife, and I wanted to be there to see it," Wil said. "To see her." He met Issy's gaze and gave a quick smile.

"Stay away from her," Dante told Wil.

The hall went silent, except for Wil, who cocked his head and let out a short, harsh laugh.

"No."

"What do you mean no?" Dante fumed.

"I mean no. I'm not staying away from Isabeau just because you say so. She's my friend. I will speak with her and spend time with her as she and I see fit, without any concern for your opinion."

Issy glared at Dante, daring him to tell her to stay away from Wil. She'd planned on telling him she wasn't interested in a courtship in private to save him any public embarrassment, but if he pushed her any further, she'd say it right here, right now, in front of everybody.

He must've sensed her anger, not that she ever hid her feelings well, if at all, for he sat back in his seat, his emotions warring across his usually placid features, and then he gave a thin, smug smile.

"I release you from your services," he told Wil. "You are no longer needed here, or welcome in my presence."

Issy sucked her breath in, ready to breathe out fire, but Wil just chuffed.

"I don't serve you, DeVittorio," he said, his demeanor calm, his voice steady. "I serve King Charles, Emperor of Rome, and I will stay here until the duty he entrusted me with is completed. Now luckily for both of us, I can do this without having to deal with you directly." He nodded at Burrell. "All of our communication can be through the stalwart Burrell here."

"Fine by me," Dante snapped.

"Thanks a lot," Burrell grumbled at Wil, who gave an apologetic shrug.

"My lady."

Issy realized Dante was speaking to her. "Yes?"

"I will not stay in this house if LeCuir does, so you have a choice. You can send him to stay elsewhere, or me."

Issy clamped down on the laugh that threatened to escape her. She glanced around the table, meeting her family's and friends' curious gazes, and let a smile slip at the amusement on her brother's face. Only two years apart in age, she and Geoff had always been close, and had been part of the pack of siblings and cousins who had grown up together, along with Wil.

She met Wil's waiting gaze and realized he wasn't as sure about what she'd do as Geoff was. Or as Dante was. The difference being, Geoff was right and Dante was wrong.

She looked directly at Dante and said, "Wil is welcome here in my home for as long as he wishes to stay."

"And me?" Dante huffed.

"You may stay or go as you choose," she told him. "Though as it stands now, my parents won't have room for you and your household until after Geoff's wedding. I suppose you could always camp out on your property. Carina and Paola are welcome to stay here, of course, regardless of where you choose to stay."

Dante went rigid, and his blue eyes went ice cold. "You would choose him over me?"

"Always." Issy caught the quick twitch of Wil's lips. "He is one of my best and oldest friends."

"How is a friend more important than your betrothed?"

Issy let out a long sigh. She'd been hoping to do this privately, discreetly. The fact that Dante assumed they were betrothed without actually asking her made this so much easier. "We are not betrothed," she told him. "Nor will we be. Ever. I told you I would think about courting you, and I have. My answer is no. You may not court me. We are not and never will be betrothed, much less married." Her appetite gone, she stood. "Now, if you'll excuse me, I have two pregnant broodmares to check on."

CHAPTER NINE

Friendship

Wil

Wil leaned back against the wall to the brooding stall and stretched his legs in front of him with a tired grin as the newborn colt suckled with vigor at Ebony's teats.

"Congratulations," he told Issy as the contented nickers of Lyts and her newborn filly were heard from the stall next door. "A colt and a filly on the same night. You and Sultan must be so proud."

"Ha ha." Issy gave a tired but happy smile. She'd been with Lyts since after supper, along with Randolph and Remi, sending Remi to let Wil know Lyts's foal was coming around midnight. Wil had made it to the stable in time to watch Lyts's ash gray filly be born, and not long after, Ebony had gone into hard labor. Wil had stayed to help alongside Randolph and Issy, who'd sent Remi to bed after he'd fallen asleep in the straw, promising to wake him in time to witness the foal's birth. They'd wakened Remi as the first gray streaks of dawn lightened the sky, and all watched in awe as Ebony gave birth to a coal black colt.

They'd left the other horses pastured all night to give the broodmares some peace and quiet while foaling, and Remi and Randolph had gone to feed and check on them a short while ago, leaving Wil and Issy alone with the mares and foals.

As expected, Dante hadn't moved out of Oloron Manor to live in a tent on his property, but had declared he would stay at the manor until after the wedding, after which he would move in to Crossroads Keep.

In the ten days since, he'd moped around the valley, complaining to anyone who would listen about how unfairly he'd been treated by Wil and Isabeau, neither of whom had spoken a word to each other about that night. Though her one-word answer, "Always," to choosing Wil over Dante had lodged in Wil's heart, creating as much peace as confusion in his mind.

He recalled the last time they'd been in the stable on her birthday and determined to concentrate on the friendship they'd lost that night and had finally reclaimed. Reaching an arm around her shoulders, he pulled her in to his side. "Happy birthday, Issy."

"Oh." She yawned. "I'd forgotten." She laid her head on his shoulder. "Thank you."

"I know you didn't want gifts or a party with your birthday being so close to Geoff and Desiree's wedding, but I'd say your horses have given you the best gifts of all. Two healthy foals out of Sultan, and one of them a colt, so you won't have to give Silver to Irene."

"That's true." Issy tried, and failed, to stifle another yawn.

"What are you going to name them?"

"Oh, I don't know. I was thinking of something twinny, like Shadey and Shadow."

"Twinny? Is that even a word?"

"I'm too tired to know or care."

"That happens when you get old."

Issy punched him in the arm.

"Ow." Wil rubbed his arm. "It's good to see you aren't feeble yet."

"Feeble?" She slung a leg over his, straddled him, and pushed him back into the wall by his shoulders, her pendant falling out from her tunic and dangling between her breasts. "I'll show you feeble."

He grabbed her by the wrists and they wrestled as they had when they were nine and ten, only she had turned twenty-three today and he would be twenty-four in another couple of months. The feel of her straddling him was nothing like it had been when they were younger. Though her skirt and his breeches were between them, it didn't stop his cock from responding to the back-and-forth, side-to-side movement of her on top of him. Torn between throwing her off or crushing her to him, he simply growled, "Isabeau. Stop. Moving."

"Why?" She stilled and her brows knit in confusion, then raised to her hairline as she obviously felt the proof of his arousal between her legs. "Oh." His cock grew harder at the O shape her delectable mouth made, and he gripped her hips and held her motionless. "I, I'm sorry," she stammered, her cheeks a rosy pink. "I didn't intend... for this..."

"It's fine," he lied, wanting nothing more than to strip their clothes off and thrust his aching cock into her beckoning heat.

She shook her head and swiped at her cheeks, the motion causing Wil to groan through grit teeth.

"I'm sorry," she apologized again, stilling instantly.

"Don't be," Wil said. "I am a man, and you're a very desirable woman."

Wide, wary gray eyes stared into his, and Wil dared not move. It took everything he had to keep from reaching out and pulling her into him, to keep from taking her mouth with his, the tensile memory of their last kiss only inflaming his desires more.

She placed her hands over his and gently pried them from her hips. "We can't," she whispered hoarsely. "I can't. I've only just got back my best friend. I don't want to lose him again." She let go of his hands and he dropped them to his sides. "And you're leaving. You're going back to serve your king, and to the life you made for yourself."

"And you're staying here, living the life you built for yourself."

She gave him a sad, bittersweet smile. "I am."

Wil nodded. "As am I."

She leaned back and held a hand out to him as he bit off a groan. "Friends?"

He took her hand in his and shook it. "Friends."

She grinned and put her weight onto her knees, his freed cock instantly missing the warmth and pressure of her. Then she stood and brushed the straw from her skirts.

"I think it's time to leave the mares and their foals alone for a while," she said. "I'm going to eat some breakfast and then I'm going to take a long, hot bath and sleep until noon."

Wil stood and watched the sway of her skirts as she walked out of the stable.

"I, on the other hand," he told a disinterested Ebony as he adjusted his still-half-hard cock in his breeches, "could use a quick dip in a cold river."

He saddled Charger and rode for the tree house oak, where he left Charger free to roam, and walked fully clad into the river up to his thighs, then fell face forward into the bone-chilling water.

When his brain took over from his cock, he stood again, only to find Talon sitting astride Bolt and watching him from the other shore.

"Only one thing causes a man to willingly freeze his stones off," Talon said as he urged the stallion into the water. "A woman." He crossed the river on Bolt and dismounted as a soggy Wil followed. "And not just any woman," he said as he tied Bolt off away from Charger. "But *the* woman."

Wil went to Charger and walked him over to a small oak, tying him off and trying to come up with an answer to Talon's observation. He had nothing.

Talon strolled over to stand under the oak's shade and Wil stripped off his soaked tunic and leaned against the old oak's trunk.

"For me," Talon said, "that woman was Lara, my wife. For you, that woman is Isabeau, my daughter." Steel gray eyes pinned Wil where he stood. "Correct me if I'm wrong."

"You're not wrong."

"What are you going to do about it?"

Wil shook his head. "I don't know. I mean, I left to get away from her, to get over her, and I thought I had. I met and wooed and…" He trailed off, aware he was speaking with Issy's father.

"Had sex with other women," Talon finished for him. He gave a wry grin. "I was a young soldier loose on the world once too."

"Who cut quite a swath through the ladies of various queen's courts," Wil said. "If the rumors can be believed."

Talon neither confirmed nor denied the rumors, which made Wil suspect they were true, not that he'd ever thought they weren't. The Count of Oloron, who had risen from soldier to emissary to captain of a troop of fast-riding, hard-fighting horse soldiers, renowned among certain circles from Gaul to Byzantium, was still a robust, handsome man. A man who, by his own admission, had never looked at another woman twice after setting eyes on his wife.

"And now that you've returned to Oloron and Isabeau again?" Talon picked up the thread of their conversation.

"I am as mad for her as ever," Wil admitted out loud for the first time in seven years. To, of all people, her father.

"As much as I hate to repeat myself," Talon said. "What are you going to do about it?"

What could Wil do about it? He was a king's guard, sworn to serve Charles and meant to return to his king once he'd seen the DeVittorios settled here in Oloron. He'd served his promised five years and could always retire from the king's service, but then what would he do? Who would he be? He had no interest in joining his father and elder brother in the leatherworking business, and while he had a good eye for and a way with horses, would he be satisfied working for the count, or any of the other landowners here in the valley?

Would he be happy settling down with Issy and raising horses and babies? Would she? Their kisses had been anything but platonic, but that didn't mean she was interested in him as a husband. Plus, he didn't dare try to start an affair with her. Her respected her too much for that, and her father would likely kill him, godson or not.

He met Talon's waiting gaze. "I will remain her friend and leave here before winter."

Talon clapped him on the shoulder. "At least she broke off her almost courtship with that preening peacock, Dante."

Wil laughed, quick and short, then turned serious. "Would you have let her marry him, if it had gone that far?"

"Who she marries is Issy's choice," Talon said. "Though I will admit her mother was certain she'd call off anything between them before it went much farther." He grinned and ran a hand back through his graying hair. "Phillipe, Dardinel, Anglbert, and I wagered on the date of their breakup, and who broke with who. We all picked her to do the breaking up, and Phillipe won the pool for the date, which he has an uncanny knack for." He chuckled and then eyed Wil. "Don't you dare tell my daughter or my wife about this."

"About what?"

"Good man."

***

Issy

Issy laid her head back on the rolled-up towel lining the tub's edge and closed her eyes with a deep sigh. If last night and this morning had been any indications, this should be a good year for her. Her mares had produced two healthy foals by Sultan. Acorn and Chestnut had branched out from the tree house oak, and Spot, whose splint had been removed a few days ago, would be able to be turned out to pasture with the horses in another few days. Geoff and Desiree's wedding was only five days away and all the planning and preparations were going well.

The DeVittorios' manor house and stable were coming along nicely, their pastures fenced, and their vineyard's earth turned over in preparation for a winter planting of the bare roots they'd brought with them. And though he remained sulky, Dante had seemed to finally accept the end of their short-lived relationship.

Issy's household and Mason's work crew continued to help keep his and Carina's not-so-secret romance from Dante's notice, and Carina had told Issy that Mason had proposed marriage and she'd accepted, that they planned to elope once the work on her family's estate was finished and paid for.

But best of all, Issy had her best friend back.

Even when, not if, but when, Wil left again, they would separate as friends, not the strangers they'd been when he left the first time, or when he'd first returned. It eased her heart to know this, to feel it in her bones, though what she'd felt earlier when she'd been straddling him and wrestling with him had done the opposite of easing her. Or him.

"I am a man, and you're a very desirable woman."

His words left her as discomfited as his arousal had, neither of which she could stop thinking about. Just the memory of his dark eyes piercing hers, his words spoken in that low, husky voice, his big, strong hands gripping her hips, the growing heat beneath her skirts and between her legs, caused her body to flush as warm from the inside as the tub's water enveloping her.

She slid her hand down her belly and touched her aching flesh, imagining it was Wil's long, blunt-tipped fingers rubbing her and not her own. *"Isabeau. Stop. Moving."* His voice growled low in her mind as she moved her fingertip through and around her folds.

She imagined Wil's hand slipping beneath the hem of her bodice, his large palm cupping her breast, his mouth covering hers, drinking from her lips. She squeezed her legs around her hand and concentrated on the nubbin of tender flesh where all sensation coalesced, rubbing back and forth, faster, harder, until she bucked her hips and bit down on her cry of release.

Her whimpers mingled with Foxy's, who sat on the bench in the bathhouse by Issy's drying linen, cocking her head back and forth at the strange sounds that had come out of her mistress.

"I'm fine, Foxy," she told the vixen. Better than fine. Apparently, she'd been more tense than she'd realized. Her only worry now was how she was going to look Wil in the eye at supper without blushing from head to toe. Of course, he had no way of knowing she'd pleasured herself while thinking of him. No one did, except her and Foxy. "I won't tell if you don't." She eyed the fox, who lay down on the bench, unconcerned. "Good. It's our secret then."

Not that it was anything to be ashamed about. Growing up with three brothers, it was impossible not to have overheard bits and pieces of their conversations about morning wood and whacking off. Though she'd never discussed it with any of her female friends, it was generally understood that everybody pleasured themselves at one point or another. She'd just never done it to a specific man before.

Her fingers pruning, she got out of the tub, dried off, and donned the clean under tunic and lavender gown with plum trimming she'd wear to her birthday supper this evening. With her birthday so close to her brother's wedding, she hadn't expected or wanted any kind of celebration other than a family supper.

Berta and Lucinda had been busy in the kitchens when she'd passed through them on the way to the bathhouse, and her mother had promised to bake a berry pie especially for Issy. Refreshed from her bath and looking forward to the evening, she left the bathhouse, walked up the stairs to her chamber, changed into a clean, gauzy night shift, and plopped down on top of her bedcovers with Foxy curling up beside her.

Issy toddled around a grassy yard after Wil, who held a dandelion tight in his pudgy little fist, leading her on a merry chase. The sound of women's laughter mingled with her own childish giggles as she and Wil ran in circles around a table covered in cloths of every color cut into squares.

"Wolf," she squealed as a large dog with reddish-brown fur came loping toward her, only to stop in his tracks as an arrow sunk into his thigh with a sickening thunk. And then another into his chest,

and another. Her mother screamed her name and Issy turned to run to her, only to watch in silent horror as she and all the other women were hit with so many arrows, they fell to the ground looking like pincushions. "Run, Issy, run," Wil yelled, holding his arms out to her, his eyes wide with terror as an arrow struck her in the back with such force that she went flying through the air.

Issy bolted upright with a gasp, staring blindly around her, her heart pounding in her ears. Her heart slowed as her chambers came into focus and she realized she was sitting on top of her bed, physically unscathed and shaking from head to toe.

"It was only a dream," she told Foxy, and herself, as the vixen crawled into her lap and licked her chin. "Only a dream."

A dream about the day the Basques had kidnapped one-year-old Issy, her mother, Wil, and several other women for Nithard Midered to exact his revenge on Issy's mother and father. A kidnapping that had left all the Basques except Inigo and Ertzi dead, as well as Nithard, his son, Ranulf, and his henchman, Lothair. A day she'd never experienced such vivid memories of before.

She stood on shaky legs, wobbled over to the washbasin, and splashed cold water on her face. By the sun outside her window, she'd slept well into the afternoon, which explained her grumbling belly. Doffing her night shift, she dressed in the lavender gown, strapped on her sandals, combed and plaited her hair into one long braid, and headed downstairs with Foxy on her heels. The common hall was empty, as was the dining hall, though the table was already set with vases full of summer wildflowers and bowls of peaches, plums, grapes, and strawberries. Issy grabbed a peach and a bunch of grapes and left through the front entrance, avoiding the kitchens, which bustled with activity from the sounds beyond the door.

Heinz greeted her outside, and she tossed him and Foxy a few grapes each and then made her way over to the stable, where Randolph was filling two buckets with ale, which would encourage the flow of milk from Lyts and Ebony.

"How's everybody doing?" she asked.

"Doing right well, Mistress," Randolph answered with a proud grin. "Both mares have taken to their youngin's and both foals are eager nursers."

"Good, good." Issy hung her arms over the gate to Ebony's stall and watched the mare nuzzle her colt. Then she went over to Lyts's stall, where the mare and her filly were lying in the straw next to each other.

"You named them yet?" Randolph asked.

"I was thinking Shadey for the filly and Shadow for the colt."

Randolph gave a cockeyed nod. "I like 'em. They fit their colors and go right well with Silver and Sultan."

Issy laughed lightly, recalling Wil's reaction to her twinny names. "Shadey and Shadow they are then."

She glanced around the stable. "Are the other horses still out to pasture?"

"They are. I was thinking, since it's figuring to be such a nice summer night, and the mares and their newborns could probably use the quiet, that we'd leave the others out for the night?"

"I agree. Let's have the guests who arrive on horseback tie their mounts to the posts outside the stable."

"Will do."

"Has Remi checked on Spot this afternoon?"

"He's there now."

Issy glanced around the organized, well-run stable. "Is there anything I can help you with?"

"We got it, Mistress. You go and get ready for your supper. Your guests'll start arriving soon and you don't wanta get your pretty gown all mussed up."

"I suppose you're right." It wasn't that she didn't enjoy time with her family; she did. It was simply that she didn't enjoy being the center of attention. Still, it was only for the evening, and there would be delicious food and her mother's strawberry pie.

She smoothed her gown, took a fortifying breath, turned for the door, and turned right back around. "Have you seen Wil?"

"I saw him riding off sometime this morning, don't know where to, haven't seen him since."

***

Wil

Wil hugged his mother good-bye.

"Tell Isabeau happy birthday for us," she said.

"I will." He gave her a quick peck on the cheek and waved to his father and brothers. Priscilla, Wyatt's wife, had taken Perrin, their chubby-cheeked son, back to their house for his afternoon feeding and a nap.

Seven years ago, Wyatt had been a randy twenty-year-old determined to never be yoked by one woman, his exact words, when there was a whole world of women to explore and enjoy, and had teased Wil for wanting to marry Issy at so young an age.

Priscilla, his wife, had been a twelve-year-old girl in side braids then, and, according to Wyatt, had caught his attention the summer she'd turned sixteen. The same age Issy had been when Wil had proposed. According to Wyatt, all it had taken was one kiss, on a dare from Geoff and Dexter, and he'd known she was the one to change his mind about being yoked to one woman. They'd married a year later and she'd given birth to Perrin a year after that. Wil had never seen his brother happier.

As happy as Wyatt and Priss were, Wil couldn't help but wonder if he and Issy would've been as happy had they married young. He'd been a boy then, a boy who'd grown and changed into the man he was today: a soldier and a king's guard who'd seen and experienced much of the world.

Though Issy had never left Oloron, she'd grown into who she was too. A smart, determined, hardworking landowner and successful businesswoman who'd made her estate not only profitable, but a home for those who lived and worked there. A home and profits she willingly shared with her brother, who ran the farming and cattle side of the business, and the rest of her household.

Not to mention a woman who'd more than grown into her natural grace and beauty.

She'd always been a pretty girl, and Wil had carried the image of her as a budding sixteen-year-old in his mind for years. But now she was a twenty-three-year-old woman in riotous bloom. All he had to do was close his eyes and her image came to him. Her thick mane of auburn waves framing her high-set brow, cut cheekbones, the fine line of her jaw. Her full lips lifting up in a smile, her gray eyes fringed with sooty lashes holding his gaze, the corners crinkling up at some jest only they understood. Her strong, agile body, always surprising for such a slim, sylphlike figure. An image that would likely stay with him for many more years to come, and would surely haunt as well as comfort him.

He dismounted Charger outside the stable, where he was greeted by Randoph asking him to pen the stallion as they wanted to give the mares and their foals an extra night of peace and quiet.

Wil walked Charger over to the pen on the far side from the one Mattone and Serge's gelding were in, with Catrina's and the other Lombards' geldings in pens between them, and settled him in for the night. There was already a bucket of clean water in a corner under the sheltering roof and fresh hay in the manger, which Wil thanked Randolph for as he passed the stable toward the manor house.

Issy's family hadn't arrived yet, so Wil went up to the room he shared with Geoff and Burrell for one last night, and changed into a clean pair of breeches and his second-best tunic, saving his best for the upcoming wedding. He and Burrell would be moving their few belongings from Geoff's chamber down to the common hall tomorrow, giving the maidservants a few days to clean the room from ceiling to floor in preparation of Desiree moving into it.

Two cots had been set up in a corner of the hall, along with a washbasin, two empty chests, and drapes across the corner to form an antechamber to afford them some privacy. Though Geoff and Issy both apologized for the meager lodgings, Wil and Burrell assured them they'd be plenty comfortable. One of the advantages of a soldier's life was learning to travel light and appreciating the chance to sleep anywhere other than on a bedroll on some hard piece of ground.

He made his way down to the dining hall as Issy's parents and two younger brothers arrived, meeting her father's amused gaze for a moment before greeting the others and finding seats at the main table. He sat across from the family and away from Dante, who, along with Carina and Burrell, took seats at the other end of the table, while the household servants took their seats at the second table.

Remi waved over at Wil, who nodded back, and then Issy walked in from the kitchens with Berta and Anglbert.

"Grandmother." Wil stood, pulled the chair out beside him, and kissed her cheek. "Anglbert." He nodded at his grandmother's husband as he took a seat beside his wife.

Issy took her seat of honor and the kitchen maids carried in trays laden with roast beef, roasted beets, turnips, and squash, along with loaves of freshly baked ryes, bowls of bitter summer greens, and tubs of churned butter.

"Thank you, Lucinda, Marie, Yvette," Issy told the cook and the maids. "It looks and smells delicious."

The staff dipped their knees and then took their places at the second table as everyone dug into the food. Conversation and laughter flowed freely with everyone seeming to enjoy themselves, except Dante, who vacillated between fake smiles and sullen frowns. And Issy, who had moments when her dancing eyes would dull and go unfocused, as if she were watching something no one else could see, something that caused her to furrow her brows and chew her bottom lip. A thing she did only when she was worried.

Wil knew she didn't like to be the center of attention, but he didn't think that was the problem, especially since it was only her family and household present. After everyone had wished her a happy birthday and congratulations on the newborn foals at the start of the meal, the conversation had turned to the upcoming wedding, but Wil didn't see Issy getting jealous over that. It wasn't her way.

He managed to catch her attention as the pies were being sliced and cocked his head at her. Issy nodded and mouthed "stable, after supper" in response. Wil relaxed back in his chair and dug into his piece of strawberry pie with clotted cream.

"Delicious, as always, Countess," he told Lara.

"Yes, thank you so much, Mother," Issy said with a smile. "Thank you everyone for the birthday supper. I truly appreciate it." She pushed her chair back and stood. "I'm going to go check on the mares and their foals, but you all stay, enjoy, I'll be back in a bit."

Wil stood too. "I'll walk out with you. I want to check on Charger."

"*Cose dolce*," Dante said, raising his cup of wine to Wil and Isabeau. *How sweet.*

Wil glared at Dante, his hand fisted at his side. He wasn't about to let the Lombard's taunts goad him into doing something stupid, but that didn't mean he was going to ignore them either.

"What, exactly, are you insinuating?" he asked Dante, who glanced from Wil to a scowling Talon and back to Wil.

"Only how sweet it is to see two childhood friends renewing that special friendship," Dante said with one of his ingratiating smiles.

"It is a special friendship," Wil told him. "One you will never experience or understand."

"Why is that?"

Wil chuffed. "You having to ask is why." He turned on his heels and strode out to the sound of coughs and sputters.

He found Issy in the stable, sitting cross-legged on the ground with her back against the wall between Ebony's and Lyts's stalls, Foxy in her lap.

He sat next to her, stretching his legs out in front of him. "What's going on, Issy?"

"What do you remember of the day the Basques kidnapped us?

Wil thought back. "It's more vague images than facts, really." He'd only been two years old. "Me holding a dandelion, you giggling, then women screaming, arrows sinking into the ground." He rubbed the back of his neck. "The rest of it is memories of riding horses, running around campfires, and then arrows sticking out of men falling off their horses. My mother crying, my father hugging me." He met Issy's serious gaze. "Why?"

"I dreamed about it today. For the first time ever." She leaned her head back against the wall and closed her eyes for a breath, then opened them and stared up at the roof. "I dreamed of you holding the dandelion, of me chasing you. Then I saw Wolf. He was loping over toward us when he was hit by three arrows and fell to the ground. I tried to run to my mother, but stood frozen in terror as she and all the other women were shot with arrows and lay on the ground like human pincushions. You yelled, 'Run, Issy, run,' but before I could, I was shot in the back... then I woke up."

Wil rubbed the goose bumps on his arms. Geoff had told Wil she'd dreamed of him leaving her the night before he'd proposed, and it was known among the countess's family and a few close friends that she had the foretelling dreams.

"Issy?"

She turned her head and met his gaze.

"Do you have foretelling dreams, like your mother?"

Tears slid down both her cheeks. "I do."

Wil's goose bumps rose again. "What do you think your dream meant?"

She shook her head. "I don't know. When I think about it, all I see is arrows. Arrows sticking into and out of everybody and everything."

Her whole body shook and Wil wrapped an arm around her shoulder and hugged her to his side. "Why do you think you dreamed of it now, all these years later?"

Issy rolled her head against his shoulder. "It feels like a warning, but about what, I have no idea."

Wil knew how much store Talon and everyone else who knew about them put in Lara's dreams. He would do the same with Issy's.

"If it comes to you, or you have any more dreams, you'll let me know?"

She sniffed and nodded into his sleeve. "I will."

"In the meantime, we'll keep our eyes and ears open and our guards up." He kissed the top of her head. "I won't let anything happen to you, Issy. I swear it."

CHAPTER TEN

The Wedding

Issy

"Congratulations, brother." Issy hugged Geoff, and then Desiree, whose doe eyes shone with happiness. "I've waited twenty-three years for a sister," Issy told her. "I'm so glad it's you." She punched Geoff in the arm. "Even if you had to marry this guy to make it happen."

Geoff laughed. "Lucky for me, then." He hugged Desiree into his side. "I'll take her any way I get her."

Wil, standing beside Issy, as he'd done throughout the marriage ceremony, held his hand out to Geoff. "Congratulations, Geoff. You're a lucky man."

Geoff shook Wil's hand. "Don't I know it."

"Desiree, you'll surely be sainted for putting up with him."

"Don't I know it," Desiree teased, then kissed her husband on the cheek.

Issy laced her hand through Wil's arm. "We'll leave you to your other guests."

She started to turn toward the tables set up in the courtyard for the wedding feast, but Wil placed his hand over hers and led her in the direction of the back gate.

"Where are we going?" she asked.

"I figured we could both use a nice walk by the river before supper."

Issy stifled a yawn. "Good idea."

He opened the gate and ushered her through, his laughter following Issy as she ran down to the river's edge, unstrapped her sandals, scooped up her gown's skirts, and waded into the water.

"No fair," Wil grumbled from the shore. "I can't go in without taking off my breeches."

"Too bad for you. It feels wonderful." The cold water refreshed her spirits and cleared her foggy mind.

"Did you have another dream last night?" Wil asked.

Issy nodded.

"Who was it this dream?"

Issy'd had variations of the same dream every night for the past five nights. They always started with her chasing Wil under Sophie's old oak, and then either the people she loved or her animals would be riddled with arrows. One night it was her mother, Patience, Doralice, and Berta. Another, her father, her brothers, and Wil.

Still another, she'd come upon Heinz lying outside the Stray's Stables, dead from the half a dozen arrows sticking out of him. Dread eating at her, she had gone inside the stable, where she'd found Foxy and Spot in the fawn's stall, their bodies riddled with arrows. Aristotle lay on the ground beneath his perch with three arrows sticking out of him, and Acorn and Chestnut had been nailed to the wall with an arrow through each of their chests. Then there'd been last night's dream.

"It started the same as the others," she told him as he paced her along the shoreline. "You and I chasing each other under Sophie's old oak as toddlers. Then we were teenagers, racing each other on foot to Oloron Manor." She stopped and stood still, as did Wil. "We went into the stable. It was quiet. Unnaturally so." She took a deep breath in and blew it out, trying to steady her voice, her shaking legs. "They were dead in their stalls. Onyx, Sultan, Silver, Ebony, Lyts, and their foals. All dead. Shot to death with a dozen arrows each, even Shadey and Shadow." She glanced down at her hands, almost expecting to see them covered in red, as they'd been in her dream right before she'd jolted awake. "There was blood soaking the straw beneath the foals. So much blood."

Wil walked into the river, soaking his good boots and leather breeches up to his knees. He held his arms wide. "Come here."

She stepped into his embrace.

"Have you told your mother yet?"

He'd been urging her to talk with her mother about her dreams since the second night she'd had them.

"Not yet. I didn't want to worry her before the wedding."

Wil leaned his chin on the crown of her head. "Promise me you will, now the wedding's over."

"I will."

"Isabeau."

She buried her nose into his chest and breathed in her new favorite scent of man and leather. "I'll tell her tomorrow, after the wedding breakfast. I promise."

"Good. Now, can we get out of the river? If this water soaks my breeches any higher, they're going to chafe."

The sun was hitting the western peak of the mountains as they returned to the courtyard, where Wil's wet breeches and Issy's arm laced through his caught more than a few curious stares. She pulled her hand from his arm and took her seat at the family table as Wil took his seat alongside his family at another table. The wedding supper of roasted beef, pork, and mutton, with bowls of summer greens and tender root vegetables, freshly baked loaves of ryes, wheels of herbed cheeses, and one table covered with nothing but pies, sweetcakes, and honeyed pears and peaches, was delicious, and Issy actually had an appetite for the first time in days.

After the toasts had been made and much ale and wine drunk, the tables were pushed back, the torches lit, and the musicians set up for the dancing to come. People started coupling up for the dances and Issy smiled with satisfaction when Carina accepted Mason's invitation to dance despite Dante's disapproving glare. Dante, who'd been openly flirting with Christine, Desiree's younger sister, asked her to dance, and Issy caught her uncle Phillipe glaring after them as Dante led Christine to the dance floor.

Dante would be a good match for Christine as far as wealth and status went, so Issy found it interesting that Phillipe so obviously didn't approve. Or maybe he simply wasn't ready to lose another daughter to matrimony.

Several of the valley's single men circled Issy, but with Wil standing guard next to her, as he'd done throughout the day, none of them dared approach any closer.

"Since you're scaring all possible dance partners away," she chided him, "the least you could do is dance with me."

Wil gave her a harassed look and then held his arm out. "Miss Isabeau Juditha Guiscard, would you care to dance?"

"Why thank you, Wilric Hugh LeCuir," she said with a dip of her knee. "I'd be honored. As long as it doesn't cause you to chafe."

"I think I can chance it."

They joined the circle of dancers, standing next to Mason and Carina as the musicians struck up the tune to a rousing circle dance. They skipped and sidestepped, holding their hands high and swinging them down, then grasping each other's hands and circling first one way and then the other, clapping and stepping as the circle closed and then opened, closed and opened, until, at last, the music stopped and they stood sweating and laughing.

Wil took Issy's hand and bent low over it. "My lady, I need ale." He kissed her knuckles, his lips warm, tender, and then he straightened and headed for the ale barrels.

Issy danced the next with her brother, Harald. At seventeen years of age, with his tall, muscular build, curly red hair, and hazel green eyes, he was quite the catch. As proved by the number of young women watching his every move as he danced with his sister.

"The silversmith's daughter, Rochelle, hasn't taken her big brown eyes off you since we started dancing," she told him as they skipped and spun.

"I know." He ran a finger along the neckline of his tunic. "She offered me a vial of love potion at the marketplace Saturday last."

"Your own mother's potion used to trap you." Issy eyed her brother's flushed cheeks, a curse of his redheaded complexion. "Did you drink it?"

"I told her I wasn't going to be drinking anyone's potion anytime soon."

Issy glanced over at the pretty brunette, who watched Harald with such a look of hopeful despair that she couldn't help but feel for the poor girl.

"You should ask her to dance after this."

"What? Why would I want to encourage her?"

"It doesn't mean you have to marry her." Issy laughed at the stricken look on Harald's face. "Have pity on the poor girl. Consider it getting to know her better. She's actually quite nice."

"Yeah?"

Issy bowed as the music ended. "Yeah."

Next, she danced with Orlando, who, at thirteen years of age, was coming out of his gangly stage and growing into his dark good looks. He'd been eight when she'd left Crossroads Keep to live at Oloron Manor, and she missed seeing his sweet face every day. Like her, he was horse crazy, and he'd ridden over to her stable to see the newborn foals three out of the past five days.

"Can I ride over to see Shadey and Shadow tomorrow?" he asked as they turned and dipped and clapped.

"How about the day after," she countered. "Desiree will be moving in tomorrow, and everyone else will either be resting up or cleaning up." She tugged on one of his dark curls. "Deal?"

"I guess."

"Come in the morning and I'll let you help me lead work Silver," she added, sweetening the deal.

He broke into a toothy grin and gave her a clumsy hug. "You know you're my favorite sister."

Issy hugged him back. "I'm your only sister."

She ruffled his hair and made her way over to an empty table, where she sat and watched her parents dance alongside Geoff and Desiree, and Phillipe and Doralice, all three couples smiling lovingly into each other's eyes. Wil came and sat beside her, nursing a cup of ale.

"If it wasn't for the age differences," he commented, "it'd be hard to tell which couple were newlyweds and which were the longtime marrieds."

His parents, Willem and Patience, stepped onto the dance floor, as did Denys and Marta, Dardinel and Annette, even Anglbert and Berta.

"Aye," Issy agreed. "We all of us have had wonderful examples of married life to look up to and learn from."

Dante led Christine onto the dance floor, and Wil scowled. "It sure didn't take the Lombard long to switch his affections."

Issy laid her hand over his. "Don't be angry on my account. Neither of us had any true affection for the other."

Wil turned his hand and twined his fingers through hers. "I'm glad to hear it, on your account. I was beginning to worry about your judgment."

"Oh you were, were you?" She leaned her shoulder into his arm. Then she yawned. Long, hard, and deep. She leaned her head on his shoulder and closed her eyes with a contented sigh. It was good to be here with her family and friends at such a joyous occasion. It was good to have her best friend back.

She woke sometime later with Wil's arm wrapped around her shoulder and her head tucked under his chin.

"Welcome back, sleepyhead."

She slowly straightened and rubbed her eyes. "How long did I nod off?"

"Long enough to start snoring."

"What?"

Wil chuckled. "Not long." He nudged her. "Do your parents still have that cot in their chamber?"

Issy yawned and nodded.

"You should go lie down on it. Get some real sleep."

"No. I don't want to interrupt their night." Her bedroll was in the common hall, along with a hundred other people's, all of whom planned to spend the night here. If she tried to sleep there, she'd likely be waking up every time someone else came in to lie down and sleep. The idea of spending the night amongst a horde of revelers suddenly didn't appeal, not when her own comfortable bed in a quiet manor house was only a league away. "I think I'm going to go home to sleep."

Wil stood and held a hand out. "I'll go with you."

She took his hand and let him help pull her up. She glanced around the courtyard, where the revelers were in full celebration. "You don't have to. I don't wish to make you leave the party."

He chuffed. "Yes, I do. If something happened to you on the ride back, my father and yours would both have my hide."

Issy scanned the crowd and found her parents and Wil's in the middle of a group of their friends, talking and laughing amongst themselves. Off on a bench in a dimly lit corner, she saw Desiree sitting on Geoff's lap, the two of them in their own little world.

She lifted her chin in their direction. "Normally, I'd go say good night, but…"

"We'll tell Oswald and he can tell our parents later."

***

Wil

It was past midnight when Wil and Issy rode onto the grounds of Oloron Manor. The horses in the pastures nickered and whinnied as if their presence disturbed them, and they'd only ridden past the house toward the stable when Heinz came running at them, snorting and squealing.

"Heinz," Issy called out. "It's me, Heinz."

The boar slowed his charge and Wil could see something poking out from its shoulder. It was an arrow, and there was another one stuck in the pig's thigh. Issy jumped down from Onyx and examined the arrows embedded in Heinz. Arrows with fletchings she and Wil both recognized.

"Basques," they said in unison.

Issy went deathly still for a breath, and then shot up and ran for the stable. Wil pulled his longsword from its scabbard at his saddle and ran after her, catching up to her and grabbing her by the arm outside of the door.

"Wait here," he whispered.

She nodded silently and pulled out her waist knife.

Sword in hand, Wil crept into the stable, where he was met by panicked pawing and snorting. He glanced over the gates to each stall as he passed, empty of horses as they'd all been ridden to the wedding, looking for any hidden enemies He came up to Lyts's stall and looked in. Her filly, Shadey, lay spread out on her side, shot through with arrows in her chest and abdomen, the straw beneath her slit throat red with her life's blood. Lyts herself looked unharmed physically as she sniffed and snorted at her dead foal, the whites of her eyes showing. He stepped over to Ebony's stall. The mare looked unharmed as well, but her colt, Shadow, lay with a slit throat and four arrows sticking out of him.

"Christ's blood."

Wil checked Sabine's stall. The mare startled and cut, her panicked whinny answered by Jolie in the stall next to hers.

"It's okay, ladies," Wil told the distressed mares. "You're okay." He turned to the open door where Issy stood craning her head and peeking in. He didn't know how to soften the blow she was about to receive, so he simply said it. "Your mares are untouched, but their foals are dead."

Issy ran in and straight to Lyts's stall. At sight of the dead filly, she clapped her hand over her mouth and took several shaky breaths in and out. Then she looked into Ebony's stall.

"I dreamed the arrows," she said, staring straight ahead into nothing, her voice barely above a whisper, her face ashen. "I dreamed the blood." She closed her eyes and then opened them with a ragged sob. "Why would Basques do such a thing? Why would they slaughter the foals?"

Wil shook his head. "It makes no sense. I mean, stealing the mares would at least make sense, but killing the foals?"

"Sultan's foals." Issy whirled around and ran to the stalls Sultan and Silver normally stabled in, out into the attached pens, and back again. "They're gone. Sultan and Silver are gone."

"Are you sure they weren't left out to pasture overnight?"

"No. I had Randolph and Remi bring them in before Randolph left for the wedding." She clutched her chest with a gasp. "Remi?" she called out. "Are you in here, Remi?" she cried, running over to the antechamber that served as his room, Wil on her heels. "It's Isabeau and Wil."

"I'm here, Mistress," a voice squeaked out, followed by Remi crawling out from under his bunk. He threw himself at Issy and clung to her legs.

"What happened, Remi?" she asked, running a hand back through his hair, stringy with sweat.

"It was bad men, Mistress," he cried into her skirts. "I, I looked out when I heard horses riding in right after dark, an' I, I saw 'em shoot Heinz, an' I, an' I didn't know what to do, 'cos there was four of 'em." He looked up at Wil, his face wet with tears. "So I, I did what you told me to, Wil, afore, when the, the bad boys was throwing rocks at me. You told me if those bad boys were to come after me agin, that I, I should hide." He lifted his head to Issy. "So I ran, an' I hid. An' I, I heard, I heard the mares screaming an', an' the foals crying, an..." His words dissolved into sobs.

"You did good, Remi," she told the lad. "Hiding was the smart thing to do."

"It was?" he sniffed.

"It was," Wil assured him. Hiding had almost surely saved the lad's life.

Remi hiccupped and swiped his runny nose on his sleeve. Issy knelt down in front of him.

"Did they take Sultan and Silver?" she asked.

Remi nodded. "I think so. I didn't see 'em, but I heard Sultan and Silver both puttin' up fusses and the men soundin' angry."

Issy helped Remi to his feet. "Let's get you into the house, where you can rest up while Wil and I check around. See what else these bandits took. Then I'll tend to Heinz, and any others that need care."

Once they had Remi calmed down with a plate of food and a cup of wine in the kitchens, they went back to the stable. Wil pulled the foals' bodies out of the stalls and behind the stable while Issy settled the mares in different stalls. Then they went to the Stray's Stables.

Issy let out a sigh of relief at the sight of Spot safe and sound in his stall, and fell to her knees as Foxy came crawling out from behind the feed pails, whining and turning circles in her lap. Aristotle was out, most likely hunting, and Wil saw Issy glance all around the stable's walls, looking he knew, for her squirrels' bodies as she'd seen them in her dream. He heaved his own sigh of relief at their absence.

She set Foxy from her lap, stood, and smoothed her best gown of gray silk, which was covered in straw and dirt. "Let's go check the horses."

They walked out to the pastures and she called Kolossus, who came trotting over, head and tail high, on alert, Lug and Maman following close on his heels. The goats and sheep stood huddled under the chestnut tree in the far corner of the pasture.

"Nobody's missing," she said. "None injured as far as I can tell." She rubbed the stallion's forehead. "Did you protect your herd, big man?" Kolossus snorted and bobbed his head up and down. Issy gave him a pat on the neck. "What a good stallion you are."

They checked the food stores and found nothing obviously missing there. They did quick checks of Berta and Anglbert's cabin, and then Lucinda and Randolph's, and found no signs of break-ins or theft in either of them.

"Why would a Basque raiding party only take Sultan and Silver and none of the other horses? None of the Frisian mares?" Issy said as they walked back to the manor house. "Inigo and my father have an agreement. We already trade with his tribe. They'd have nothing to gain and a lot to lose by breaking that agreement."

"Turkmene stallions like Sultan and Silver are worth enough coin each to feed a village for a year," Wil offered.

"If you lived long enough to collect it."

"True." Inigo had already felt the wrath of Talon and the men of Oloron once. As well as their mercy. "Inigo's smarter than that. If he'd been responsible, he wouldn't have been so obvious about it."

"I agree." Issy stopped and held Wil's gaze. "Which means it's likely another tribe." She started for the manor again. "I'm going after them. As soon as I've tended to Heinz and put a pack together, I'll give Remi a message to take to my father and then I'm going after them." She looked to Wil. "I can't afford to lose the time it would take to gather a tracking party."

Wil nodded. She wasn't wrong about losing time, and he knew better than to try to talk her into waiting. Or staying put and letting others chase the thieves and her horses down.

"I'm going with you," he told her.

She flashed a grim grin. "I was hoping you'd say that."

***

The moon was only a night out from full, casting enough light for Wil and Issy, riding Charger and Onyx, to follow the trail of four horses with riders and two without from the stable west to the river. They crossed the river, where Wil rode south along the shore while Issy rode east, until Wil sighted their quarry's tracks a hundred paces downriver. He gave three short whistles and waited for Issy to catch up with him, then they followed the tracks another hundred paces to where they turned onto a game path heading up into the foothills.

"So far, they don't seem too worried about being tracked," Wil said.

Issy eyed the game path. "Most likely because they expected to have more of a head start. Nobody was expecting us back at Oloron until late tomorrow, or rather, this morning. Which means whoever they are, they knew about my brother's wedding and everyone's plans to sleep over at the keep."

Wil nodded. "There is that. Not that it was a big secret. We can use it to our advantage, that and the fact they'll be expecting to be followed by a band of riders kicking up dust, not just the two of us."

Wil wore his armored vest over a leather jerkin, lacquered wrist guards and helmet, and was armed with his long sword, waist knife, boot knife, and two short swords strapped across his back. Issy wore a leather vest and pair of leather breeches she'd had made special for her to ride in, and she carried a short sword, her waist and boot knives, and a bow and quiver of arrows that, if memory served, she was a deadly shot with.

As foolhardy as Wil knew taking off with only Issy after the bandits was, he also figured a band of four thieves weren't likely to have a man near as deadly wielding a sword as he, a battle-hardened soldier, and none of them would be riding a trained and armored warhorse like Charger, who was a weapon in his own right.

And, as Issy pointed out, the thieves wouldn't be expecting anyone coming after them so soon.

They started up into the foothills as the first gray streaks of dawn lightened the sky to their backs. At midmorning, they stopped at a stream to rest and water the horses, and he and Issy broke their fast with some bread and cheese and apples. They'd packed enough fresh food for two days and dried tack enough for another five, as well as a small bag of oats mixed with mutton fat to supplement their horses' grazing. He wondered how well supplied the thieves were, since he hadn't seen any signs of a fifth pack horse, or if they'd be meeting up with more men at a base camp somewhere. All things to be aware of and for which he made plan after plan for in his head.

Issy's message to her father had asked him to ride straight to Inigo's village in case the horses were being taken there, and if not, to ask Inigo for any information he had, and to watch for any riders crossing their mountains, or any Turkmene horses being sold. She asked that Geoff stay back with his new wife to run Oloron while she was gone, and to send Oswald, Gil, and any other fighting men who could be spared after her and Wil, though the storm clouds building to the east might well wash their tracks away before anybody following them got ahead of the brewing storm.

"You ready to ride?" he asked when she came back from behind a hedge of bushes.

She bent over to tug the hems of her breeches down over her boots, and Wil was torn between looking away for propriety's sake and staring at the lovely shape of her backside in those breeches, which clung to the rounded tops of her buttocks down the sleekly muscled length of her thighs to her shapely calves.

Staring won out.

She straightened and eyed him as he clamped his mouth closed. "I'm ready."

They followed the tracks due west up the mountain until noon, when the hoofprints doubled up and circled back and forth. As the sound of thunder boomed and lightning lit the eastern sky, Wil backtracked to where the hoofprints turned onto a game path, and whistled for Issy to join him. The path turned southwest, away from the direction of the pass to Inigo's town, which meant either the thieves were trying to lead anyone tracking them on a wild-goose chase, or they weren't working with or for Inigo.

They could be working for another Basque, or someone else altogether, as Inigo had been working for Nithard all those years ago. But why steal only Sultan and Silver, and none of Issy's mares? Why kill her two Turkmene-Frisian crossbreed foals? It didn't make sense. Any of it.

The only thing that made sense at this point was to catch the thieves and beat it out of them, if need be, and by the darkening sky and smell of rain from behind them, it would be up to Wil and Issy.

Issy rode Onyx abreast of Charger, her breeches-clad legs hugging the mare's sides, her seat easy even after half a night and day of riding, her eyes constantly scanning the path ahead and the woods surrounding them, when they weren't drooping shut. He knew she hadn't slept well for the past five nights. In fact, the few moments she'd fallen asleep against him at the wedding party was the only sleep she'd gotten at all last night. She had to be exhausted.

When her eyes fell shut again and her head drooped down, her chin touching her chest, Wil reached over and took hold of Onyx's reins.

"Whoa, Onyx. Hold up, girl."

"What?" Issy jerked her head up. "Where?"

"You fell asleep," Wil told her. He doffed his armored vest, stuffed it in his saddlebag, and then reached back and untied his bedroll and folded it over Charger's withers. He held his arm out to her. "Come sit here, ride before me." He could tell it was on the tip of her tongue to tell him no. "This way we can keep riding while you sleep without falling off."

She let out a grudging sigh, and then slung a leg over Charger's withers and slid over, settling onto the bedroll and draping her thick braid over the front of her shoulder. Wil tied Onyx's reins to the end of Charger's, then wrapped one hand around Issy's waist and held Charger's reins in the other. He urged the stallion onward and steeled himself against the feel of Issy's back against his chest, the scent of lavender emanating from her hair.

He felt her body relax and soften against his before they'd gone a quarter of a league, and she was sound asleep before they'd gone another. Wil had never felt such a mix of contentment and agitation in his life.

"Keep to your mission, LeCuir," he told himself. "Keep to your duty and honor." Duty and honor. Duty and honor. He kept repeating the words in his mind until they synced to the rhythm of the horses' hoofbeats.

The path led onto an open meadow as the sun started to lower in the western sky. With Issy cradled in his arms, Wil pulled the horses up at the edge of the tree line and watched for any sign of the raiders lying in wait. When he was certain as he could be that they weren't, he spoke low into Issy's ear.

"Time to wake up."

"No." She shifted in his embrace and buried her nose into his shoulder. "Not yet."

"I'm afraid so, sleepyhead." He jiggled his arm. "We have an open field to cross, and we both need to be awake and aware to do it."

She let out a heavy sigh and sat upright, rubbing her eyes and gazing out onto the meadow. She looked northeast, at the rainstorm washing away their tracks, and then shaded her eyes and looked west to the sun, which was quite a bit lower in the sky than when she'd fallen asleep.

"Thank you for letting me sleep," she said with a yawn. "Apparently I needed it." She swung her leg up and over Charger's withers and dropped to the ground, leaving Wil's body craving her warmth. "I'm going to go..." she pointed to a bramble and disappeared behind it.

Wil dismounted and relieved himself behind a tree on the opposite side of the path and then met her back at the horses.

"What's the plan?" she asked.

"I'll follow the tracks out into the meadow while you stay in the tree line," Wil told her while donning his vest of armored ringlets. "I haven't seen any signs of the thieves, and I doubt they left anybody behind to watch for us, but I want you to have an arrow notched and ready to shoot. Just in case." She nodded, and he grinned. "Just not at me."

She gave his shoulder a playful shove. "I would never shoot you. Not by accident."

"Uh-huh."

Issy adjusted her thick leather jerkin and then mounted Onyx. She edged the mare up to the tree line, slung her quiver of arrows over her saddle horn, pulled her bow, nocked an arrow to it, and nodded to Wil, who urged Charger out into the open field. He followed the tracks west to a small stream running along the meadow's edge, where he found signs the raiders had stopped to rest and eat and let the horses drink and graze. He waved Issy over, grinning to himself as she rode out with the arrow notched and ready to shoot.

Wil dismounted and pulled his food stores out of his saddlebag, and then left Charger loose to drink and graze. Issy rode up and did the same with Onyx. Wil pointed to boot prints next to a log that lay along a rocky section of shoreline and to two spots of flattened grass the size of men's backsides a few paces from the log.

"They stopped here for a bit," he said. "By the looks of things, we haven't lost any ground to them, but we haven't gained any either."

"Do you think they know we're tracking them?"

"I think they expect to be followed at some point, and for us to come after them with numbers, so either they mean to outrun us, not knowing the jump you and I got on them, or they're planning to meet up with numbers of their own. Though if they are, I'd have expected them to have already met up." He rubbed his jaw, the back of his neck. "I'm thinking they're trying to outrun us."

"Which is good for us," Issy said. "Bad for them. Sultan and Silver can run like the wind, but I doubt the raiders' horses can outrun our Frisians. When it comes to strength and endurance, few can."

"True," Wil agreed. He tore off a chunk of bread and cheese and chewed on them while he circled around the area, his circles getting larger each time around as he looked for more tracks. Issy did the same, eating as she searched, and then she took her jerkin and boots off and rolled her breeches up to her knees, exposing her shapely ankles and calves as she crossed the stream.

"Duty and honor, LeCuir," Wil reminded himself as he enlarged his circle and Issy searched the opposite shore with her breeches still rolled up. "Duty and honor."

"Over here." She pointed to a game path about a hundred paces upstream. "They went up here."

Wil walked up to where the stream narrowed and jumped over it, then he joined Issy in inspecting the tracks turning onto a path heading due west up the mountain.

"I count six different sets of hoofprints," he said. "All still heading toward Basque lands."

"Then we'd better get going."

She crossed back over the stream and knelt next to the water and splashed handfuls onto her face and the back of her neck. The silver and ruby pendant he'd given her fell out from under her tunic and dangled over the water. She stood, her wet tunic plastered to her breasts, her nipples showing through the linen fabric. Wil snapped his mouth shut and knelt at the stream's edge, then dunked his entire head in the cold water.

He stood and shook the water from his head, then ran his hands back through his hair.

"You fill the waterskins," he told Issy. "I'll check our packs and weapons are good and secure."

CHAPTER ELEVEN

The Chase

Issy

Issy lay her bedroll on the ground alongside Wil's and then stretched out on her side facing him. It had been years since they'd slept together along with their siblings, piled on and over each other like a litter of puppies, or, as her parents had been fond of calling them, a wolf pack.

In some ways it felt like only yesterday, familial and familiar. In other ways it felt new and strange and anything but familial, lying there, staring into Wil's handsome face, so like the boy she'd known and yet so different.

The soft planes of youth had been honed and hardened into masculine lines and angles, the faint white of a scar visible beneath his short beard, deepening the cleft of his chin. His lips, still full and pillowy, contrasted with the strong line of his jaw and cut cheekbones, and his thick, dark brows could still convey his humor with a twitch. Then there were his eyes. Looking into them was like looking into a pool at midnight. Deep, dark, reflective.

They were staring into hers now, stirring up feelings and emotions she'd been trying to tamp down since the day he'd ridden back into her life. Feelings and emotions she'd be a fool to give in to now. Now, she and Wil needed to concentrate on chasing the raiders down and getting her horses back. On staying alive.

They'd ridden until it was too dark to see the horses' tracks, and then they'd stopped in a small glen off to the side of the path. They'd tied Charger and Onyx to a line so they could graze and set up a cold camp for the night, eating the last of their bread and cheese along with an apple each.

Tomorrow it would be jerky, nuts, and apples or dried fruit. Issy was no stranger to camping out; her parents had taught all their children how to survive in the wilds. They would journey up to the Hollow for a different month every year as a family to stock and maintain the place, as well as enjoy the peace and solitude, and while there, her parents would take Issy and her brothers into the wilds for three to four days at a time, where they'd teach them how to survive on their own.

The Hollow. How she'd love to be there now in her cozy bed with Foxy curled up beside her. She rolled onto her other side with a sigh and drifted off to sleep dreaming of lying in the grass at the Hollow on a warm summer day, and woke up in the first graying of dawn with Wil's arm tucking her tight into him, his nose in her hair, his big, warm body curled around her, the hard length of him pressing against her buttocks.

She craned her neck and watched his eyes slowly open and focus on hers.

"Good morning, Little Dove." His voice was rough with sleep, the smile in his eyes warm. He removed his arm from around her and Issy shifted, rubbing her backside against his pelvis. Wil groaned and Issy swore he blushed. "Uh, sorry about that," he mumbled, scooting back from her.

Issy's cheeks were flushing hot too. "I have three brothers. Don't worry about it," she said, trying to make light of it even as her body flushed as hotly as her cheeks.

"I'll, ah, I'll see to the horses." He stood and turned his back to her, but not before she caught sight of the bulge in his breeches that had been pressed up against her moments before.

"I'll see to our breakfast."

Which didn't take long or much effort, but it gave her something to do besides dwell on the sight and feel of Wil's erection.

When he returned, the manly bulge in his breeches more its usual size, they ate their meager breakfast of jerked meat and apples in silence, avoiding each other's gazes. Issy walked over to Onyx and gave the mare her apple core, then approached Wil. It was ridiculous for them to be so awkward around each other. There was a time they could and did tell each other everything. Why shouldn't they be able to do that again?

"So, ah, do you, ah, wake up like that every morning?"

Wil raised one brow, giving her his *are you serious?* look. Then he burst out laughing.

"Not every morning," he said, still chuckling. "But certainly any morning I'm lucky enough to wake up next to a beautiful woman."

Torn between wanting to ask him if he really thought her beautiful and feeling a prick of jealousy at the idea of his waking up next to another woman the way he'd been curled around her, Issy went with the jealousy.

"How many other women have you woken up next to?"

Both of his brows shot up. "Are you asking me how many women I've slept with?"

"No." Issy gave a vehement shake of her head. "Of course not," she said, even though that'd been exactly what she'd asked him. She waved her hand dismissively. "How about we forget about this entire morning and get back on the trail?"

"I think that would be the smart thing to do," he said, his eyes lit with amusement. "I'll saddle the horses."

The horses. Find and save her horses. Issy repeated the words in her head as she packed up their saddlebags and made sure everything was tied down. She spoke the words under her breath as they followed the trail up the path west into the mountains and she found herself staring at the cut of Wil's jaw, the breadth of his shoulders, the muscled length of his thighs. The horses. Find and save her horses.

They came upon the raiders' overnight camp at noon, and where they'd stopped to rest, most likely for their noon repast, by midafternoon, which meant they were gaining some ground. By late afternoon, they followed the tracks onto another game path that veered south, and followed it until dark.

"South is away from Basque territory," Issy said as they ate their supper of dried meat, walnuts, and raisins. "So, who are they taking my horses to?"

Wil shook his head. "I don't know. Someone with a sense of horse flesh, lots of coin, and no morals about stealing horses."

"Which could be anybody, anywhere." Issy gnashed her teeth. "At least if it had been Basques, my father would have had some bargaining power."

"We still have a chance to get them back," Wil told her. "If we keep pushing hard, we can catch up to them by tomorrow night."

Issy glanced north and east, back the way they'd come, where a summer storm had raged all day. "How long do we wait for the others to catch up with us?" She met Wil's gaze. "Do we wait for them to catch up before we try to take the horses back, considering the storm likely washed our tracks away?" Making it hard, if not impossible, to follow her and Wil.

"First, we catch up to the raiders," Wil said. "Then what we do when will depend on what we find."

What he said made sense. Issy nodded. "Agreed."

"Until then, we should try to get a good night's sleep."

Issy's heart did a flip in her chest. She'd known this moment was coming all day. She'd been waiting for it with a mixture of dread embarrassment and happy anticipation that made her legs shake and her hands tremble now as she unfurled her bedroll and Wil laid his out alongside hers. Though the summer night was warm, she was shivering as she lay down. Wil reached an arm out and pulled her in close, cocooning her with his body.

"No kicking in your sleep, Little Mule," he whispered into her ear.

Issy giggled. Warm and safe.

166

***

Wil

Wil woke with Issy in his arms and the iron rod between his legs nestled in the soft heat of her buttocks. He lay there throbbing with yearning as the night sky morphed into dawn, not daring to move lest he wake her and lose this bittersweet respite before spending another day in the saddle. He nuzzled her hair, breathing in the faint fragrance of lavender and earthy woman, and she stirred, arousing his cock to a new level of exquisite agony.

She stirred again, and Wil groaned through his gritted teeth. Fighting the urge to nip her neck and push his erection deeper into her softness, Wil rolled over and away from her, grinding his teeth at her little mewl of disappointment as she scooted her backside closer to where he'd been a moment ago, her body instinctively seeking his.

He was up and walking as best he could with his cock rubbing against his breeches over to a bush to relieve both his cock and his bladder as she stretched her sinuous body with a yawn and then opened her eyes, looking this way and that until she spied him standing behind the bush.

"'Morning, Wil."

"'Morning, Issy."

She grinned at him then rolled onto her knees, stretched her arms out in front of her, lowered her forehead to the ground, and pushed her backside over her heels.

Christ. Was she trying to kill him?

He tucked his randy cock in and laced up his breeches, then went over to check on Charger and Onyx, giving them each a carrot and an apple and keeping his back to Issy. When he heard her walking over to the bushes, he went back over to their bedrolls and started packing them up.

"I'm thinking if we push hard today, we can catch up to the raiders by late afternoon, early evening," he said, mentally chastising his errant cock for twitching at the mention of pushing hard.

"Then we can sneak into their camp and get Sultan and Silver back tonight," she said with a glint in her eyes.

"What we do when is going to depend on many different things."

He hated dulling her excitement, but he wasn't going to encourage her to jump into a dangerous situation without looking at it from all angles first. She had a rash side to her, which Talon often attributed to Lara, and with only the two of them going after the raiders, this was as far as Wil was going to indulge it. The closer they got to catching up to the raiders, the less likely it was the men Talon had sent after them would catch up in time to help in the fight to come, especially after the rains had likely washed all their tracks away. And no matter how or when they went after the horses, Wil would lay odds on there being a fight.

Same as he'd lay odds Issy would jump into any fight that broke out. No matter what he made her promise.

They followed the trail south across the mountain's face and came upon the thieves' overnight camp by midmorning. Pushing themselves and their horses hard, they caught sight of the riders leading Sultan and Silver across a meadow in the late afternoon. Pulling back, they kept their distance until dark, when Wil left Issy with Charger and Onyx and made his way to the outskirts of the raiders' camp.

There were still only four raiders. They looked to be supplied enough for a journey of several more weeks, and from what he could see, their weapons consisted of short swords, waist knives, two bows, and two quivers of arrows. There wasn't a long sword or battle axe to be seen, which was good for Wil, bad for them.

If he thought he could handle fighting them and taking the horses by himself, he would have. But as much as he hated the thought of putting Issy in danger, he knew the odds of successfully rescuing her horses would increase greatly with her involved.

Not to mention, his little falcon would kill him if he fought the raiders without her.

Her stallions were tied to a separate line about ten feet away from the raiders' horses, which should make retrieving them easier. All the horses, including Charger and Onyx, had been ridden hard over the past three days, but Sultan and Silver hadn't had to carry any riders, so they would be a bit fresher. Where Charger was used to long, hard rides, Wil would bet coin the raiders' horses weren't. Onyx wasn't either, but as Issy said, few horses could match a Frisian in strength and endurance.

"Jean Luc," one of the raiders said. "You take first watch. Aubin, you take second. Jean Paul, you take third, I'll take fourth."

"Sounds good, Lance."

Wil was putting faces to the raiders' names as they responded, when it hit him, they were speaking in the Frank tongue. He edged closer, taking in their looks and clothing. The only thing Basque about them was the fletches on their arrows.

The thieving bastards were Franks.

"Get some sleep while you can," the one called Lance, who seemed to be in charge, said. "We turn due east tomorrow." He looked up into the sky. "It looks like more rain coming. And it doesn't look like it'll stay behind us this time."

"Aye, much as I hate being wet," Jean Luc said, "it does help cover our tracks. That last storm surely seems to have."

"Good for us," Aubin said, lying down on his bedroll. "Bad for anyone tracking us."

"Aye, and luckily for us," Jean Paul said, "our buyer doesn't care when we get the Turkmenes to him. Only that we deliver them."

Edging back into the woods, Wil made his way back to where Issy waited, bow in hand and arrow notched and pointed at the footpath's entrance to the glen where they'd made camp.

"It's Wil," he said, waiting for her to lower the arrow before stepping into the glen.

"Well?"

"Sultan and Silver are fine."

She let out a relieved sigh.

"There are still only four raiders, and from what I could see, they're only armed with short swords, waist blades, and arrows."

"Which is good for us."

Wil nodded. "There's one more thing. They're not Basques, they're Franks."

"What?"

"They were speaking the Frank language amongst themselves. Their clothing, horses, gear, it's all Frank."

"Are they working for themselves or someone else?"

"They spoke of delivering the Turkmenes to a buyer, and they're turning due east tomorrow."

Issy nodded and set her chin. "What's the plan?"

"From what I heard, they split guard duty between the four of them each night. We sneak up on their camp at midnight, which is when the third shift starts, wait for that guard to get bored and the others sleeping deeply. You'll shoot the guard and I'll take the other three while you get your horses."

Issy grinned and her eyes narrowed fierce as a falcon's spotting their prey. "Sounds easy enough."

Wil chuffed. "Yeah. Doesn't mean it will be." He'd seen too many battle plans go awry to expect anything to be easy. "Which is why I need you to promise me something."

"What?"

Wil chuckled. He should've known she wouldn't promise him anything without knowing what it was first. Not that he blamed her. He'd have done the same.

"I need you to promise me that if anything goes wrong, if I'm killed, or injured, or even look to be losing the fight—"

"No."

"What?"

"No." She pressed her lips and shook her head. "I will not promise to cut and run if you're killed or hurt or losing."

Wil quizzed his brows at her. "Even if I'm killed?"

"How would I know for certain you were dead?"

"Uh, throat slit, stabbed in the heart, hamstrung."

She tilted her head at him. "Okay. Throat slit and bleeding out, I'll take my horses and run; otherwise, I'm not leaving you until I see the breath leave your body."

"Damn it, Issy. If they catch you, they'll kill you, or worse."

"They'll try."

"Christ." A low growl rumbled up from his chest and out his throat. "I should tie you up on Onyx and head back to Oloron right now. Your horses are not worth your life."

"You can try," she challenged. "Besides, it's my choice. My decision. If you don't agree with it, why didn't you try to stop me back at Oloron?"

"Because…" *Because you're the one person in the world I can't say no to. Because I still love you, you beautiful, maddening woman. I always have. I always will.* "Because I knew you'd come anyway, Little Mule."

"You were right. So let's prepare for our own raid."

***

Issy

Issy stood with her left shoulder to the tree she'd been hiding behind, her quiver of arrows slung over her shoulder, one arrow loosely nocked to her bow. She glanced over at the three men sleeping on their bedrolls, waiting for Wil to make his move, which would be her signal to shoot the guard sitting with his back propped against his saddle.

A shadow moved in the tree line by the sleeping men and Issy aimed for the guard's chest. She saw movement from the corner of her eye and let the arrow fly. It sunk into the guard's chest. "Wake up," he rasped before slumping over.

One of the thieves jumped up, drawing his short sword as Wil leapt out from the trees with his long sword high. Wil swung his sword down and the thief was able to get the flat of his short sword onto his shoulder, preventing Wil's slash from severing his arm. The other two thieves were up and circling Wil, who twisted and turned as he parried their jabs, fighting three against one.

"Get the horses and run," he yelled. "Now."

Issy froze. If she went for the horses, Wil would surely be injured, if not killed. If she went to help him, they could get the horses after the fight. She nocked another arrow and aimed it at the back of one of the men jabbing at Wil and let it fly. The man twisted to the side to avoid Wil's thrust and her arrow only nicked his arm.

"Jean Luc," that same man shouted. "Take care of the horses."

Issy nocked another arrow as one of the thieves broke away and ran for the horses. She aimed and let fly as he dove headfirst onto the ground. Her shot grazed his shoulder and he came up behind Silver. She nocked another arrow and was trying to find a shot she could make without hitting the colt when Silver let out a scream that sent shivers down her spine.

She glanced over at Wil and saw one of the thieves lying on the ground with a longsword sticking out of his chest and the other backing up as he parried an onslaught of double-fisted blows from Wil's short swords. Pulling her waist blade, she ran over to her horses. Silver was hobbling around on three legs, while Sultan kicked at the thief who was standing behind him.

Issy stood on the other side of the tie line, grabbed the rope to Sultan's bridle, and yelled. "Hey."

The thief glanced away from Sultan to Issy, who jerked the rope hard to the right. Sultan swung his body to the left, knocking the man to the ground between him and Silver. Issy let go of Sultan's line and the stallion reared and stomped the man's head and chest with his front hooves until the man stopped screaming and thrashing and lay still and lifeless.

"Wil?" Issy swung around as Wil twisted his short sword in the last standing thief's belly, then pulled it out. The thief crumpled to the ground.

"Issy?"

"I'm all right. But Silver's been hurt." She held her hand out to the yearling colt to sniff, and then rubbed her hand up and down his nose as Wil walked over. "It's all right, Silver," she crooned. "You're going to be all right."

She ducked under the line and stood next to the still-anxious colt, running a hand down his neck as Wil reached under, grabbed the dead man by his shoulders, and pulled him out from between the horses. The horses immediately settled. Issy ran her hand down Silver's back to his rump, which twitched as she touched the side of his back right leg, which he was holding up.

Issy inspected further. A deep, bloody gash ran high across the back of the colt's thigh. They'd tried to hamstring him. She prayed they hadn't been successful.

"How bad is it?" Wil asked, and she realized he was standing next to her.

"I don't know. I'll have to wait until daylight to see it better."

She started to step over to check on Sultan and her legs went boneless.

"Whoa there." Wil wrapped an arm around her waist and caught her before she hit the ground. "I've got you." She threw an arm around his shoulders and hung on. "That's it, lean on me. I won't let you fall."

He walked her over to a log and eased her down onto it, then he took her numb, freezing hands in his and rubbed some blood flow back into them.

"It's always after a battle that the nerves hit," he said, rubbing his hands up and down her arms. He laid his hands on her shoulders and gave them a gentle squeeze. "Sit here. I'm betting these thieves have a wineskin or two around." He started to stand and Issy grabbed his hand, afraid to let go. "I'm not leaving you, Little Mule."

"It's my fault."

"What is?"

Tears welled in her eyes and spilled down her cheeks, hot and salty. "I, I saw movement, and I, I thought it was you. I sh-sh-shot too early. It's m-my fault Silver's hurt. M-maybe crippled."

"No, Issy." Wil pushed a stray strand of hair back behind her ear. "It's not your fault. Things happen, there's no way to predict them, no way to keep them from happening." He wiped her cheek with his thumb and smiled, his dark eyes soft. "We're alive, they're dead. Right now, that's all that matters."

He chucked her chin and Issy sucked a ragged breath in and blew it out. "You're right," she said, her voice shaking as badly as her body. She sucked another breath in and blew it out, let go her hold of Wil's hand and tried to smile. "I'm all right. Go." She lifted her chin. "Find some wine. I could use a good drink or ten."

She concentrated on her breathing, slow, deep, and steady, while watching Wil search through the dead men's gear. He came back carrying two skins, opened one, and handed it to her.

"Slow and easy does it," he said as she lifted the skin and took three long swallows.

She handed the skin to Wil and he did the same. They repeated it twice more before Wil capped the skin.

"How you feeling now?" he asked.

She gave a stupid grin and nodded. The wine's warmth had spread from her belly out to her limbs and had dulled her nerves enough to calm her. "Better."

"Good. I'm going to drag the bodies away from the camp, then start a fire."

Issy stood and tested her legs, which were still wobbly, but held her up. "I'll gather wood. A fire will be nice after two nights of cold camps."

"Once we've got a fire going," Wil said, "I'll go get Charger and Onyx." He looked up into the late-night sky, which had clouded over. "We should be able to get a bit of sleep in before day breaks."

***

Wil

Wil woke to the sound of horses pawing and snorting, his body wrapped around Issy's, her face buried in his chest, her knees tucked up against his thighs, his hands cupping her backside, his cock hard and seeking her heat. He hadn't had this many erections without a release his entire life. Yet disappearing behind the trees to help himself didn't feel right.

"You're killing me, Issy," he whispered hoarsely as he rolled onto his back and stared up into the dawning sky. A sky that promised rain.

He got up and glanced around the camp. The horses stood with their ears pricked, and Wil swore he heard a predator's snarl from the direction he'd dumped the bodies. He relieved himself behind a tree and then he crouched down beside Issy and stared at her face in repose.

Her skin was smooth and unblemished underneath the smeared dirt and dried blood, her brow unfurrowed, her mouth slightly open, her breath warm and steady. Gone were the rounder contours of her youth, honed by age and nature into a firm jaw and high cheekbones. If her eyes had been open, he wondered what he would see, the soft gray of a dove's breast or the fierce, flashing silver of a falcon's wing.

Another snarl brought him out of his reverie.

"Issy." He gently shook her shoulder. "Time to get up."

Eyes the color of the sky about to rain down on them opened and focused on his. She smiled, slow and sweet, and then she shot up. "Silver?"

"He's still standing." Wil glanced up at the sky. "We need to get moving before the rain hits."

Issy yawned, ran a hand back through her wild mass of curls, and stood. "I have to check on Silver's injury first."

"I'll go through the thieves' gear, take what we can use and pack up the other horses while you tend to Silver."

He'd set the horse blankets and saddles in one pile, the thieves' bedrolls and extra clothing in another, their weapons in a third, and was putting their foodstuffs, water-, and wineskins in a fourth pile when Issy called him over to the horses.

"They tried to hamstring Silver." She pointed to the gaping slash across the colt's outer thigh. "I don't think they managed to cut deep enough to sever the tendon, but they caused quite a bit of tissue and muscle damage. It's still seeping blood and serum. I can cauterize it here, but it needs to be cleaned out, sewn up, and wrapped up with a mending poultice to heal." She met Wil's gaze, her own full of worry. "I don't have any of the tools or medicines I need to do that with here."

"Can he walk?"

She nodded. "He can, but it's going to be slow going, with lots of stops to rest his leg." She ran her hand over the colt's rump. "I figure it'll take us three times as long as normal to travel with him."

"Which means it would take six to seven days to make it back to Oloron." Wil eyed the wound. It was deep and raw, and the odds of the colt walking on it for that long without becoming lame or infected were slim to none. Which were still better odds than asking Issy to even consider leaving the colt here or putting it out of its misery. He rubbed the back of his neck. "Well, if that's what it's going to take…"

"There's somewhere closer we can take him. Somewhere that has everything I'll need to heal him. Where we can all rest up."

Wil cocked his head. "Is this the same somewhere your family goes to for a month every year? Your secret hiding place from the world?" He'd heard the name spoken by Issy or her brothers through the years, but nothing more. "The Hollow?"

"It is. And it's only about a day or two's ride from here due north on a healthy horse."

"So, only two to four days walk for Silver versus six to seven to Oloron."

"And a quiet, peaceful place to heal."

Wil nodded. "I'll start packing up while you get what you need ready to cauterize the wound."

CHAPTER TWELVE

The Hollow

Issy

"Someone's here."

Issy and Wil crouched down behind the hedge of bushes that bordered the Hollow's southwest edge. From there, they could see the doors to both the stable and the cabin were open, and what looked and smelled to be a haunch of venison roasting on a spit over the fire pit in the yard. Two Frisians grazed in the paddock to the other side of the stable. Issy let out the breath she'd been holding.

It had taken her and Wil three and a half days to get the horses here, traveling at a pace Silver could manage with at least six rest breaks a day. Plus, it had rained the first day and night, not enough to stop them from their journey, but enough to slow them down even further, and erase any signs of theirs or the thieves' tracks for anybody following them.

Silver had been a champ through it all. Issy knew the colt was hurting with every step he took, and she had done what she could to help ease his pain, separating the oats from the globs of sheep fat and smearing the fat around the edges of his cauterized wound to keep them soft and pliable, then feeding him the oats after.

She would massage the muscles around his wound when they rested, and would cover him with extra saddle blankets they'd taken from the thieves' horses at night. Once the ground had dried enough they weren't walking in puddles, she'd padded the hoof of his injured leg with pieces of the dead men's bedrolls to help absorb some of the shock as it hit the ground.

Now they were finally here at the Hollow, safe and relatively sound.

She stood and gave three short whistles. A large, black and tan, rough-coated dog came loping out of the stable, followed by a tall, redheaded young man.

Issy grinned. "It's Harald and Lucan." Another, older, giant of a man came out of the cabin. "And Tree."

She whistled again and Lucan came running over, tail wagging, as Issy and Wil led the horses out from behind the bushes into the open yard.

"Hey, Lucan." Issy patted Harald's dog, a descendant of their mother's wolf dog, who had passed a year after Harald had been born.

Lucan walked up to Wil, sniffed and wagged his tail, and then circled around the herd of eight horses. He circled closer to Silver, no doubt smelling the colt's injury, and Issy shooed him away.

"Lucan, come here." Harald called his dog to heel, and then wrapped Issy in a welcoming hug. "It's good to see you, sister."

She hugged him back. "It's good to be seen, brother."

"Wil." Harald clasped Wil's forearm. "Thanks for bringing her back in one piece."

Wil gave Harald's arm a shake. "We brought each other back."

"Uncle Tree." Issy squealed like a little girl as she was picked up off her feet and twirled around in the giant's arms. She kissed his cheek and he set her down, grinning from ear to ear.

"I see you've brought both of the Turkmenes back with you," he said. "Not that we ever doubted you would."

"Aye," Harald chortled. "Only because we all knew you were both too stubborn to ever come back without them."

"Did Father ride to Inigo's?" Issy asked, ignoring her brother's and Tree's jests.

"He did. He rode there with Phillipe and Wyatt."

"Wyatt?" Wil interjected.

"Aye, he said he could help look for you while also doing some trade." Harald gave an apologetic shrug.

"That sounds like him." Wil didn't sound too insulted.

"Oswald, Gil, and Dante's man, Sergio, went after you," Harald continued. "We all left together the afternoon after the wedding and split up the next morning where your tracks turned southwest. Father wanted me and Tree to stay here in case you showed up." He grinned. "Good thing, apparently."

"The others never caught up with us," Issy said. "Last week's rainstorm almost certainly washed away any tracks they were following. Hopefully, they've already headed back to Oloron."

"The thieves led us southwest for two days before turning almost due south," Wil told them. "We caught up to them on the third afternoon and took back the horses that night."

"What happened to the Basque bastards?" Tree asked.

"They weren't Basque," Wil said. "They were Franks."

"What?" Tree and Harald exploded in unison.

"They were Frank," Wil repeated. "The only thing Basque about them were the arrows they left to make it look like Basque raiders had been responsible."

Harald and Tree looked to Issy. "It's true. Wil heard them speaking it when he spied on their camp. It was what they yelled at each other during the fight."

She started shaking, her body's memories taking over. Wil wrapped an arm around her waist and pulled her into his side, holding her upright.

"They spoke of already having a buyer for the Turkmenes," Wil told them. "Unfortunately, there weren't any survivors left to question." He lifted his chin toward the thieves' saddled horses. "Maybe someone in the valley will recognize their horses and who they belonged to."

"You didn't recognize any of them, Issy?" Harald asked.

"No." She drew a deep breath in, blew it out, and stepped away from Wil. "Right now, I need to set Silver up in a clean stall and tend to his wound."

"Silver's hurt?" Harald started for the colt. "What happened?"

"They tried to hamstring him rather than give him up to us," Issy told him. "But they cut too high, thank God. They tried to hamstring Sultan too. He trampled the man to death."

"Well done, Sultan." Harald saluted the stallion, then took in the thieves' horses and Charger and Onyx. "There's clean stalls in the stable," he told Issy. "You take care of Silver and we'll take care of the others."

"Onyx, Sultan, and Charger could use some oats. You can pasture the thieves' horses."

Harald gave her shoulder a brotherly shove. "Don't you ever get tired of being a bossy big sister?"

Issy laughed, the heaviness of the past several days lifting from her. "Nope. Never."

The original stable had been built by their great-great-grandfather with stalls for eight horses, enough for the mounts and pack horses of a hunting party. It had been added on to over the past twenty years by her father and mother, and now had stalls for a dozen horses, plus a storage room for feed and tack. She settled Silver in a stall near the door facing the house where the summer breezes could be felt without overheating the colt, and where she could hear him from the house if he was in distress.

She grabbed an empty water bucket as Wil led Charger and Onyx into the stable, followed by Harald and Sultan, then she went to the stream and filled the bucket, hauled it back to the stable, and set it in Silver's stall. She went into the tack and feed room, to the shelf where a myriad of herbal remedies were stored, and pulled out a vial of belladonna, a bar of lye soap, a tub of knitting balm, a small, sharply honed knife, and the sewing kit. She tossed a couple handful of oats into a pan, mixed a dose of belladonna into it, drizzled it with honey, and stirred it with a spoon.

"Here you are, Silver." She held the pan up to him, making sure he ate every last morsel. Then she left him alone to give the belladonna time to take its sedating effect.

Sultan, Onyx, and Charger were contentedly munching away on their oats as she went back to the tack room and put the knife, sewing needle, thread, and small scissors in another pan and set it, along with the knitting balm, on a stool outside the gate to Silver's stall.

Wil, Tree, and Harald were busy unpacking the thieves' horses as she crossed the yard toward the house. She hadn't come with her family on their monthly sojourns here for the past two years, having been busy with her own property and livestock, and she hadn't realized how much she'd missed her time here until she stepped up onto the porch and through the door.

Like the stable, her family had built onto the house through the years to accommodate their growing numbers. When she'd been a young child, it'd been a one-room cabin with a worktable, a hearth, a bed, and two cots for her and Geoff. By the time Harald came along, her parents had added on a room large enough for four beds, a master bedchamber for themselves, and a kitchen large enough for a supper table that sat eight.

Issy, Geoff, and Harald had helped to enlarge the common room the summer she was twelve, and they'd all been taught how to repair the thatching over the house and stable roofs, as well as the feeding and care of the animals, mucking out the stalls, keeping the house clean, the larder stocked, and the gardens producing. As well as how to hunt, skin, and cook wild game. All the things they had help for back at Oloron as the children of the count and countess.

Staying at the Hollow had been some of the happiest times of Issy's life.

She took the pot of simmering water they'd been taught to keep handy from over the hearth spit, grabbed a couple of clean kitchen linens, and headed back to the stable.

"You need any help with Silver?" Wil called out as he shut the gate to the pasture where the thieves' four horses were being watched over by Harald and Tree as they integrated with their horses.

"I do. If you could restrain Silver while I work on his wound."

"You did sedate him, right?" Wil asked as he strode over.

"I did. He should be feeling the effects any time now."

Silver's head was hanging low and his third eyelids were covering the inside corner of his eyes by the time Issy had soaked her tools in the hot water and assembled her surgical tray. Wil laid three saddle blankets over the colt's back for cushioning, and then led him headfirst to the corner where the gate hinged and pushed the gate in, up against Silver's side, pinning him tight.

He pushed against the gate with one hand and patted Silver's neck and head with the other while Issy gently washed the colt's wound with the lye soap, then rinsed, repeated the process, and dabbed it dry with a clean cloth.

"Good boy, Silver." She tossed the cloths in a basket set aside to collect the dirty linens and tools, then met Wil's gaze. "He's not going to tolerate the debriding as well as he did the washing."

Wil pushed his shoulder into the gate. "I've got him."

Issy took the knife in hand and started scraping the dead flesh away from the wound, worried that the colt wasn't putting up more of a fight.

"How's he doing?" she asked Wil.

"He tenses when you scrape, relaxes when you stop."

"Good. That's good. Though I'd feel better if he tried to kick me at least once."

"I can let up the pressure on the gate if that'd help, Little Mule."

Issy laughed softly. "I'm sure you would."

"You know me," he chuckled. "I'd do anything for you."

She chanced a glance at Wil, who flashed a teasing grin at her. "Uh-huh." She concentrated on debriding the wound, else she cut Silver or herself. When she got down to the pink, healthy flesh, she washed and rinsed the wound again and packed it with a knitting balm of comfrey and St. John's wort.

"You can let up for a bit, give Silver a rest before I start sewing."

She stood and stretched her back, neck, and fingers, then scrubbed her hands with the lye and dried them on a clean linen, then she sat back down on the stool, threaded the needle with the boiled thread, and looked to Wil.

"Ready?"

He pushed on the gate and patted Silver on the withers. "Ready."

Issy pushed the needle through the edge of Silver's wound and the colt tried to bolt forward but had nowhere to go.

"Pat harder," she told Wil. She pushed the needle through the other edge to the thump, thump, thump of Wil's pats, and Silver flinched, but didn't move otherwise. "Good. That worked. I'll tell you go and you pat until I say stop."

"Got it."

Issy positioned the needle. "Go," she said, and pushed the needle through. "Stop." She gave them all a moment's rest, then said, "Go," and pulled the thread through. "Stop."

Thirteen stitches later, the wound was closed. Issy smeared a healing salve of lemon balm, thyme, and juniper over the suture line and then stood to inspect her work.

"It's not pretty, but I think it'll hold and heal," she said.

She started to clean up and Wil shifted his hold on the gate so he could see the wound.

"I'm impressed. I've seen field surgeons without half your skills."

"Aye, well, I did have my mother and Denys as teachers."

"So you did. So did we all. But it took with you."

"As far as treating animals goes. People, not so much."

Wil laughed, low and near. "You always were partial to the furry and the feathered."

"And you."

Issy could have bit her tongue as soon as she'd said it, especially as Wil's eyes changed from teasing to serious.

184

"Issy…"

"How's it going in here?"

Wil stepped back as Harald sauntered into the stable.

"We're done," Issy said as she collected the basket full of dirty linens and tools. "Come take a look before Wil lets Silver out of the chute."

***

Wil

Wil pushed his chair back from the supper table with a satisfied groan. "That's the most I've eaten in one sitting since Geoff and Desiree's wedding feast. I can't tell you how good that fresh venison tasted after six days of jerky and nuts."

"I remember existing on camp food for months at a time," Tree commiserated. "One of many things I don't miss about being a soldier." He winked at Issy. "Though I do recall one march where the food was more than tolerable thanks to a cook's lad called Hamm."

"Too bad Issy didn't inherit our mother's and aunties' abilities in the kitchen," Harald teased, and was rewarded by her throwing a chunk of bread at him and hitting him square in the chest.

"Who's been cooking between the two of you?" Wil asked.

Tree jutted his chin toward Harald. "The lad has. He's not half bad." He grinned and then grimaced. "He's not half good either."

"I haven't noticed your girth shrinking any," Harald groused.

Tree gave a good-natured harumph and then helped himself to another piece of bread.

"Don't worry," Harald said as Tree drizzled honey over the bread. "We brought a cart full of supplies with us, including six tubs of Issy's honey."

Wil recalled that the family always left for their sojourns with a cart full of dry goods, and often came back with a supply of different fruits and vegetables, depending on the time of year. He'd always wondered where they went, but it had been the one secret Issy had never shared with him, until now.

"Are Tree and I the first non-family members to be here?" he asked.

"Other than our father when our mother brought him here to heal after their fight with Nithard's men almost twenty-four years ago," Issy answered. She pointed her knife at Wil and then Tree. "So you both must swear to keep our secret."

Wil looked to Tree and they both raised their right hands. "We swear."

"Good." Harald gave a serious nod. "Now we won't have to kill you."

"You could try, lad." Tree puffed out his considerable chest. "You could try."

They all laughed and Tree made a show of licking the honey off his fingertips.

"Was Father planning on stopping here on his way back to Oloron?" Issy asked Harald.

"No. He wanted to keep everyone else away and unaware of the Hollow. Tree was to ride to Inigo's, or to intercept Father on his way back from there, if needed. But since you made it here safe and sound, we'll ride straight back to Oloron as soon as you're ready."

"There's no reason for you to wait for me to ride back," she told him. "I'm staying here with Silver until he heals up, which will be at least ten to fourteen days, maybe more."

"And I'm staying here with Issy," Wil declared.

Issy smiled her approval, and neither Harald nor Tree argued the propriety of the situation. Not that it would have done them any good.

"We'll stay through tomorrow then," Harald said. "Help restock firewood, cut some hay. We'll head back to Oloron the day after, take the raiders' horses with us, so they don't decimate the pasture grass, see what we can find out about their dead owners."

"If nothing else, they'll stir up some interest." Tree pulled on his beard. "What do we say about you two and the Turkmene stallions?"

Wil looked to Issy. He knew what he would do, but it'd been her horses stolen, her home raided, her foals killed.

"We tell the truth," she said. "That way we don't have to remember any lies. The thieves were killed, my stallions recovered, and Wil and I are making our way home with them."

"Agreed," Wil said. He eyed Harald and Tree. "However, you two don't tell anyone but the count and countess that the thieves were Franks who died without spilling their guts about who they stole the horses for. If anybody else asks, you tell them all will be revealed in time."

"Clever." Harald grinned and slapped Wil on the shoulder.

"And if anyone else in the valley's involved," Tree added, catching on, "they'll be worrying about what you do or don't know."

Wil sat back. "Exactly."

Harald pushed back from the table and tossed his meat scraps to Lucan while Issy watched, a faraway smile on her face.

"Do you remember Wolf?" she asked Harald.

"I don't. I was too young when he passed, though I've heard plenty of stories about him."

"I remember him right well," Tree offered. "Nobody messed with your mother when that beast of a wolf-dog was nearby. Even your father had a healthy respect for him, though they took to each other pretty quick."

"Do you remember him, Wil?"

"I have vague memories of him herding us if we strayed too far from our mothers."

"For some reason," she said, "I remember him very clearly here at the Hollow. I swear, I can see him sitting guard next to me, his huge head in profile against a blue sky as I lay in a basket." She stared off into the distance for a moment, then shook herself. "Most likely I'm simply remembering the stories Mother told me about my infancy here."

Wil rubbed the goosebumps that rose on his arms. From what he'd witnessed of her dreams, he had no doubt she was recalling her own memories and not her mother's tales.

Issy yawned, and then yawned again. "I assume you've been sleeping in our old room?" she asked Harald.

"We have."

"I'll sleep in Mother and Father's room then." She gave Wil a fleeting glance and swiped at the pink spreading across her cheeks. "I'm ah, I'm going to check on the horses first."

Wil stood. "I'll go with you."

The sun had set below the mountain and the dusky sky was slowly darkening as they crossed the yard.

"I'll check on Charger and Sultan," Wil offered as they reached the stable. "Make sure they're settled for the night."

"My father taught you well."

"Yes, he did." Wil lowered the tenor of his voice. "A good horseman always sees to his horse first. If your horse can't walk, you can't ride. Take care of your horse and they'll take care of you." He wagged his brows at Issy. "Did I miss any?"

"So many," she said, laughing. She stopped at Onyx's stall and rubbed the mare's nose. "All of them true."

She pulled a carrot from the bucket and entered the mare's stall, offering her the treat. Wil grabbed a carrot and moved on to Sultan's stall first. Charger was more likely to accept Wil smelling like Sultan than the other way around. He'd been working on making friends with Sultan since he'd first arrived at Oloron Manor, and the stallion trusted Wil enough now to let him enter his stall and handle him.

Wil gave Sultan the carrot and ran his hands up and down the stallion's neck, withers, back, and legs. "Good boy, Sultan," he spoke slow and low as he lifted a hoof and checked for cracks, swelling, or bruising, and then repeated with the other three hooves. He stood and gave the stallion a pat on the rump. "Looking good, Turk."

He checked the water and feed buckets, which were both half full, and then went to Charger's stall.

"How you doing, old man?" He gave Charger a carrot and did his inspection of the stallion who'd been with him since the day he'd left Oloron seven years ago. Charger had been Talon's gift to Wil on his seventeenth birthday. A gift he could never thank his godfather enough for, along with the years of teaching and advice on riding and tending to horses, as well as weaponry and fighting.

Talon, Wil's father, and King Charles were the three men Wil admired most in the world. They'd all taught him by example how to be not just a man, but a good man. Something he strived for every day.

Shutting the gate to Charger's stall, he leaned against the gate to Silver's and ogled Issy's breeches-clad backside as she was bent over retying Silver's padded boot. He felt a stab of guilt, wondering how pleased his godfather would be at Wil's obvious lust where Talon's daughter was concerned. But then he recalled stories of how badly Captain Talon Guiscard had pined for Lara when she'd been his lidi.

Wil adjusted his tightening breeches, determined to act honorably. Problem was, when it came to Issy, his body and mind were at odds.

She turned and caught him staring. "What?"

He considered lying to her; it'd certainly make some things smoother between them, especially considering they were going to be alone here together for the next two to three weeks. Still, no matter what else, they'd always been able to count on each of them being honest with the other, even when it would have been easier to lie.

Wil held her gaze and hid nothing in his. "I already miss waking up with you in my arms."

Her cheeks turned the same rosy pink they had when she'd mentioned the sleeping arrangements earlier. "I already miss waking up in yours."

Their eyes locked and Wil took a step toward her, meaning to kiss her. To show her exactly how much he missed having her in his arms. By the look in her eyes, she was ready to be shown.

He stopped in his tracks as Lucan came bounding through the open door, followed by Harald. Wil clamped his jaw shut and willed his eager cock down. He glared at Harald, who either took no notice or had and was ignoring Wil as he hung over the gate to Silver's stall. Was he purposely interrupting Wil and Issy for the second time today?

Wil gripped the gate. Harald and Tree would be gone day after tomorrow. Then it would be Wil and Issy. Alone. Together.

"How's Silver doing?" Harald asked.

Issy swiped at her cheek. "So far, so good." She tugged on her jerkin. "The next week will be the real test. If infection is going to set in, that's when it'll happen." She gave Silver a pat on the neck and reached for the gate, causing Harald to step off and back.

"Would you rather Tree and I stay here until you know he's out of the woods?" Harald asked. "In case you need one of us to fetch a medicine or relay a message to Oloron."

Issy glanced at Wil, who purposely kept his expression blank, though the words *please say no, please say no,* repeated in his mind.

"That won't be necessary," she told Harald. She gave Wil a quick flash of a grin. "I've got everything I need here."

CHAPTER THIRTEEN

Healing

Issy

Issy waved good-bye to Harald and Tree as they rode away from the Hollow leading the dead thieves' four horses, Lucan loping along behind them. She turned to Wil standing beside her, suddenly nervous about being alone with him, though she'd been eagerly awaiting this moment for the past two days and nights.

"Shall we start the laundry?" she asked.

"You really know how to sweet-talk a man."

She swiped at her cheeks, which had recently taken to flushing at nothing more than a look or grin from Wil. "It's a fine, sunny day for it," she said. "Things should dry quickly."

Wil shaded his eyes and looked up into the cloudless sky. He rolled up the sleeves to her father's borrowed tunic. "Let's get started."

They stripped the linens from their beds, as well as Harald's and Tree's, and filled a basket with their clothes from the six days they'd been on the chase along with three skirts and tunics Issy kept stored at the Hollow, which hadn't been out of her chest for three years.

She and Wil had both bathed in the pool downstream from the house yesterday and had both dressed in her parents' clothes after. Luckily, Wil was as tall as Issy's father, if not as thickly built, and his clothes fit reasonably well. Issy wasn't nearly as tall as her mother, or as curvy. She wore her mother's tunic, which hung down to her knees, tucked into her skirt's waist, and the skirt's hems, which dragged on the ground otherwise, tucked up between her legs and into her waist belt.

Her mother and Issy had worn their skirts tucked high like this whenever they were here at the Hollow, away from the prying, judging eyes of the world, as it was both freeing and practical. Her father and brothers were so used to their manner of dress, they'd never even raised their eyes at it.

Tree had stood, mouth agape, the first time Issy had tucked her hems high, and then ignored it as if she'd dressed this way every day of her life. Wil, on the other hand, had a pained expression on his face every time he looked at her dressed like this, which she caught him doing about a hundred times a day.

She tossed two bars of soap into the basket of dirty laundry, and then Wil took one handle, Issy the other, and they hauled it down to the bathing pool.

"We should wash the bed linens first." Issy kicked off the pair of sandals she kept at the Hollow, grabbed a linen and a bar of soap, squatted on the stream's rocky bank, dunked the linen until it was wet through, and rubbed the soap onto a section of it. She rubbed the soap in, dunked, rinsed, and repeated the process with another section of the linen while Wil watched.

He doffed his boots, rolled his breeches up to his knees, and did the same with another of the bed linens. Though it was obvious he wasn't used to washing linens, he tackled the job without complaint, or finesse.

She caught herself stealing glances at the muscles working in his corded forearms as he scrubbed and dunked and wrung out the linens, and she laughed quietly as he tried to fold the damp linen into a neat square, finally rolling it up into a ball and tossing it into the basket on top of the neatly folded linen she'd set in it, his tunic and breeches almost as damp as the bed linen.

"What's so funny?" he groused.

"You." Issy tried to suppress her giggle and failed. "Wilric Hugh LeCuir, king's warrior, bested by a soggy bed linen."

Wil puffed up and out. "Bested? Hah. My foe lies vanquished there." He pulled his tunic off over his head, threw it down into the basket with the linen, and set a bare foot on the basket's edge, arms akimbo. "While I stand here victorious."

Issy's laugh died in her throat at the sight of Wil's bare, broad shoulders and how the breadth of his chest narrowed to a waist ridged with muscles. She took note of a ragged scar that ran from his left shoulder to his chest and tried hard not to stare at the patch of dark, curly hair nestled between his well-formed pectorals, or the line of dark hair that led from his navel down past the waist of his breeches, which clung damply to his thighs.

Swallowing hard, she grabbed her dirty tunic from the pile, dunked it in the pool, and then threw it at Wil, grinning as it hit him square in the chest with a satisfying thwack.

His brows rose, then narrowed.

Issy laughed nervously. "You wouldn't dare."

"Wouldn't I?"

He grinned as he approached her, slow, purposeful, step by step, until he was nearly upon her. He wagged his thick brows and Issy jumped back, squealing as he grabbed for her, and then squealing louder as she tripped over a rock and fell backward into the pool.

She came up sputtering and thrust her hand out to Wil, who stood on the shore laughing heartily. "The least you can do is help me out."

He grasped her hand and she tugged with all her might, laughing as he tumbled face first into the pool. Wil came up spitting, wiped the water from his eyes, and focused them on Issy. The slow grin that spread across his face had her backing away from him, her skirts dragging heavily in the water.

"Wil—" She shrieked as he lunged for her and caught her around the waist, sending them both back under water.

Her skirts wrapped around her legs and his as they twisted and turned, tangling them even worse. Issy was a strong swimmer, but she hadn't taken that deep of a breath before going underwater and her lungs were starting to run out of air. She stopped struggling and felt Wil untangle her skirts and separate his legs from hers, then he grabbed her under her arms and pulled her to her feet.

"Sorry, Issy." He steadied her as she sucked in air and found her footing. "Those damned skirts of yours tried to drown us."

She shoved him off her and trudged out of the pool onto the rocky shore, where she unstrapped her waist belt and let her soggy skirt drop to her bare feet. She stepped out from the wet pile of skirt, her legs bare up to her knees, her wet tunic clinging to her body, her skin flushing from head to toes as Wil's gaze traveled the length of her.

A muscle ticked on the side of his clamped jaw, and her nipples, already pebbled from the cold water, grew taut at the intensity of his gaze. Issy dropped her gaze to his nipples, as taut as hers, the light brown skin around them framed by the perfect symmetry of his pectorals, and her breath hitched.

Wil's belly sucked in, his wet linen breeches plastered to him and showing the outline of his hips, thighs, and the bulge between them as he walked out of the pool.

Issy couldn't take her eyes off him.

He unclasped his waist belt and tugged the breeches down over his legs, kicking them off his feet and standing there in nothing but a breechcloth. His legs were long, well-muscled, and well-proportioned, with a light covering of dark hair that hadn't been there the last time she'd seen his bare legs when they were still children.

And there wasn't anything childlike in her response to the sight of his body now. He'd grown into a man sculpted by the hard, physical life of a soldier. A man whose body made her aware of her own.

He closed the distance between them, standing so near he could reach out and touch her. A dull ache began to throb between her legs, and her breasts grew full and needy, a need Wil's fathomless gaze only intensified. Set spinning by her growing lust yet pinned by Wil's gaze, Issy clasped her pendant, trying to center herself, her world.

Wil's gaze shifted to her hand holding the pendant he'd given her for her sixteenth birthday, the night he'd proposed marriage to her and she'd refused his love. A love she'd give anything for now.

He reached out and touched the pendant with his fingertip. Then he lifted his gaze to Issy's, pressed his lips together, and slowly shook his head. He dropped his finger, stepped back from her, and rubbed the nape of his neck.

"We should get back to the laundry," he said, his voice low and hoarse.

***

Issy rode Onyx beside Wil on Charger, picking their way along a thickly wooded mountain path onto an open meadow where Sultan and Silver ran loose, their coats glistening white in the sunlight. Urging their mounts forward, they chased the Turkmenes across the meadow, its borders never growing closer. They chased them from sunup to sundown, unable to close the gap between them, no matter how hard they rode. They chased them under the light of the moon, ghostly shadows slipping through the night, never gaining or losing so much as a stride. Then, as the moon hung directly above them in a starless sky, Sultan and Silver disappeared into a dark, dense wood guarded by four men bristling with arrows, two of them holding knives to the throats of the foals Shadow and Shadey.

"Please don't." Issy's plea blew away on a gust of icy wind.

She watched in horror as the men slit the foals' throats and their lifeless bodies slumped to the ground. A hooded man stood apart from the other four. He lifted his head, his face nothing but shadows.

Issy woke with a start, sitting upright in a bed that wasn't her own, her hands feeling for Foxy's warm, furry body, finding nothing but the bed's tangled linens.

Her racing heartbeat echoed from her chest to her ears as she took in her surroundings and recognized her parents' bedchamber at the

Hollow. Her memories from the past week came rushing back to her, mixed in with her dream.

She took a deep breath in and blew it out, and then another, more slowly this time as she sorted out the jumble in her mind into what was real and what wasn't. A low, guttural moan tore its way out of her throat as she realized anew that Shadow and Shadey had been killed, followed by a sob of relief.

She and Wil were here at the Hollow together, and Silver and Sultan were in the stable, safe and relatively sound, along with Onyx and Charger.

She kicked off her bed linens and was instantly back in the pool, her heavy skirts wrapping around her and Wil's legs, his strong arms pulling her up out of the water, his fathomless gaze plumbing hers, drinking in the sight of her tunic hugging her every curve, her mouth practically watering at the sight of his muscled body glistening wet, clad only in a breechcloth. She'd thought he was going to kiss her then. She'd been sure of it. And she'd wanted him to. She still did.

"Damn you, Wilric Hugh LeCuir," she cursed. "I was doing just fine until you showed up again."

Except she wasn't. She simply hadn't known what she was missing.

She gave the bed linens another kick for good measure, then swung her legs over the side and stood. There was no sense in trying to get back to sleep. Not with her mind and her body strung taut as a bow string with an arrow set to fly.

Padding on tiptoe past the open door to the bedchamber she normally shared with her brothers, where Wil now slept, she opened the door to the front porch, slowly, quietly, so as not to wake Wil. She stepped out into the warm August night and looked up at the waning moon hanging high in a night sky brilliant with stars, then let out the breath she'd been holding while rubbing her bare arms.

"It was only a dream," she reassured herself. And not a foretelling dream either. Everything she'd dreamt of had already happened. Though the faceless, hooded man niggled at her.

"Issy?"

"Sweet Mary, mother of Jesus," she yelped as Wil rose from the bench on the porch. She glanced about, looking for what, she couldn't have said. "What are you doing out here?"

He walked over so he was standing shoulder to shoulder with her, staring out into the night. "I'm guessing the same thing you are."

"Which is what?"

"Trying to figure out why I didn't kiss you at the pool."

Issy side-eyed Wil. "Figured it out yet?"

He turned to face her, his eyes glowing dark under the night sky. He reached out and hooked the chain to her pendant with his finger and pulled it out from under the bodice of her night shift, holding the pendant in his palm, the backs of his fingers resting against her chest. "I have."

Her breath hitched. "Care to explain it to me?"

"If I start kissing you, I won't want to stop."

Warmth surged through her. "Then don't."

He dropped his hand and stared hard into her eyes. "What I mean is, I won't want to stop at kissing."

"Oh." She hung her head to hide her blazing cheeks, though it was the pitch of night. "I see."

"Do you?" He cupped her chin and lifted her gaze to meet his. "Because I want you, my fierce little falcon. More than I've ever wanted any woman."

Issy's heart swelled. As did her nipples, which seemed to be perpetually hard whenever she was around Wil these past few days, or even thought about him. She smiled and opened her mouth to say, what? That she wanted him too?

Wil gently closed it. "But I respect you too much to take your virtue without intending to marry you."

Her heart dropped to her feet as she stepped back from him. "And you don't intend to marry me."

"I don't intend to marry anybody. Not while I'm in service to the king." He gave her a lopsided grin, softening the blow a bit. "Not to mention if we did become lovers without marrying, your father and brothers would kill me."

"No," she assured him. 'They wouldn't." She grinned, trying to make light of the matter, as he had. "They might maim you though."

***

Wil

Wil stuck the axe in the stump, picked up his tunic from the porch, and wiped the sweat from his brow. He snuck a look over at the clothesline where Issy was hanging a basketful of rags and linens she'd been using to tend Silver's wound, and caught her watching him, both of them quickly looking away.

They'd been playing this game since their midnight talk on the porch last night, which was making today awkward. Wil pulled the axe from the stump, set another section of log on it, chopped it into quarters and tossed them onto the wood pile. Not that the wood pile wasn't already well stocked, but he needed to do something to work off his energy. Normally, he'd jump on Charger and ride it off, but the stallion had earned a few days of lazing and grazing.

Now that the other horses were gone with Harald and Tree, Charger and Onyx had free reign of the pasture. Issy had mentioned trying Sultan in the pasture with them today or tomorrow. The Turkmene had gotten along with Charger and Onyx on the trail, so she and Wil were hopeful they'd get along in the pasture as well. Onyx wasn't in season, which would help. Still, they'd have to keep a close eye on them for the first couple of days.

When Silver was healed enough, he'd join them. The yearling's hind leg was weak and tender, but so far, he hadn't come up lame. If he continued to recover as well as he had been, thanks no doubt to Issy's healing skills, the colt should be able to make the daylong journey back to Oloron in another two weeks or so. Stealing another glance at Issy's slender calves as she hitched the basket to her hip and sauntered toward the stable, her skirt hem tucked high into her waist belt, Wil honestly couldn't have said if he hoped their stay here would be more or less than those two weeks.

He'd told her the truth when he'd said he wanted her more than he'd ever wanted any woman, and had since the night of her fifteenth birthday when she'd come down the stairs in a gown of gray silk clinging to her young womanly curves that he'd been oblivious to until that moment. The same gown she'd worn a year later for her sixteenth birthday celebration, the night she'd sworn she only saw him as a brother and that she couldn't foresee ever thinking of him any differently.

Watching the sway of her hips as she disappeared into the stable, Wil remembered the way she'd looked at him yesterday and last night. The way she'd been looking at him ever since he'd returned to Oloron.

Not at all like a sister looking at her brother.

She wanted him too. Of that he was certain. As certain as he was that they shouldn't become lovers, no matter how much they wanted to. He'd hurt her last night, and he was sorry for that, but he was adamant about not marrying as long as he served Charles. As adamant as he was about not bringing shame to Issy, her family, or his, by taking her as his mistress for however short a time he'd be remaining in Oloron.

Truth be told, he was as wary of her mother, Countess Lara, as he was of her father, brothers, and assorted honorary uncles. Her male relatives might do him bodily harm, but her mother was a known witch. He didn't even want to think about what she could do to him.

Not that he was especially superstitious, but he'd heard too many stories about Lara and Sophie the Sixth growing up. Stories corroborated by too many of the valley's people to take lightly. Plus, he knew how much credence Count Talon, a man not prone to flights of fancy, put in his wife's healing arts and foretelling dreams. Dreams that always came true one way or another. Like her daughter's had.

Issy hadn't had the foretelling dreams as a child, else she'd have told him. In those days they'd told each other everything. But Geoff had said she'd dreamed of Wil leaving the night before he'd proposed. The night he'd decided to leave Oloron after she'd refused him. She'd told Wil her recurring dream about the foals, Shadey and Shadow, and those had come true too.

Wil shivered, though the summer sun was beating down on his bare back. Issy had her mother's gift of foretelling dreams. He was sure of it, and she'd admitted as much.

He was also fairly sure she hadn't had any more dreams since, because if she had, she'd have told him about them. Of course, they weren't exactly talking right now, and he wasn't completely sure of anything except he wanted her and she wanted him, and he'd hurt her last night by refusing her.

If he were a petty man, he might relish inflicting a small portion of the pain she'd inflicted on him seven years ago. But there was nothing to relish in denying them each other. Only more pain.

Picking up another piece of wood, he set it on the stump and took a swing with the axe as Issy rode out of the stable on Sultan, bareback, and bare-legged from the thighs down. Luckily, the axe hit its target.

"Damned fool," Wil cursed himself. "Pay attention to what you're doing." He stuck the axe in the stump to safely admire Issy's seat and the lean length of her legs wrapped around Sultan's girth as she rode the stallion in a sedate walk around the yard. "Christ," he grumbled, half hard. His almost continuous state these past several days and nights. "She really is trying to kill me."

Leaning over Sultan's withers, her auburn rope of a braid falling down her back, Issy whispered something into the stallion's ear and pressed her cheek to his neck while Wil contemplated the foolishness of being jealous of a horse. She sat back up, catching Wil's gaze, and turned Sultan so their backs were to Wil. She urged the stallion into a trot, making figure eights around the yard, and then put him into a canter, reversing the direction and refusing to even look Wil's way though she rode right past him for several loops.

"He's looking good," Wil called out the next time they cantered by.

Issy dipped her head in response but didn't say a word. Wil went back to chopping wood. This was going to be an interesting two weeks.

He heard the change in Sultan's hoofbeat and looked over in time to see Issy riding the stallion straight for the fence to the pasture. Damn her, she was going to jump the five-foot-high fence, bareback. Wil dropped the axe and ran for the fence. She was a good rider, better than good, but jumping a horse bareback was mad.

"Issy," he yelled. "Don't."

She glanced over her shoulder at him as Sultan lifted his forelegs and then away as the stallion pushed off his hind quarters and sailed over the fence. Wil stopped as horse and rider landed, and then sprinted as Issy slid off Sultan and fell with a thud and a grunt as her back hit the ground at Sultan's feet.

"Issy." Wil vaulted over the fence as Sultan shied away from her prone form. "Are you all right?"

"I would have been," she said, pushing herself up to sitting and scowling at Wil, "if you hadn't yelled right when we jumped."

Wil raised his brows at her and offered her his hand, leaving it hanging as she glared at it before finally taking it and letting him help her to her feet. She swayed a bit and he held her by her upper arms, peering into her eyes and making sure they focused.

Eyes as gray and fierce as a falcon's wing stared back into his, and then she shook his hands from her arms. Wil grinned. "There's my little mule."

"Be glad I've stopped kicking irritating boys in the shins," she grumbled.

"I'm just glad you're talking to me again."

"Yeah, well." She rubbed her backside and looked around the pasture. Sultan was grazing on a patch of grass ten paces from them, his reins dangling, seemingly unconcerned with either his rider's fate or Charger and Onyx, who grazed close by. "At least the horses are getting along."

Wil chuckled, knowing he'd been forgiven for yesterday. Issy had never been the type to hold a grudge for long. He was glad to find that was still true.

"I'll go unhook Sultan's reins," he said. "You go sit on a cushion while I watch and make sure they continue to get along."

***

"Fooxxyy."

Wil woke to Issy's scream with a jolt.

"Please, no. Not Foxy."

He jumped out of his bed, grabbed his short sword, and ran from his room to hers, bursting through the door.

"Issy?" he called out, his eyes focusing on her thrashing around in her bed. "Issy!"

She went still and then sat upright with a gasp.

"Issy?" He glanced around the room as he strode over and stood next to her bed. "Isabeau," he said more softly as she stared straight ahead at something Wil couldn't see. He sat on the bed beside her. "Are you all right?"

She turned her gaze to Wil as if in a dream, her eyes slowly focusing on his. "Wil?" She looked around the room and her breath came out in a half gasp, half sob. "It was only a dream," she whispered hoarsely. "Only a dream."

"What happened in your dream?" Wil asked, his gut twisting with dread.

She focused her eyes on Wil, still wide with lingering fear. "The faceless man tried to slit Foxy's throat."

The small hairs on Wil's entire body stood on end. "The faceless man?"

She didn't answer, yet there was something about the way she'd said "faceless man."

"Have you dreamt of this faceless man before?"

She nodded, her hands clasped tightly in her lap.

Wil laid his hand over hers. They were ice cold. "Isabeau, look at me." He gave her hands a gentle squeeze. "Tell me."

She shivered, and nodded, and licked her lips. "You and I," she said, her voice a hoarse whisper, "we were riding Charger and Onyx, chasing after Sultan and Silver over fields and mountains for leagues on end, always far enough behind them to just spy them ahead of us, never getting any closer, until finally, in the middle of a starless night, they suddenly stop at the edge of a woods."

She let out a shaky breath and Wil rubbed her chilled hands with both of his. She glanced down at their hands and lifted her gaze to Wil's.

"You can tell me, Issy. You can tell me anything."

She drew a deep breath in and let it out. "Four men stepped out from the woods, two of them leading Shadey and Shadow, their lead ropes so short and tight around the men's fists, the foals are struggling to walk and breathe. The men jerked the foals to a stop, pulled out short swords, and held the blades to the foals' throats. I, I begged them not to do it, but they slit the foals' throats and let their lifeless bodies drop." She sniffed and blew out a shaky breath. "There's another man, a hooded man, standing alone, apart from the others. He, he looks directly at me, but his face is in complete darkness."

A shudder shook her body and her eyes welled with tears. Wil reached out and pushed an auburn tress back behind her ear. He kept his palm on her cheek and wiped the tear that fell with his thumb.

"What happened then?" he asked gently.

"I woke up," she said. "The first time."

Another tear fell and Wil brushed it away with the backs of his fingers. "And this time?"

"This time the faceless man held Foxy by her scruff with one hand and a knife to her throat with his other. I screamed and begged him to stop and then I woke up." Her tears fell freely. "What if she's killed too? Like Shadey and Shadow were?"

Wil pulled Issy into his embrace and whispered fiercely into her ear. "We took care of the thieves who took Sultan and Silver. And Foxy didn't die in your dream. She's much too smart and sly to be caught as easily as a penned foal."

She sniffed and nodded into his shoulder, and then she lifted her gaze to his, her face no more than a hair's breadth away.

"There was pure hatred emanating from the faceless man toward me," she said, her voice catching. "And I don't know why. What have I done to make anyone hate me so much?"

"I don't know, my dove. I can't imagine you doing anything to cause such hate. But I intend to find out."

"Why would they hurt innocent animals?"

"To hurt you."

He watched his words sink in and her eyes fill with grief and anger. He touched his forehead to hers. "I swear to you here and now, my fierce little falcon, I will protect you from this faceless man. I will never let anybody harm you as long as I have breath in my body."

She sniffed and nodded, touching her nose to his. "I know."

CHAPTER FOURTEEN

A Thousand Little Deaths

Issy

Issy shaded her eyes from the early morning sun as she walked out onto the porch, still groggy from being up half the night. She was glad she'd told Wil about her dreams, gladder still for his promise to protect her.

Wil always kept his promises.

Between Wil's promise and the light of day, the dark menace of the faceless man was pushed to the back of her mind, if not completely forgotten. Taking a deep breath of the warm August air, Issy blew it out, ready for a new day. A quick, furtive movement at the tree line bordering the eastern edge of the Hollow caught her eye. She stepped back into the doorway and grabbed the bow and quiver of arrows that had been stationed there for as long as she could remember.

She pursed her lips to whistle for Wil, who'd gone into the stable after breaking their fast, when a small, reddish head with upright ears and a white chest poked out from under the trees.

"Foxy?" With a loud yip, the vixen came running across the field and leapt into Issy's open arms, chittering and licking her face as she wriggled in her hold. "What are you doing here, girl?"

Wil came charging out of the stable, a short sword in each fist. "Issy?"

"It's all right," she said, clutching the fox to her chest. "Foxy's here."

"By herself?"

Issy glanced over at the woods edge. "I think so."

"Bring her into the stable," Wil said, still holding his short swords at the ready and scanning the Hollow's visible borders.

She set the vixen down, grabbed the bow and arrow, and trotted over to the stable with Foxy following. Wil shut the door behind them and peered through the arrow slit. Issy set an arrow to the bow and looked out of another slit.

"I don't think Foxy was followed," she told Wil. "She would've given anyone trying to follow her the slip leagues ago."

"You're likely right." Wil changed his angle looking out of the slit. "Still, I'd rather be safe than sorry."

"Agreed."

The horses hadn't been put out to pasture for the day yet, and Issy watched them for any signs of hearing intruders as Wil continued to keep watch through the arrow slits while Foxy reacquainted herself with the smells of the stable. She sniffed at Issy's bare feet, and Issy noticed a patch of matted fur on the right side of her neck.

"What's this?" She sat down and Foxy crawled into her lap. Beneath the fur, which was matted with dried blood, was an open laceration the size of Issy's thumb. By the crusted edges of the wound, it was at least a day old. "Wil." She got his attention. "Foxy has a wound."

"Man-made?"

"I'm pretty sure. The edges are too clean cut to be a tear." Issy's dream last night came to her. "I think someone tried to slit her throat. That's why she ran here. To hide away at a safe place and heal." Or die of infection.

"You have what you need here to tend to her?" Wil asked.

"I do."

"Can you do what you need to do by yourself?"

"I should be able to. She's always let me before. Why?"

Wil stepped away from the slit. "I'm going to ride around the area, make sure nobody's skulking around."

Issy set Foxy off her lap and stood. "I'm going with you. Foxy's wound can wait a bit longer."

"Issy."

She placed her hands squarely on her hips. "Wil."

"What if something happened to you?"

"It's my family's home. I have the right to defend it. Besides, what if something happens to you? If I'm with you I can help fight or heal as the need arises."

Wil furrowed his thick brows. "Have you dreamed of anything happening to me?"

"No."

"You would tell me if you did?"

"Yes."

He narrowed his eyes so that his brows almost touched. "Say you promise."

She narrowed her eyes right back at him. "I promise."

"Right then. We'll saddle Charger and Onyx and walk between them to the house for our jerkins, your breeches, and my long sword."

***

Issy sat across the table from Wil, eating their supper of roast venison, carrots, and turnips from the vegetable garden and fresh plums from the orchard. She wasn't anywhere near as good a cook as her mother or Wil's, but she knew the basics, as did Wil. Between the two of them, they cooked up a decent meal.

They hadn't found any signs of anybody lurking in the area when they'd ridden around earlier in the day, and though Issy hadn't expected they would, it was reassuring to know the sanctity of the Hollow held.

Having Foxy with her somehow made it feel more normal to be here, even alone with Wil. The vixen's wound would heal without needing stitches, and Issy hoped it meant the end of her dreams about the faceless man.

Dreams that had warned her of the dangers to come. And come they had.

"You all right?"

She met Wil's worried gaze. "Yes. I'm trying to sort things out in my mind."

"Anything in particular?"

She chuffed. "Only everything."

Wil laid his hand over hers on the table. "Anything I can do to help?"

Issy stared at their hands, suddenly, ridiculously, close to tears. She twined her fingers through his, drawing from the solid strength of his grip. "You already have."

It was true. Other than her father, Wil was the best person she could've been with through all this. Of course, unlike her father, Wil was also part of what she needed to sort out. Her feelings for him ran deeper than friendship, as she knew his did for her, and she had no idea what to do about it.

Wil lifted their hands and pressed his lips to the back of hers. "You look tired," he said, setting their hands down and letting go of his hold. "I'll wash the dishes and check on the horses. You should try to get some sleep."

"Thanks." She gave him a tired smile. "I think I will."

Foxy followed her to her parents' bedchamber, where Issy closed the door, stripped off her boots, breeches, and tunic, dipped a washrag in the water basin, lathered it with a bar of lavender soap, and did a quick wash and rinse. She slipped on a thin linen nightshift, drew the window drapes closed over the shutters, and climbed onto the bed, pulling only the bedsheet up over herself. She stroked Foxy's head as the vixen tucked into her chest and closed her eyes with a bone-weary sigh.

She drifted in and out of fitful sleep, tossing and turning and waking up every time she started to dream, chasing Foxy to the foot of bed with her inability to settle down, until she finally tossed the tangled sheet off and got up out of bed.

She paced the confines of the dark room, wanting nothing more than to go to Wil one moment and cursing herself for being a needy fool the next. Because she not only wanted Wil, she needed him. She needed to hear his low, resonant voice in her ear telling her everything would be all right. She needed to be safe in his arms, cocooned by his body, where her dreams couldn't find her.

Tiptoeing into his room, she watched him sleep, smiling at how much he looked like the boy she'd known without all the worries he carried on his broad shoulders. She stood staring at the soft pillow of his lips and how they contrasted with the hard line of his jaw when his eyes flew open. He grabbed her by the wrist, and yanked her down to him with one hand and pressed the edge of his waist blade to her throat with the other.

She froze as he focused on her face.

"Christ, Issy." He dropped her wrist and lowered his blade. "Did I hurt you?"

She shook her head.

Wil placed the knife back under his pillow and pushed himself up to sitting. "I'm so sorry."

"Don't be." Now that the danger had passed, her voice shook as badly as her knees. "I shouldn't've loomed over you like that."

"Why are you here?" He swung his legs over the side of the bed, sitting on the edge in nothing but his breechcloth, scanning the dark chamber. "What's wrong?"

"Nothing." Issy clasped her pendant. Now that she was standing here next to his bed in her flimsy night shift, aware of his mostly naked body, she felt beyond foolish.

He reached out and touched her hand. "Tell me."

"I, ah, I came to ask, to ask you, if you would sleep with me."

Wil's jaw dropped.

"Like we did on the trail," she added hastily.

Wil eyed her from head to toe and rubbed the back of his neck. "We had a lot more clothes separating us on the trail," he said. "I'm not sure it would be wise for us to sleep together half naked."

"Please, Wil," she pled. "It seems I can't sleep without you. You keep the faceless man from my dreams."

He stood, his body no more than a hair's breadth from hers, his eyes reflecting the storm of emotions brewing inside Issy. He touched his knuckles to her cheek and pushed a stray lock of hair behind her ear, and then his hand was on the back of her neck and his mouth was on hers. There was nothing hesitant, polite, or safe about his kiss. His lips took hers, moved over hers with a bone-melting need and knowledge that coursed through Issy's blood. He was claiming her with his kiss, and she gave herself over to it, to him.

A mewl of surrender rose up and out her throat. Wil broke their kiss, and another, pathetic mewl followed. He grinned, a pure male smirk, before scooping her up into his arms to carry her back into her parents' bedchamber.

Fearing he would drop her on the bed and leave her, she opened her mouth to protest only to be silenced with another kiss. Gentler this time, and gentler still as he spread featherlight kisses over her mouth, her jaw, her cheeks, and her eyes.

She clung to his neck as he lifted his head and lowered her to the bed, and then she smiled with satisfaction and anticipation as he laid his body over hers. He rolled them onto their sides, facing each other. Issy could have happily stared into his dark, fathomless eyes for eternity, if it weren't for the delicious feel of his big, warm hand roaming down her back to her buttocks, her thigh, the back of her knee. He pulled the hem of her night shift up to her waist and skimmed his fingertips back down her buttocks and thigh. Then he grasped her thigh and hitched it up over his.

Issy gasped and went still at the feel of her flesh pressed against the bulge of his breechcloth.

"Are you all right?" Wil asked, his voice low and ragged.

He moved his hand up her thigh, stopping when his fingertips brushed her private parts. A warm heat rushed through her.

"I don't know what I am," she rasped.

"Do you want me to stop?"

"God, no." She shifted her leg so his fingers touched more of her flesh, the sensations coursing through her coalescing between her legs.

He moved his hand from her thigh to her head, running it back through her hair as he kissed her again, slowly, leisurely, cradling her face in both his hands now. His kiss became more insistent. Issy opened her mouth to him and he filled it with his tongue, touching hers, tasting hers as she tasted him. He was all warm, wet, salty, sweet heat, and she could happily feast on his kisses for eternity.

Trailing kisses from her mouth, across her jaw, and down her neck, he pushed the thin strap of her night shift off her shoulder, exposing her breast to the night air, followed by his mouth. Issy gasped and arched her back as he took her nipple in his mouth and gently suckled. The he pushed her onto her back and did the same with her other breast, the night air caressing the still-wet nipple. He ran the pad of his thumb over the nipple and Issy groaned.

He sat up and straddled her, staring down at her naked breasts, her nipples straining toward him, missing his ministrations. He smiled that same pure male smile he'd given her before scooping her into his arms and carrying her to bed. Issy stared at the breadth of his chest, the muscled ridges of his belly, and the dark line of fur disappearing beneath his breechcloth. She reached out a tentative finger and touched the bulge straining the confines of the leather, and Wil growled. A deep, low, guttural growl that resonated to Issy's core.

"Are you sure?" Wil asked, his eyes holding hers, watching hers. "If we go any further, there's no turning back."

"I don't want to turn back. I want to take this journey with you, only you."

He said nothing for so long she feared he'd changed his mind.

"Sit up," he said, still straddling her.

Issy complied.

"Arms up."

Issy lifted her arms, and he pulled her night shift up and over her head, tossing it onto the floor. Then he unfastened his breechcloth and tossed it too. Issy had grown up with three brothers, twice as many non-blood cousins, a mother who was a healer, and she herself was a horse breeder. But none of that had prepared her for seeing Wil at full arousal.

He was, "Magnificent." She swore his cock jumped at her voice, and again when she reached a finger toward it. "May I?"

Wil's Adam's apple worked up and down as he nodded wordlessly. Issy touched the tip of his cock, marveling at the soft firmness as she ran her fingertip over the domed head. A drop of warm, thick liquid beaded at the center, and she dipped her finger in it and then rubbed it over the soft flesh.

Wil groaned.

Issy grinned and slowly trailed her fingertips from the tip of his cock down to the root, up and down, up and down, and though she hadn't thought it possible, his cock grew even larger and harder. She wrapped her hand around its thickness and felt his blood pulsing. She had no idea what she thought a man's erect cock would feel like, but she'd never thought it would feel so … alive.

Wil pushed his cock forward and Issy gripped tighter. He pushed and she gripped again and again. He bent over her and took her mouth with his in a searing kiss, his cock pressed against her belly. Issy held on to his shoulders, raising her head to meet his kisses. He placed a hand between her shoulder blades and held her close so that her nipples rubbed against his chest, their bellies touching with every gasp of breath.

Issy pressed harder, closer, thrilling at the feel of his skin on hers. Mewling with disappointment as he stopped kissing her, then panting with anticipation as he slowly nipped and kissed his way down her neck to her breasts.

Arching her back, she moaned with pleasure as he suckled first one breast and then the other, then he lifted his head and held her gaze, hazy with want and need. He shifted over her and pushed his erection between her legs, which seemed to open for him of their own volition. He reached down and took his cock in hand, rubbing the warm, firm head of it against and around her cleft.

"You feel so good, Issy," he rasped. "So wet. So ready."

He centered the head and gently pushed into her, a little bit at a time, holding still and letting her flesh accommodate him before he pushed farther, rubbing her cleft and her clit until she was begging him for more with her body, not quite having the words. She had no idea how deep into her he was, other than not deep enough, when he stilled.

"This last may hurt," he whispered, "but only for a moment. Then it will feel much better. I promise."

Issy licked her lips and nodded.

"Wrap your legs around me, my little enchantress."

She lifted her legs and wrapped them around Wil's back, bringing him deeper into her. Wil lowered his mouth to hers, kissed her, and plunged into her. Issy gave a quick yelp into his mouth, which Wil swallowed, then continued to kiss her apace with his pelvic strokes, slow and steady at first, then building in speed and depth and friction. He lifted his head and stared down into her eyes and she unwrapped her legs and braced her feet, meeting him stroke for stroke, thrust for thrust. As his strokes grew faster and harder, he balanced on one bulging arm while reaching down with his other and pressing his thumb against her nubbin of flesh where every nerve in her body had gathered.

Together, they crested and rode wave after wave of pleasure, clinging to each other and crying out with release.

***

Wil

Wil woke hugging a naked Issy to him, her head on his shoulder, one arm splayed across his chest and a leg hooked over his thigh. He still couldn't believe that after years of wishing and wanting and learning to come to terms with the fact that it would likely never happen, he was lying in bed with Issy after making love to her. With her.

He'd always known they'd be good together, in life and in bed, even before he'd known much about sex. He'd since learned with many different women, most of them ladies of one court or another, from experienced widows to young wives married off to old men, all happy to have a young, virile man in their bed. Yet with all those women, it had only been sex. With Issy, it had been making love. And she'd made love with the same natural, unbridled passion she lived her life with. Three times.

There had been no acting or artifice in her lovemaking, no schooled tricks or responses. Her obvious surprise as she'd stared, open-mouthed, calling his cock "magnificent." Her touch, tentative at first, quickly growing bolder as she explored his body with her hands and her mouth. The way she'd responded to his kisses, his touch, opening to him and taking him all in, sheathing him stones deep, so hot and wet and tight, learning their sensual rhythm and matching him thrust for thrust. The sound of his name on her lips as she cried out in release. All of it had been natural and spontaneous. All of it had been pure Issy.

His rolled onto his side and nuzzled her neck, his cock straining toward the heat of her body. He ran a hand down her shoulder to the nip of her waist and the swell of her hips. She sighed and nestled in closer as he cupped her taut, round backside and scooted her closer, until his erection pressed against the soft warmth of her belly.

Her eyes fluttered open and found his. She smiled. A new, sated, knowing, woman's smile. A smile only for him.

"Good morning, Little Dove," he said, running his hand back through her sleep and sex tousled hair.

"Good morning, my fine, Frank stallion."

His cock surged at her words, and she slung a leg over his, pressing her wet heat against his thigh.

"Something I can do for you this fine summer morn?" he asked with a cocky leer.

"Oh, so many things," she purred, running her fingertips up and down his back.

Wil hiked her leg higher, freeing his cock from between their bellies and pressing the tip to her cleft. "Would this be one of them?"

She took him in hand and lowered herself over him so only his head was inside her. "You know me so well," she said, moving in tiny, tantalizing circles.

"I know if you keep this up," he growled, "you're going to kill me yet."

"Only to bring you back to life again."

She let go her hold of his cock and he thrust into her, groaning at the feel of her intimate muscles contracting around him.

"Make love to me, Wil," she whispered hotly. "Make love to me so we both die a thousand little deaths and then come back to life."

CHAPTER FIFTEEN

Eden

Wil

Wil sat on the porch bench, watching Issy playing chase with Foxy in the yard under the late morning sun, certain he'd died and gone to heaven. If not heaven, then certainly the Garden of Eden. He understood now why the Hollow was such a special place for the Guiscards, and not only because it was a place to hide away from the rest of the world, but because it was a world of its own. Complete and replete with everything a person needed.

Or, in Wil's case, wanted. What and who Wil wanted was Issy. He always had. The miracle of it all was that she wanted him too.

They spent their days and nights wrapped up in and around each other. Foxy's wound was healing well, as was Silver's. The yearling had been let into the pasture with the other horses five days ago and had yet to show any sign of lameness. Charger and Onyx were both content lazily grazing away, seldom leaving each other's sides, and Sultan thrived on the open wilds and mountain air. Issy said she'd never seen him so calm and happy. She rode him daily, racing him across the field and meadow, jumping him over hillocks and logs and letting him splash around in the stream and swim in the pool.

The stallion had even let Wil ride him a few times. He was used to riding Charger, his powerful Frisian stallion; riding Sultan was like harnessing the wind. The fastest horse Wil had ever seen, much less ridden, the Turkmene was swift and sure-footed, sailing over any jump his rider pointed him toward.

But by far the best part of being here in the Hollow was Issy. He not only had his best and longest friend back, he had a lover who matched him in need and want and passion. They were a match physically and emotionally, and here in the Hollow, they were able to indulge their compatibility any time they felt like it, which was several times a day and night, every day and night for the past week.

Wil hadn't felt so content since his childhood, before he'd starting having sexual urges and desires that, apparently, no other woman could fulfil like Issy. While the other women had provided some satiety for his body, they'd never filled the Isabeau-size void in his soul. Coming back to Oloron, to Issy, had truly been coming home for him.

And as luck, or God, or the fates would have it, he was the same for her.

The only shadow over their days and nights here together in the Hollow was the knowledge that their time was running out. The original two-week time period she'd given Harald and Tree for their return to Oloron was up in two days, though she had warned them it might be longer.

Silver had healed enough to make the trek back, but, as Issy pointed out, it would only do him good to rest another week here. Which Wil had seconded. They hadn't decided on a definite day of departure yet, neither of them in a hurry to leave their own private Eden.

Issy came up onto the porch and plopped down on the bench next to Wil with a happy smile on her face.

"What?" she said as he stared at her with a stupid grin on his.

"All you need is side braids and you'd look like you did at twelve years of age."

She shoved his shoulder and stuck her tongue out at him.

"There's my little mule," he teased, tugging the thick auburn plait hanging down to the middle of her back. "Reverting to about eight years old."

She gave him a sidelong look that had nothing of the young girl in it and crawled over his lap, straddling him. "Good thing for you, I'm not a young girl anymore."

"Yes," he rumbled as she wriggled suggestively. "It is very good for me."

"I was conceived here, you know," she said. "Born here too, as was my mother."

Her speaking of conceiving and birthing cooled Wil's ardor a bit. He'd been kicking himself for not taking any precautions against impregnating Issy, but, truth be told, when he was stones deep inside her, pulling out was the last thing on his mind.

Pregnancy was a possibility they hadn't spoken about yet, along with what they would do when they returned to Oloron. Or when Wil returned to his duty as a king's guard. Both of which they'd need to discuss sooner than later.

Wil heaved a sigh. Now was as good a time as any.

"Wil," Issy spoke before he could. "There's someplace I'd like to take you today. Someplace special."

"Someplace we can talk?"

"Put your boots on," she told him. "We'll be walking."

She led him across the pasture, Foxy on their heels, their herd of four horses following them to the fence line, then upstream to a small, ferned glen. A bier of stacked stones covered in moss and vining blood red roses sat in the center of the glen, a slab of shale standing sentinel at the western end of the bier and facing east.

There was a hushed, almost sacred quiet to the glen as Issy stood at the shale slab and touched her hand to the bier. "Hello, Grandmother," she said, her voice and manner reverent. "I'm sorry it's been so long since I've come to see you." She looked up and met Wil's gaze. "This is Wilric Hugh LeCuir."

Wil stepped up beside Issy and bowed his head. "It's an honor, Lady Isabeau." He knew how deeply and intricately linked Issy was to her grandmother and namesake, that her grandmother had died giving birth to her mother here. That Issy's mother had given birth to her here, alone and hiding from Nithard Midered, the Count of Oloron at the time. He'd been the man responsible for Wil and Issy's kidnapping along with their mothers and several other women, all in an effort to regain the Midered estates in Oloron, which now belonged to Issy, her grandmother's heir.

He took her hand in his and lifted it to his lips. "Thank you for introducing me."

She smiled. "I wanted her to know the man I love."

Wil stood stunned. They'd been making wild, passionate, soul-searing, bone-melting, physical love with each other for the past week, but this was the first time she'd spoken the word.

"So," he whispered, "you love me?"

Issy chuffed. "Of course I do, you stubborn ass. As it turns out, I always have, I just didn't know it."

Wil chucked her chin. "Or *you* were just too stubborn to admit it."

Issy shrugged. "Perhaps." She wrapped her arms around Wil's neck. "Do you still love me?"

Wil pressed his lips together and shook his head, then grinned at the confusion in her eyes. "Of course I do, Little Mule. Always have, always will." However, as he'd learned seven years ago, loving somebody didn't guarantee a happy ending. "The question is, what do we do about it?"

"Good question."

"One we should figure out the answer to before we go back to Oloron and our families, our lives."

Issy dropped her hands from around Wil's neck. "Our very different, separate lives."

Wil dropped his head. "Yeah."

He'd made it clear from the day he'd ridden into Oloron with the DeVittorios that he'd be leaving again as soon as they were settled and his duty done, which shouldn't be too long after he and Issy got back to the valley. The DeVittorios' house had been halfway finished when he and Issy had chased after the thieves who'd taken Sultan and Silver, and that had been three weeks ago. The house should be close to finished by now, as long as Dante hadn't done anything stupid while they'd been gone, like letting Mason and his crew go because of Carina.

Wil couldn't wait to put the whole business with Dante behind him. He completely disliked the preening peacock and had thought more than once he might have something to do with Sultan and Silver getting stolen, simply because the man's ego couldn't stand the humiliation of Issy ending their short-lived and ill-suited relationship.

"Can I ask you something a bit off topic?"

"You can ask me anything, Wil, you know that."

"Why did you tell Dante you'd think about a courtship?"

She gave a short, quick laugh. "Because you warned me against it."

"I figured it was something like that."

"Oh you did, did you?"

"Yeah, I did." He considered whether to bring up his suspicions about Dante and the horses now or wait until they got back to Oloron and set their trap for him or whoever else was involved. In the end, he wanted only truth between them, now and for however long there would be a them. "Issy…"

"Wil?"

"I don't like the man, never have, that's no secret, but my gut's telling me he has something to do with your foals being killed and your horses being stolen."

She seemed to think on this for a moment. "He hasn't been circumspect about showing his jealousy of my having them," she said. "Or his anger at my family not agreeing to breed any broodmare of his with our stallions on nothing but his say-so. Still." She shook her head. "Why would he be part of such a scheme?"

"I don't know," Wil admitted, glad she hadn't outright defended Dante. "But I intend to find out and deal with whoever it was when we get back."

Issy gave a determined nod. "On that, we agree." She met Wil's gaze, her own questioning. "As for the other topic. What do we do about us when we get back?" She hesitated, then blurted out, "What do you want to do? Do you still intend to return to your life as a king's guard? Or are you willing to stay in Oloron, with me, married to me?"

Wil's jaw dropped. "Are you asking me to marry you?"

"I am."

"Christ, Issy. It's not like I haven't thought about it." Only about a thousand times through the years. "But I don't know if I'm ready to settle down to a life in the countryside yet."

"I understand," she said, her jaw as hard as her eyes.

"Do you?"

She nodded curtly. "I turned you down, you built a life for yourself, as have I, and neither of us is willing to change our lives for the other."

"Yet," Wil reiterated. "I said yet."

"So, what? I'm supposed to wait for you another seven years?"

He said nothing. She was hurt and angry, and all the things he'd felt when she'd refused him seven years ago.

"Well, you certainly got your revenge on me," she hissed. "Well done you."

Now Wil was angry.

"Do you really think that's why I'm here? Why I've done what I've done with and for you?" he rumbled. "Because if you do, then you don't know me at all."

"Obviously, I don't," she seethed.

"Horseshit."

"What?"

"That's horseshit and you know it. God damn it, Issy, I love you and you love me, but I can't stay in Oloron with you. Not yet. I've sworn an oath to my king, one my honor and the honor of my family requires I fulfill. I can't ask you to marry me and stay in Oloron while I go off to God knows where, for God knows how long, fighting God knows who for the king."

"But—"

He took her by the shoulders and held her pleading gaze square on. "I will not marry you only to leave you and possibly make a widow of you and any children we might have orphans." He heaved a heavy sigh. "Now, do you understand?"

"No." She shook her head vehemently. "I don't. Don't I get a say in whether I'm willing to take the chance of becoming your widow? Plus, no child we have would be an orphan. They'd have me, my family, your family."

"If and when I have a child, I want to be around to raise it."

"Then why…" She puffed her cheeks and blew the air out of them. "Why didn't you stay away from here, from me, until you were ready?"

Wil scoffed. "You think it was my idea to come here? I refused when Charles asked me, then he ordered me. He said I had unfinished business to tend to here."

"Like what?"

"Damned if I know."

Except he did know. Charles fancied himself a matchmaker. He even bragged about how he'd helped get Talon, who swore he'd never marry, and Lara together. He'd also told Wil to his face that he should reconnect with their famously beautiful daughter. And reconnect they had.

"Issy, there's something else we need to consider."

"Whether or not I'm already pregnant?"

Wil could barely look her in the eye. Between the two of them, he was the one experienced in sexual matters, he should have known better than to have spilled his seed in her so many times. He did know better, but he'd lost control in the moment. Which was still no excuse.

"I'll stay until we know for certain whether you are," he said. "If you are, we'll be married and I'll leave the king's service."

Gray eyes as sharp a falcon's wing cut him as she shouted, "Leave."

"Leave?" Here? The Hollow? Oloron?

"Leave this glen. I want to be alone with my grandmother."

***

Issy

Issy held her tears in until Wil disappeared beyond the ferns, then she let them fall freely. Hot, bitter tears of frustration.

"What am I to do now, Isabeau?" she asked her namesake, buried some forty years ago. A woman who had lost her parents to murder, her husband to war, and her life to childbirth here in the Hollow with no one but Sophie the Sixth by her side to help bring Lara into this world, and then to raise her.

It was here in the glen Issy felt closest to these women. Women who had faced the trials life had thrown at them with determination and strength. Who had forged lives of their own, both with and without the men they loved.

As would she.

Wil would leave Oloron, would leave her, again, and she would survive as she had before. Though this time, she'd be losing not only her best friend, but her lover, her life's mate. The realization of which brought forth a new cascade of tears. She let them flow. Better to cry herself out here in the glen with only her grandmother to witness than to let Wil see her cry. To let him see how much he'd hurt her. As she'd hurt him.

She sniffed and swiped at her wet cheeks. "Damn you, Wil."

With him, she'd discovered wonderfully soul-bending intimacy and passion, a rare and special connection according to Wil, who swore he'd never found anything close with any other woman. Which was something to hold on to. Something to hope would help bring him back to her sooner than later. Because as things stood between them now, hope and wait were all she could do once he left.

Unless she was pregnant. God help her, she didn't know which she wished for more, to be pregnant, marry Wil, and keep him in Oloron with her, or to let Wil go and hope he returned to Oloron and her someday of his own accord.

Yet even as she thought it, she knew she'd never wish to trap him, to force him to marry and stay penned up in the valley before he was ready to settle down. He was like one of the wild animals she took in. At some point, she had to set them free. To let them go out in the world and live the life they were meant to.

A few, like Foxy and Aristotle, chose to stay, but like them, if Wil stayed, it had to be his choice, freely made. Her own decision made, she laid a hand on her grandmother's bier.

"Keep watch over him, Grandmother," she said fervently. "Keep him safe and bring him back to me, if he's meant to be mine as I am his."

She left the dappled light of the secret glen and walked out into clear skies and bright sunlight as if waking from a hazy dream to the cold, hard light of day. She supposed that's what their time here at the Hollow had been, a wonderful dream filled with love, lust, passion, and a peace between her and Wil that they hadn't had for a long time.

A dream that wouldn't last in the world outside of the Hollow.

Not yet.

It was the yet she would have to hold on to without losing herself in the waiting. She sighed and climbed over the fence into the pasture. She'd been waiting for Wil these past seven years without realizing it, and had built her own life in the process, a life she loved. She could do it again.

The big difference being she knew what she was missing this time, leaving a huge, Wil-size hole in her soul.

A horse whinnied and she looked over to where Sultan, Silver, and Onyx were grazing, with no Charger. Quickening her pace, Issy trotted across the pasture and into the stable, but Charger wasn't in there either, and neither was his saddle. Her heart dropped to her feet. Had Wil left the Hollow for good?

No. He wouldn't do that. No matter how angry he was with her, he wouldn't leave her and the horses alone here. He must have taken Charger for a ride to patrol the area and have some time to think by himself.

"Come on, Foxy," she told the vixen trying to get into the bucket of carrots. "Let's go make supper."

She kept an eye out for Wil as she chopped up carrots, turnips, celery, and parsley for the last batch of venison stew she'd be cooking here. Silver was healthy enough to make the journey back to Oloron.

Time to leave the Hollow and return home.

She figured one last day to prepare the gardens for autumn, and then a day to pack up and clean, and they could be on their way on the third day and home by the fourth or fifth. The ride could be made in a day if they rode from dawn to dark with brief stops to rest and water the horses, but she didn't want to push Silver too hard too soon.

Wil rode in as the sun hit the western peak and Issy was pulling a loaf of rye bread from the oven.

"Smells good," he said as he rode Charger past the outdoor kitchen and into the stable.

Issy had already taken the other horses in from the pasture and set them up in the stable for the night, including filling Charger's bucket with fresh water and his manger with hay and oats. Her way of telling Wil she knew he'd be back.

He came out shortly and unhooked the pot of stew from over the fire and set it on the outdoor table as Issy set two bowls and plates on the table. It had become their habit to cook and eat outside in the August heat, and they did so without speaking tonight.

When they were finished, Wil took the wash bucket to the stream to fill with water while Issy set the uneaten stew and bread inside to store for tomorrow night's supper. She heard Wil washing the dishes outside, and went out and sat on the porch bench, watching his big, strong hands that knew every inch of her body as he rinsed and set them to dry. Then he came and sat beside her.

"How soon?" he asked.

Issy turned her head to meet his gaze. "Before we leave here? I figured tomorrow to prepare the gardens and store the root vegetables and fruit, the next day to clean the cabin and stable, do the laundry, then leave first thing in the morning the day after."

Wil nodded. "Tell me what you want me to do."

What she wanted him to do was take her in his arms, kiss her until she couldn't think, and make mad, passionate love to her, but her pride wouldn't let her. Instead, she stood and called for Foxy, who came running from the wood's edge.

"I'll see you tomorrow morning," she told Wil.

He stood, as if to retire to her parents' bedchamber with her as he normally would.

Issy held her hand up. "You can sleep in Geoff's old bed. I wouldn't want you to have to worry about my getting with your child in order to trap you into a marriage you don't want."

***

Wil walked out of the dark, dense woods into the open meadow leading Silver, the yearling limping badly on his hind leg. Two newborn foals black as pitch wobbled out behind them on long, knobby legs, whinnying loudly as they struggled to keep up. Wil looked across the meadow at Isabeau, met her gaze and held it. Issy stepped forward and was caught short by a sharp, stabbing pain to her ankle. She looked down at her leg, tied to a stone bier with a vine of thorns, blood trickling down her foot where the thorns stuck her flesh. She looked up at Wil and tried calling to him for help, but her throat constricted and no sound came out.

A shadow moved at the edge of the woods, snaking out toward Wil and the horses, growing in size and menace until it was suspended over him like a black storm cloud. Again, Issy tried calling out, to warn Wil of the danger descending on him, but her voice was no more than a strangled cry.

The amorphous shadow swirled and morphed into the shape of a hooded, faceless man hovering over Wil, spreading his black mantle wide, his hands clawed like a wild beast's. A sword appeared in one of his hands, shining dully in the night's shadows. The faceless man looked at Isabeau and smiled, his teeth metallic and pointed like a saw's blade, as he held a knife to Wil's throat.

Issy screamed.

***

Wil

Wil jolted upright, grabbed his short sword from under his pillow, and was on his feet before he realized it was the sound of Issy screaming his name that woke him. He bolted from his room to hers, where she lay in her bed flat on her back, her body as stiff as death, her eyes wide open and staring at something that only she could see, her scream having turned into a keening moan. He laid his hand on her bare shoulder, which was cold and clammy, and gently shook her.

"Isabeau, wake up. Issy, it's me, Wil. Wake up, my love. You're having a bad dream."

A dream that had her screaming out his name.

Her keening stopped as her eyes focused on his, and Wil cupped her cheek with his palm.

"Wil?"

"Welcome back."

She gave a tremulous smile, and he wrapped his arm around her shoulder and pulled her into his embrace, running his fingers back through her hair and whispering into her ear.

"You're safe now, Issy. I've got you. I won't let any harm come to you."

She shuddered in his arms and let out a shaky sigh.

"Can you tell me what happened in your dream?"

She rolled her forehead against his shoulder.

"It might help to talk about it." He leaned back and cupped her chin, waiting until her gaze lifted to his. "Tell me."

Her eyes welled with tears. "It was the faceless man," she said, her voice quaking as badly as her body. "You, you were walking Silver, Shadey, and Shadow out of a deep wood, and a darkness followed you. I tried to warn you, to call out to you, but…" She held her hand at her throat. "Nothing, not a sound came out."

She squeezed her eyes shut tight, and tears slipped out and down her cheek. "The darkness grew into the shape of a hooded man. It, he, was pure evil." She drew in a shaky breath and blew it out. "It hovered over you, like a hawk mantling its prey, and then, then it looked up at me. It was the faceless man, smiling at me. He had no eyes, no nose, but his teeth were sharp, metallic." She shuddered and Wil felt a chill race down his spine. "Then it, it held a knife to your throat." She clasped her pendant. "All I could do was scream your name."

Wil held her close, his hand pressing her head into his shoulder, the scent of her lavender soap wafting over him. "The faceless man is never going to get me, Little Mule," he told her. "Want to know why?" She nodded into his shoulder. "Because I'm going to catch and kill the bastard, whoever he is, first." He tucked her head under his chin. "He won't be haunting your dreams again because I'm sharing your bed every night until he's dead."

She nodded and sniffed. "Even when we return to Oloron?"

"Unless you don't want me to, in which case I'll be camped out at your door."

She wrapped her arms around his waist and swung her legs over his, burrowing her nose into his chest. "I do want you to," she said. "You know I do."

He did, but it was still good to hear her say it, especially after their argument in the glen earlier. Wil kissed the top of her head and rocked her in his arms, whispering soothing words into her hair until her breathing slowed and her head lolled against his chest.

He woke in the early morn to the pleasurable feel of his cock being stroked with a featherlight touch. "That feels good, Little Dove."

Rolling onto his back, he hugged Issy into his side, his erection growing apace with her stroking. When he was about to burst in her hand, he rolled her over onto her back and lay on top of her, pressing his iron-hard cock into her soft belly.

She wrapped her legs around him, her warm, wet flesh cradling his cock.

"Are you sure, Issy?"

"I'm sure I want you inside me." She slid her hand down and grasped his throbbing cock, then shifted and settled the tip just inside her.

Wil groaned and pushed in a little deeper. "You don't play fair, Little Mule."

Issy thrust her pelvis up and he slipped stones deep into her. "Fair has nothing to do with this, you stubborn ass. I'm getting as much of you as I can for as long as I can."

He lowered his mouth to hers, started moving inside of her, fast, deep, and hard, taking as much of her as he could for as long as he could. Which wasn't going to be long. This was sex, raw, rough, carnal, their bodies straining toward climax.

Wil applied his thumb to her clit, making sure she reached hers first, and then he plunged into her, again and again, pulling out at the last possible moment and spilling his seed into the bed linens.

They both lay on their backs staring up at the ceiling, their bellies rising and falling with each breath, the sweat cooling off their skin.

Wil took Issy's hand in his and kissed the backs of her knuckles. "How's this going to work back at Oloron, when we can't keep our hands off each other?"

She placed their hands over her heart and rolled her head back and forth. "I have no idea." She rolled onto her side, facing him, his hand still clutched in hers. "I don't think we can hide this from my parents. One look at us and my father will know, and my mother." She gave a nervous little laugh. "She's likely already dreamed of it, of us."

Wil chuckled too, though it really wasn't funny. "True enough. Plus, my mother has a hound's nose for these things. She knows people are a couple before they do half the time. Even without one of them having bought a vial of Sophie's love potion."

Issy rolled onto her belly and propped herself up on her elbows. "We could say I offered you a vial of potion and you accepted. That we're simply courting. That way, we don't have to hide our feelings for each other."

Wil gave her taut behind a pat. "Only that we're sleeping together."

"Nobody needs to know that. And if my parents figure it out, well, they lived together at the keep before they were married. They'd understand."

"They may understand," Wil said, "but that doesn't mean your father is going to approve." In truth, her father finding out about them was one of the things that most concerned Wil. Issy may have been born out of wedlock, but that didn't mean Talon would approve of her having a child out of wedlock, and Wil wouldn't purposely leave her in that condition. "When is your next menses due?"

"You mean, when will you know if you'll be forced into marriage with me?"

"Issy."

"My menses should arrive about the same time we return to Oloron."

She glanced down at Wil's drying seed on the bed linen, then got up and out of bed. Wil admired her lovely backside as she walked over to the washbasin, splashed water on her face, and ran her wet hands back through her hair. Then she donned her work tunic and skirt and walked out of the bedroom.

Wil ran a hand back through his hair and over his bearded jaw, unsure if he'd been allowed to stay in Eden a bit longer or if he'd fallen from grace.

CHAPTER SIXTEEN

Plans

Issy

Issy closed the door to the Hollow's cabin and the strangest two weeks of her life. Three, if she counted the week that she and Wil spent chasing the horse thieves. So much had changed in that short time. Everything, really. She and Wil had gone from best friends to strangers to wary combatants to friends to lovers to... She had no idea what they would be once they returned to Oloron. Or after.

For now, though, they had two more days alone together while they made the trek back to Oloron. Mounting Onyx, she led Silver on a lead as Wil led Sultan, Foxy trotting alongside them.

She stared openly at Wil as they rode side by side across the yard toward the path through the woods, admiring his strong nose and jaw, his broad shoulders, straight back, slim waist, and long, well-muscled legs. His big, strong hands holding Charger's reins, hands that knew her body better than she did.

He was pure male and he'd brought out the woman in her. A woman of sensibility and sensuality. A woman she liked.

A woman whose pride, courage, and determination she would need once he was gone. She sat up straighter and looked forward. Forward to forging ahead with her new life as this woman, with or without Wil, for however long it took him to come back to her.

Unless she was pregnant.

She placed a hand over her belly, trying to feel if she could sense life growing in her womb. Trying to sense how she felt about the possibility of bearing a child of Wil's. She'd been thinking about it almost incessantly for the past three days, ever since their argument in the glen, yet she still couldn't put a name to her feelings, other than unsure and confused.

"Enough," she chastised herself. *Don't make yourself crazy worrying about what might be. Deal with the here and now. Be here with Wil now.*

They rode in companionable silence, abreast when the path allowed, Issy following the familiar trail, Wil, she knew, studying it, memorizing it. She trusted him to keep her family's secret, as would Tree, the only two people in the world other than her family to know of the Hollow. It comforted her to know Wil could find his way back to the Hollow if he ever needed to.

Dappled sunlight shone through the forest canopy as they made their way down the mountain, taking short breaks to let Silver rest. The yearling had been healing well, but a cut that deep into the muscle would take more time to heal completely, and Issy didn't want to press it.

At high noon, they stopped by a small creek to eat and rest and let the horses graze and drink.

After a small meal of cheese, the last of a rye loaf, and apples, Wil sat with his back against the trunk of an oak, his long legs sprawled in front of him, watching Issy as she splashed water from the stream over her arms and face with a lazy grin on his.

"Come here, Little Dove." He crooked a finger and wagged it toward himself.

Issy knew that grin. She gave him one of her own as she sauntered over and straddled him. Dressed in her leather breeches, she could still feel the bulge of his cock growing between her legs. She wiggled her buttocks and then moved her pelvis in slow, undulating circles. "Is this what you were hoping for, my randy buck?"

Wil's grin turned roguish. "Always."

Issy untied the leather strip from her braid, shook her hair out, and placed her hands on his shoulders, grinding her pelvis against his. His chest rumbled and she kissed him, slow and purposeful, pushing his hands down every time he tried to pull her closer.

"What are you doing, Little Mule?"

She grinned into his lips. "Having my way with you."

He chuckled and leaned back, his arms loose at his sides. "Do what you will. I'm all yours."

"Oh I intend to." She lifted her chin. "Arms up," she said, and pulled his tunic up over his head and tossed it to the ground. She kissed and nipped her way from his mouth to his jaw to his chest, suckling his nipples as she ran her hands over the breadth of his shoulders and back.

She kissed and tasted his skin from his chest down his belly, grinning with satisfaction as he sucked his breath in when she untied the laces to his breeches and laid open the flap, releasing his erect cock.

She licked her lips and Wil groaned.

Issy met his dazed gaze and smiled, then she dipped her head so that her hair fell over his cock. Slowly swinging her head side to side, she gently dragged her hair back and forth across the tip of his erection, her core throbbing with anticipation as his belly sucked in and his cock jumped with each pass of her hair.

She lifted herself onto her knees. "Spread your legs."

Wil's brows rose to his hairline and he spread his legs wide enough for Issy to kneel between them, then she braced her hands on his thighs and kissed the tip of his cock, licking the first drop of his milky seed away. She swirled the tip of her tongue over and around the soft, fleshy head, then ran it up and down the length of him, from stem to root, gently fondling his testicles with one hand as she suckled the head.

Wil's moan reverberated from her mouth to her core.

Opening her mouth wider, she lowered it over and around his cock, sucking as she pulled back up.

"Christ, Issy."

His hands in her hair, Wil moved with her, pushing his cock up and down in time with her mouth and her hand until she felt his cock pulsing in her hand. Then he went rigid and spurted his seed into her mouth. And Issy, who'd always before swallowed his yeasty seed, turned and spat it out onto the ground.

Wil stared at his seed seeping down into the grass. "Fair enough," he said. Issy stood and started to step away, but Wil grabbed her by the hand and shook his head. "My turn."

He knelt on his knees and untied the laces to her breeches and let them drop to her ankles. He cupped her buttocks with his hands and buried his nose into her thatch, teasing her clit with the tip of his tongue.

Issy half gasped half moaned. Her feet trapped by her breeches around her ankles and Wil's strong hands holding her backside, she arched her back as he licked and sucked her flesh. Her legs stiffened and then trembled as he brought her to climax, her guttural moan reaching up to the skies.

Gazing down at him, she ran her hands back through his curls. "Help me out of these breeches," she said, lifting one leg as he pulled the leggings down over her foot, and then the other. She doffed her tunic, relishing the sun's warmth on her bare skin, then grinned and ran into the knee-deep stream, yelping from the cold as she dropped and sat in the water. "You coming in or not?"

Wil stood, the flap to his breeches still open, his cock hanging out, and eyed the stream. "You trying to give me blue bollocks?"

Issy feigned outrage. "I would never."

He drew his brows together and up, then he stripped off his breeches and ran into the stream, knees high and splashing water at her.

Foxy danced along the shoreline, yipping and yapping as Issy stood. She and Wil chased each other, splashing and laughing as they grabbed for wet, slippery limbs, their laughter dying as Wil caught her and pulled her to him. Issy leaned into him, pressing her body against his, the sun warming their chilled skin, his cock nestled into her belly.

She reached a hand down and grasped his thickening rod. Wil pushed into her hold, back and forth, back and forth, his erection growing with each thrust.

The throbbing between her legs was as needful as his cock in her hand, and she lifted a leg to press her flesh against his thigh. Letting out a throaty rumble, Wil cupped her buttocks and lifted her.

She wrapped her legs around his waist and he held on to her with one arm around her back. He positioned his cock at her core with his other hand and they groaned in unison as she slid down over and around his cock, taking him deep inside her. They rocked up and down, back and forth, in delicious, tortuous circles, clinging to each other, driving each other mad until they both screamed out the other's name in a frenzied release.

With Wil still holding her tight, Issy took his face in her hands and kissed him longingly. "You know I love you, Wilric Hugh LeCuir."

He kissed her back, smiling against her lips. "I do, Isabeau Juditha Guiscard. I do."

***

Wil

Between taking their time for Silver's sake and stopping four times yesterday and three times today for everything between rough, carnal sex play to making sweet, tender love, it was late in the afternoon when Wil and Issy crossed the river and headed for the back gate of Crossroads Keep.

The guard at the watchtower called out their arrival before they made the gate, where they were greeted by the count and countess, Harald, Tree, Phillipe, and Dardinel as soon as they rode in.

Issy jumped down from Onyx and was enveloped by both her mother and father almost as soon as her feet hit the ground, while Wil dismounted to a few slaps on the back by Harald and Tree, and a good sniffing-over by Harald's hound, Lucan.

Count Talon disengaged from his wife and daughter and walked over to Wil, offering him his hand. "Thank you for helping return our daughter safe and sound."

"She helped me as much as I helped her," he told Talon, trying not to think about what else they'd helped each other with and to.

Talon grinned. "I'm sure she did." He clapped a hand on Wil's shoulder as Issy and her mother walked over to them. "Harald and Tree told me what you'd discovered about the thieves," he said, holding his arm out and tucking his wife into his side. "Come inside, we have much to discuss."

Wil let the count and countess walk ahead, following them alongside Issy, touching his little finger to hers.

"Hah! I told you," Harald crowed from behind them. He held a hand out, palm up, and waved it toward Tree, Phillipe, and Dardinel. "I got the day and them together. Pay up."

Issy stopped in her tracks and turned on her brother and the others. "You wagered on us?"

Harald shrugged and Phillipe laughed as Dardinel tossed a copper piece to Harald.

"It's tradition," Phillipe said with a wink .

Wil clasped Issy's hand in his and gave it a squeeze. "It was inevitable," he said. "If surprisingly fast."

Issy twined her fingers through his. "I really thought my mother or father would be the first to notice."

"Oh, we did," her mother said over her shoulder. "We were simply being more circumspect about it."

Wil lifted their clasped hands to his lips and kissed the back of hers with a slow grin. "Welcome home, Issy."

Talon led them into the manor house, through the common room, and into a side room he'd had built when Wil and Issy were young.

It was where the count dealt with the business of running his estates and the valley, and as such, was supposed to have been off limits to anybody not expressly invited. Which meant, of course, Wil and Issy had snuck in every chance they'd gotten as children.

Wil glanced around the familiar room and sat beside Issy on a cushioned bench on one side of a low table while Harald, Tree, Phillipe, and Dardinel took seats along the other side, Lucan settling at his master's feet.

The count took a cushioned seat at a higher table, its top covered with stacks of parchment, a pot full of ink, another with quill pens of varying size and sharpness, and a vase with a single red rose. The same table Wil and Issy had been caught playing under too many times to count.

Talon waited until the countess entered, followed by maidservants carrying cups and pitchers of ale and wine. The countess took her seat at the table beside her husband and the maidservants poured the wine and ale and then left, closing the door behind them.

Talon lifted his cup. "To my headstrong daughter and godson. Well done."

They all lifted their cups and drank to the count's toast, though Wil wondered if Issy's father would still be saying well done if he knew *all* they'd done.

"Tell us what you know," Talon said.

Issy and Wil took turns telling them about discovering the slaughtered foals and missing Turkmenes, of tracking the horse thieves and how once they'd caught up to the thieves, Wil had heard them speaking the Frank tongue, talking of already having a buyer. They told them of the fight, of how, instead of running for their lives, the thieves had tried to hamstring Silver and Sultan, how Sultan had stomped the one to death and Wil and Issy had killed the others. None of them Basque.

Issy told them of Foxy showing up at the Hollow with a neck wound, without telling them about her dreaming it the night before, or about any of her dreams of the faceless man. So, neither did Wil.

He did tell them of his intent to set a trap, using Silver and himself as bait when the yearling was strong enough for them to set off for Byzantium, and tried not to dwell on Issy's dream of the faceless man cutting his throat. Forewarned was forearmed.

"You think the person responsible will still go after the yearling then?" Talon asked.

"I do," Wil said. "Whoever's behind this seems to want the Turkmenes as much as they don't want Issy to have them. Why else would they have killed the two newborn foals and tried to hamstring Sultan and Silver when we came at them?"

"Any suspicions who?" Talon asked.

Wil turned to Issy. "Dante," they said in unison.

Nobody in the room looked surprised.

"Why do you suspect him?" Talon asked.

"A gut feeling," Wil admitted. "Though one brought about by the way the entitled prick reacted when you and Issy both refused to agree to breed your studs to his mares or your mares to his stallion without vetting them first. I don't trust him. Never have. Again, just my gut feeling."

"I see," Talon said. "Isabeau?"

"I don't trust him either," she answered. "Plus, my animals don't like him."

"Neither does Lucan," Harald added, patting the dog at his feet on the head. "His instincts about people have always proved out."

"We can all agree he's an unpleasant man," Talon said. "But that doesn't mean he's responsible for hiring the thieves."

"No," Wil agreed. "It doesn't. Which is why we need to set our trap."

"You have a plan, I assume?"

Wil and Issy nodded.

"Well, what is it?"

"You tell it," Issy said to Wil.

Wil took a drink of his wine. "As soon as we walk out these doors, we intend to let it be known that once the DeVittorios are in their new residence, Burrell and I will be taking Silver back to Byzantium, with a stopover in Toulouse, where Charles is staying the summer. Hopefully, word will get back to whoever hired the first thieves and they'll try again, someplace between here and Toulouse."

"Why do you think they'll try to take the colt before Toulouse?" Phillipe asked.

"Because if they were successful, I'd either have to return here without the colt, or continue on to Toulouse and admit to Charles that I lost the colt Isabeau owes Irene. That I mucked up the deal he made with the empress. If it's Dante who's responsible, the chance to humiliate me would be too much for him to pass up."

"And once you've caught whoever it is that comes after you?" Talon said.

"We'll try our best to capture them alive and make them tell us who hired them."

"Then what?"

"That'll depend on who it turns out to be," Wil said.

Talon held Wil's gaze, his own dead serious. "If it is Dante?"

"My preference would be to kill him. But, of course, I would leave his punishment up to you, Count Guiscard."

Talon said nothing, his tight jaw showing he was well aware of how fraught the situation would be if Dante was, in fact, behind the attempted thefts. The count glanced at his wife, and then at Phillipe, Dardinel, and Tree, his oldest and most trusted friends, who each nodded their assent in turn.

"I'll agree to this plan," he said at last. "But I'm sending Tree with you. We can say he's carrying a message from me to Charles."

"Send me, Father."

All eyes turned to Harald.

"It would make more sense that I'd be carrying a message from my father to the king."

"You're too young," his mother said.

Harald stood at his full, impressive height and squared his shoulders. "I'm seventeen. The same age Father and Wil were when they joined the king's army." He met and held his father's gaze. "I want to go. Besides," he added with a quick grin, "my young back can handle sleeping on the hard ground better than Tree's these days. You should have heard him moaning and groaning every morning on the trail."

"Why, you scurrilous young rascal," Tree threatened good-naturedly.

"We'll discuss your going later," Talon decreed. He looked to Issy. "This is what you want to do?"

Issy nodded. "It is."

"Very well then."

***

Issy

The wine drunk and their plans made, Issy's father adjourned their meeting.

"I'm going to stay and speak with my mother for a bit," she told Wil.

"About your dreams?"

"Yes."

"Good. If anyone can help you unravel them, it's your mother."

He kissed her on the cheek. A kiss that earned them her father's furrowed brows and her mother's knowing smile as the other men filed out of the room.

"Mother," Issy said. "May I speak with you in private?"

"Of course." Her mother gave her father a slight push toward the door. "Go. Our daughter and I have some things to discuss."

"But—"

"Female things," her mother said, shooing him out the door, shutting and bolting it behind him.

She sat in one of the chairs and Issy sat in the chair beside her, shifting uncomfortably on the cushioned seat.

"What is it, child?"

Child. Her mother hadn't called her child in years, and Issy hadn't felt like a child for many years, until this moment. Suddenly nervous about where this conversation could go, she took a deep breath in and let her words spill out.

"Wil and I are…"

"Lovers?"

Issy nodded, too embarrassed to look her mother in the eyes.

"It was inevitable," her mother said, sounding more amused than angry or disappointed. She laid a hand over Issy's, clenched together in her lap. "As a wise woman once told me, everyone in the valley could see it but you two, and then only because you both spent so much energy fighting it."

"Sophie the Sixth?"

Her mother gave a sad smile. "She and I had a conversation much like this on the night Wil was born." She met Issy's gaze and held it, her own serious. "I'm going to ask you the same question she asked me. Do you love him?"

"I do. Very much."

"Does he still plan on leaving here again?"

"He does." Issy was suddenly, ridiculously, close to tears.

"Has he said anything about coming back to you?"

"Eventually," Issy sniffed.

Her mother squeezed Issy's hands and gave an encouraging smile. "Then all you can do is stay true to your love and his, my darling girl. Or should I say woman?"

Issy swiped at her threatening tears. "I can't wait another seven years. Not now, now that I know."

"How it can be between a man and a woman who love each other?"

Issy gave up trying to hold her tears back and let them spill. Her mother wrapped an arm around her and hugged her into her shoulder.

"He's not gone yet," she whispered.

"Have you dreamt of him staying?" Issy asked hopefully.

"No. Have you?"

The fear she'd been pushing down for weeks rose from her belly into her chest, filling it with a great, gaping nothingness. She swallowed past the lump in her throat and managed a rasping whisper. "Not of him staying, but of him being engulfed by an encroaching darkness, held helpless by a faceless man who emanates pure evil and holds a knife to his throat."

Her mother went still, and Issy wasn't sure who the shudder that passed through the both of them started with.

"I dreamed of seeing your father die, over and over again for weeks on end," her mother said, her voice low, hushed. "I saw him shot through with an arrow. Watched him fall off his horse and lie in a pool of his own blood, his eyes glazed over and unseeing."

"What did you do?"

"I ran scared, refused to let myself love him because I was so afraid of losing him. And then it happened. Nithard sent his men to kill me and I ran for the Hollow. Your father came after me and in the ensuing fight, he was shot, twice, and fell to the ground as I'd seen him fall in my dreams." She took a slow, deep breath in and let it out just as slowly. "Only, he didn't die.

"What I saw in my dreams happened, just not the way I'd interpreted it." She gave a bittersweet smile. "Though Talon did leave to finish out his duty to Charles, he came back to Oloron, to me, eventually. And unless I'm completely wrong about Wil, a man I've known since he was in his mother's womb, it will take more than an evil man or the king's duties to keep him away from you for long."

CHAPTER SEVENTEEN

Segreti

Issy

Foxy ran into the stable and hid behind Issy's legs as Dante and Sergio rode in.

"Lady Isabeau, you are back," Dante exclaimed, dismounting and tossing his horse's reins to Sergio. "I am so happy to see you have returned safe and sound." He strode over to her, eyeing Sultan and Silver in their stalls. Foxy scooted under the gate into Charger's stall, where Wil was, watching. "And with your stolen horses too. *Grazie Dio*." He held his arms out, as if about to hug her, then dropped them when Wil stepped out of Charger's stall. "We heard of your adventures in retrieving your horses. That you killed the Basque thieves before you were able to make them talk."

Wil furrowed his brows. "You heard wrong," he said. "The thieves were Franks, not Basque." Which, according to Harald and Tree, they'd already made known. "And they did talk."

"Oh?" Dante glanced from Wil to Issy and back to Wil. "What did they say?"

"That they were taking the Turkmenes to the man who'd paid them to steal the horses."

"Did they say who this man was?"

Wil leaned in close to Dante. "Can you keep a secret?"

"Of course."

"So can we."

A loud guffaw came from Silver's stall, where Randolph was settling the yearling in for the night, and Issy swore Sergio's shoulders were shaking as he walked Mattone into his stall.

"No need to be like so." Dante flicked a dismissive hand at Wil. "I only meant to offer my help."

"We've got it taken care of," Wil told him before stepping over to Issy and laying a possessive arm around her shoulder.

Dante's smile was tight as he dipped his head to her. "My offer of help still stands."

"Thank you." Issy's smile was only slightly less tight than Dante's. "Randolph." The stable master came to the gate of Silver's stall. "I want an armed guard on Silver and Sultan night and day until Wil takes Silver back to Byzantium."

Randolph tipped his cap. "You got it, Mistress."

Wil tucked her into his side. "I can't wait to eat some of Lucinda's home-cooked food," he said, heading for the stable's door. "Camp food gets old fast." He gave Issy a smacking kiss on the cheek. "Especially when you're cooking it."

She gave him a playful elbow in the side, both of them laughing heartily as they walked out of the stable, Foxy zipping out ahead of them.

"How many daggers are stuck in my back?" Wil whispered in her ear.

She gave a quick glance over her shoulder at Dante, standing and glaring at their backs. "Oh, a hundred at least."

"Good. That means he bought it. Still, just to twist my knife in a bit deeper."

He stopped and turned to stare into Issy's eyes, grinning like he used to when they were young and he was about to dare her to do something risky. He held her face in his hands and touched his lips to hers, moving them over hers, slowly, purposefully, running one hand down her back and pressing her close. Issy wrapped her arms around his neck and melted into him, kissing him back. Wil rumbled, low and deep, his arms like iron bands around her waist as their kisses grew in need and intensity.

"Ahem."

They broke their embrace to find Geoff and Desiree walking toward them from the kitchens.

"So, it's true," Geoff said, giving Wil a hearty slap on the back before hugging Issy. "We ran into Harald on our way home. He told us you won him a few copper pieces. That you two finally resolved your differences." He grinned, looking back and forth between Issy and Wil. "So, when's the wedding?"

Issy gave her brother's shoulder a shove. "Shut up."

"What'd I say?"

Issy met Desiree's questioning gaze and shook her head.

Desiree took her husband's arm. "I'll explain later," she told him. "For now, it looks like Issy and Wil could both use a hot bath and a warm supper."

Issy and Wil walked hand in hand into the kitchens, where they were greeted by smiling faces, "welcome backs," and Lucinda's promise of a welcome-home supper.

They continued into the empty dining hall and into the common room, where the drapes to Wil and Burrell's little antechamber were pulled closed.

She glanced from the closed drapes to Wil and made a sad face. "I already miss you," she said, then leaned in close and whispered, "I'll leave my door unbolted tonight."

She kissed him on the cheek and slowly let her fingers slide away from his, then made her way up the stairs as he headed for the antechamber. Once in her room, she plopped down onto her bed and stared up at the ceiling, glad to be home again, yet already missing the seclusion of the Hollow. Foxy jumped up and squirreled into her side.

"You really don't like Dante, do you?" Issy said, recalling how the vixen had hidden behind her legs when Dante came into the stable. How she'd hidden in Charger's stall with Wil. She ran her fingers over the scab from the knife wound on Foxy's neck. "Did he do this to you? Is he the faceless man?"

She sat up and cross-legged, feeling the stretch in her hips as Foxy nestled in her lap. Dante was, without question, a preening peacock, but was he truly evil like the man in her dreams? Would he really try to have Wil killed? Would he try to kill Wil himself?

Personally, she didn't think Dante had it in him to bloody his own hands, but she wouldn't put it past him to hire somebody else to. As she suspected he'd done with the theft and attempted maiming of her horses. She hoped whoever it was would take the bait and fall into their trap.

Ruffling Foxy's fur, she lifted the vixen from her lap and stood next to the bed. She raised her arms over her head and leaned back, then side to side. She bent over to touch her toes, groaning at the pull from her thighs to her neck. Then she doffed her riding tunic and breeches and went to the water basin, wetting the wash rag and giving herself a quick wipe-down, deciding to wait on a bath until after supper.

She grinned, thinking of how she and Wil had stripped naked and splashed around in a creek they'd stopped at earlier today on their way down the mountain, how they'd stopped at every rill, creek, stream, or river they'd crossed to play.

She dressed in a clean under shift, dusky blue, sleeveless gown, and her sandals, then ran a comb through her tangled hair and plaited it into one long braid. She tucked her pendant under her bodice, kissed Foxy on the nose, leaving the vixen to sleep on her comfortable bed, and headed downstairs.

The smell of fresh baked bread and roasted meat and vegetables wafting up from the dining hall set Issy's belly to growling. She smiled a greeting at Carina, who sat to her brother's left, and took her seat at the center of the long table between Geoff and Dante, with Wil and Burrell sitting directly across from her, alongside Oswald and Gil and Dante's men.

"This looks and smells delicious," she told Lucinda as the head cook set a platter of roasted mutton in front of her. "I can't tell you how much Wil and I have missed your cooking."

"Wil here's told me three times already," Lucinda said with a pleased grin. "Though it never hurts to hear it again."

"Lucinda has been teaching Paola and me some of your local dishes," Carina said. "She also has recommended a village woman to work as the head cook and housekeeper for our new home, as well as some maidservants."

"I'm glad to hear it." Issy gave a nod of approval to Lucinda. "You can be sure they'll be good workers if Lucinda recommended them."

Carina smiled as Dante helped himself to a slab of mutton, the talk of household help apparently beneath him.

"Is your manor house ready to live in yet?" Wil asked.

"It is," Dante answered, though Wil had been looking at Carina when he asked. Dante turned one of his charming smiles on Issy. "We were waiting for Lady Isabeau's safe return before we moved in." He laid his hand over hers on the table, earning a scowl from Wil. "The DeVittorios can never thank you enough for your gracious hospitality."

Issy slipped her hand out from beneath Dante's. "You're most welcome," she told him, spearing a slice of mutton and placing it on her plate before passing it on down the table.

"Once we are in our new manor," Dante said to Wil, "you will be free to leave Oloron, will you not?"

Wil took his time chewing a mouthful of food before he answered. "We will," he said, looking to Burrell beside him. "As soon as you're in your new home and Silver is able to make the journey from here to Toulouse to Byzantium."

"To Toulouse?"

"Aye," Wil answered. "We'll stop in Toulouse where the king is summering before we go on to Byzantium." He winked at Issy. "Charles will want to see the Turkmene Frisian crossbreed for himself. As well as hear how well you and your sister have settled here in Oloron, thanks to the Guiscards' help and hospitality."

Issy lifted her cup to her lips, hiding her smile behind its rim. Wil was spreading his bait pretty thick. By Dante's pressed lips and tight jaw, he wasn't liking the smell of it one bit. The big question was, if he was the faceless man of her dreams, would he bite?

She glanced at Burrell, whom she assumed Wil had apprised of their plan, but Burrell was looking at Carina with something of a proprietary gaze, not, in Issy's opinion, like a man about to leave the woman he wanted, possibly forever.

It'd been obvious to anyone who paid attention that Burrell had feelings for Carina beyond friendship. Feelings she didn't reciprocate. She was more than sweet on Mason, as he was on her, of which Burrell was fully aware.

Issy took a sip of her wine. Either Burrell had come to terms with his unrequited feelings, or they weren't as deep as she had thought. Or, much like Wil, Burrell was resigned to his duties as a king's man usurping his personal wants.

Supper finished and her belly sated, Issy made a point of announcing she was going upstairs to her room for a bit before heading to the bath chambers. She was standing at an open window, looking out across her estate, which Geoff and Randolph had kept running and in good shape while she was away, when there came a light knock on her door.

"Enter."

Carina slipped through the door and quickly closed and bolted it behind her. Issy indicated the table and chairs and took a seat as Carina did the same.

Issy jumped right into it. "How's it going with you and Mason?"

Carina blushed prettily. "He has asked me to marry him, and I have accepted. But we cannot marry until after my brother pays Mason what he owes him."

"You don't trust your brother to pay him otherwise?"

Carina shook her head. "I do not."

"Does your brother suspect anything?"

"I do not think so. Mason and I have been very careful to keep our, *segreti*, our secrets, hidden. Only he and I, and now you, know of our intention to marry."

Issy laid a hand over Carina's on the table. "I'm so happy for you. If you need help with anything, you can ask me."

Carina laid her other hand over theirs. "And Mason and I thank you." She frowned. "I worry that my brother will make it impossible for Mason to get work after I leave my family for him."

Issy clapped her hand over theirs with a conspiratorial grin. "This is Oloron, not Lombardy. Your brother doesn't have the power he thinks he does. Here, my family and others loyal to the count and countess do."

She pulled her hands away, wishing she could tell Carina of their plans for her brother, knowing she couldn't. She must keep her *segreti* too.

***

Wil

Wil waited until the manor was dark and the only sounds he heard were Burrell's snores before he crept out of his bed and slowly made his way across the common room, up the stairs, and down the hallway to Issy's room. He gave her door three soft knocks and waited.

Her door creaked open a crack and she peeked out. "What took you so long?"

"It was hard to hear anything over Burrell's snoring," he said as she opened the door and let him into her room. She was wearing a gossamer-thin night shift that draped lightly over her sylphlike figure. "You look like an enchantress," he whispered as he wrapped her in his arms and buried his nose in her hair, breathing in the fresh, clean scent of her lavender soap. "You smell like one too."

"You've had occasion to smell an enchantress?"

"Every time you're in my arms."

Issy stood on her toes and kissed him, her lips featherlight on his. "I have something to tell you."

Wil met her uncertain gaze. "What is it?"

"I started my menses tonight."

Wil said nothing, his thoughts and emotions rushing through him, relief being the first and foremost. Her not being pregnant made everything going forward less complicated. Neither of them would be forced into marriage before they were ready, meaning Wil was free to return to his life as a king's man. To leave Oloron at any time once the DeVittorios were in their new home and he'd caught the man responsible for killing and stealing Issy's horses.

To leave Issy.

A deep sadness hollowed his chest at the thought of leaving her again, even if he didn't mean to stay away for years this time. This time, he intended to come back to her after taking her colt to Irene. This time he'd be leaving her knowing she loved him too. He wouldn't be leaving with happy childhood memories and a dream of what could have been between them; he'd be leaving with his memories of Isabeau the woman, of the physical and soul-binding love she'd given and shared with him. Of what would be between them when he returned.

Bittersweet regret swept through him. Regret for a country life he hadn't realized he'd missed until this very moment. For leaving Issy and Oloron, hoping she would wait for him. Knowing in his bones she would, which somehow made it even worse. But the most surprising thing he felt was regret over there not being a child. Their child. Not yet.

He pulled Issy into his arms and kissed the top of her head. "Truthfully," he whispered into her hair, "I feel as sad as I do relieved."

She nodded and sniffed into his chest. "Me too."

He cupped her chin and lifted it until she met his gaze, her big gray eyes wet with welling tears. "You know I love you, Isabeau Juditha Guiscard. Always have, always will."

She smiled. "I do."

"You know, too, I would marry you tomorrow, but for the chance of leaving you my widow. Of making you wait for a dead man and keeping you from finding happiness with another."

"Wilric Hugh LeCuir, you idiot," she chided. "Married or not, I would still be your widow in my heart." She grinned, though her eyes shone with unshed tears, and gave him a playful slug on his shoulder. "So, don't die."

Wil chuckled. "I'll do my best."

"Swear it."

He took her hand in his and placed it over his heart. "I so swear."

"Good." She kissed him on the cheek. "Now, can we go to bed? I'm exhausted."

"Are you sure?" Wil had intended to slip in, make love with her, and slip out again before anyone woke and saw him leaving her room.

Issy took him by the hand and led him to her bed. "I want every moment I can have with you for as long as we have."

"What if someone sees me coming out of your room? It's one thing for a man to have a lover, quite another for a woman."

Issy chuffed. "My parents are fine with this, with us. What's anybody else going to do other than talk? I'm my own woman, with my own estates; talk isn't going to hurt me. Besides," she added with a grin, "according to my mother, most of the valley's had us as lovers since the day you rode back into Oloron."

***

Wil stood at the fence railing with Geoff, Randolph, Burrell, and Dante, watching Issy take Sultan through his paces. It'd been two days since he and Issy had returned with the Turkmene stallions, two nights of sleeping with her in his arms, and two mornings of walking out of her bedchamber alongside her.

Geoff had only raised a brow in amusement the first morning they'd stepped out into the hallway from Issy's room at the same time as he and his wife walked out of theirs, while Desiree had simply smiled and wished them both a good morning.

There'd been some whispering among the servants, along with smiles and nods, and Burrell, who'd woken alone in his and Wil's antechamber, had sat at the breakfast table chuckling into his morning cup of ale when they walked down together, arm in arm. Carina had stared at them longingly, until she caught her brother's expression. Wil chuckled silently as he recalled how Dante's scowl and pursed lips made him look like he'd drunk soured milk.

"Well," Randolph said as Issy took Sultan over a low jump. "The stallion sure don't look any the worse for what he's gone through."

"He's tougher than he looks." Wil watched the pair take another, higher, jump. "As is his colt."

They all glanced over at the next pasture where Silver grazed alongside his dam, Sabine, under Remi's and Heinz's watchful eyes.

"Aye," Randolph agreed. "The mistress was smart to crossbreed 'em with her Frisian mares. I reckon the empress'll be quite pleased when she's given Silver." He sniffed and swiped his nose with his sleeve. "I'm gonna miss 'em when he's gone. 'Specially since we won't be having any more foals to raise 'til next year, thanks to whatever evil, thieving bastard had poor Shadey and Shadow kilt. I mean, who would do such a thing? Killing poor, innocent foals like that?"

He looked to Wil and the others as if waiting for an answer.

"I don't know," Wil said through gritted teeth. He glanced at Dante and then Geoff for good measure. "We may never know. We're just lucky we got the yearling back and can take him to the empress and fulfill Isabeau's deal with Irene and Charles."

"I'd say it was more my sister's stubborn determination than luck," Geoff opined as Issy and Sultan sailed over a four-foot-high jump.

"You're not wrong," Wil agreed. "Our little mule has plenty of both."

Dante sneered. "*Abbondanza*, plenty of kick in the bedroom too, I would imagine."

Wil closed the distance between them in three short strides, grabbed ahold of Dante's tunic at the neck, and twisted it in his fist. "You shut your mouth, or I'll shut it for you."

"Are you going to let him treat me like this?" Dante appealed to Geoff.

Geoff stepped up and stood nose to nose with Dante. "Talk about my sister like that again and I'll cut your tongue out myself. Do we have an understanding?"

Dante licked his lips and nodded. Wil shoved him so he stumbled back into the fence. Geoff clapped Wil on the back as Dante turned heel for the stable, and Randolph stalked after him, mumbling about how the Lombard better not go in there and disturb the horses.

"Was that part of your setup?" asked Burrell, whom Wil had told of the trap they were planning.

"No," Wil said, clenching his fists and fighting the urge to go after Dante and pummel him. "The Lombard set himself up for that."

"Though I'd say it helped stoke his hatred of you and our family," Geoff added with his Guiscard pragmatism.

The sound of hoofbeats turned their attention back to the paddock, where Issy pulled Sultan up next to the fence.

"What was that about?" she asked.

"Wil here threatened to pummel Dante to a pulp," Geoff said, ratting Wil out.

"And Geoff threatened to cut out his tongue," Wil told her.

She raised her brows. "Because?"

Wil and Geoff looked at each other with sheepish grins.

"Because the Lombard said something he shouldn't have," Burrell told her.

"Which was?"

Burrell looked to Wil, who gave a quick shake of his head, before he answered. "He insulted your horses."

"Did he now?"

They all three nodded, not saying another word. She eyed them one by one, then reined Sultan toward the jumps.

***

Wil escorted Issy into the main hall of the DeVittorios' manor for the housewarming feast. Dante, Carina, and their household had moved out of Oloron Manor and into the estate they had named *Nuovo Lombardi* three days ago, two days after Wil and Geoff had threatened Dante with bodily harm for slandering Issy.

They'd been the most pleasant three days Wil had spent in Oloron since he'd returned, and he'd have gladly skipped this feast altogether, except for the social mores and politics of the situation. He and Issy needed to be seen together at this celebration, their relationship openly accepted by their families and others of import in the valley like Phillipe's and Dardinel's.

Most importantly, they needed to show Dante that his disapproval meant nothing to them, that they were able to rise above the disapproving whispers spread by him and a few others.

This feast was the perfect occasion to accomplish all the above, as well as lay the trap wider for whoever was responsible for the thefts and deaths of Issy's horses.

Wil, Harald, and Burrell would be leaving with the Turkmene yearling in two days, and had been spreading the information of their departure date and route around the valley for days now, in case it wasn't Dante. If it was, as Wil still suspected, he intended to spread as many clues as he could tonight without giving his game away.

Though it was only the last day of August, the heat of summer had already given way to the chill of early autumn nights, and the supper was being held in the dining hall rather than the courtyard. Carina had admitted to Issy that this had given Dante the perfect excuse for only inviting the landowners of the valley and none of the common folk, including Mason and his crew, who'd actually built the manor house and outbuildings. They'd done a good job of it from what Wil saw.

The manor home, like most in this area of Gaul, was a sturdy, two-story building of stone and wood built to house a large family and their household, with both indoor and outdoor kitchens and a bathhouse. Dante and Carina had brought some furniture with them, a bedframe each, a set of chairs, an ornately carved cabinet that was a part of Carina's dowry, and numerous chests full of household goods and clothes. The rest, they'd commissioned from local artisans who'd set up shops in what was still known as Tent City, though there'd been more buildings than tents for years.

Paola ushered Wil, Issy, Geoff, and Desiree from the common room to the dining hall where the Guiscard family was already seated. Carina greeted them with a genuine smile, her brother's less so.

"When does Carina plan to leave her brother's house for Mason's?" Wil whispered to Issy, who'd told him of their plans.

"As soon as Dante pays Mason all he owes him. He's been stalling paying him off. My father says he'll give him another week to pay, then he'll intervene as count if he has to."

"Do you think Dante's stalling because he knows of Carina's plans?"

"No." Issy shook her head, her auburn waves shining in the candlelight. "I think Dante would do something far more punitive to them if he knew. I think he's trying to get away with whatever he can."

Wil chuffed. "He definitely has more wrongful pride than brains. Which is good for us."

The newly hired maidservants carried out pitchers of wine and filled the guests' cups, and then Dante stood.

"Welcome, Count Talon, Countess Lara." He held his cup out toward them, then turned to the table at large. "Welcome, my honored guests, to *Nuovo Lombardi,* my," he inclined his head to Carina, "our, new home here in this wonderful province of Oloron."

Cups were raised and drinks taken. Dante sat and Talon stood.

"Thank you for welcoming us into your home." He raised his cup to Dante and to Carina. "May you be as happy and fruitful here as we have been."

More cups were raised, more wine drunk, and then Count Talon took his seat beside his wife. The maidservants brought out platters of roast beef and pheasant, autumn squashes and peas, bitter greens, loaves of rye breads, and churned butter.

"This looks and smells delicious, Lady Carina," Countess Lara said.

"Thank you, Countess. The women you and Lucinda recommended for household positions have worked out quite well."

"I'm so glad to hear it."

"How are the men I recommended for preparing your vineyards?" Dardinel asked Dante.

"They have cleared a quarter of the land already," Dante told him. "I will be sending Sergio and Marco back to Lombardy for more of my family's vines to be planted along with the vines we brought with us this spring, as well my stallion and six broodmares."

"Six?" Phillipe said.

"Yes, well, while my family consider them superb mares, I am aware that you and Count Talon may disagree, so I am hoping you will find at least half of them to your breeding standards."

"Here's hoping." Phillipe raised his cup and took a drink.

"Yes," Talon agreed. "New blood can be a good thing."

"Are you still hoping Isabeau will breed Sultan with one of your mares?" Wil asked.

"I am always hopeful when it comes to Lady Isabeau," Dante answered with a smug smile.

Wil clenched his table knife tight, resisting the urge to gouge Dante's pretty blue eyes out with it.

Issy dipped her head with a gracious smile. "I look forward to seeing your family's mares when they arrive."

"I have another proposition for you, Lady Isabeau," Dante said. "I would ask permission for Sergio and Marco to travel with Wil and the others taking your yearling to Irene as far as Toulouse, where my men will turn south and east for Lombardy."

Issy looked to Wil, who pretended to think on it, and nodded his approval.

"Of course, they may," she told Dante.

Wil raised his cup to Dante. "Though I don't expect any trouble on the road, the extra company will be welcome."

CHAPTER EIGHTEEN

Promises

Issy

Issy watched Wil sleep as the inexorable gray of dawn crept in through the open shutters of her bedroom window. She slowly pushed the bed linens down to his hips, admiring the ridged muscles of his belly, the light furring of his broad chest and the breadth of his shoulders. She ran a fingertip lightly over the scar that ran down his left shoulder, fighting the urge to continue her path down below the bed linens.

They'd made love last night for the last time for only God knew how long. Days, weeks, months, years, forever. It all depended on what happened on the road from Oloron to Toulouse to Byzantium and back. Though Issy knew he would wake and respond to her touch, she wanted last night's tender, bittersweet lovemaking to be the last memory they had of their physical love. She sighed; as much as she would miss their physical connection, it was the melding of their hearts and souls she would miss the most.

She'd heard the term soulmate many times in her life, but now she knew what it meant to have one. Though Wil had forgiven her for refusing him seven years ago, and she'd forgiven him for leaving her then, it didn't lessen her regret for all that time they'd lost to be together. For the time they were about to be separated again.

All she could do now was hope it wouldn't be for another seven years.

Her eyes welling with tears she'd promised herself and Wil she wouldn't shed, she gazed upon his beloved face. At the strong line of his stubbled jaw, the soft pillow of his lips, his perfectly shaped nose, long, full eyelashes, thick, expressive brows, and high, wide forehead, topped by a head of close-cropped, earthen brown curls. Choking back a sob, she laid her palm over his bare chest and felt the strong, rhythmic beating of his heart.

He clasped his hand over hers and gave it a gentle squeeze. "'Morning, Little Dove."

Issy snuggled in closer to him and he lifted his arm so she could lay her head on his shoulder, kissing the top of her head as she burrowed her nose into his neck and breathed in the scent of his warm skin. Searing it into her senses.

Wil wrapped his other arm around her and held her close, his breathing short and strained, as if he too was choking back tears. After his breathing slowed and lengthened, he loosened his hold, though Issy still clung to him.

"This was so much easier when I was angry with you," he said with a hoarse chuckle.

Issy rolled her forehead against his shoulder. "I can pick a fight, if that would help."

"It might, Little Mule." He cupped her chin and lifted her face, his gaze meeting hers. His dark eyes reflecting everything she was feeling. "But I never want to feel like I've lost you forever again."

"You never will." She kissed him, sweet and tender, whispering into his lips. "I'm yours, always."

"As I'm yours."

Held tight in each other's embrace, they lay together in the tenuous peace of their chambers until the sounds of people moving around the manor could no longer be ignored.

Wil hugged Issy into him and then let go. "It's time."

He rose from her bed and Issy lay there admiring his taut backside as he walked over to the washbasin and splashed water on his face. With a heavy sigh, she too rose and went to her chest, where she pulled out a linen packet.

"For you," she said, handing it to Wil. "So that a part of me will always be with you."

He opened the packet and pulled out a lock of auburn hair twined around a sprig of dried lavender.

"Thank you." He kissed her forehead. "I'll keep it with me always." Folding the lock back into the linen square, he picked up his tunic and tucked it into the chest pocket. "It'll be my lucky talisman."

They dressed and descended the stairs arm in arm to the dining hall where a breakfast feast of cured pork, fried eggs, porridge, rye bread, and apple pies awaited them.

"You and your staff have outdone yourself, Lucinda," Wil complimented the head cook.

"Can't have you and Burrell riding off on half-filled stomachs," she said, her cheeks pink from Wil's praise.

"I'll be lucky if I'm able to mount my horse after eating my fill of this delicious meal," Burrell told Lucinda.

"I've packed up a wheel of your favorite herbed cheese too," she told him with a wink. "Be sure to grab it on your way out of the kitchen before you leave."

Burrell gave a gruff nod. "Thank you. I will."

Issy met Wil's lifted brows. "I think that's the most words I've heard Burrell speak at one time since he's been here," she said.

Wil chuckled. "While a man of few words, he's also a man of hearty appetite."

Issy didn't have much of one herself this morning, pushing food around her plate more than actually eating, while Wil ate a full plate of cured pork, eggs, bread, and two pieces of apple pie.

She recalled her father's tales of camp food and what a good, home-cooked meal meant to a soldier, tales Wil had seconded as they'd eaten their meager camp food while chasing her horses, so she knew not to take it as a personal slight that he could eat a full meal while her belly was tied in knots over his upcoming departure.

When he and Burrell finished and pushed back from the table, Issy's belly dropped to her feet. Wil offered her his hand and she stood on stiff, wooden legs and walked beside him on feet of stone as they made their way to the stable.

She went to Silver's stall and petted the yearling's muzzle as Randolph gave him one last look over and Remi saddled Onyx. Wil and Burrell saddled and packed their horses and then led them out of the stable, Randolph and Remi following with Silver and Onyx.

They tied them to the post outside the stable as Issy's and Wil's families rode into the courtyard, Lucan loping alongside Harald's Frisian stallion, Ajax, a sixteenth birthday gift from their parents. Orlando jumped off his gelding and ran over to Issy.

"Guess what, Issy? Harald gave me Lucan to watch over while he's gone."

"Well, of course, he did." Issy ruffled Lando's black curls. "Who else would take such good care of Lucan?"

She looked over to where Harald had dismounted and knelt beside his dog, petting him and whispering into his ear. He met her watchful gaze and dropped his own. She walked over to her mother and father, who handed their horses' reins over to Randolph and Remi, and saw her mother's eyes were red-rimmed and her father's jaw clamped tight.

"Harald isn't planning on coming back to Oloron, is he?" she asked them.

"No," her father answered as her mother fought to keep more tears from spilling. "He wants to stay in Toulouse and join the king's army."

"Like his father and Wil did," her mother choked out.

Issy took a deep breath in and forced a smile. "And like his father and Wil, he will succeed at it and come back a self-made man."

"From your lips to God's ears." Her mother lifted her chin, lengthened her spine, and met her husband's steely gaze with a shaky smile. "We have farewells to say."

Issy walked with them to where Harald stood next to Wil, who was hugging his teary-eyed mother good-bye, while his father and brothers looked on.

She hugged Harald. "You take care of yourself, brother."

"I will, Issy. I promise." He hugged her back. "And I swear we'll get whoever it was that went after your horses."

"I know you will. Make me another promise?"

"Of course."

"Tell the Empress Irene thank you from me, personally, for sending me Sultan."

"I will, if the king lets me be part of his company."

"He will," she assured him. From what her father and Wil had told her, Charles had a soft spot for the Guiscards. She gazed in awe at her middle brother. "The wide world awaits you."

"I'm not sure the wide world is ready for him," their father said from behind Issy. He clasped Harald's forearm with one hand and laid his other on Harald's shoulder. "I'm proud of you, son." He clapped him on the shoulder and grinned. "The things you're going to see and do."

Harald beamed with pride as their father stepped back and their mother opened her arms, welcoming her son into them.

"I love you, son."

"I love you too, Mother."

She sniffed and nodded and kissed him on the cheek. "Now, go and show the world what Harald Rousell Guiscard is made of."

"I will, Mother."

"And stay alive."

He laughed and snuffled. "I'll do my best."

She chucked his chin. "You'd better.

"Where's that grandson of mine?" Anglbert's voice boomed out as he and Berta arrived. "Thought you'd leave without saying good-bye, did you?"

"Never, Grandfather." Wil clasped Anglbert's arm, and then he hugged Berta. "I was going to come by your house before I rode out, I swear."

"I know you were, dearie," Berta clucked and patted him on the arm. "You know how Anglbert likes to blow and bluster."

Wil kissed his grandmother on the cheek. "Take care of each other," he said, then added in a whisper, "and Isabeau."

"We will, dearie." Berta gave Issy a sympathetic smile. "We will."

They moved on to Harald, their godson, as Dante rode up with Sergio and Marco, the two servants leading a pack horse each. They didn't bother to dismount, but sat waiting on their horses.

Their good-byes finished, Wil gave Issy a boot up onto Onyx and mounted Charger as Randolph tied Silver's lead rope off to Harald's saddle.

"Ready?" Wil swung Charger's head east.

"We are ready," Dante answered.

"We?" Wil said.

"I have decided to travel with you and my men as far as Toulouse," Dante announced. "There is some family business I must discuss with King Charles."

Wil furrowed his brows as he met Issy's surprised gaze for a brief moment, cocked his head, and then shrugged. "Let's go then."

With one last wave good-bye to their family and friends, Wil led the way onto the road leading east out of Oloron, Issy riding beside him, and Harald following with Silver. Dante and his men rode behind Harald, and Burrell took rear guard.

As they approached the foothills, which was as far as Issy would ride with them, she glanced back at Dante, not at all surprised to see that the eyes she felt boring into her back were his. She sidled Onyx closer to Charger.

"Do you believe Dante's stated reason for traveling with you?" she whispered.

"No. I think he's planning on making sure the job gets done right."

"You mean stealing Silver?"

"And killing me. As well as any other witnesses. I think once he's accomplished this, he does plan on meeting with Charles, to tell the king how we were ambushed and he managed to survive."

The vision of the faceless man holding a knife to Wil's throat came unbidden to Issy. A cold chill swept through her, as if she'd ridden through a ghost.

"I don't like this, Wil," she said, her voice shaking. "Not one whit."

Wil reached over, took her hand in his, and gave it a reassuring squeeze. "Don't worry. He's not as smart as he thinks he is. According to your father's spies, he hasn't approached any men about going after us, and no strange men have been seen entering or leaving the valley. Which they will continue to watch for and go after if any leave after us. Odds are, Dante plans to take the three of us with his three. When he makes his move, we'll be ready for him."

Issy wished she felt as sure as Wil sounded. "Be careful. He's as sneaky as a snake in the grass. And Wil? Please watch out for Harald."

He lifted her hand and pressed his lips to the back of her knuckles. "I will. I promise."

He held on to her hand for the remaining quarter of a league until they were at the base of the pass through the foothills, neither of them speaking a word, though their clasped hands and gazes said plenty.

"Ride on ahead," Wil told the men as he and Issy stopped their mounts. "I'll catch up with you."

Issy said good-bye to Sergio and Marcos as they rode by, and dipped her head in response to Dante's "*Arrividerci*." Harald sidled Ajax next to Onyx and gave his sister a one-armed hug.

"Be safe, brother," she said with a forced smile.

"I will, Issy."

She turned Onyx around and held her hand out to Silver, rubbing his forehead. "Do me proud, Silver," she told the colt. "If any bad men try to hurt you, remember your sire and stomp them into the ground."

"Farewell, Lady Isabeau," Burrell said as he rode past them.

"Farewell, Burrell. Take care."

She and Wil dismounted, and Wil hugged her into his side as she stood watching her brother and yearling colt ride away.

"They'll be fine," Wil said. "I promise."

She leaned her head on his shoulder. "So many promises have been made today."

He kissed the top of her head, then stood facing her and held her by the shoulders. "I can make you one more promise," he said. "I promise to love you, and only you, Isabeau Juditha Guiscard. That I will come back to you. I'm yours as you're mine, always."

Issy smiled through sudden tears. "I'm holding you to that promise, Wilric Hugh LeCuir."

***

Wil

Riding away from Issy as she stood watching was the hardest thing Wil had ever done. When he'd left her seven years ago, he'd left in anger, determined to start a new life and forget her. While he'd been successful at forging a new life for himself, a good, productive life as a king's soldier and then a king's guard, he'd never been able to forget Issy.

Growing up together, she'd been as much a part of him as he was of her, and now that they'd found each other again, found their love for each other, he knew he never would forget a single moment with her.

He'd meant what he told her. He would return to her, whether in this world or the next. He touched the pocket where her lock of hair was and prayed that it would be in this world, and that he could, in fact, keep Harald safe as well. He glanced back over his shoulder at the line of men and horses behind him, taking in Sergio and Marco, sizing them up as adversaries in a fight he was certain would come.

In his early thirties, Sergio was the man chosen by Dante's father to come to Oloron with his son and keep an eye on him. He was the only man other than Dante's father the Lombard seemed to listen to, and in the time that Wil had spent in Sergio's company, he'd come to like the man, and had great respect for his steadiness and his sword arm. Built much like Burrell, he was stout, though not overly so, and as quick-footed as he was quick-thinking. While he served Dante well, he didn't seem to particularly like him.

Where Sergio was the smartest of the three Lombards, Marco had the muscle. In his mid-twenties, he was as tall as Wil and Harald, but muscled like Sergio and Burrell. Unlike Sergio, Marco followed Dante's orders without thought or hesitation.

In a fair fight, they were the two Wil would worry most about, but he wasn't expecting Dante to fight fair. He was, as Issy had described him, a snake in the grass. One Wil looked forward to catching in his own trap, while knowing Dante would do everything he could to strike Wil and slither away from any consequences.

As it stood, their numbers were even at three against three, though there was always the chance that an ambush awaited them, which Wil, Burrell, and Harald were well aware of and ready for. They might end up outnumbered in the fight that was sure to come, but they wouldn't be surprised. Forewarned was forearmed.

Plus, Issy hadn't had any more dreams of Wil or Silver at the mercy of the faceless man. Which eased his mind about the outcome somewhat.

This being the dry season, it should take them six days to make Toulouse. Wil figured Dante would make his move at day three or four, when they were far enough away from Oloron yet not too close to Toulouse. Still, he kept his eyes and ears open to every flash of movement or snapping of a twig, as did Harald, which could be put to excitement over his first adventure out in the world.

Burrell rode as he had the entire journey from Tours to Lombardy, and from Lombardy to Oloron, quiet but watchful, his left hand holding his mount's reins, his right hanging loosely by the hilt of his sheathed war axe.

They crossed over the foothills and made camp at dark, eating a cold supper of rye bread, cheese, and apples before tucking in for the night. Wil had Harald take first watch, and he took second, which meant he spent most of the night staring up at the star-filled sky thinking about Issy. Remembering how they'd slept together under the stars while chasing down Sultan and Silver, cocooned but chaste, and then their passion-filled nights at the Hollow.

He pulled the packet with her hair out of his pocket and breathed in the scent of lavender, and of her, and wondered how she was faring in her bed without him, recalling how she'd come to his room in the Hollow and asked him to sleep with her. Told him she couldn't sleep without him.

"Ahh, Issy, my little dove. I miss sleeping with you too."

He woke Burrell for third watch and managed to get some fitful sleep in before dawn broke. Sergio was already up and about when Wil rose from his bedroll, but Dante, Marco, and Harald were all still soundly asleep.

They woke the others and Wil checked Charger and Silver while a cold breakfast of cheese and the last of the rye bread was served up. Both horses looked good, and Wil nodded in approval at Harald as he came over and checked his stallion, Ajax.

"Your father taught us well," Wil said as Harald ran his hands over Ajax and lifted a hoof to check it for soundness.

"Aye. Some lessons you never forget." He set the hoof down and lifted another. "A horse soldier without a horse is—"

"A foot soldier," Wil finished.

Their chuckles died down as Sergio came over to check on his, Marco's, and Dante's horses, and Wil walked away shaking his head.

They were mounted and on the road as the sun broke over the horizon, passing a tinker's wagon heading west and nothing more until they stopped at noon to rest and water the horses after crossing a bridge over a river that ran from north to south.

"How is the colt handling the journey so far?" Dante asked Wil as he held Silver's lead in one hand and Charger's reins in the other, letting them drink.

"He's holding up fine," Wil answered. He glanced downriver to where Sergio was watering his and Dante's horses. "How's Mattone?"

Dante shrugged. "He seems fine. Sergio will let me know if he is not."

Wil turned his back to Dante, clamping his jaw tight so he didn't say something he shouldn't to the spoiled, selfish prick. He didn't want to antagonize him yet.

There would be time for that soon enough.

***

Issy

Issy sat at the supper table staring at the empty seat across from her where Wil usually sat. He'd only been gone for a day, but it had been the loneliest day of her life.

"You need to eat something, Mistress." Lucinda's concerned voice broke Issy out of her broodings, as did the mouthwatering aroma of the freshly baked strawberry pie she set on the table in front of Issy. She cut a piece and handed Issy the plate, then stood there, hands on hips, watching until Issy took a bite, and then another.

"Mmm," Issy murmured, taking a third bite. "This is delicious. Thank you, Lucinda."

"You're welcome, Mistress." Lucinda patted her on the shoulder before heading back into the kitchen with a pleased smile.

Taking another bite, Issy realized that everyone there was watching her.

"I'm fine," she assured them. "I mean, I'm worried about Silver…"

"Only Silver?" Geoff challenged.

Issy glanced around the table. Of the people there, only she, Geoff, Desiree, and Randolph knew of the plan to trap Dante, or whoever it was trying to steal Silver. It wasn't that she didn't trust her household, but the fewer people who knew a secret, the more likely it was to remain a secret.

She gave her brother a warning glare. "I miss Harald and Wil," she said. "But I'm worried about Silver. It's a long journey to Byzantium. He could still go lame at any time."

"Do you trust your knowledge and instincts as an animal healer?" Geoff asked her.

"For the most part," she answered.

"Then you must trust all the work and planning you put into his journey."

Issy nodded with understanding, then purposely gave her brother a teasing grin.

"And people say you're the dense brother."

Desiree tried to smother her giggle, then gave up. "Don't worry, husband," she said with a smile meant only for him. "To me, you're thick in all the right places."

Issy's mouth dropped open and Geoff's cheeks turned an unmanly shade of pink.

Issy burst into laughter as Oswald and Gil choked and sputtered.

"Well done, sister," she told Desiree. "Well done, indeed."

She finished her pie, excused herself, and headed for the stable as was her habit. Foxy came running from behind the stable with a dead mouse in her mouth and dropped it at Issy's feet.

"What a good huntress you are, Foxy." She petted the vixen's head and ruffled her ears. "But you keep it."

She entered the stable she'd been in every single day for the past five years, minus the three weeks spent with Wil recovering the Turkmenes. The stable she'd rebuilt from the ground up that housed her Frisians and Sultan, and all she felt was as empty as the stalls that Silver and Charger had filled until this morning.

As proud as she was that her years of hard work were coming to fruition, it wasn't the same without Wil to share it with. To say she missed him was the understatement of a lifetime. There was a Wil-size hole in her heart that only he could fill. She would simply have to learn to live with it until he returned. If he returned.

It wasn't that she didn't believe Wil loved her and meant to come back to her. It was that any number of things could happen to him, or even her, in the time it took him to fulfill his duty to Charles. And now that she knew what it was to love and be loved, to be Wil's woman and he, her man, she wanted every moment of every day and night she could have with him.

She checked on her broodmares, Lyts, Ebony, and Sabine, all of whom had lost their foals, Lyts and Ebony in a horrible, abrupt way, and let her tears for them and herself fall freely. She pressed her forehead to Onyx's, remembering the night the mare was born, the night Wil first proposed marriage to her, and was deluged by an overwhelming sense of loss that left her as empty as a hollowed-out piece of driftwood.

Her legs suddenly as wobbly as wet river grass, she entered Onyx's stall and plopped down in the straw, her back against the wall. Foxy skittered in, chattering away as she climbed into Issy's lap and Onyx folded her legs and laid down beside them. Issy let out a heavy sigh and closed her eyes with a silent prayer to God to keep Wil, Harald, and Silver safe from harm.

Desiree lay in bed holding a swaddled, newborn babe while Geoff stood beaming down at them, a young boy with black curls standing beside him and holding his hand.

"Talon Geoffrey Guiscard," Desiree said to the boy, "meet your brother, Phillipe Wilric Guiscard."

Geoff looked up and saw Issy watching from the doorway. He let go of the boy's hand and took a step toward Isabeau.

"You cannot come with me, brother," she said. "Your family needs you."

She turned from the door and was standing at the edge of a ferned glen with a stone bier in the middle of it. Two women stood next to a vine of red roses, one young, beautiful, with long blonde curls and eyes the color of the sky, the other old and leaning on a staff, her snow-capped head tilted as her wizened gaze held Issy's.

"Who is it you seek, child?" the old woman asked.

"Wil. I can't see Wil."

The glen was enveloped with a dank, heavy darkness, the air thick and musty as a tomb. The low glow of a dying campfire's embers illuminated the figure of a man standing by the fire, staring down into the ashes.

"Wil?"

He looked up, his face pale as a ghost. "Issy?"

The cowled figure of a man crept up behind Wil, a knife's blade gleaming dully in his gloved hand. Isabeau tried to scream, to call out a warning, but no sound came from her throat as the man plunged the blade into Wil's back. Frozen with horror, Issy watched as the man pushed the hood back from his head and smiled.

Issy jolted awake, her scream still stuck in her throat. Foxy leapt out of her lap as she scrambled to her feet and stumbled out of the stall, sucking in air. Holding her hands out to her sides, Issy staggered out of the dark stable into the night, chills running up and down her body.

She bent over and braced her shaking hands on her wobbly knees, trying to calm her breath enough to not pass out. After several slow, purposeful breaths in and out, she straightened and glanced around. There were no lights shining anywhere, and by the almost full moon starting to descend in the western sky, it was closer to dawn than midnight.

She ran into the manor house and took the stairs two at a time, stopping at the door to Geoff and Desiree's chambers.

"Geoff, wake up." She banged on the door with her fist. "It's me, Issy. Wake up."

"Quit banging." Geoff's muffled voice came from beyond the door. "I'm coming."

He opened the door, dressed only in a pair of breeches, as Oswald and Gil came out of their room, hastily dressed the same.

"What is it?" Geoff asked, taking in her wild eyes and disheveled appearance.

"I'm going after Wil and Silver."

"Now?"

"Yes. Now. I have to get to Wil, to warn him. I've seen the faceless man."

Geoff leaned against the door jamb, staring at her as if she'd lost her mind. "Who?"

"The faceless man in my dreams. The one trying to kill Wil and steal Silver."

Geoff stood straight up. "You have the dreams?"

"I do."

He held her gaze for a moment and then nodded. "Right." He squared his shoulders. "I'm going with you."

"No. You need to stay here. Your wife and sons need you alive."

"Sons?" Desiree said, stepping out from behind Wil in her night shift. She laid her hand over her flat belly. "How do you know? I'm not even sure yet."

"I dreamed them too," Issy told her. "Your oldest will be Talon Geoffrey Guiscard, and your second will be Phillipe Wilric Guiscard."

A beatific smile lit Desiree's face while Geoff stood stunned.

"I need you to go to Crossroads and let Mother and Father know I've gone after them, and to ask Father to send men after them as well." She turned to Oswald and Gil. "You two, pack enough supplies for four days and saddle up; you're riding with me."

"Issy," Geoff said. "Wait. At least until Father and his men can ride with you."

"I can't. There's no time to lose."

CHAPTER NINETEEN

Treachery

Issy

Issy glanced back at the cloud of dust on the road behind her that was Oswald and Gil and dismounted from Sultan. She'd chosen the stallion to chase after Wil and Dante for his endurance and speed, and though it was only noon, she and Sultan were already a good league ahead of her men. She'd warned them she wasn't going to slow down or wait for them, that she meant to ride all day and night until she caught up to Wil and Harald, and she'd meant it.

Wil had told her he expected Dante to make his move on the third or fourth day of the journey, which meant she had one, maybe two days to catch up to them and warn him who was the faceless man of her dreams.

She led Sultan to the river and let him drink while she stretched her legs and back, then pulled two apples out of her saddlebag, one for her and one for Sultan. When Sultan finished drinking, she walked him over to a hedge of bushes, tied him off, and gave him his apple while she relieved herself behind the bushes. Eating her apple, she let Sultan graze for a bit, then remounted and rode east, Oswald and Gil now only half a league behind her.

The road wasn't a well-traveled one, and the hoofprints from Wil's company were faint but readable, Charger's and Ajax's larger, heavier prints easy to discern from the others, as were Silver's smaller, lighter ones. Though the hoofprints were a day old, they still gave her some comfort as she rode on, trying not to think of her dream and how the faceless man had stabbed Wil in the back. Praying and hoping she could reach Wil in time to warn him.

"Come on, Sultan," she told the stallion. "We have two days of riding to get done in one day and a night."

***

Wil

Wil sat on his bedroll staring at the moon rising low in the eastern sky, wondering if Issy was looking at it too. If she was thinking about him as he was of her. Cursing himself for leaving her after finally finding her again. He told himself he'd had to. He had his duty to the king to fulfill, his duty to Issy to save Silver, and to turn the yearling over to the Empress Irene. That when all that was accomplished, he would return to his one true love.

She'd told him she understood, that she stood by his decision to fulfill these duties and promises, and he knew the pragmatic side of her did, but the part of her that ran on pure heart didn't understand in the least. Apparently, neither did his. Else there wouldn't be an empty, cavernous hole where his heart should've been.

"Mooning over Isabeau?" Harald said, sitting down on his bedroll next to Wil's.

"Funny."

Burrell laid his bedroll out on the other side of Wil and sat. "What are we talking about?"

"Wil, mooning over my sister."

Burrell chuffed. "He's been mooning over her since the day we received orders to accompany the DeVittorios to Oloron. I just didn't realize it until the day we rode in and he saw her again."

"The way you've been mooning over Lady Carina since the first time you laid eyes on her?" Wil countered. Which wasn't very kind of him. At least Issy loved Wil back. Carina was in love with another man. A man she intended to marry once her brother was dealt with, though Burrell didn't know about that part. "I'm sorry, Burrell." Wil clapped him on the shoulder. "I know what it's like to want a woman who doesn't feel the same about you."

"Yeah," Burrell huffed. "Unrequited love may be the inspiration of poets, but for an old soldier looking to find a wife and settle down...not so much."

"Maybe she'll change her mind," Harald, unaware of Carina's love for Mason, said. "Like my sister did about Wil."

"Maybe," Burrell said. "But I'm not as patient a man as Wil here is."

"Maybe you'll meet a beautiful, exotic Byzantium woman when we take Silver to the empress," Harald offered. "Maybe you two'll fall madly in love and she'll run away with you and come back to Gaul with you and give you six sons and four daughters."

"And how am I supposed to feed ten children and a wife on a soldier's pay?" Burrell groused.

"Maybe she'll be a princess," Harald said.

Wil laughed.

"What is so funny?" Dante demanded as he and his men laid out their bedrolls on the opposite side of the campfire.

"Young Harald here has me marrying a Byzantium princess and having ten children," Burrell told him.

"Only ten? A healthy, virile man like you?" Dante tsked. "Think how many children you could sire with a Byzantium harem."

Burrell shook his head and pulled on his beard. He met Dante's teasing gaze and held it. "I'll happily settle for one special wife and however many children she's able to bear."

"*Accorto*," Dante said. "Smart man. Keep your expectations within reach."

Burrell dipped his head. "I always do." He turned to Wil. "How about I take second watch tonight and you take third. That way you can get a stretch of uninterrupted sleep."

"Sure," Wil agreed. "We can switch off every other night."

"Sounds good." Burrell lay down on his bedroll. "Don't fall asleep on your watch and forget to wake me up," he told Harald.

Harald stifled a yawn. "I'm going to go splash some stream water on my face before my shift starts."

"Tell you what," Wil said. "I don't think I'll be falling asleep anytime soon, so why don't I take first shift and you can take third."

"Great," Harald agreed. "I could fall asleep where I'm standing right now."

Wil nudged Burrell with the toe of his boot. "You hear that?"

"Yeah," Burrell grunted. "I wake Harald up for third shift instead of you."

Wil set his saddle at the foot of his bedroll and leaned back against it, his short and long swords at the ready, watching the path that led from the road to their camp and listening to the sounds of the night while missing Issy's sweet body so much his actually ached.

He looked over to where Dante, Sergio, and Marco looked to be sleeping soundly, and tried to think of every possible way they could try to steal Silver and kill him, Harald, and Burrell. Because no matter if Dante had hired more mercenaries to attack them and take Silver, or he and his Lombards planned on doing it themselves, he couldn't afford on leaving any witnesses alive.

Wil stood and stretched, keeping alert. His plan was to live through this while saving Issy's brother, horse, and her deal with Charles and Irene. He walked the edges of their camp, went over to the line of horses and checked on them, sat for a while, and repeated the routine over and over again until it was time to wake Burrell for second shift.

"No signs of anyone or anything happening so far," he told Burrell.

"Tomorrow night or the next morning would make more sense anyway," Burrell said, setting his saddle up on the foot of his bedroll, ready to take his watch.

"Let's hope we're right, and ready for them when it happens."

Wil adjusted his waist blade and set his short sword to one side of his bedroll and his long sword to the other, then lay on his back and stared up at the moon overhead. He fell asleep thinking of Issy and woke to Burrell's gruff voice telling him to stay down, the edge of his axe pressing against Wil's throat.

***

Issy

Issy jerked awake as her chin hit her chest. She shifted in her saddle and sat up straighter, sucking a deep breath of night air in and blowing it out. She looked up at the full moon making its descent in the western sky, grateful for the light that still shone on the road ahead of her, enabling her and Sultan to ride through the night. Grateful too for Sultan. The Turkmene's speed and endurance had carried her leagues ahead of Oswald and Gil, easily covering two days' worth of riding in a day and a night. If she estimated Wil's rate of travel correctly, she and Sultan should be catching up to them soon.

She went over the story she meant to tell them one more time. That she'd forgotten to send a tub of salve for Silver, and wanted to get it to them before they got any farther, in case he started showing signs of lameness during the journey. She would then tell Wil that Burrell was the faceless man, and that Oswald and Gil weren't far behind her, as well as the count and his men. She could only hope and pray they hadn't already been ambushed, and that she and the others got to them in time to stop it or help them fight.

She knew Charles had handpicked Burrell for this duty along with Wil because Burrell spoke Lombard and Charles trusted him. So why had he gone against his king's trust? And Wil's. As well as her father's. All of them men who wielded the power to punish him if he was caught. End his life even.

Had it been his intention from the start to steal her Turkmenes? Or had he formed his plan after arriving at Oloron? Was he doing this for himself, or had somebody bought him off?

Then there was the question that had plagued her from the start. Why kill the crossbred foals? That had always felt personal. She'd never even heard of Burrell before he'd come to Oloron, so why would he have a personal grudge against her or her family?

Whatever his reasons, if Burrell would kill Wil to keep his part in this treachery, then he wouldn't hesitate to kill Harald.

She patted the short sword sheathed at her waist belt and the bow and quiver of arrows tied off with her bedroll to her saddle, silently thanking her father for teaching her the basics of sword fighting, and her mother for the many times they'd practiced archery together. For not only letting her, but encouraging her to be who she was, an animal-crazy girl who ran wild with a pack of boys and more than held her own.

Of course, looking back, she was never really on her own. Wil had always been there at her side. She intended to be by his.

The first gray streaks of dawn were lighting the sky when Sultan snorted and pricked his ears forward. Issy pulled the stallion up and breathed in the faint scent of ash and smoke. "I smell it too, boy," she whispered.

Keeping the stallion to a slow walk, she kept her eyes peeled on the road, looking for side paths into the woods. A hundred paces farther up, she spied a game path and horses' hoofprints. Dismounting, she slung her bow and quiver of arrows over her shoulder and led Sultan onto the path.

Fifty paces in, she heard voices. Angry, male voices. She turned into a thicket of trees and tied Sultan to one, then crept closer to the voices, slowly, carefully, avoiding stepping on any twigs or dry leaves. She stopped at the edge of the tree line and crouched behind a thick trunk, peering out into the fireless camp.

The horses were tied to a line, close to the stream, and Wil and Harald were bound at the wrists, sitting back-to-back in the dirt,

Burrell, Dante, Marco, and Sergio standing in a loose circle around them. Sergio standing farther back than the others.

"How do you think you're going to get away with this, DeVittorio?" Wil challenged. "Count Talon already suspects you. How are you going to explain his dead son to him?"

"*Semplice*," Dante answered. "We were attacked in the middle of the night by overwhelming numbers. We fought, you and Harald fought especially bravely, but alas, were overcome, along with Sergio and Marco. Burrell and I managed to hold off the thieves until they took the Turkmene colt and ran. Burrell and I will give each other a few superficial wounds, while Sergio and Marco take the Turkmene to my father in Lombardy."

Wil glared at Burrell. "I hope he's paying you well for your treachery. Because you're going to be spending the rest of your sorry life on the run and in hiding."

"No, I won't," Burrell said. "I'll be married to the lady Carina and living a life of comfort in *Nuevo Lombardi*."

"You sold me, Isabeau, the Guiscards, and your king out because Dante promised you Carina in marriage?"

"That I did. Beats a retired soldier's miserly life alone."

"She doesn't love you, Burrell. She loves Mason."

"My sister will marry who I tell her to," Dante stated. "She will forget her love for the lowly tradesman once she is married to Burrell."

"Don't be so certain," Wil told them. "She and Mason were planning to marry as soon as you left on this journey."

"That is a lie," Dante spat.

Wil lifted his brows. "Is it?"

Burrell stomped up to Wil. "Get up," he snarled, yanking Wil up by the jerkin as Harald scrambled to his feet too. Issy notched an arrow to her bow.

"Can I ask something before you kill us?" Harald said to Dante, sounding remarkably calm. "Why are you doing this? Why go to so much trouble to steal a horse?"

"I would not have had to if your *puttana* of a sister would have agreed to marry me and breed her stallions with my mares," Dante answered.

A person didn't need to know the Lombard language to understand what Dante had called Issy. She grit her teeth and gripped her bow and arrow tighter.

"Why kill her newborn foals?" Harald asked.

"Because my father," he bit off the words, "wants the Turkmene's bloodline for his line of horses. That is why he asked Charles for the land in Oloron. He had heard of your sister's stallions. Now, he will have Silver to breed and I will have Sultan."

Harald chuffed. "How do you figure that?"

"I will comfort and console your sister over the deaths of you and LeCuir. She was enamored of me once, before you," he stabbed in the air at Wil, "interfered. She will come to care for me again after I offer to marry her, a spoiled woman whose man is carrion for the crows."

Wil let out a short, harsh laugh. "You so don't know her. She despises you. She will never marry you. Or breed Sultan to your Lombard nags."

Dante shrugged. "Then I will simply have Sultan killed."

Issy aimed her arrow directly at Dante's heart.

"I am tired of all this talk," Dante said with a flick of his hand. "Kill them."

Burrell gripped his axe and stepped to Wil as Marco stepped to Harald, short sword in hand. Issy changed her aim.

"Sorry, Wil," Burrell said. "Nothing personal."

"Go to hell, Burrell."

"You first." Burrell stepped back and hefted his axe toward Wil's chest.

Issy let her arrow fly.

***

Wil

I'm sorry, Issy.

Thwack.

Wil stood gaping at the quivering arrow shot through Burrell's ear, then watched his body drop to the ground.

"Move," he yelled to Harald as he dropped to his knees. His wrists bound, he grabbed ahold of Burrell's axe handle with both hands and wrenched it from the dead man's hold as he rolled to avoid Dante's wayward stab and came up onto his feet.

Dante screamed as an arrow struck him in the chest, and then screamed louder as Wil sliced his belly open with Burrell's axe. Wil pivoted to defend Harald in time to see him kick Marco in the groin and then plow his tied fists into Marco's jaw as he doubled over, with Sergio holding Marco in a bear hug from behind. Sergio let go of Marco, who crumpled to the ground, and Harald gave him another kick to the kidneys, then reached down and took his short sword.

Wil whirled around as Issy walked out from the tree line, an arrow pointed at Sergio, who held up both hands, palms out. Issy kept her arrow pointed at his chest.

"Issy." Wil had never been so happy to see anybody. Ever. "How are you here?"

"I had a dream about the faceless man, only he showed me his face." She dipped her chin toward Burrell, her arrow sticking out of his ear. "I had to warn you."

"You saved us," Wil told her.

"Saved our sorry hides for certain," Harald seconded. He stepped over to Sergio and held Marco's short sword to his throat.

Wil held the axe he'd taken from Burrell by the handle and lifted his bound hands up toward Issy. "Could you help us out a bit more?"

Issy grinned and pulled her waist blade. She stepped up to Wil and started cutting his ties.

"Gods, I love you, my fierce little falcon."

"You'd better." She cut through the last tie and Wil enveloped her in his arms and felt her body shaking.

"Everything's all right now," he whispered hoarsely into her hair. "We're all right." She nodded into his shoulder, and he hugged her close, kissed the top of her head, then let go his hold of her. "Cut your brother loose."

Wil held the axe to Sergio's chest as Issy cut Harald's ties, then the three Franks stood staring at the lone Lombard.

"Why did you help us?" Wil questioned him.

"It was the right thing to do," Sergio answered. "I never wanted any part of this. I had no choice. He threatened to send Paola away if I did not."

Wil had always liked Sergio the best of Dante and his men. Had thought him a good man stuck with a bad master. He looked to Issy. "What do you think?"

"I think Harald would be injured or dead if not for what Sergio did here today."

"I agree," Harald said.

"We'll have to take what happened today, and what happened with Isabeau's horses to Charles," Wil told Sergio. "Do you swear to tell the king exactly what Dante planned, what he did, and what happened as a result?"

Sergio raised his right hand higher. "I so swear."

Wil tapped the axe's blade on Sergio's shoulder. "Go back on your word, try to run off, or help Marco escape, and I will kill you. Do we have an understanding?"

"We do."

Wil lowered the axe. "You and Harald tie up Marco," he told them. "Then we'll pack Dante's and Burrell's bodies. We need to show them to Charles." He stared hard at Issy. "Did you come alone?"

"Oswald and Gil started out with me, but I rode Sultan and he outran them. My father and his men should be coming too."

Wil raised his brows at her.

"I wasn't going to slow or wait. I knew I had to get to you as soon as I could."

Wil nodded and took her hands in his. So small and delicate-looking, yet so capable and tough. "Your dreams."

"For once, I'm glad of them."

Wil raised her hand to his lips. "As am I."

She smiled. Sweet and tender, fierce and fearsome. Everything she was. Then her eyes went wide.

"I should go get Sultan. I tied him to a tree along the path."

She started to pull her hands from Wil's, but he held tight.

"I can get him by myself," she assured him.

"I know you can, Little Mule. But I'd feel better going with you." She made a face, and he chuckled. "I'm not letting you out of my reach, much less my sight, until I have to."

He looked over at Marco, still unconscious, bound and tied to a tree, and then at Sergio, who was gathering tinder for a campfire alongside Harald.

"Issy and I are going to get her horse," he told them. "We won't be gone long."

Harald waved them off. "Take your time. We'll be starting some breakfast. I don't know about you, but I'm starving."

"You're always starving," Issy teased. "Be careful Charles doesn't see how much you eat, or he'll send you back."

She led the way back to where Sultan stood dozing in the rays of morning sun breaking through the trees, twitching his ears and giving a soft snort at their appearance.

Issy ran a hand down the proud arch of his neck and along his back, praising the Turkmene for his swift legs and courageous heart, a sentiment Wil shared.

"Thank you, Sultan," he told the stallion, who deigned to let Wil rub his nose. "Thank you for getting your mistress here so quickly and safely."

Issy started to untie Sultan's reins, but Wil shook his head with a slow smile. "Not yet, my dove."

He pushed her gently by the shoulders until her back was against the tree's trunk, and then he cupped her chin and kissed her, a starving man granted the sweetest nectar.

He'd been two days and nights without her, and the more he tasted her sweetness, the more his hunger gnawed at him. His kisses grew ravenous, his hands bold, his cock rock hard.

Her kisses as hungry and needy as his. Issy untied the flap to his breeches and freed his erection. She moved her hand up and down his pulsing cock as he pushed her breeches down past her hips and ran his fingers through her thatch, groaning at the wet heat between her legs. They kissed and nipped and bit and rubbed until they both cried out into each other's mouths.

Then they leaned forehead to forehead, catching their breath and laughing lightly.

"How close on your heels do you think the others are?" Wil asked.

"Too close," Issy said with an exaggerated sigh. She stood on her toes and kissed his cheek. "That one was for the road ahead."

"And a long, lonely road it's going to be without you." Wil didn't have to exaggerate his sigh.

"How long?"

Wil knew what she was asking. "As long as it takes to deal with Charles and the DeVittorios," he said. "Then to deliver Silver to Irene. After that's done, I'll be free to return to you."

"Do you, personally, need to take Silver to Byzantium?"

Wil pulled her pendant out from under her tunic, the pendant he'd given her seven years ago, and hoped it wouldn't take another seven years to return to her again.

"It was the duty Charles swore me to," he told her. "The only way I can make sure your horse is delivered to the empress and your deal with Irene and Charles satisfied."

Issy rolled her forehead into his chest and gave him a half-hearted punch in the shoulder.

"Of course it is, you stubborn, honorable ass."

CHAPTER TWENTY

Waiting

Issy

"I now pronounce you husband and wife."

Issy cheered along with half the valley gathered for Carina and Mason's wedding, truly happy for them. She stood with her parents, Orlando, Geoff, and Desiree, trying not to be jealous of Desiree's happy, pregnant glow and failing miserably.

She looked around Mason's property, at the sturdy house of wood and stone and the two workshops, both the size of the house, at the tables and chairs set out for the marriage celebration, the fire rings to ward off the mid-October chill, and back at the beaming couple accepting congratulations from their friends and neighbors. Carina had chosen to dwell in her husband's house, more than content, she'd said, to live in a cozy house five times smaller than the manor house Mason had built for her and her brother.

Her father, forced by Charles's hand, had agreed to pay Carina's dowry, which would afford them the luxury of a cook and housemaid, a position quickly filled by one of the valley's widows eager to support herself and her two teenage children.

Count Talon and his men, along with Oswald and Gil, had caught up to Issy, Wil, and the others by noon the day of Burrell's betrayal. After one last night sleeping next to Wil on their bedrolls, Issy had left for Oloron the next day accompanied by Oswald and Gil, while the count and two of his men had traveled with Wil, Harald, Sergio, Marco, and Silver from there to Toulouse, where they'd met with

Charles and told him everything that'd happened. Charles had not only absolved Wil and Isabeau of Dante's and Burrell's deaths, but had declared the DeVittorios' claims on the land in Oloron forfeited. Then he'd gifted the land to Wil, who had expressed his intent to retire from the king's guard after fulfilling his duty to deliver Silver to the empress Irene.

Marco had been pressed into the Frank army for his part in his master's deceit, and Sergio was given the choice of returning to Lombardy or Oloron. He'd chosen Oloron and Paola, and the two of them had agreed to stay on at *Nuevo Lombardi* to assist Geoff and Desiree, whom Wil named as stewards of his new estate.

Wil, Harald, and four of Charles's men, handpicked by Wil, had left a month ago for Byzantium with Silver and messages from Charles to Irene. Wil and his men intended to cross the Alps before winter set in. After his return to Oloron, Issy's father had told her this, along with passing along a private message from Wil.

I will come back to you. Always.

She held Wil's message as close to her heart as the pendant dangling between her breasts. She clasped the pendant beneath her gown's bodice of heather wool and sighed. As much as it meant to her, it was a poor substitute for Wil himself. Still, the pendant, her memories, and her hopes for their future together were all she'd have of him for the next year at least. Even with good weather and no issues along the road, a year was the minimum amount of time it would take Wil to get to Byzantium and back. A year's time in which anything could happen.

"You look sad for such a joyous day, sister." Geoff laid his hand on Issy's shoulder and gave it a squeeze.

"Oh. No. I'm happy for Carina and Mason. Truly."

"She's missing Wil," Desiree said with a sympathetic smile.

"And you two, now that you're living in the new manor." Issy glanced over at Sergio and Paola, holding hands and smiling as they talked with Dardinel and Annette. "How are things working out with them and your new staff?"

"Good," Geoff said. "Without Dante around, Sergio's shown himself to be a man of many talents. He's got lots of ideas about the vineyard, which I'm sure is what he's discussing with Dardinel as we speak."

"Paola's got the house and kitchen well under control," Desiree added. "She and I get along quite well."

Issy smiled. "I'm glad. Wil always said he liked Sergio the best of Dante's company."

"Wil's a good judge of character," Geoff said. "Well, except for Burrell. And you can't blame Wil for that one. That one was on Charles."

She closed her eyes and took a deep breath. It wasn't that she regretted killing him, she'd do it again in a heartbeat, but the memory of her arrow striking through his earhole and sinking into his head, of his body dropping to the ground, still haunted her, which killing the thieves who'd stolen Sultan and Silver never had.

She'd never even seen the thieves before, but in his time at Oloron, living in her house, she'd gotten to know Burrell, at least she'd thought she had, and she'd actually liked him. As had Wil.

Burrell's treachery had cut deeper than Dante's for them all, but especially for Wil, who'd considered him a brother-in-arms.

It eased Issy's worried mind some knowing Wil was with Harald now. Though Harald had been too young to be a close friend with Wil growing up, her brother was as true of heart as they came. He would become a good friend to Wil on the road, someone he could talk to about their families and friends, of growing up in Oloron. And Wil would protect Harald, teach him about the world and how to be a good soldier. This much Issy knew instinctively. What she didn't know was how she was going to manage to wait a year or more to hold Wil in her arms again.

The line of well-wishers congratulating Mason and Carina had thinned, and Issy made her way over to them.

"Congratulations." She shook Mason's hand. "You've married the loveliest of women."

"Thank you, Lady Isabeau." Mason beamed. "I will strive to be worthy of her."

"I'm sure you will," Issy told him. "As I'm sure you will prove to be."

He dipped his head and she turned to Carina and clasped her hands. "You deserve every happiness, my friend."

Carina threw her arms around Issy and hugged her tight. "Thank you, Isabeau," she whispered. "For everything."

"You're most welcome," Issy whispered back. Carina let go her hold and Issy stepped back, swiping at the tears threatening to spill. "For everything."

She wandered around the courtyard for a bit, mingling and making small talk. Everywhere she looked she saw people smiling, talking, laughing. She was surrounded by people she knew and loved, yet she'd never felt so alone.

Her mother waved her over to the table where her family was sitting.

"I'm not feeling well," Issy told her. "I think I'm going to go home and go to bed." *For a week.*

"Are you sure?" Her mother peered into Issy's eyes and laid her palm on Issy's forehead. Her sympathetic smile told Issy she'd seen the truth of her ailment. She kissed her daughter's cheek. "We'll stop by on our way home to check on you."

Ridiculously close to tears for the second time that afternoon, Issy nodded.

She untied Onyx from the wagon Randolph, Lucinda, and the rest of the manor's staff had ridden over on and mounted up. She urged the mare into a canter until they were out of sight of the celebration, then she turned Onyx onto the path leading to the tree house oak and gave the mare her head. Onyx broke into an easy gallop and Issy breathed in the brisk October air and shook her hair out of its braid, letting the breeze blow through it. She leaned forward over Onyx's withers and sent the mare racing across the field.

"Thanks, girl." She patted the mare's neck as they pulled up to the oak. "I needed that."

She looped the reins over Onyx's neck and left her loose to graze, then walked to the river's edge as two squirrels chattered away at her from the oak's branches.

"Acorn? Chestnut?" The squirrels ran halfway down the tree's trunk and stopped, upside down and blinking their beaded eyes at her. "It is you." She held her empty hands out palms up. "Sorry, I didn't bring any treats with me. But now that I know you're still here, I will next time."

The squirrels ran back up into the high branches and Issy sat with her back against the trunk, staring at the river and remembering the many times she and Wil had splashed and played and made love in the pool at the Hollow and the streams they'd crossed riding from the Hollow to Oloron. A familiar ache began to grow between her legs, but she didn't have the desire to do anything about it.

"I miss Wil," she sighed. "More than I thought humanly possible."

Soul sick and bone weary, she closed her eyes to the waning sunlight and imagined a pair of eyes as deep and rich as the loamy earth smiling into hers.

Wil paraded around on his stubby little legs, holding a dandelion high in the air as Issy toddled after him, laughing and trying to grab the white puff from Wil's hand.

"Like dis, Issy," he said, and blew the dandelion seeds into the air.

Issy watched them float in the air around her, and when she looked down again, Wil was running in circles around a campfire in the dark of night. Laughing and squealing, she chased after him as he changed and grew with each circle until he was a boy on the cusp of manhood. Suddenly, he stopped and turned to face her, his once-familiar smile changing, growing serious, making her nervous. He held a silver pendant with a ruby twirling in the middle of it out to her, but when she reached for it, he snatched it away.

They were riding Onyx and Charger bareback across an open field, chasing a dark shadow into a deep wood, where it dissipated among the trees and then disappeared altogether. A herd of white and gray dappled horses came running out of the woods, and she and Wil raced with them across the field, sailing over logs and rills.

Issy laughed, happier than she'd been for a long, long time. A red light danced before her eyes, and Wil was holding the pendant and smiling.

Issy woke to eyes so brown they were almost black, smiling into hers.

"Wil?"

* * *

Wil

Wil knelt on the ground beneath the oak, staring into eyes as gray and soft as a dove's breast.

"Yes, love, it's me."

She blinked and shifted against the tree trunk. "But you're on your way to Byzantium. My father said he watched you leave with Harald and Silver." Her eyes went wide. "Are they all right? Where are they?"

"They're fine," he said, "and I'll tell you all, but first things first." He pulled her up onto her knees and embraced her, the feel of her heart beating against his, in time with his. "I've missed you, my little dove," he murmured into her hair, breathing in the clean, fresh scent of lavender. He leaned back and cupped her chin, then he kissed her, sweet and tender, every moment of longing he'd felt over the past month and a half making it even sweeter. "And I'm back for good."

She caught her breath. "Truly?"

"Truly." He took her hands in his and kissed them, then he sat back on his heels and eyed her. "You're entirely too far away from me," he said, and motioned for her to scoot. He positioned himself with his back against the tree and pulled her into his lap, her head resting on his shoulder and her legs draped over his. "Now, to answer your questions, Harald and Silver were both well the last I saw them, which was a week into our journey east to Byzantium, when I turned back and they continued on."

"Why did you turn back?" she asked, almost shyly.

"Because, before I left Toulouse, a very wise man told me again of how he'd once been like me. How he thought it more important to fulfill his duty to the king than to be with the woman he loved. How that decision had almost cost him his love and their child, and how the only thing he regretted was each and every moment spent apart from them."

Issy smiled up at Wil. "My father."

"Your father." Wil shifted her in his lap and hugged her tight. "I, of course, being the stubborn ass I am, left for Byzantium anyway. But a week into our journey, I was so miserable from missing you, from contemplating not being with you for another year, I just up and told the others that I was done. I was going back to Oloron. I was going home. To you."

"Oh Wil." She threw her arms around his neck, the smile on her face as warm and bright as the sun in summer. "I'm so glad you did."

"Poor Charger," he said. "I almost ran him into the ground to get back here as soon as I could, though I did make a stop in Toulouse to give Charles my official resignation and to buy this." He pulled a small, intricately carved box out of his breeches pocket and opened it, revealing a ring of gold encircling an oval ruby. "Isabeau Juditha Guiscard, will you marry me?"

"Yes." She nodded her head fervently. "Yes, Wilric Hugh LeCuir, I will marry you."

She held out her hand and Wil slipped the ring on her finger.

"I love you, Issy. Always have, always will. I swear from this day forward, I will never leave you again."

EPILOGUE

Issy

"Happy birthday, Issy." Wil leaned closer and pressed his warm lips to her cheek as they stood gazing into the brooding stall, where Pearl, her Turkmene mare, a gift from Irene in return for Silver, had given birth. "Your mares have a knack for gifting you foals on your birthday." He grinned at their first foal out of Pearl and Charger. "She's a gorgeous filly, exactly like you dreamed. That makes you, what?"

Issy touched her pendant. "Ten for ten."

Since her marriage to Wil, she'd only dreamt of good things happening, like the sex of foals about to be born, or her own children while pregnant with them. She shifted two-year-old Sophie on her hip as four-year-old William came running into the stable with Foxy nipping at his heels.

"Is the baby horse born yet, Papa?" he asked, running into Wil's legs.

Wil pointed through the slats in the stall gate and William peered in. "The baby horse is a she."

"What's her name, Mama?" William asked.

"Hmm." Issy put a finger to her lips. "I don't know yet. What do you think we should name her?"

"Horsie," Sophie chirped.

"You can't name a horse Horsie," William told her.

"Oh." Sophie, who took her big brother's word as truth, squirmed to get down, immediately toddling over to stand next to William and look into the stall at the white and gray dappled mare and her ash gray filly.

"Can we name her Smokey?" William looked up at Issy and Wil.

"Why Smokey?" Wil asked his son, his twin in looks and, as Issy liked to tease her husband, stubbornness.

"'Cos she looks like smoke."

"Smokey." Issy pretended to think about it, then grinned. "I think Smokey is a wonderful name."

"Mokey, Mokey, Mokey." Sophie jumped up and down, her auburn curls bouncing.

"Shh, Little Monkey." Wil scooped up Sophie into his arms. "We need to be quiet so Pearl and Smokey can rest."

Sophie nodded solemnly, then looked down at William. "Shh, Wiwem."

Issy took her son's hand and led them out of the stable into the courtyard as Randolph and Remi were walking back from the dining hall after breaking their fast, tossing Heinz slices of apple as they went.

"Guess what, Ranolph?" William said. "I named the baby Smokey."

"An' a fine, good name that is, young master." Randolph ruffled William's brown curls and gave him a slice of apple to feed to Heinz.

"Can we help Ranolph and Remi, Mama?"

"Not today," Issy told William. "Today we're going to Uncle Geoff and Aunt Desiree's house. It's baby Lara's first birthday, remember?" A date she shared with her Aunt Issy.

"Yippee." William started running in circles around Issy and Wil, Sophie chasing behind him. "We get to play wif Talon an' Phillipe."

"Tawon and Phiweep," Sophie parroted. "Pway wif Tawon and Phiweep."

Geoff and Desiree still lived at *Nuevo Lombardi,* renamed The Vineyard, as full partners with Wil, who had chosen to live with Issy at Oloron Manor, where they concentrated on breeding horses. Dardinel had taken over running the vineyards along with Sergio, while Philippe and Geoff ran the livestock.

"Will Granmama Lara, Granpapa Talon, Granny Patience, and Grandy Willem be there too?" William asked.

"They will," Wil told him. "Would you like to tell them about Smokey?"

William's brown eyes grew wide. "Can I?"

"Of course you can."

Lucinda came out of the kitchen and waved the children over to her. "Come on, you two," she said. "Let's get you cleaned up and ready for your mama's and baby Lara's party."

Wil started to follow, but Issy laid a hand on his arm. "Not yet," she said. She led them over to the pasture fence where they could see their Turkmene Frisian crossbreeds grazing under the July sun, Sultan keeping watch over his herd.

Issy leaned against the fence, grinning. "I had a dream last night."

Wil furrowed his brows. "About?"

She took his hand and laid it over her belly, only beginning to swell with the new life growing in her womb. "Meet Hugh Guiscard LeCuir."

Eyes as deep and brown as loamy earth warmed by the summer sun smiled into hers. He took her hand in his and lifted it to his lips.

"Thank you, my Issy," he said, kissing the backs of her fingers. "Thank you for waiting for me, for loving me, for giving me this wonderful life and family. Thank you for being mine."

Issy smiled, her love for him a tangible thing. "Always."

ABOUT THE AUTHOR

Michele James lives in a southern California beach town with her understanding husband, one mini panther, and two crazy cattle dogs.

A retired veterinary technician, she writes historical romances with elements of fantasy that are full of adventure and romance with swoon worthy heroes and strong-willed heroines. You might find a bit of medicinal lore and an animal character or two in her books.

She enjoys watching movies without commercials, cooking, gardening, walks on the beach (especially in winter), and practicing yoga.

CONNECT WITH MICHELE:

website: michelejamesauthor.com
tiktok: @michelejamesauthor
IG: @michelejamesauthor
FB: /michelejamesauthor
pinterest: /michelejamesauthor
goodreads: /19960951.Michele_James

www.BOROUGHSPUBLISHINGGROUP.com

If you enjoyed this book, please write a review. Our authors appreciate the feedback, and it helps future readers find books they love. We welcome your comments and invite you to send them to info@boroughspublishinggroup.com.

Follow us on TikTok and Instagram, and be sure to sign up for our newsletter for surprises and new releases from your favorite authors.

Are you an aspiring writer? Check out www.boroughspublishinggroup.com/submit and see if we can help you make your dreams come true.

Love podcasts? Enjoy ours at www.boroughspublishinggroup.com/podcast.

www.ingramcontent.com/pod-product-compliance
Lightning Source LLC
Chambersburg PA
CBHW020256200626
46816CB00001BA/319